D1168216

The SUPERNATURALIST

THE GRAPHIC NOVEL

The SUPERNATURALIST

THE GRAPHIC NOVEL

ADAPTED BY EOIN COLFER AND ANDREW DONKIN

ART BY GIOVANNI RIGANO

COLOR BY PAOLO LAMANNA

Color separation by Studio Blinq

Disney • HYPERION BOOKS

NEW YORK

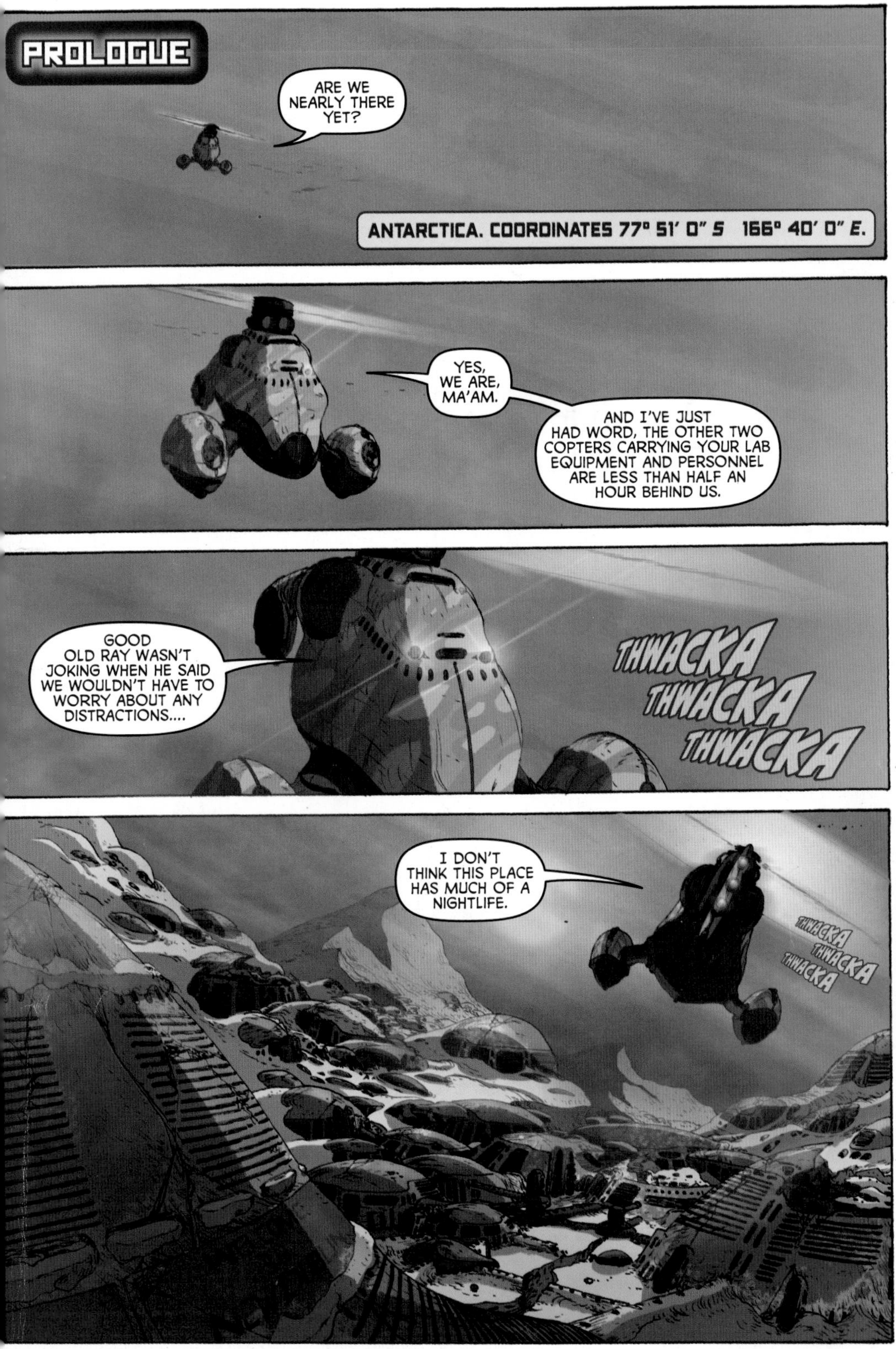
PROLOGUE
ARE WE NEARLY THERE YET?
ANTARCTICA. COORDINATES 77° 51' 0" S 166° 40' 0" E.
YES, WE ARE, MA'AM.
AND I'VE JUST HAD WORD, THE OTHER TWO COPTERS CARRYING YOUR LAB EQUIPMENT AND PERSONNEL ARE LESS THAN HALF AN HOUR BEHIND US.
GOOD OLD RAY WASN'T JOKING WHEN HE SAID WE WOULDN'T HAVE TO WORRY ABOUT ANY DISTRACTIONS....
THWACKA THWACKA THWACKA
I DON'T THINK THIS PLACE HAS MUCH OF A NIGHTLIFE.
THWACKA THWACKA THWACKA

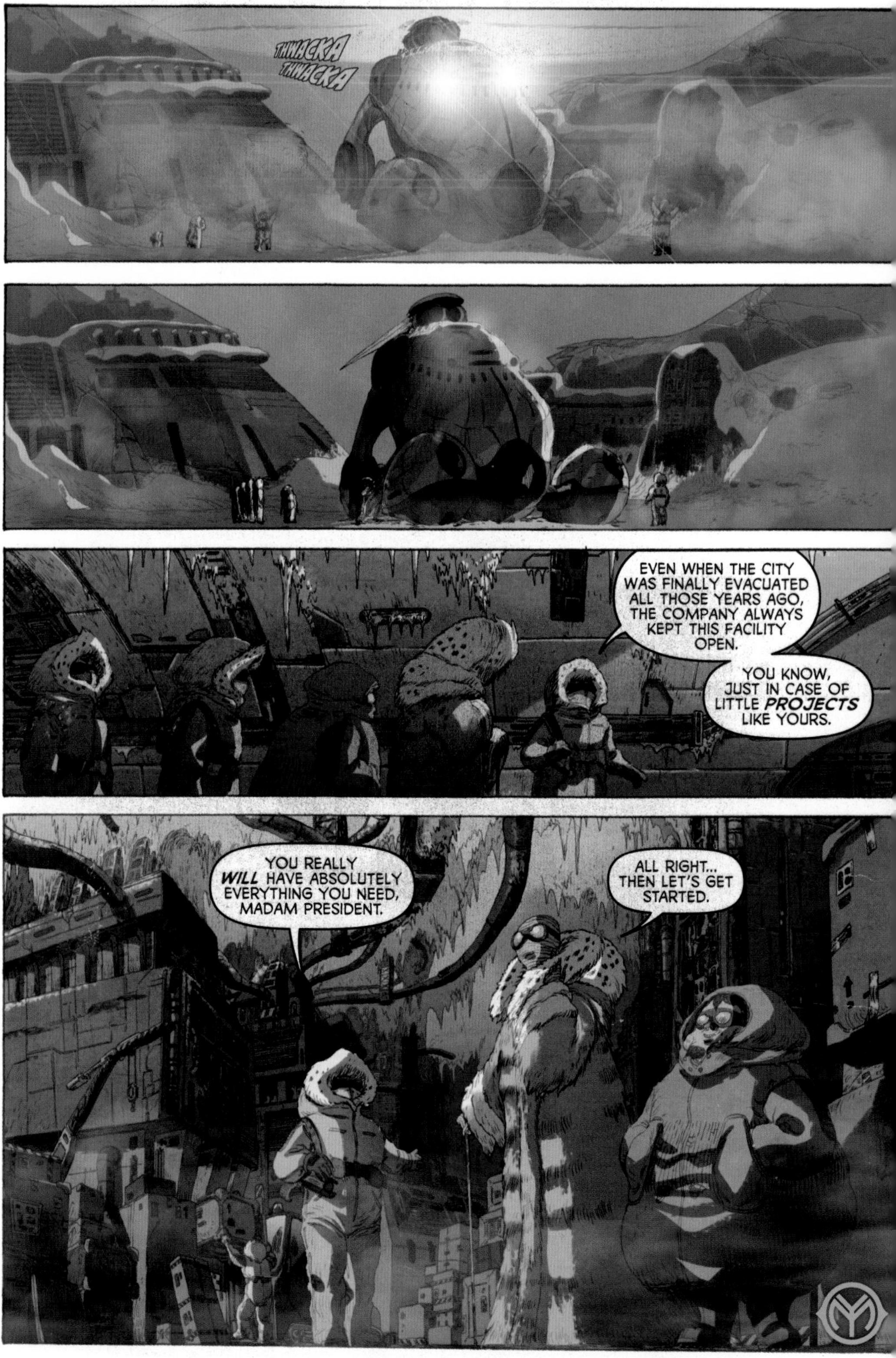
THWACKA THWACKA
EVEN WHEN THE CITY WAS FINALLY EVACUATED ALL THOSE YEARS AGO, THE COMPANY ALWAYS KEPT THIS FACILITY OPEN.
YOU KNOW, JUST IN CASE OF LITTLE PROJECTS LIKE YOURS.
YOU REALLY WILL HAVE ABSOLUTELY EVERYTHING YOU NEED, MADAM PRESIDENT.
ALL RIGHT... THEN LET'S GET STARTED.

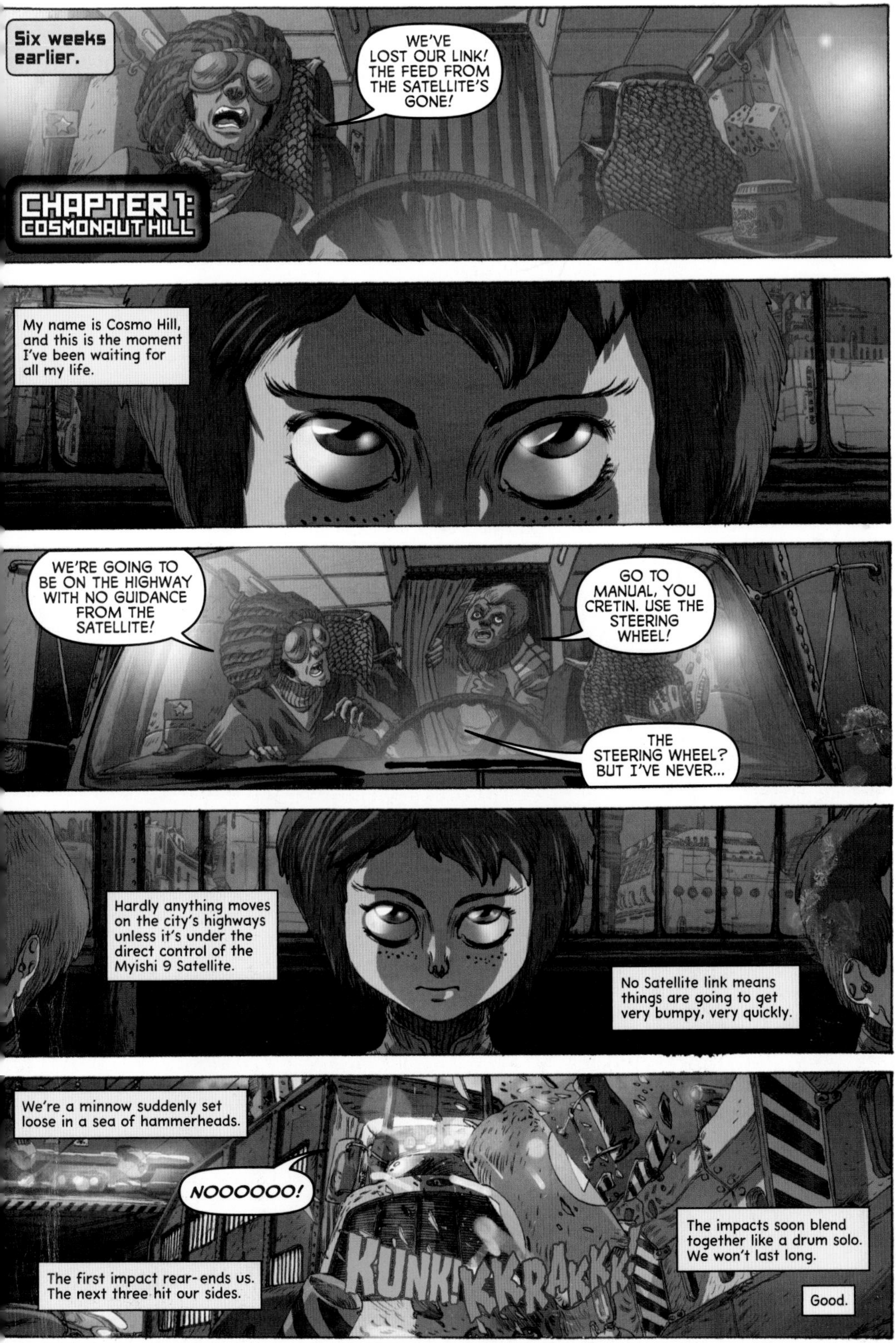

Six weeks earlier.
WE'VE LOST OUR LINK! THE FEED FROM THE SATELLITE'S GONE!
CHAPTER 1: COSMONAUT HILL
My name is Cosmo Hill, and this is the moment I've been waiting for all my life.
WE'RE GOING TO BE ON THE HIGHWAY WITH NO GUIDANCE FROM THE SATELLITE!
GO TO MANUAL, YOU CRETIN. USE THE STEERING WHEEL!
THE STEERING WHEEL? BUT I'VE NEVER...
Hardly anything moves on the city's highways unless it's under the direct control of the Myishi 9 Satellite.
No Satellite link means things are going to get very bumpy, very quickly.
We're a minnow suddenly set loose in a sea of hammerheads.
NOOOOOO!
KUNK! KKRAKKK
The first impact rear-ends us. The next three hit our sides.
The impacts soon blend together like a drum solo. We won't last long.
Good.

SATELLITE CITY—Northern Hemisphere.

"The City of the Future" proclaim the billboards.

A metropolis completely controlled by the Myishi 9 Satellite hovering overhead like a floating man-of-war

My name is Cosmo Hill, and this is the moment I've been waiting for all my life.

All fourteen years.

SSSKRRREECCHH!

WUMP!

KKRANKK!

KRUNK!

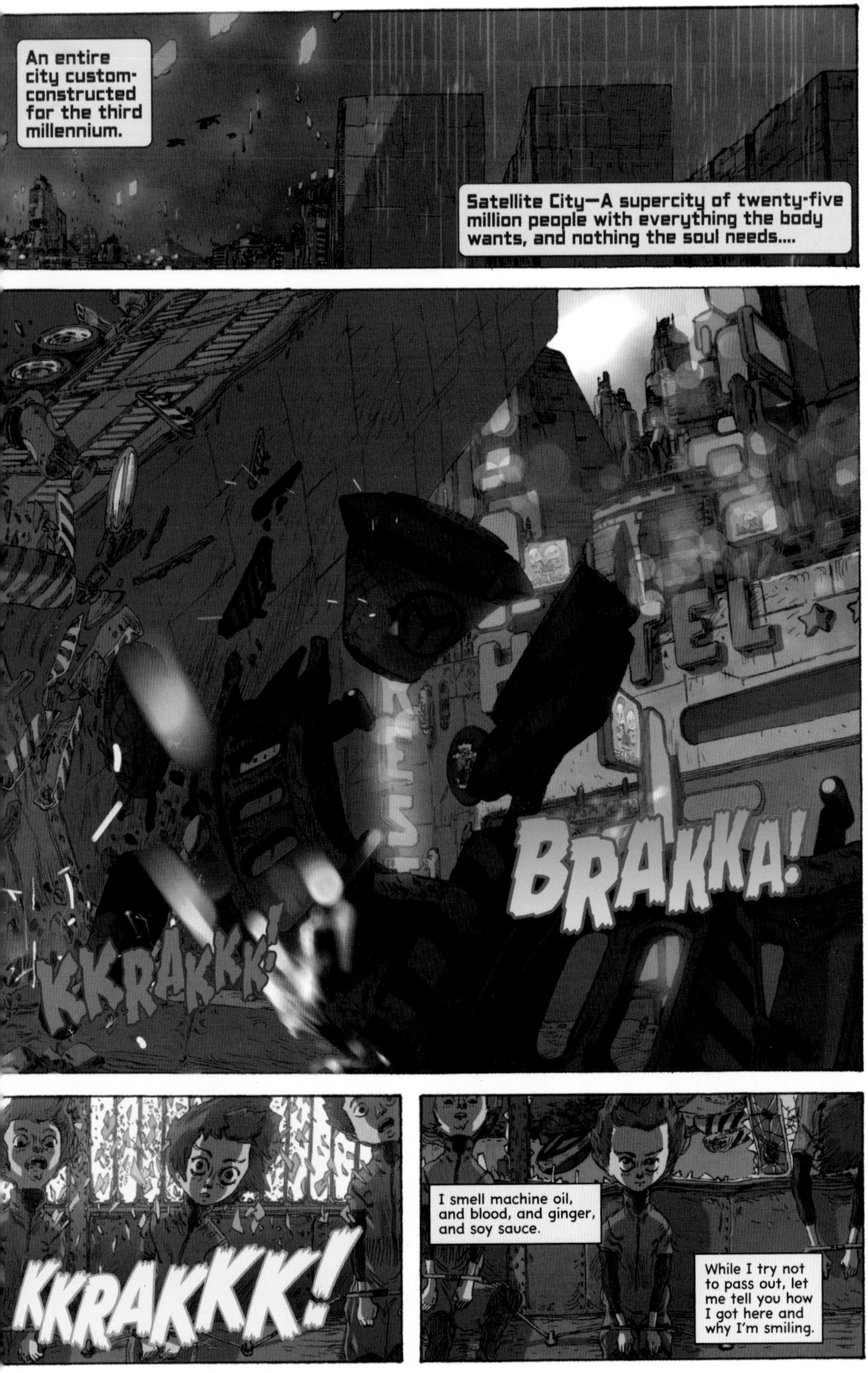
An entire city custom-constructed for the third millennium.
Satellite City—A supercity of twenty-five million people with everything the body wants, and nothing the soul needs....
BRAKKA!
KKRAKKK!
KKRAKKK!
I smell machine oil, and blood, and ginger, and soy sauce.
While I try not to pass out, let me tell you how I got here and why I'm smiling.

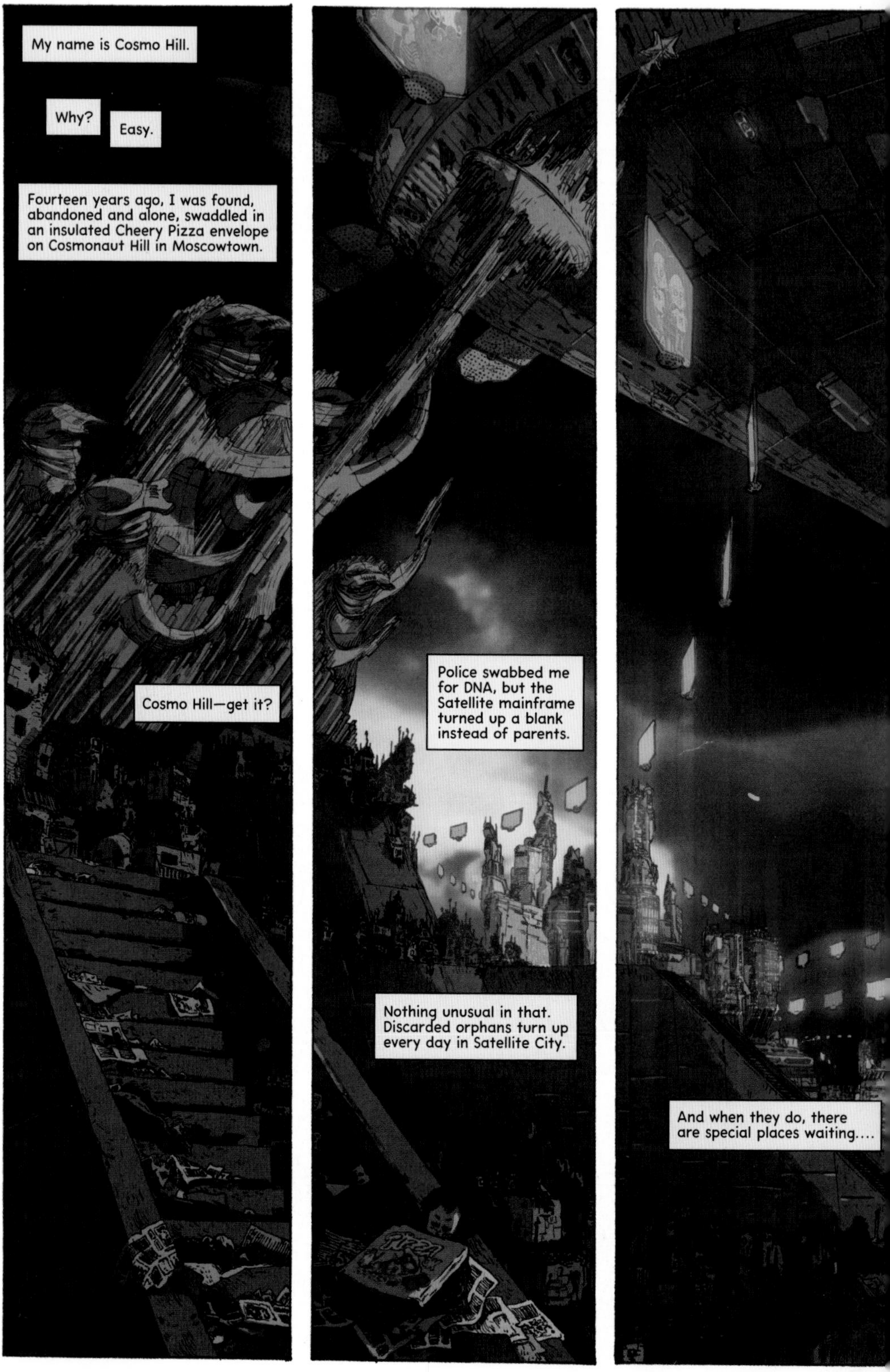
My name is Cosmo Hill.
Why?
Easy.
Fourteen years ago, I was found, abandoned and alone, swaddled in an insulated Cheery Pizza envelope on Cosmonaut Hill in Moscowtown.
Cosmo Hill—get it?
Police swabbed me for DNA, but the Satellite mainframe turned up a blank instead of parents.
Nothing unusual in that. Discarded orphans turn up every day in Satellite City.
And when they do, there are special places waiting....

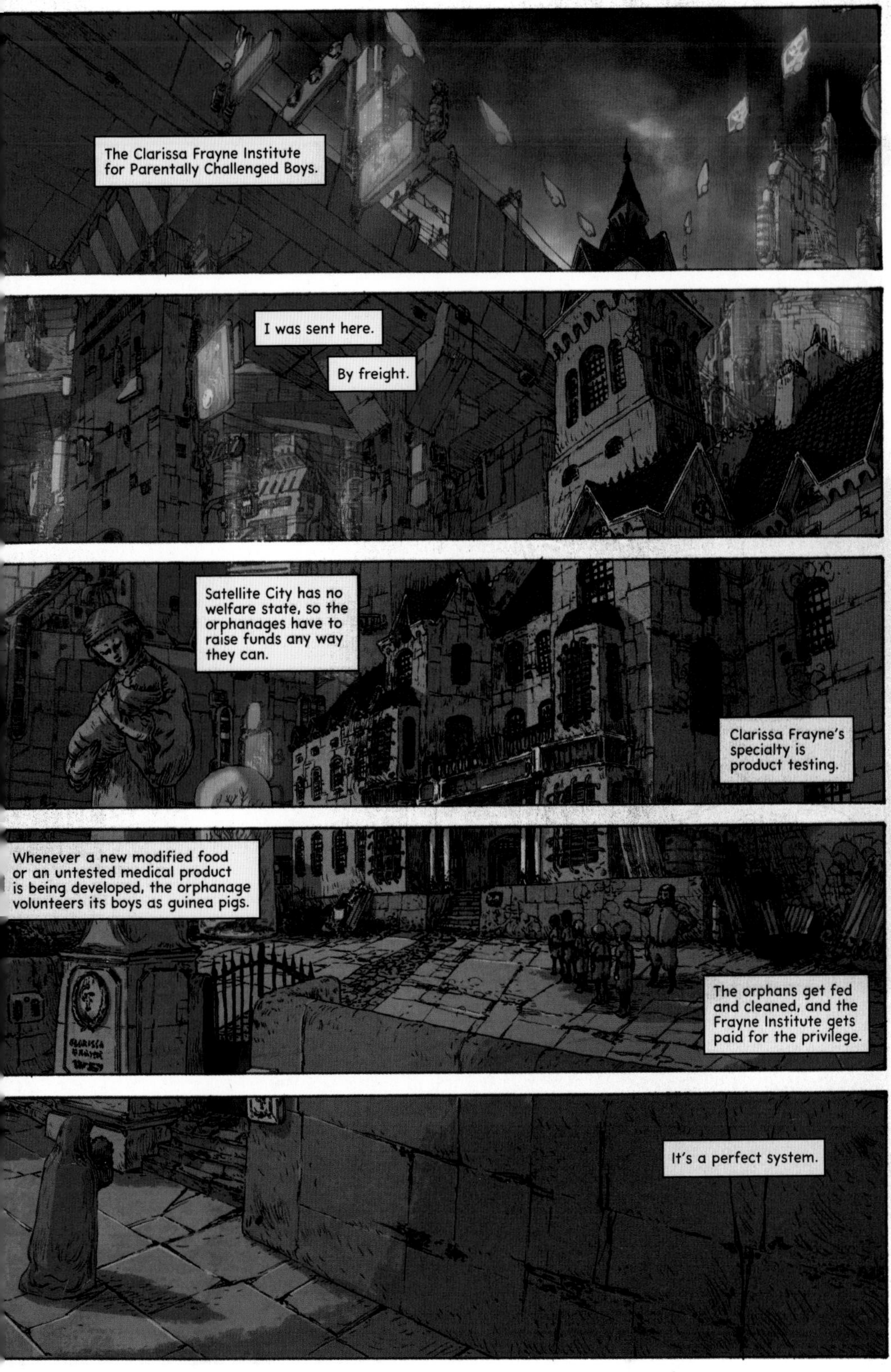
The Clarissa Frayne Institute for Parentally Challenged Boys.
I was sent here.
By freight.
Satellite City has no welfare state, so the orphanages have to raise funds any way they can.
Clarissa Frayne's specialty is product testing.
Whenever a new modified food or an untested medical product is being developed, the orphanage volunteers its boys as guinea pigs.
The orphans get fed and cleaned, and the Frayne Institute gets paid for the privilege.
It's a perfect system.

As long as it isn't being done to you.

GLAAAAGHLGIG!

They tested shampoos on me until my hair was lustrous and flake-free. And toothpastes until my teeth were whiter than white.

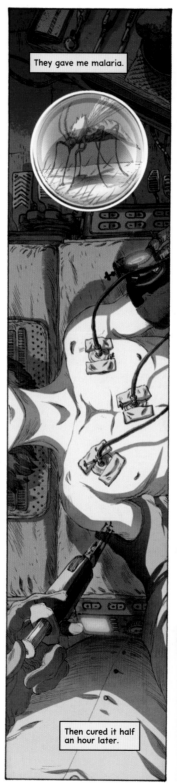

They gave me malaria.

Then cured it half an hour later.

Toxic pollution caused the rain molecules in Satellite City to bond together more efficiently until they fell to earth like rock-hard little missiles.

Anyone foolish enough to look up in a rainstorm could easily lose an eye.

Naturally, we got to test new reinforced raincoats and umbrell to make sure that they worked one hundred percent.

Surprise.

They didn't

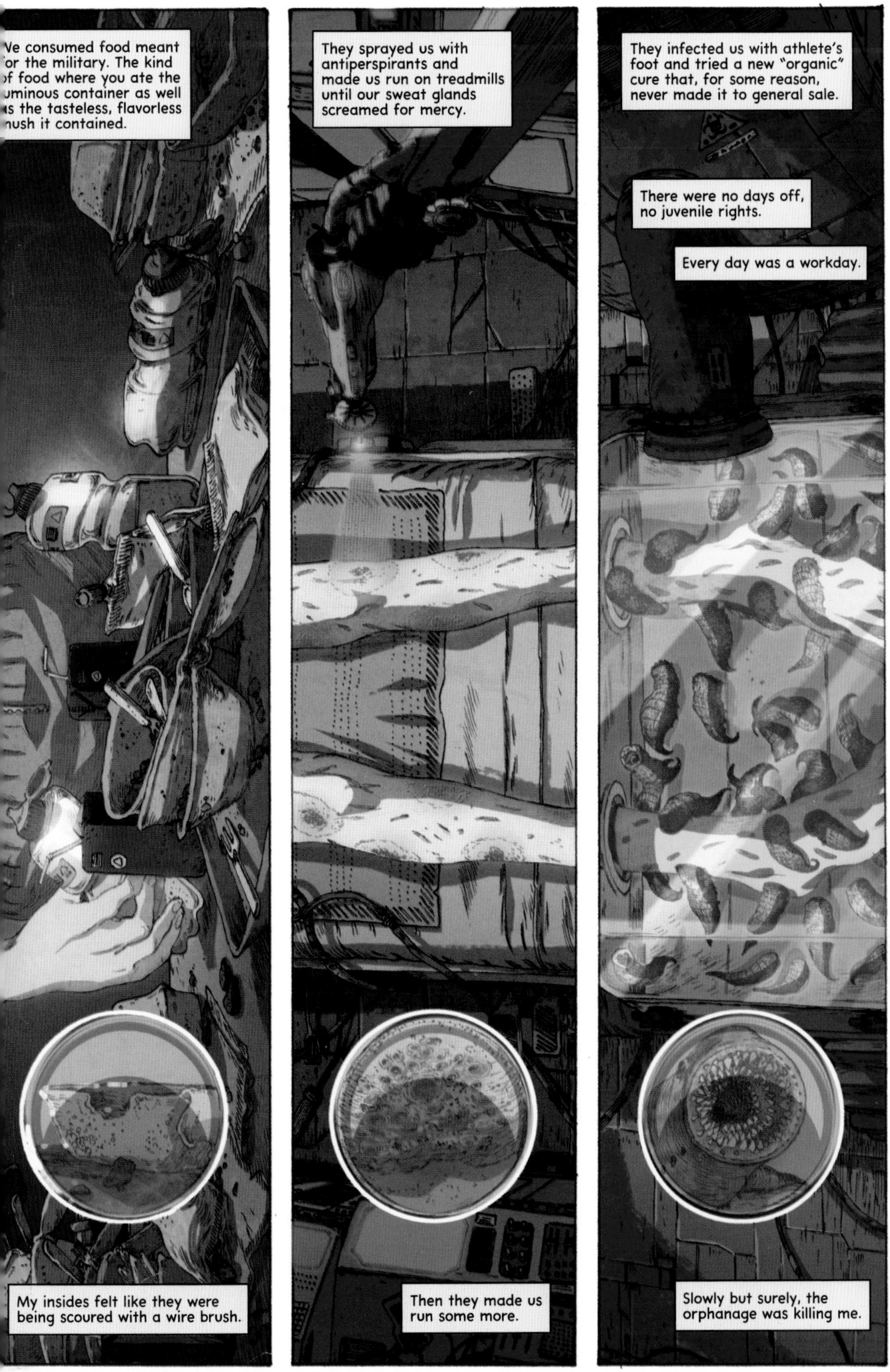
Ve consumed food meant 'or the military. The kind of food where you ate the uminous container as well as the tasteless, flavorless nush it contained.
My insides felt like they were being scoured with a wire brush.
They sprayed us with antiperspirants and made us run on treadmills until our sweat glands screamed for mercy.
Then they made us run some more.
They infected us with athlete's foot and tried a new "organic" cure that, for some reason, never made it to general sale.
There were no days off, no juvenile rights.
Every day was a workday.
Slowly but surely, the orphanage was killing me.

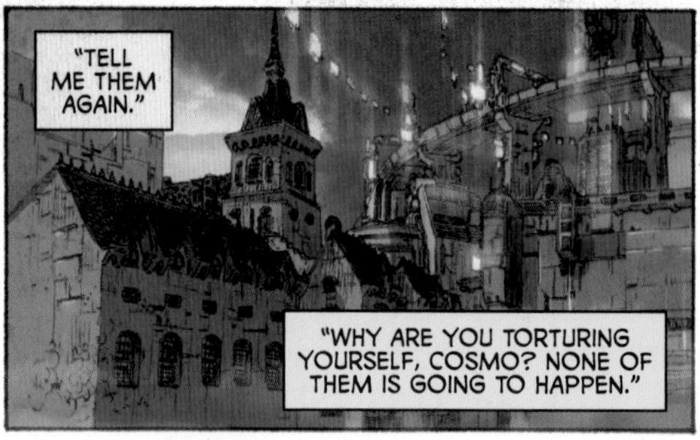
"TELL ME THEM AGAIN."
"WHY ARE YOU TORTURING YOURSELF, COSMO? NONE OF THEM IS GOING TO HAPPEN."

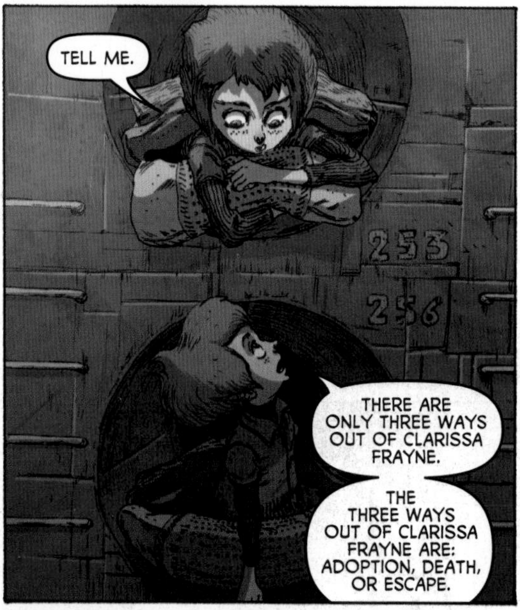
TELL ME.
253
256
THERE ARE ONLY THREE WAYS OUT OF CLARISSA FRAYNE.
THE THREE WAYS OUT OF CLARISSA FRAYNE ARE: ADOPTION, DEATH, OR ESCAPE.

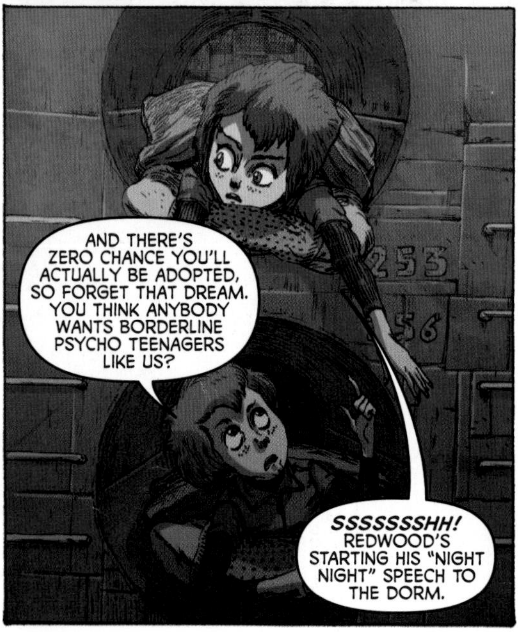
AND THERE'S ZERO CHANCE YOU'LL ACTUALLY BE ADOPTED, SO FORGET THAT DREAM. YOU THINK ANYBODY WANTS BORDERLINE PSYCHO TEENAGERS LIKE US?
SSSSSSSHH! REDWOOD'S STARTING HIS "NIGHT NIGHT" SPEECH TO THE DORM.

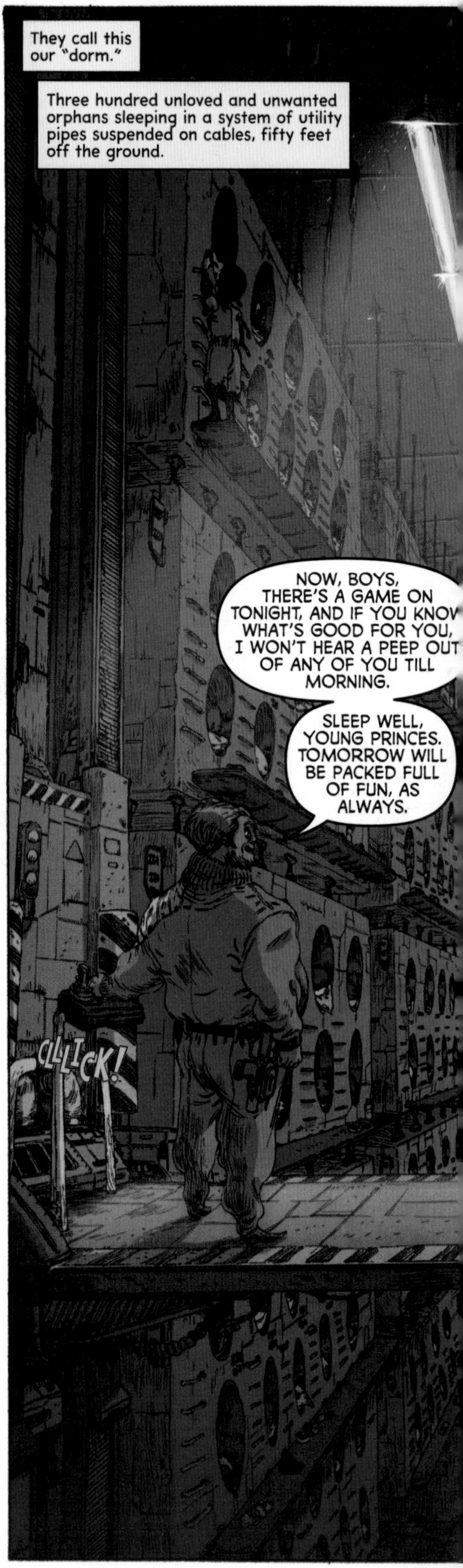
They call this our "dorm."
Three hundred unloved and unwanted orphans sleeping in a system of utility pipes suspended on cables, fifty feet off the ground.
NOW, BOYS, THERE'S A GAME ON TONIGHT, AND IF YOU KNOW WHAT'S GOOD FOR YOU, I WON'T HEAR A PEEP OUT OF ANY OF YOU TILL MORNING.
SLEEP WELL, YOUNG PRINCES. TOMORROW WILL BE PACKED FULL OF FUN, AS ALWAYS.
CLLLICK!

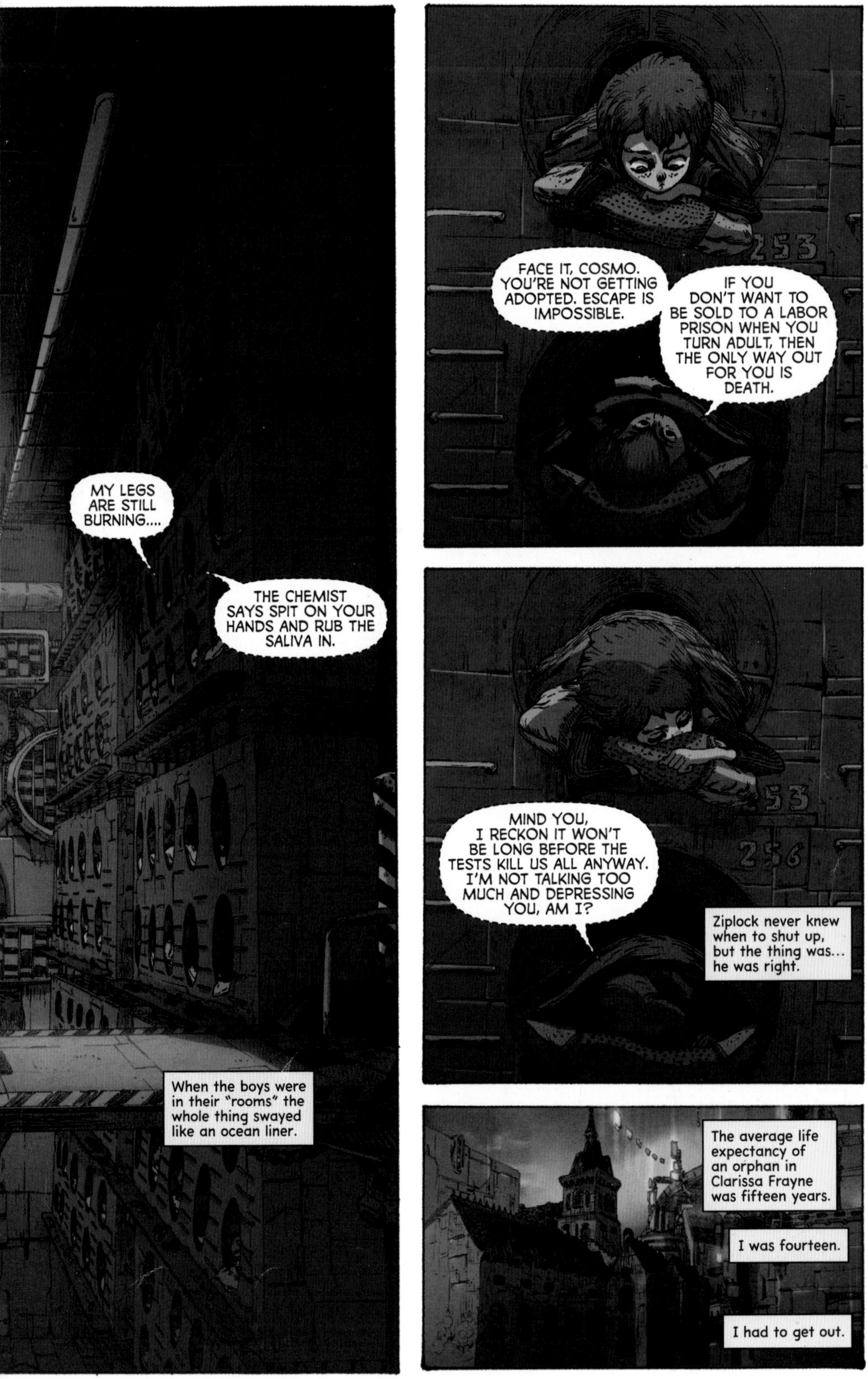
MY LEGS ARE STILL BURNING....
THE CHEMIST SAYS SPIT ON YOUR HANDS AND RUB THE SALIVA IN.
When the boys were in their "rooms" the whole thing swayed like an ocean liner.
253
FACE IT, COSMO. YOU'RE NOT GETTING ADOPTED. ESCAPE IS IMPOSSIBLE.
IF YOU DON'T WANT TO BE SOLD TO A LABOR PRISON WHEN YOU TURN ADULT, THEN THE ONLY WAY OUT FOR YOU IS DEATH.
256
MIND YOU, I RECKON IT WON'T BE LONG BEFORE THE TESTS KILL US ALL ANYWAY. I'M NOT TALKING TOO MUCH AND DEPRESSING YOU, AM I?
Ziplock never knew when to shut up, but the thing was... he was right.
The average life expectancy of an orphan in Clarissa Frayne was fifteen years.
I was fourteen.
I had to get out.

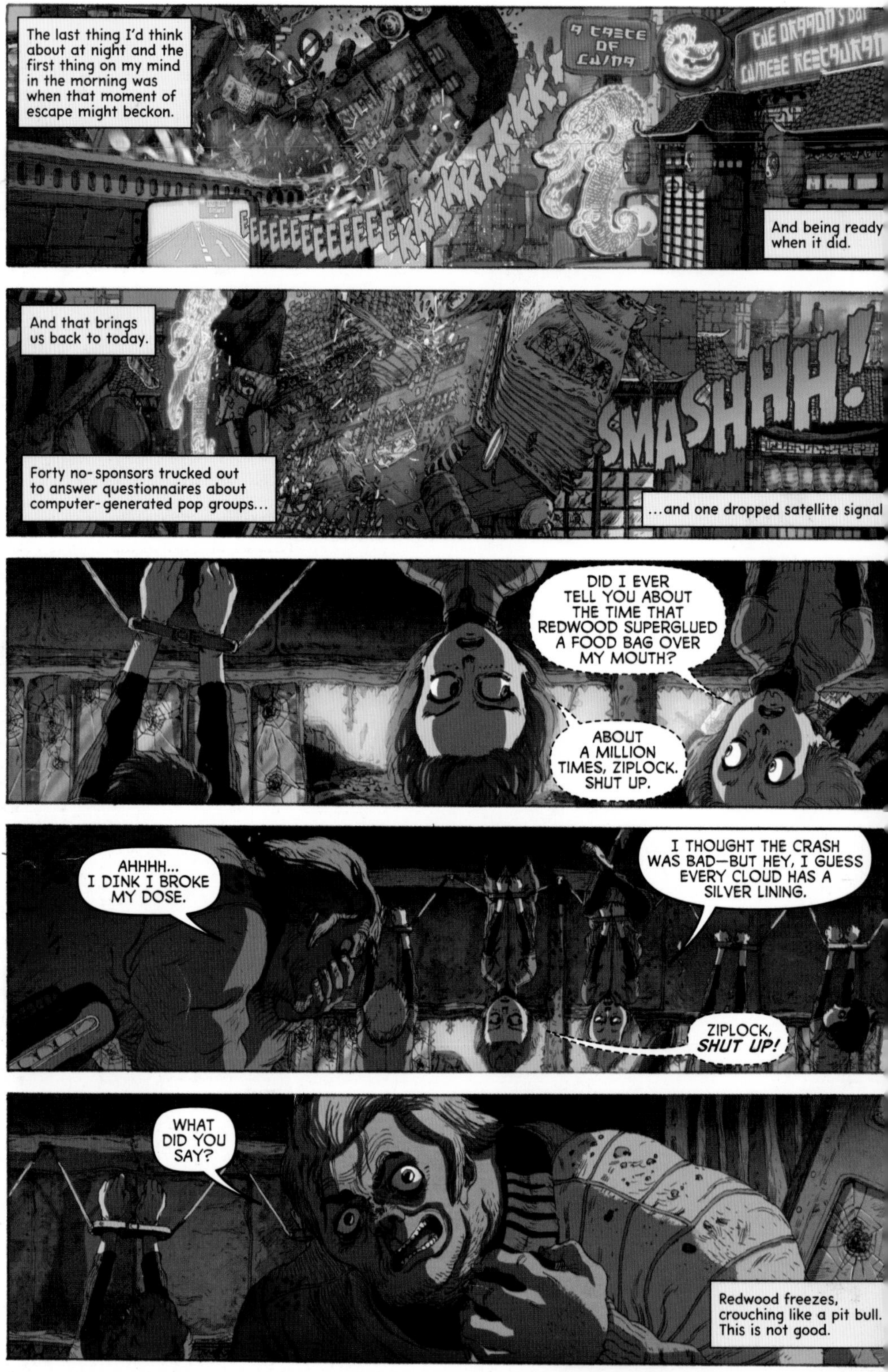
The last thing I'd think about at night and the first thing on my mind in the morning was when that moment of escape might beckon.
EEEEEEEEEEEEEKKKKKKKKK!
And being ready when it did.
And that brings us back to today.
Forty no-sponsors trucked out to answer questionnaires about computer-generated pop groups...
SMASHHH!
...and one dropped satellite signal
DID I EVER TELL YOU ABOUT THE TIME THAT REDWOOD SUPERGLUED A FOOD BAG OVER MY MOUTH?
ABOUT A MILLION TIMES, ZIPLOCK. SHUT UP.
AHHHH... I DINK I BROKE MY DOSE.
I THOUGHT THE CRASH WAS BAD—BUT HEY, I GUESS EVERY CLOUD HAS A SILVER LINING.
ZIPLOCK, SHUT UP!
WHAT DID YOU SAY?
Redwood freezes, crouching like a pit bull. This is not good.

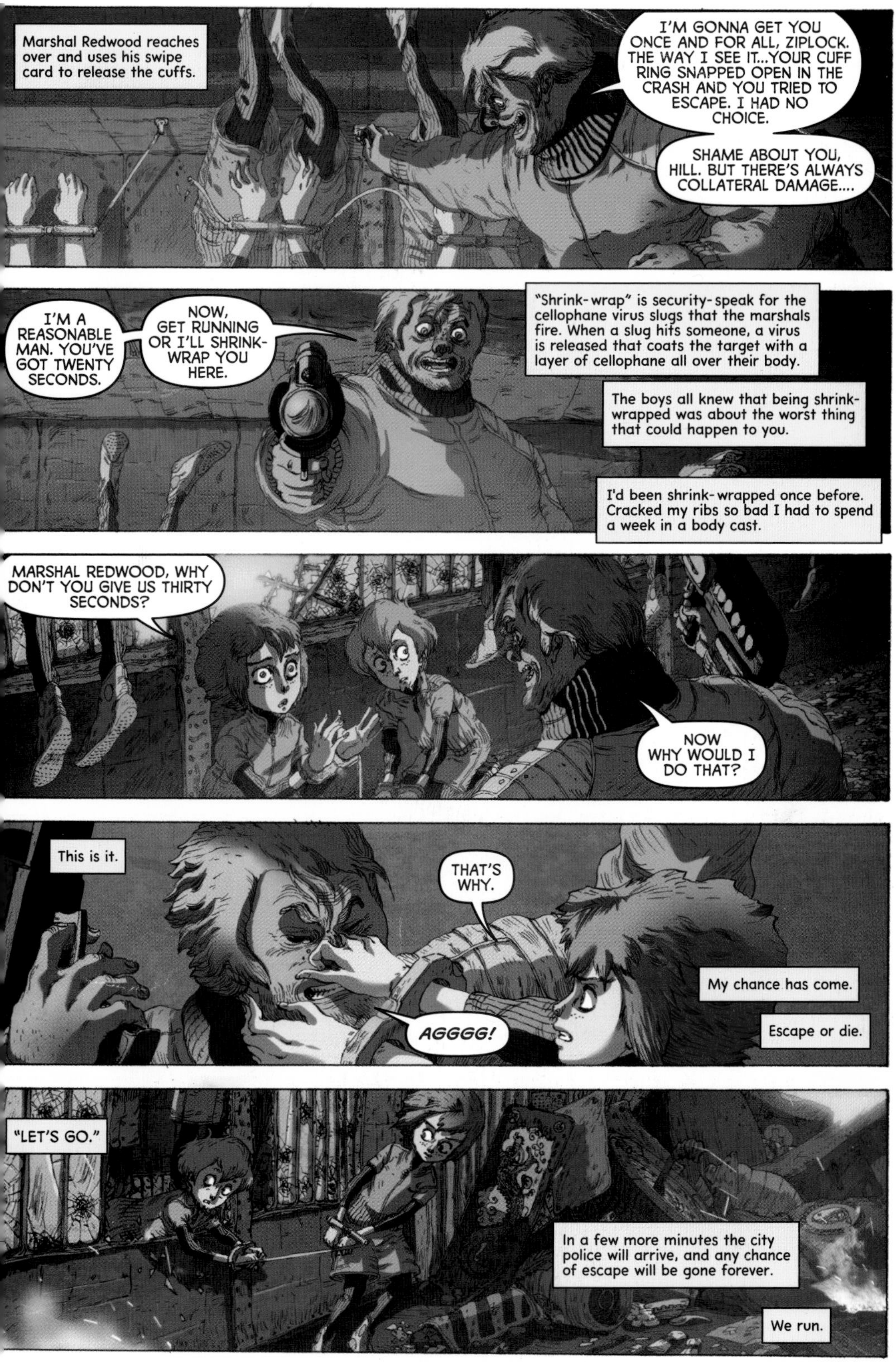

Marshal Redwood reaches over and uses his swipe card to release the cuffs.
I'M GONNA GET YOU ONCE AND FOR ALL, ZIPLOCK. THE WAY I SEE IT...YOUR CUFF RING SNAPPED OPEN IN THE CRASH AND YOU TRIED TO ESCAPE. I HAD NO CHOICE.
SHAME ABOUT YOU, HILL. BUT THERE'S ALWAYS COLLATERAL DAMAGE....
I'M A REASONABLE MAN. YOU'VE GOT TWENTY SECONDS.
NOW, GET RUNNING OR I'LL SHRINK-WRAP YOU HERE.
"Shrink-wrap" is security-speak for the cellophane virus slugs that the marshals fire. When a slug hits someone, a virus is released that coats the target with a layer of cellophane all over their body.
The boys all knew that being shrink-wrapped was about the worst thing that could happen to you.
I'd been shrink-wrapped once before. Cracked my ribs so bad I had to spend a week in a body cast.
MARSHAL REDWOOD, WHY DON'T YOU GIVE US THIRTY SECONDS?
NOW WHY WOULD I DO THAT?
This is it.
THAT'S WHY.
AGGGG!
My chance has come.
Escape or die.
"LET'S GO."
In a few more minutes the city police will arrive, and any chance of escape will be gone forever.
We run.

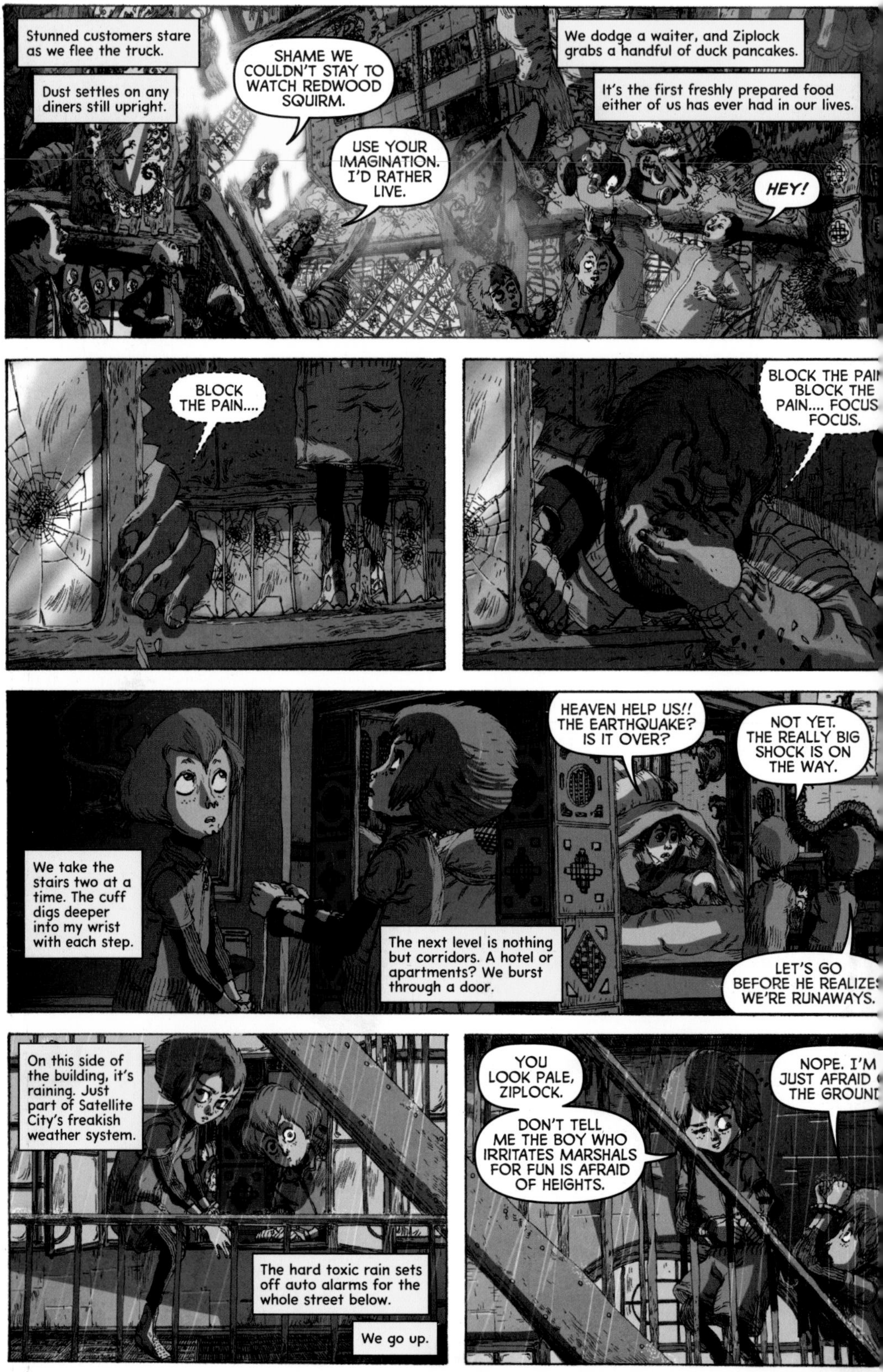
Stunned customers stare as we flee the truck.
Dust settles on any diners still upright.
SHAME WE COULDN'T STAY TO WATCH REDWOOD SQUIRM.
USE YOUR IMAGINATION. I'D RATHER LIVE.
We dodge a waiter, and Ziplock grabs a handful of duck pancakes.
It's the first freshly prepared food either of us has ever had in our lives.
HEY!
BLOCK THE PAIN....
BLOCK THE PAI
BLOCK THE PAIN.... FOCUS
FOCUS.
We take the stairs two at a time. The cuff digs deeper into my wrist with each step.
The next level is nothing but corridors. A hotel or apartments? We burst through a door.
HEAVEN HELP US!! THE EARTHQUAKE? IS IT OVER?
NOT YET. THE REALLY BIG SHOCK IS ON THE WAY.
LET'S GO BEFORE HE REALIZE
WE'RE RUNAWAYS.
On this side of the building, it's raining. Just part of Satellite City's freakish weather system.
The hard toxic rain sets off auto alarms for the whole street below.
We go up.
YOU LOOK PALE, ZIPLOCK.
DON'T TELL ME THE BOY WHO IRRITATES MARSHALS FOR FUN IS AFRAID OF HEIGHTS.
NOPE. I'M JUST AFRAID
THE GROUN

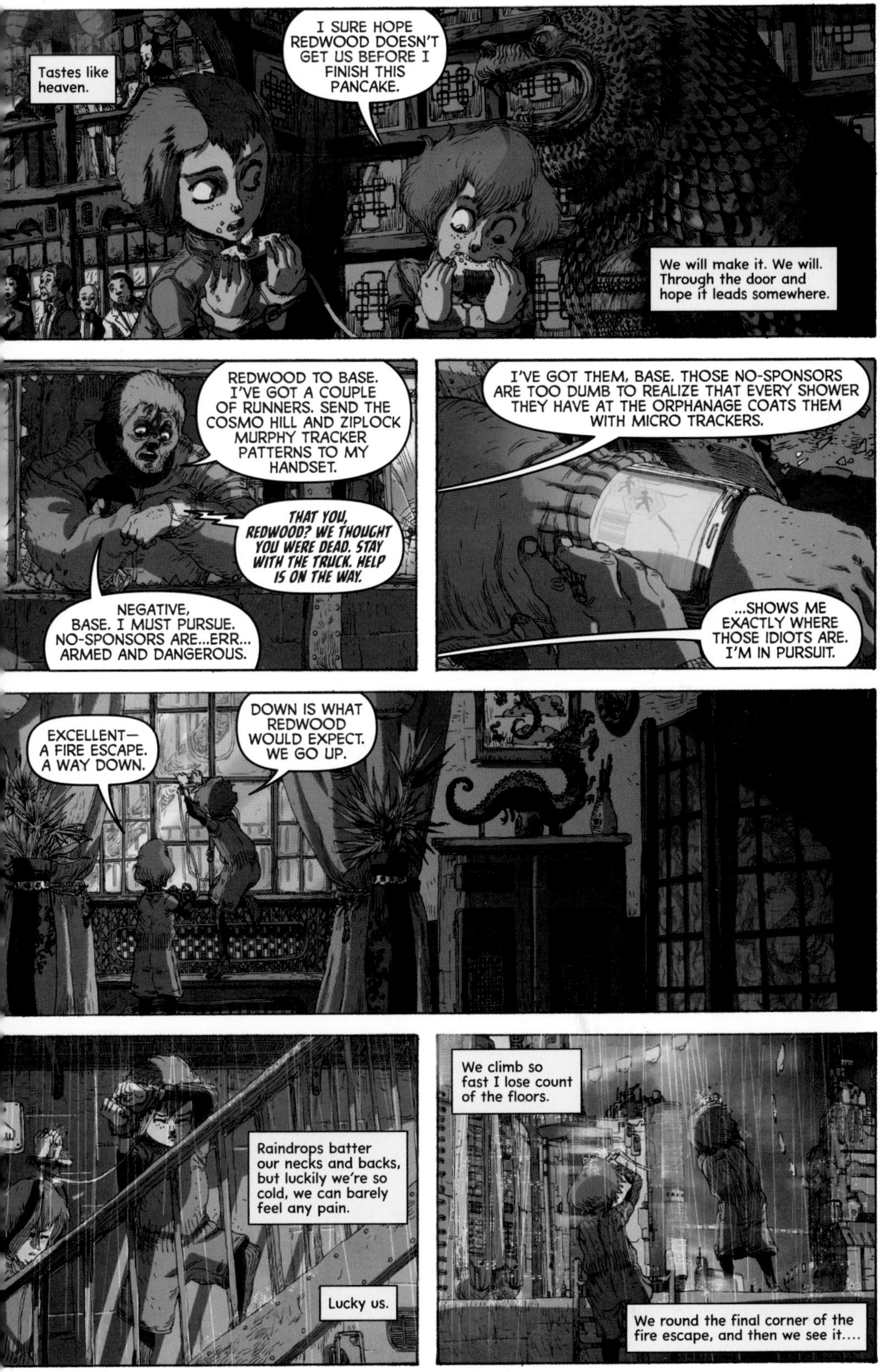

Tastes like heaven.
I SURE HOPE REDWOOD DOESN'T GET US BEFORE I FINISH THIS PANCAKE.
We will make it. We will. Through the door and hope it leads somewhere.
REDWOOD TO BASE. I'VE GOT A COUPLE OF RUNNERS. SEND THE COSMO HILL AND ZIPLOCK MURPHY TRACKER PATTERNS TO MY HANDSET.
THAT YOU, REDWOOD? WE THOUGHT YOU WERE DEAD. STAY WITH THE TRUCK. HELP IS ON THE WAY.
NEGATIVE, BASE. I MUST PURSUE. NO-SPONSORS ARE...ERR... ARMED AND DANGEROUS.
I'VE GOT THEM, BASE. THOSE NO-SPONSORS ARE TOO DUMB TO REALIZE THAT EVERY SHOWER THEY HAVE AT THE ORPHANAGE COATS THEM WITH MICRO TRACKERS.
...SHOWS ME EXACTLY WHERE THOSE IDIOTS ARE. I'M IN PURSUIT.
EXCELLENT— A FIRE ESCAPE. A WAY DOWN.
DOWN IS WHAT REDWOOD WOULD EXPECT. WE GO UP.
Raindrops batter our necks and backs, but luckily we're so cold, we can barely feel any pain.
Lucky us.
We climb so fast I lose count of the floors.
We round the final corner of the fire escape, and then we see it....

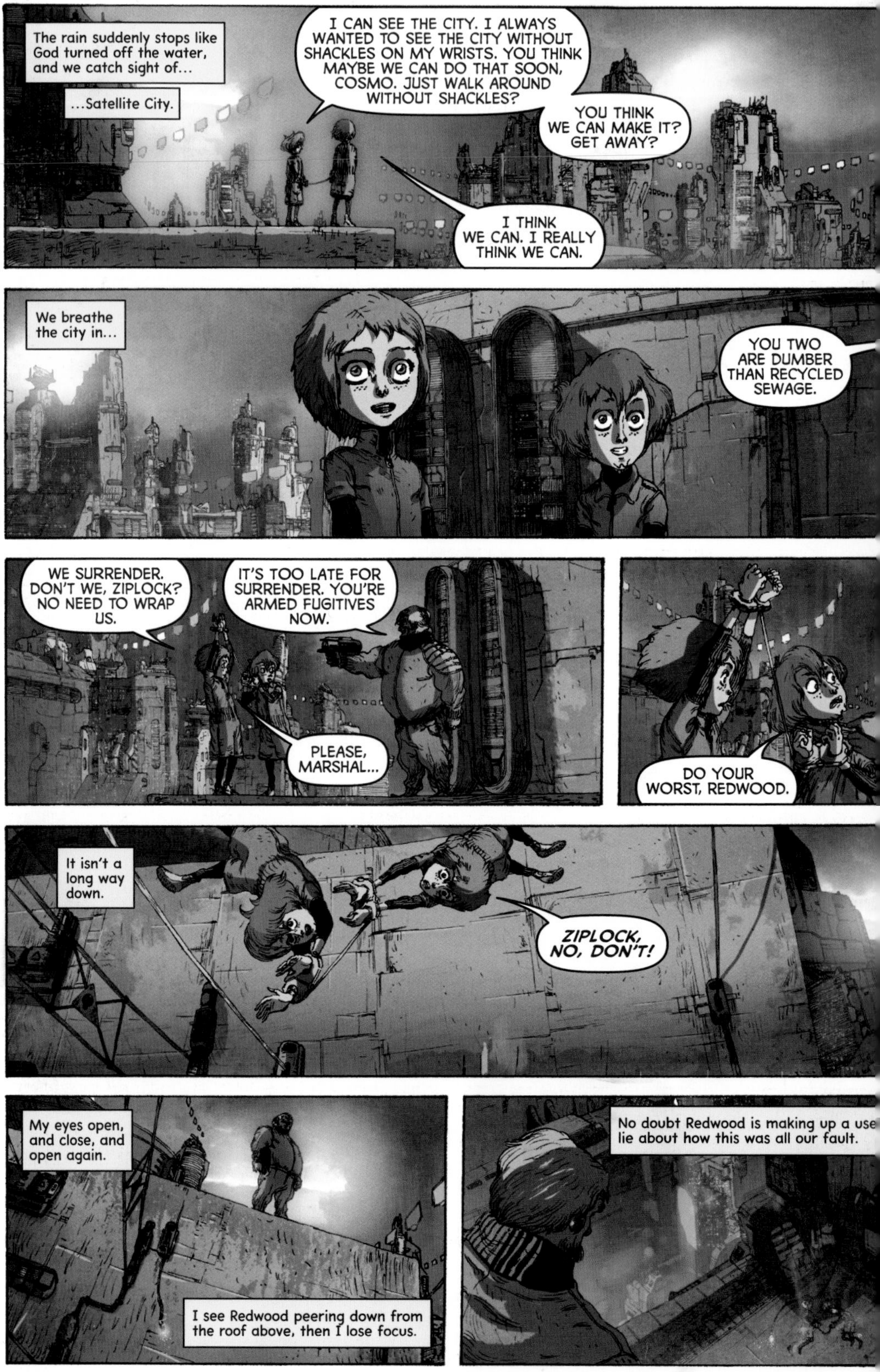

The rain suddenly stops like God turned off the water, and we catch sight of...
...Satellite City.
I CAN SEE THE CITY. I ALWAYS WANTED TO SEE THE CITY WITHOUT SHACKLES ON MY WRISTS. YOU THINK MAYBE WE CAN DO THAT SOON, COSMO. JUST WALK AROUND WITHOUT SHACKLES?
YOU THINK WE CAN MAKE IT? GET AWAY?
I THINK WE CAN. I REALLY THINK WE CAN.
We breathe the city in...
YOU TWO ARE DUMBER THAN RECYCLED SEWAGE.
WE SURRENDER. DON'T WE, ZIPLOCK? NO NEED TO WRAP US.
IT'S TOO LATE FOR SURRENDER. YOU'RE ARMED FUGITIVES NOW.
PLEASE, MARSHAL...
DO YOUR WORST, REDWOOD.
It isn't a long way down.
ZIPLOCK, NO, DON'T!
My eyes open, and close, and open again.
I see Redwood peering down from the roof above, then I lose focus.
No doubt Redwood is making up a use
lie about how this was all our fault.

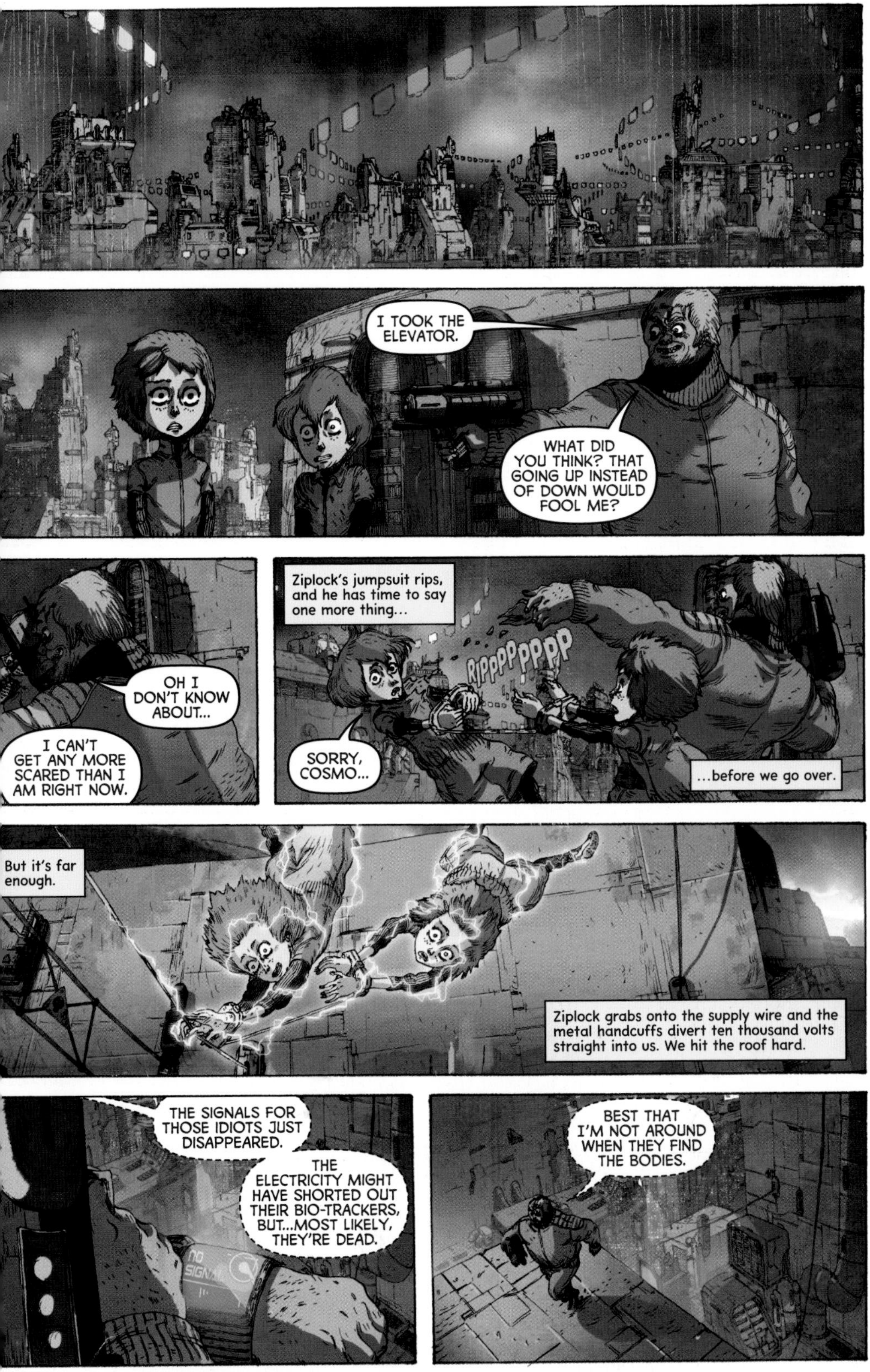
I TOOK THE ELEVATOR.
WHAT DID YOU THINK? THAT GOING UP INSTEAD OF DOWN WOULD FOOL ME?
OH I DON'T KNOW ABOUT...
I CAN'T GET ANY MORE SCARED THAN I AM RIGHT NOW.
Ziplock's jumpsuit rips, and he has time to say one more thing...
RIPPPPPPPP
SORRY, COSMO...
...before we go over.
But it's far enough.
Ziplock grabs onto the supply wire and the metal handcuffs divert ten thousand volts straight into us. We hit the roof hard.
THE SIGNALS FOR THOSE IDIOTS JUST DISAPPEARED.
THE ELECTRICITY MIGHT HAVE SHORTED OUT THEIR BIO-TRACKERS, BUT...MOST LIKELY, THEY'RE DEAD.
BEST THAT I'M NOT AROUND WHEN THEY FIND THE BODIES.

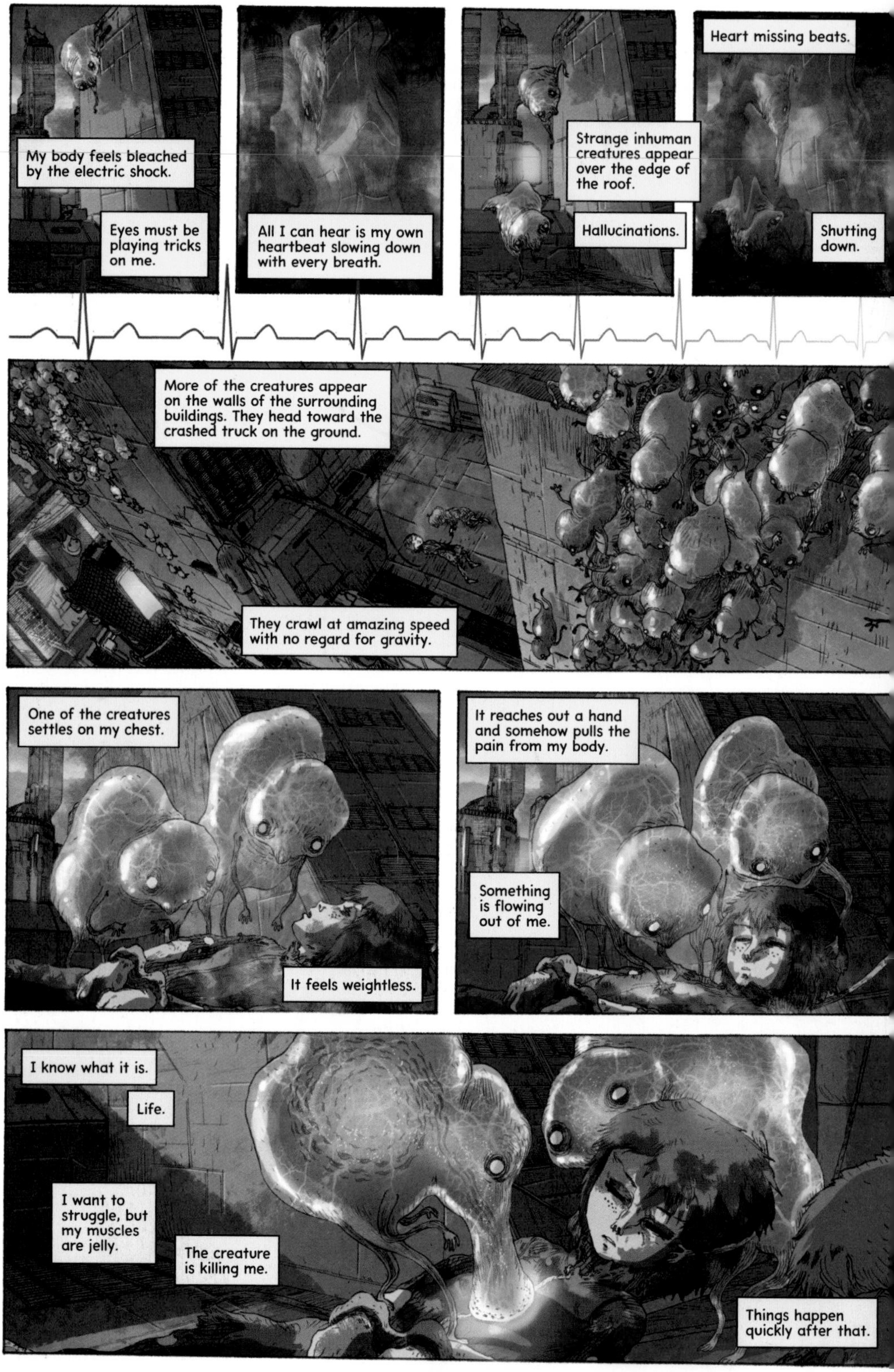
My body feels bleached by the electric shock.
Eyes must be playing tricks on me.
All I can hear is my own heartbeat slowing down with every breath.
Strange inhuman creatures appear over the edge of the roof.
Hallucinations.
Heart missing beats.
Shutting down.
More of the creatures appear on the walls of the surrounding buildings. They head toward the crashed truck on the ground.
They crawl at amazing speed with no regard for gravity.
One of the creatures settles on my chest.
It feels weightless.
It reaches out a hand and somehow pulls the pain from my body.
Something is flowing out of me.
I know what it is.
Life.
I want to struggle, but my muscles are jelly.
The creature is killing me.
Things happen quickly after that.

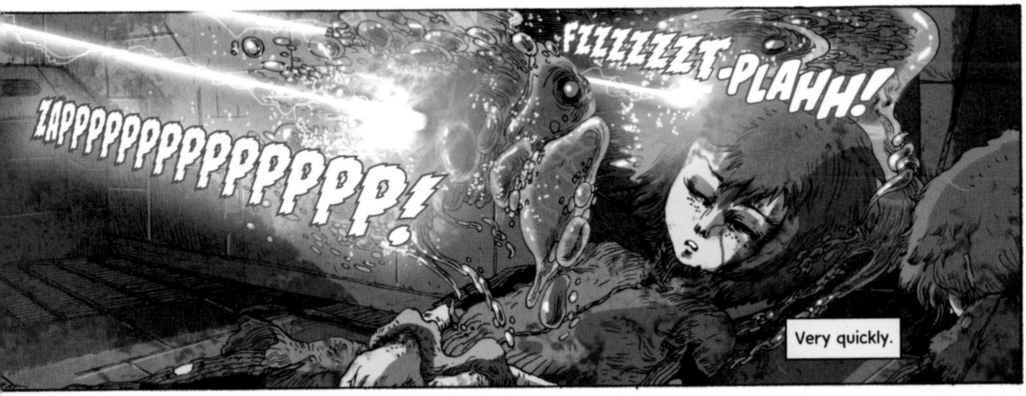
ZAPPPPPPPPPPPPPPP!
FZZZZZZZT-PLAHH!
Very quickly.

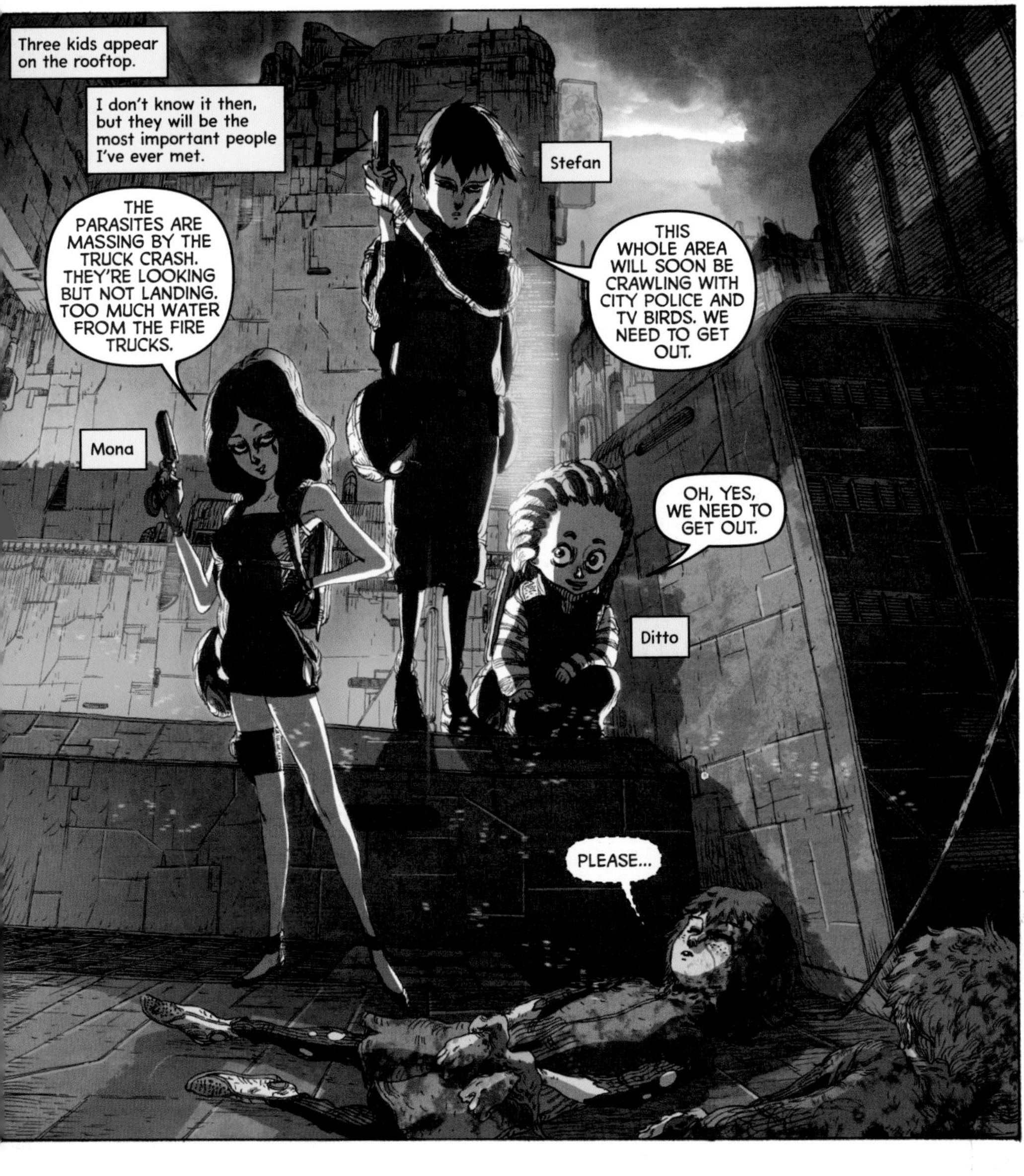
Three kids appear on the rooftop.
I don't know it then, but they will be the most important people I've ever met.
Stefan
THE PARASITES ARE MASSING BY THE TRUCK CRASH. THEY'RE LOOKING BUT NOT LANDING. TOO MUCH WATER FROM THE FIRE TRUCKS.
THIS WHOLE AREA WILL SOON BE CRAWLING WITH CITY POLICE AND TV BIRDS. WE NEED TO GET OUT.
Mona
OH, YES, WE NEED TO GET OUT.
Ditto
PLEASE...

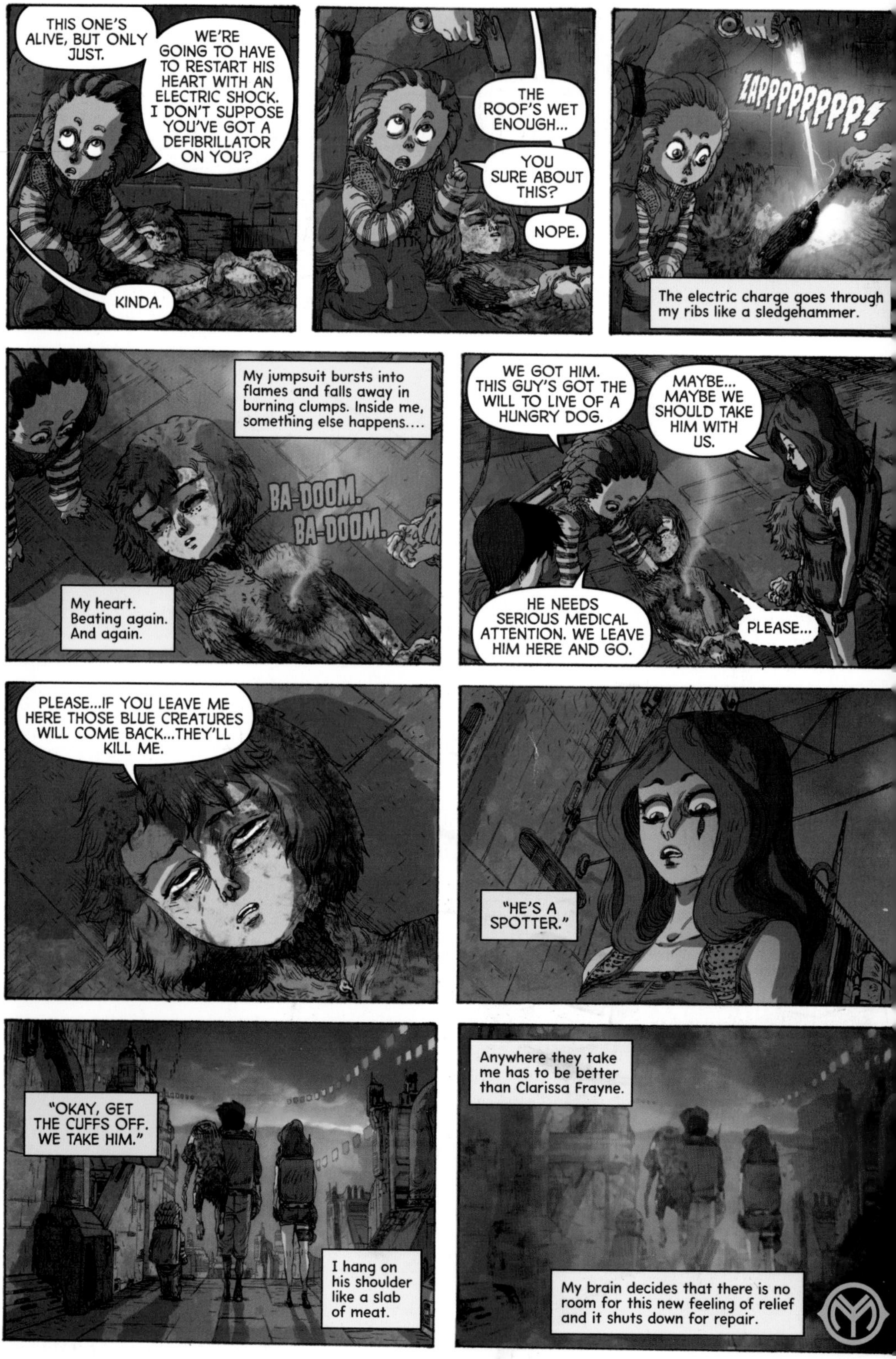
THIS ONE'S ALIVE, BUT ONLY JUST.
WE'RE GOING TO HAVE TO RESTART HIS HEART WITH AN ELECTRIC SHOCK. I DON'T SUPPOSE YOU'VE GOT A DEFIBRILLATOR ON YOU?
KINDA.
THE ROOF'S WET ENOUGH...
YOU SURE ABOUT THIS?
NOPE.
ZAPPPPPPPP!
The electric charge goes through my ribs like a sledgehammer.
My jumpsuit bursts into flames and falls away in burning clumps. Inside me, something else happens....
BA-DOOM.
BA-DOOM.
My heart. Beating again. And again.
WE GOT HIM. THIS GUY'S GOT THE WILL TO LIVE OF A HUNGRY DOG.
MAYBE... MAYBE WE SHOULD TAKE HIM WITH US.
HE NEEDS SERIOUS MEDICAL ATTENTION. WE LEAVE HIM HERE AND GO.
PLEASE...
PLEASE...IF YOU LEAVE ME HERE THOSE BLUE CREATURES WILL COME BACK...THEY'LL KILL ME.
"HE'S A SPOTTER."
"OKAY, GET THE CUFFS OFF. WE TAKE HIM."
I hang on his shoulder like a slab of meat.
Anywhere they take me has to be better than Clarissa Frayne.
My brain decides that there is no room for this new feeling of relief and it shuts down for repair.

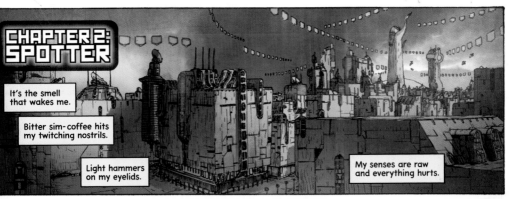

CHAPTER 2: SPOTTER

It's the smell that wakes me.

Bitter sim-coffee hits my twitching nostrils.

Light hammers on my eyelids.

My senses are raw and everything hurts.

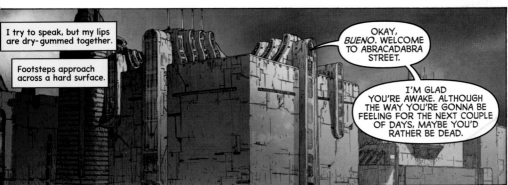

I try to speak, but my lips are dry-gummed together.

Footsteps approach across a hard surface.

OKAY, *BUENO*. WELCOME TO ABRACADABRA STREET.

I'M GLAD YOU'RE AWAKE. ALTHOUGH THE WAY YOU'RE GONNA BE FEELING FOR THE NEXT COUPLE OF DAYS, MAYBE YOU'D RATHER BE DEAD.

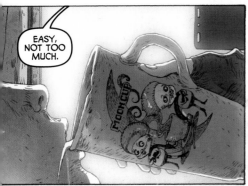

EASY, NOT TOO MUCH.

MOON CUP

The girl from the roof.

Then I remember it all. The crash, the climb, the fall.

ZIPLOCK?

"ZIPLOCK"?

YOU GOT THE ENERGY FOR ONE WORD AND THAT'S THE WORD YOU PICK?

She sees my face and winces at her own blunder.

I'M SORRY.

ZIPLOCK, WAS THAT YOUR FRIEND'S NAME?

SORRY, KID. HE WAS GONE WHEN WE GOT THERE. WE HAD TO LEAVE HIM BEHIND, REMEMBER?

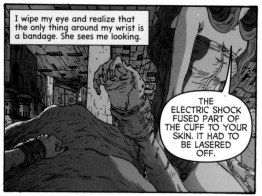

I wipe my eye and realize that the only thing around my wrist is a bandage. She sees me looking.

THE ELECTRIC SHOCK FUSED PART OF THE CUFF TO YOUR SKIN. IT HAD TO BE LASERED OFF.

There's a tattoo under her eye. It's in the shape of a DNA strand—signature of one of the city's many street gangs.

DITTO SAID YOU WERE LUCKY THE VEIN DIDN'T POP.

The tattoo ink is loaded with a scannable isotope to prevent police infiltration.

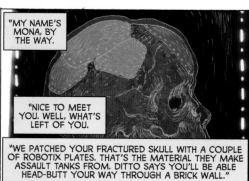

"MY NAME'S MONA, BY THE WAY.

"NICE TO MEET YOU. WELL, WHAT'S LEFT OF YOU.

"WE PATCHED YOUR FRACTURED SKULL WITH A COUPLE OF ROBOTIX PLATES. THAT'S THE MATERIAL THEY MAKE ASSAULT TANKS FROM. DITTO SAYS YOU'LL BE ABLE HEAD-BUTT YOUR WAY THROUGH A BRICK WALL."

DITTO? THE LITTLE BOY?

SHHH! DON'T CALL HIM THAT. HE'S VERY TOUCHY.

DITTO IS A BARTOLI BABY. THAT LITTLE BOY IS TWENTY-EIGHT YEARS OLD.

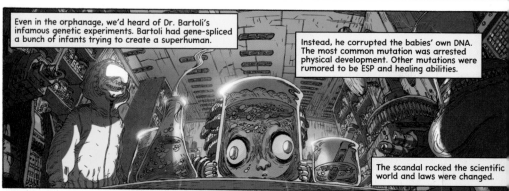

Even in the orphanage, we'd heard of Dr. Bartoli's infamous genetic experiments. Bartoli had gene-spliced a bunch of infants trying to create a superhuman.

Instead, he corrupted the babies' own DNA. The most common mutation was arrested physical development. Other mutations were rumored to be ESP and healing abilities.

The scandal rocked the scientific world and laws were changed.

THIS SEDATIVE PATCH WILL HELP.

THE BEST THING FOR YOU NOW IS REST AND RECUPERATION.

NO, I DON'T WANT TO....

Too late. I just have time to tell her my name, but the sedative is already seeping into my bloodstream.

NIGHTY NIGHT.

The world drips away like wet paint down a canvas.

My eyes close.

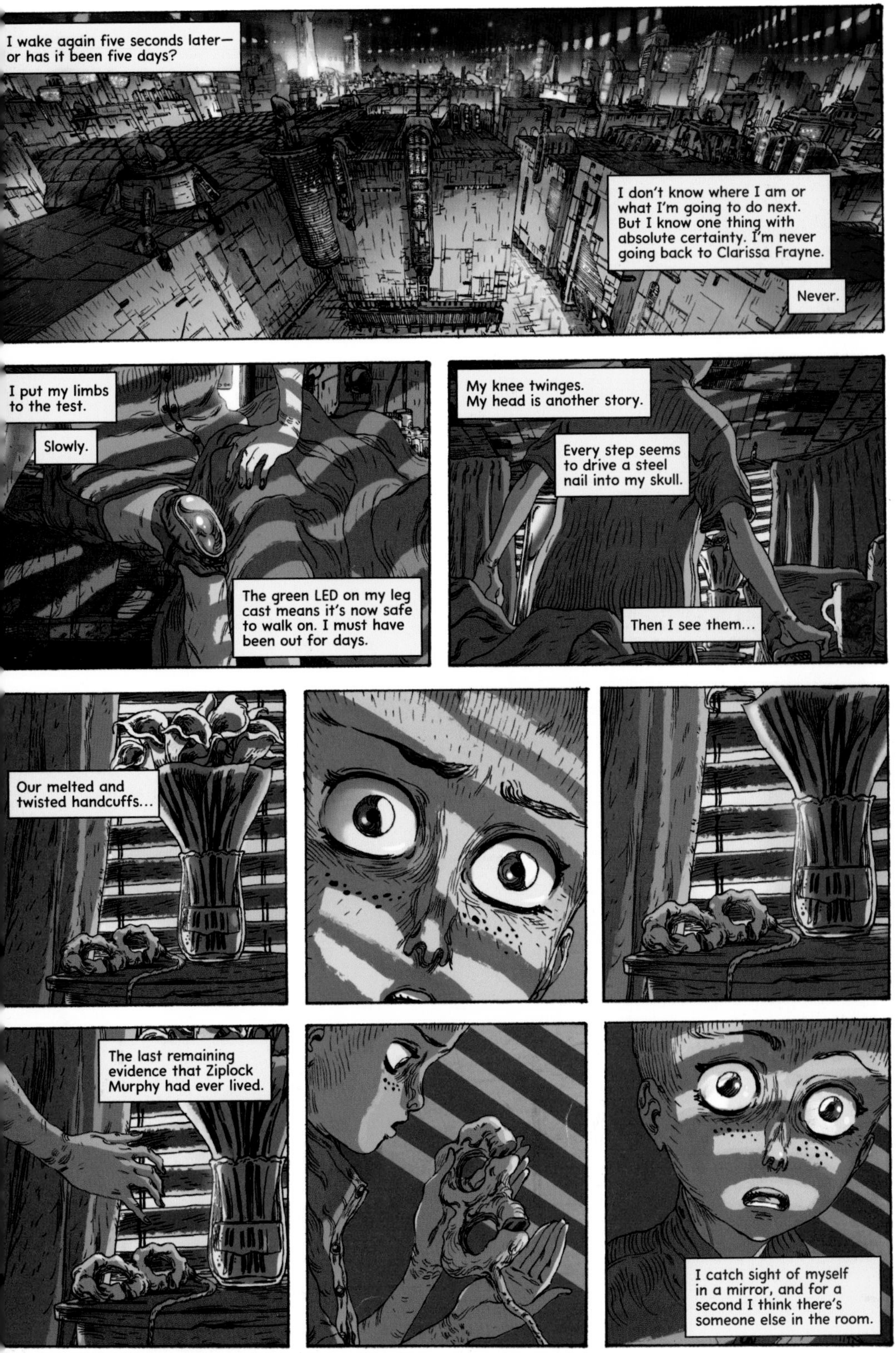

I wake again five seconds later— or has it been five days?
I don't know where I am or what I'm going to do next. But I know one thing with absolute certainty. I'm never going back to Clarissa Frayne.
Never.
I put my limbs to the test.
Slowly.
The green LED on my leg cast means it's now safe to walk on. I must have been out for days.
My knee twinges. My head is another story.
Every step seems to drive a steel nail into my skull.
Then I see them...
Our melted and twisted handcuffs...
The last remaining evidence that Ziplock Murphy had ever lived.
I catch sight of myself in a mirror, and for a second I think there's someone else in the room.

The robotix plate in my forehead bulges slightly beneath my swollen sk

I can feel a hundred or so staples in various cuts and bruises. Ribs feel like they've been opened up.

Right knee replaced with a grown-bone

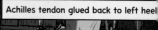

Achilles tendon glued back to left heel

Everything is being fixed, I tell myself.

It is all temporary.

OH...

Looking back at me is a miniature Frankenstein's monster.

A war child from a history vid.

The only thing I recognize are the eyes.

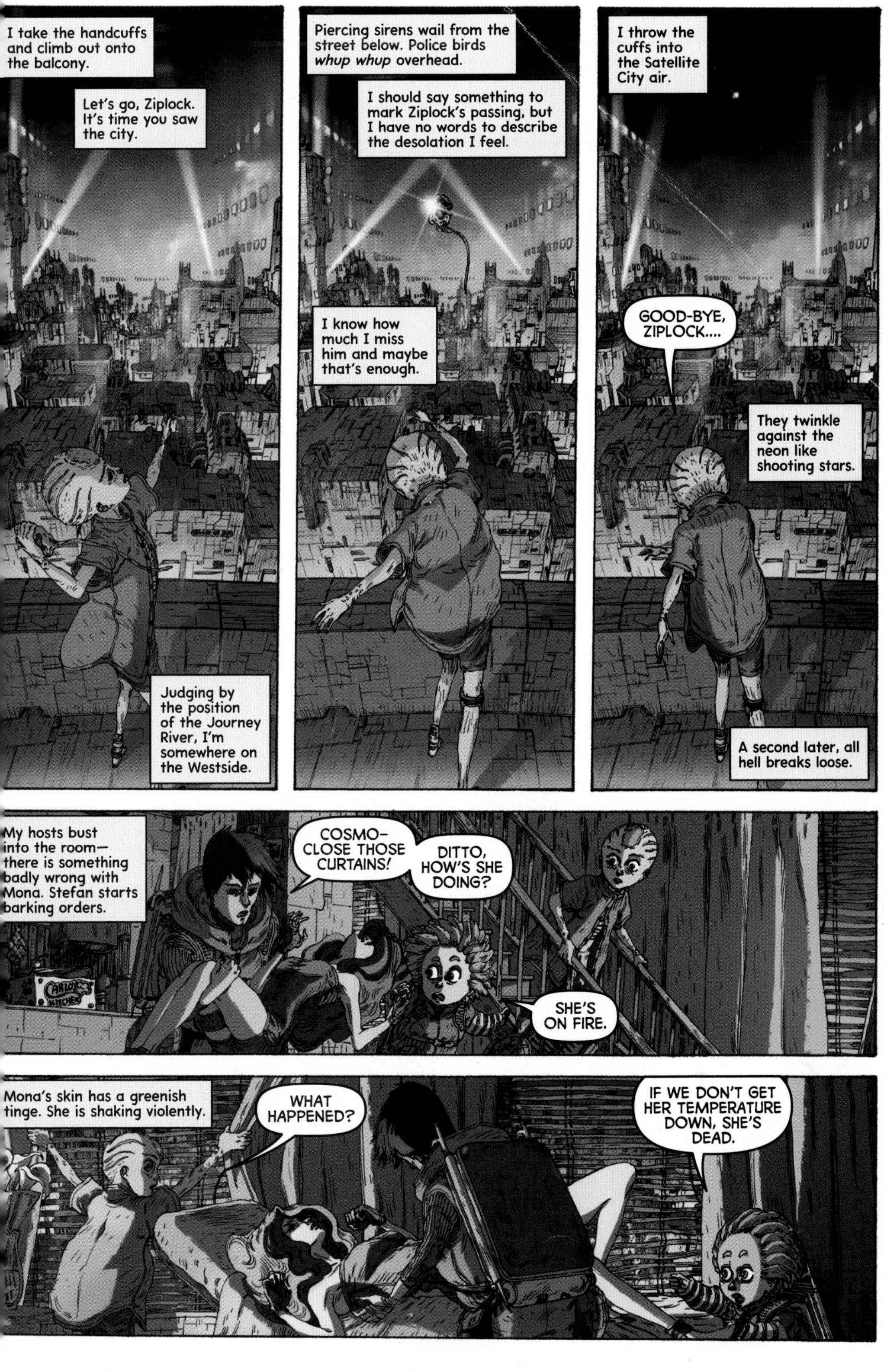
I take the handcuffs and climb out onto the balcony.
Let's go, Ziplock. It's time you saw the city.
Judging by the position of the Journey River, I'm somewhere on the Westside.
Piercing sirens wail from the street below. Police birds *whup whup* overhead.
I should say something to mark Ziplock's passing, but I have no words to describe the desolation I feel.
I know how much I miss him and maybe that's enough.
I throw the cuffs into the Satellite City air.
GOOD-BYE, ZIPLOCK....
They twinkle against the neon like shooting stars.
A second later, all hell breaks loose.
My hosts bust into the room—there is something badly wrong with Mona. Stefan starts barking orders.
COSMO—CLOSE THOSE CURTAINS!
DITTO, HOW'S SHE DOING?
SHE'S ON FIRE.
Mona's skin has a greenish tinge. She is shaking violently.
WHAT HAPPENED?
IF WE DON'T GET HER TEMPERATURE DOWN, SHE'S DEAD.

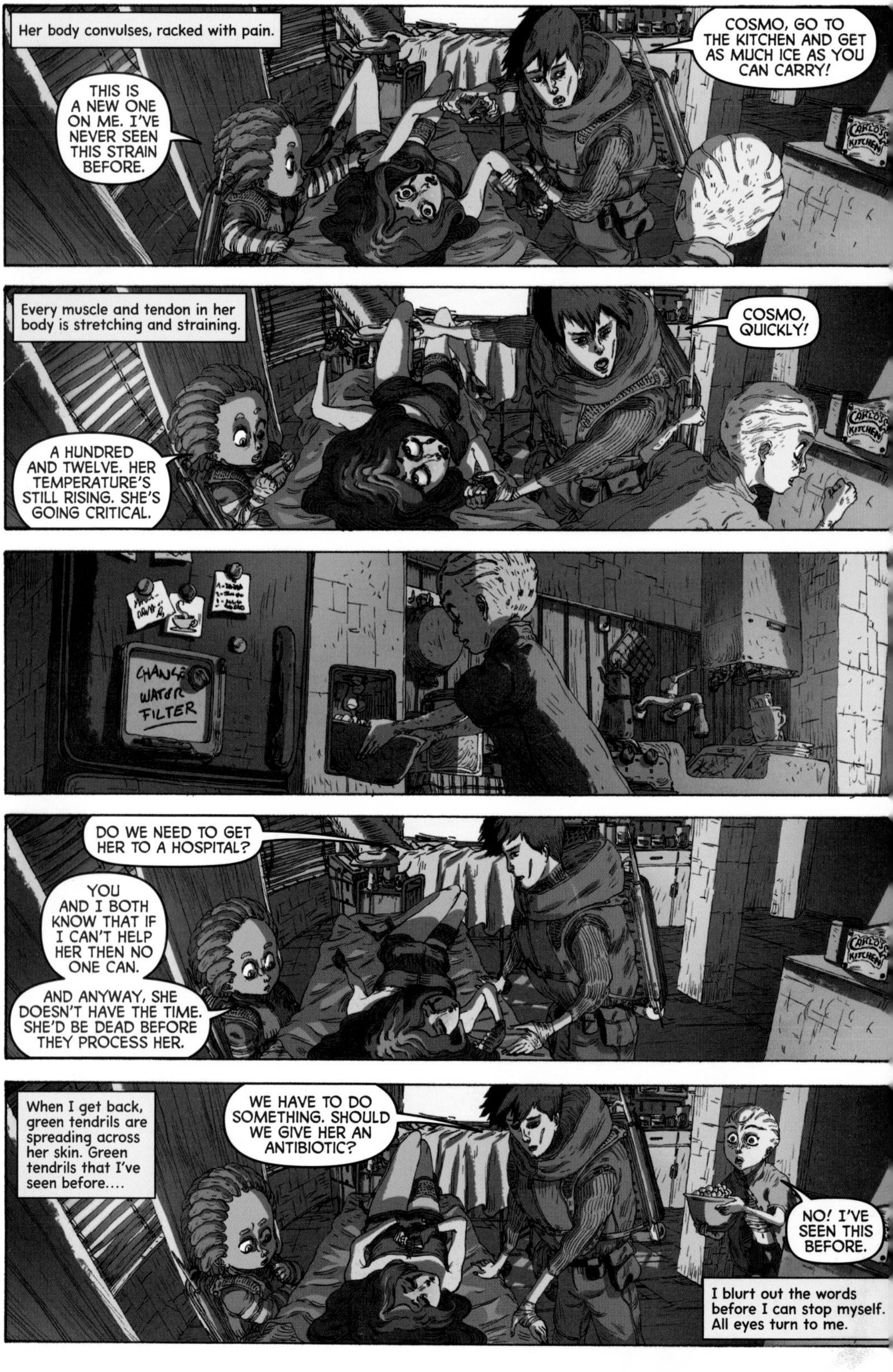

Her body convulses, racked with pain.
THIS IS A NEW ONE ON ME. I'VE NEVER SEEN THIS STRAIN BEFORE.
COSMO, GO TO THE KITCHEN AND GET AS MUCH ICE AS YOU CAN CARRY!
CARLOS'S KITCHEN
Every muscle and tendon in her body is stretching and straining.
COSMO, QUICKLY!
A HUNDRED AND TWELVE. HER TEMPERATURE'S STILL RISING. SHE'S GOING CRITICAL.
CHANGE WATER FILTER
DO WE NEED TO GET HER TO A HOSPITAL?
YOU AND I BOTH KNOW THAT IF I CAN'T HELP HER THEN NO ONE CAN.
AND ANYWAY, SHE DOESN'T HAVE THE TIME. SHE'D BE DEAD BEFORE THEY PROCESS HER.
When I get back, green tendrils are spreading across her skin. Green tendrils that I've seen before....
WE HAVE TO DO SOMETHING. SHOULD WE GIVE HER AN ANTIBIOTIC?
NO! I'VE SEEN THIS BEFORE.
I blurt out the words before I can stop myself. All eyes turn to me.

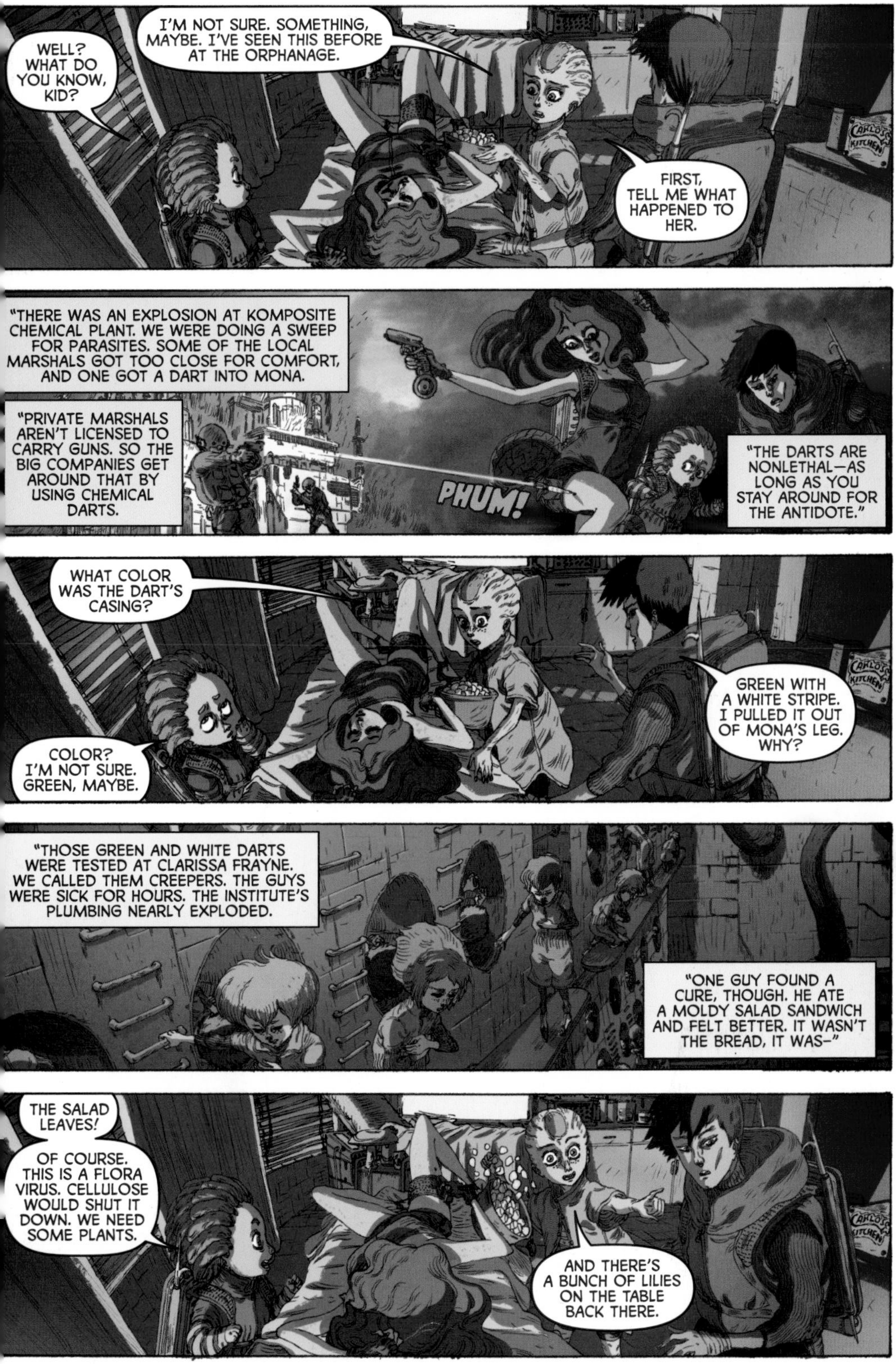
WELL? WHAT DO YOU KNOW, KID?
I'M NOT SURE. SOMETHING, MAYBE. I'VE SEEN THIS BEFORE AT THE ORPHANAGE.
FIRST, TELL ME WHAT HAPPENED TO HER.
"THERE WAS AN EXPLOSION AT KOMPOSITE CHEMICAL PLANT. WE WERE DOING A SWEEP FOR PARASITES. SOME OF THE LOCAL MARSHALS GOT TOO CLOSE FOR COMFORT, AND ONE GOT A DART INTO MONA.
"PRIVATE MARSHALS AREN'T LICENSED TO CARRY GUNS. SO THE BIG COMPANIES GET AROUND THAT BY USING CHEMICAL DARTS.
PHUM!
"THE DARTS ARE NONLETHAL—AS LONG AS YOU STAY AROUND FOR THE ANTIDOTE."
WHAT COLOR WAS THE DART'S CASING?
COLOR? I'M NOT SURE. GREEN, MAYBE.
GREEN WITH A WHITE STRIPE. I PULLED IT OUT OF MONA'S LEG. WHY?
"THOSE GREEN AND WHITE DARTS WERE TESTED AT CLARISSA FRAYNE. WE CALLED THEM CREEPERS. THE GUYS WERE SICK FOR HOURS. THE INSTITUTE'S PLUMBING NEARLY EXPLODED.
"ONE GUY FOUND A CURE, THOUGH. HE ATE A MOLDY SALAD SANDWICH AND FELT BETTER. IT WASN'T THE BREAD, IT WAS–"
THE SALAD LEAVES!
OF COURSE. THIS IS A FLORA VIRUS. CELLULOSE WOULD SHUT IT DOWN. WE NEED SOME PLANTS.
AND THERE'S A BUNCH OF LILIES ON THE TABLE BACK THERE.

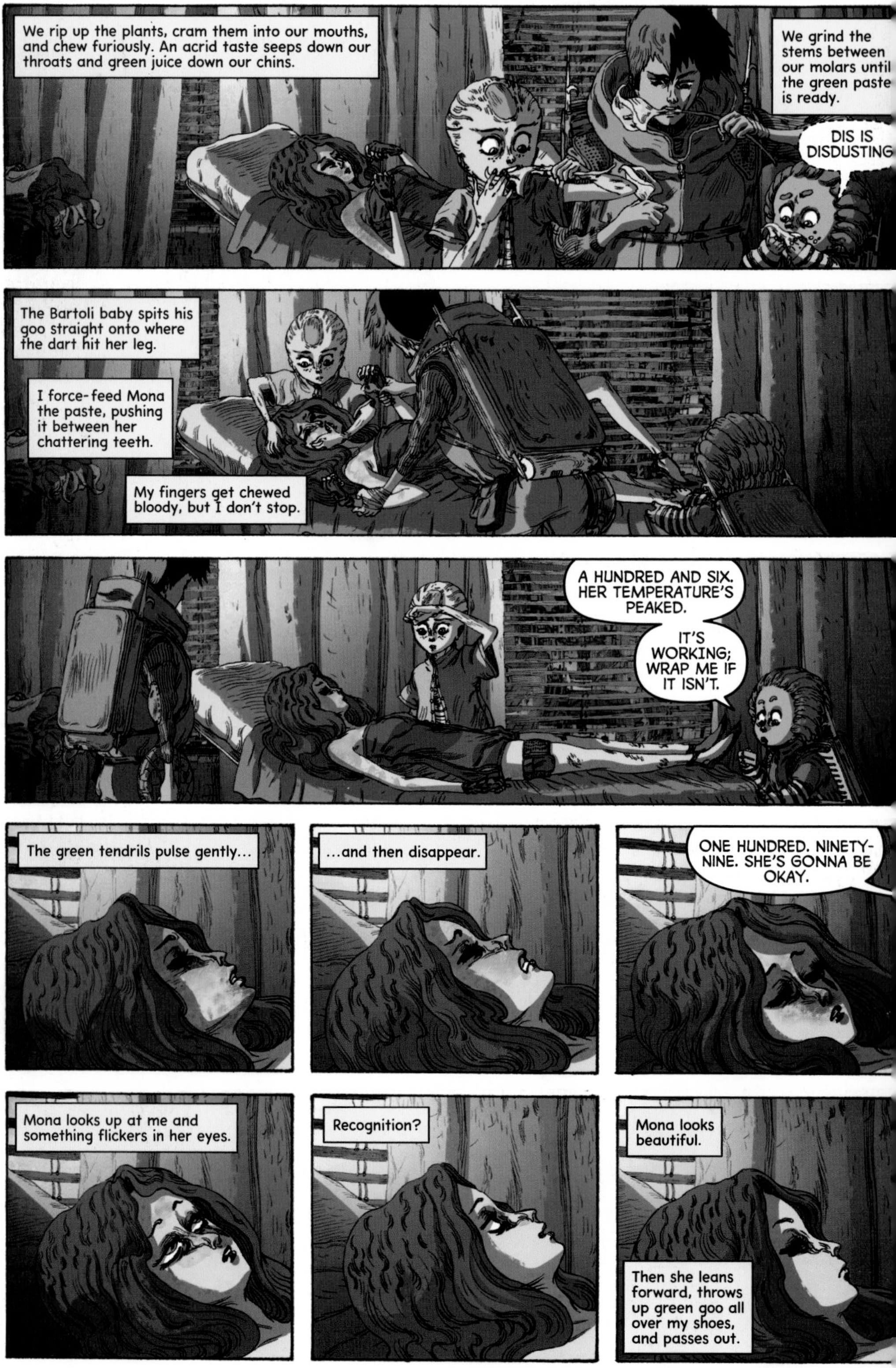
We rip up the plants, cram them into our mouths, and chew furiously. An acrid taste seeps down our throats and green juice down our chins.
We grind the stems between our molars until the green paste is ready.
DIS IS DISDUSTING
The Bartoli baby spits his goo straight onto where the dart hit her leg.
I force-feed Mona the paste, pushing it between her chattering teeth.
My fingers get chewed bloody, but I don't stop.
A HUNDRED AND SIX. HER TEMPERATURE'S PEAKED.
IT'S WORKING; WRAP ME IF IT ISN'T.
The green tendrils pulse gently...
...and then disappear.
ONE HUNDRED. NINETY-NINE. SHE'S GONNA BE OKAY.
Mona looks up at me and something flickers in her eyes.
Recognition?
Mona looks beautiful.
Then she leans forward, throws up green goo all over my shoes, and passes out.

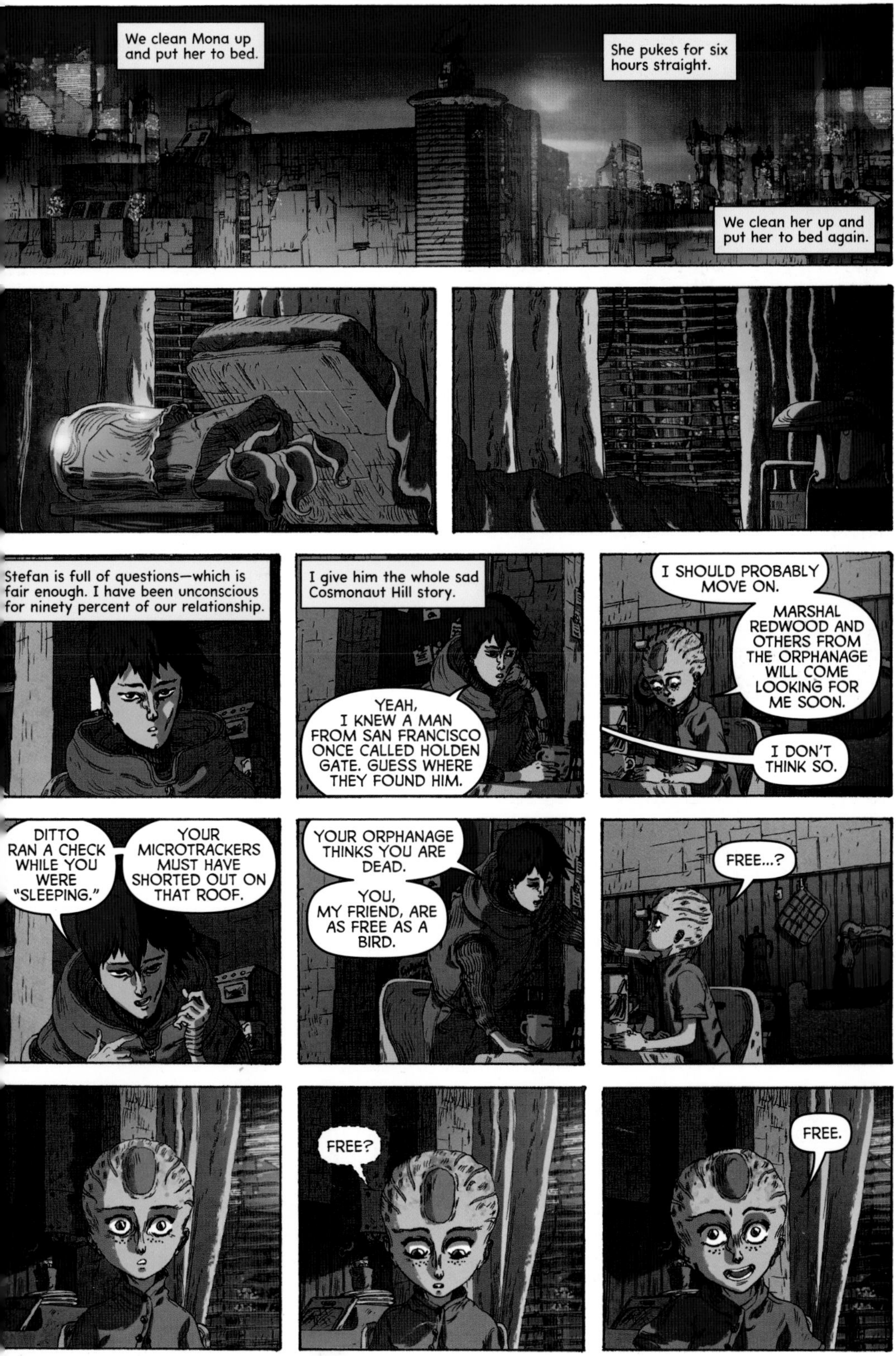
We clean Mona up and put her to bed.
She pukes for six hours straight.
We clean her up and put her to bed again.
Stefan is full of questions—which is fair enough. I have been unconscious for ninety percent of our relationship.
I give him the whole sad Cosmonaut Hill story.
YEAH, I KNEW A MAN FROM SAN FRANCISCO ONCE CALLED HOLDEN GATE. GUESS WHERE THEY FOUND HIM.
I SHOULD PROBABLY MOVE ON.
MARSHAL REDWOOD AND OTHERS FROM THE ORPHANAGE WILL COME LOOKING FOR ME SOON.
I DON'T THINK SO.
DITTO RAN A CHECK WHILE YOU WERE "SLEEPING."
YOUR MICROTRACKERS MUST HAVE SHORTED OUT ON THAT ROOF.
YOUR ORPHANAGE THINKS YOU ARE DEAD.
YOU, MY FRIEND, ARE AS FREE AS A BIRD.
FREE...?
FREE?
FREE.

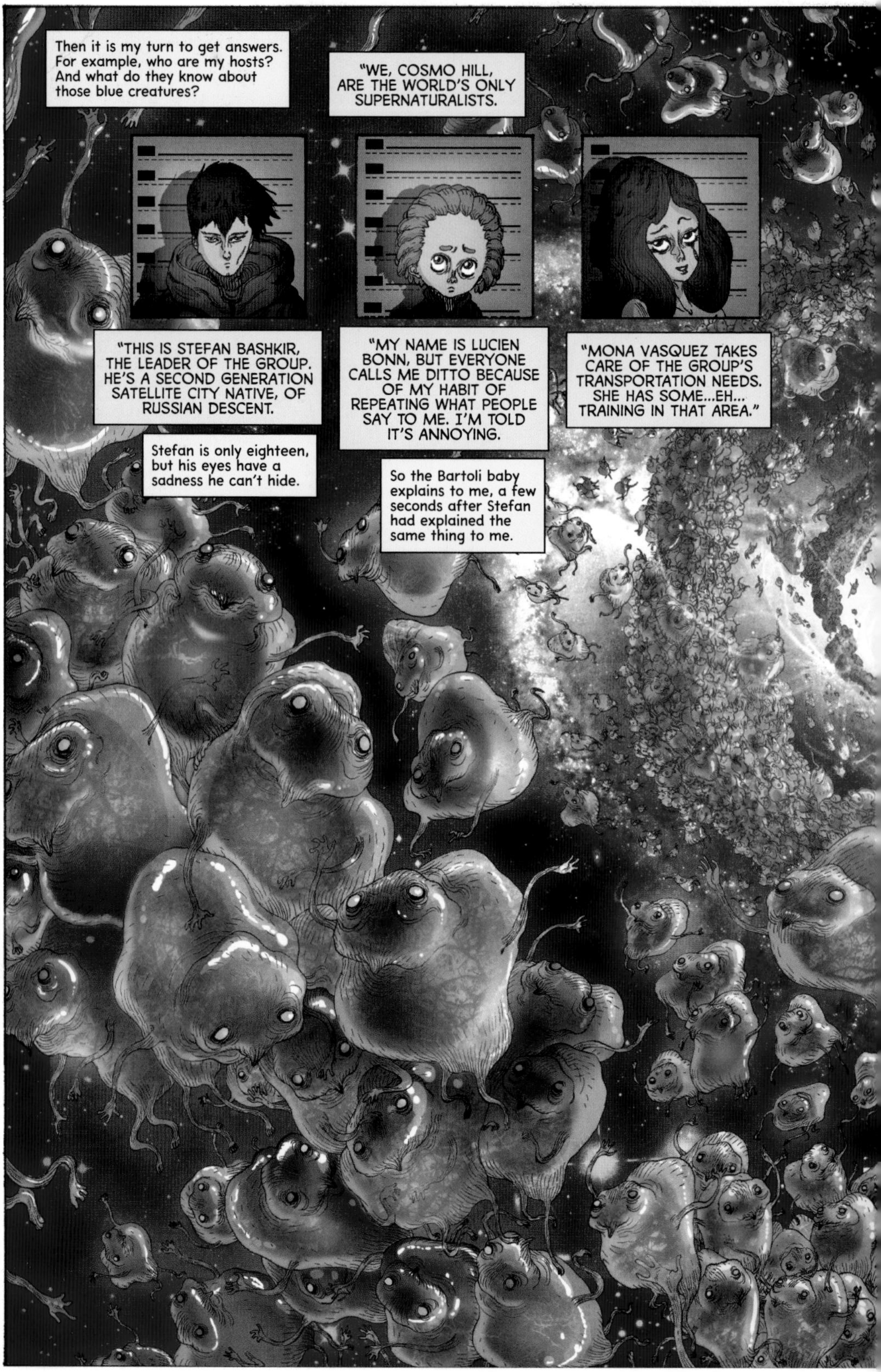
Then it is my turn to get answers. For example, who are my hosts? And what do they know about those blue creatures?
"WE, COSMO HILL, ARE THE WORLD'S ONLY SUPERNATURALISTS.
"THIS IS STEFAN BASHKIR, THE LEADER OF THE GROUP. HE'S A SECOND GENERATION SATELLITE CITY NATIVE, OF RUSSIAN DESCENT.
Stefan is only eighteen, but his eyes have a sadness he can't hide.
"MY NAME IS LUCIEN BONN, BUT EVERYONE CALLS ME DITTO BECAUSE OF MY HABIT OF REPEATING WHAT PEOPLE SAY TO ME. I'M TOLD IT'S ANNOYING.
So the Bartoli baby explains to me, a few seconds after Stefan had explained the same thing to me.
"MONA VASQUEZ TAKES CARE OF THE GROUP'S TRANSPORTATION NEEDS. SHE HAS SOME...EH... TRAINING IN THAT AREA."

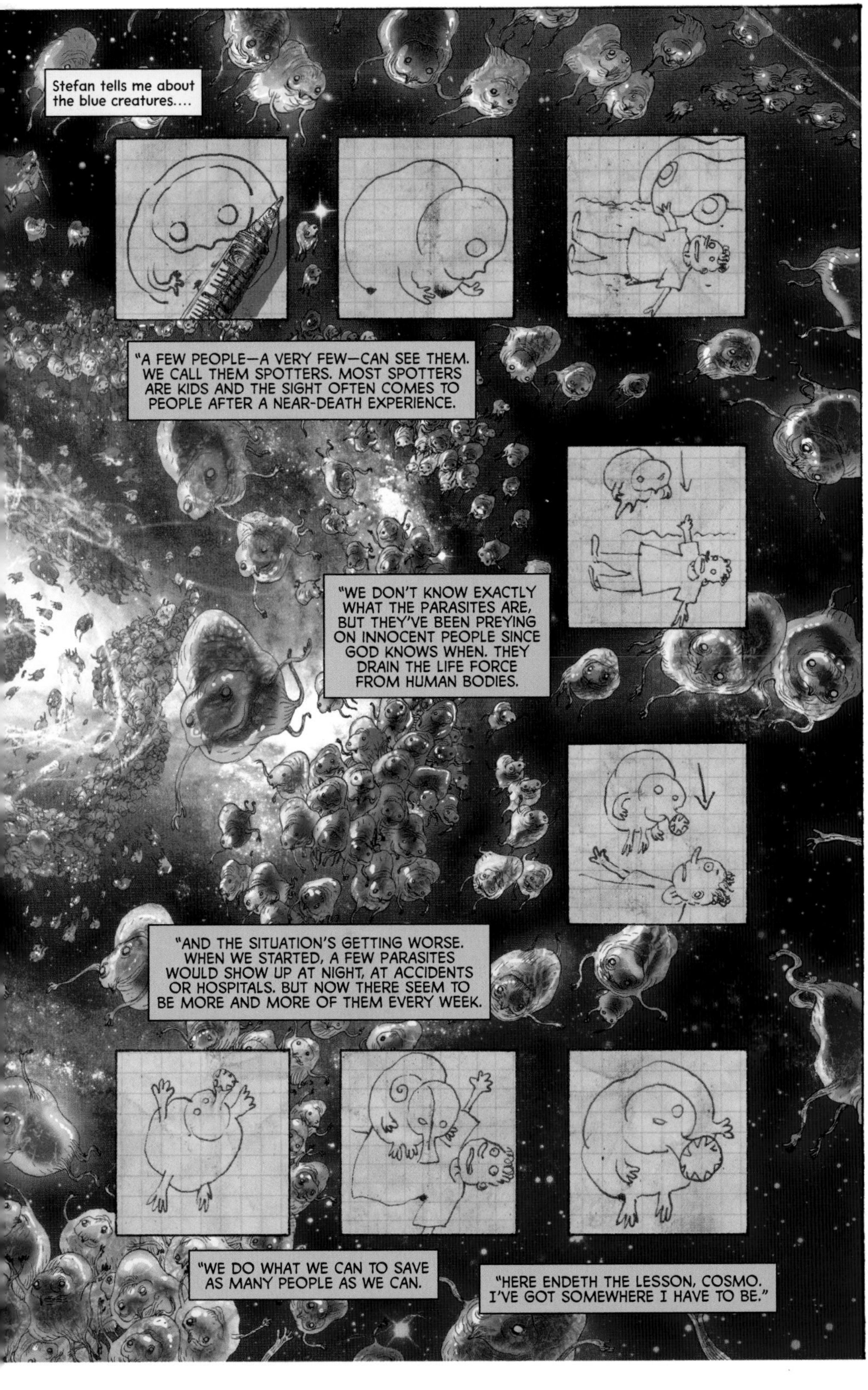
Stefan tells me about the blue creatures....
"A FEW PEOPLE—A VERY FEW—CAN SEE THEM. WE CALL THEM SPOTTERS. MOST SPOTTERS ARE KIDS AND THE SIGHT OFTEN COMES TO PEOPLE AFTER A NEAR-DEATH EXPERIENCE.
"WE DON'T KNOW EXACTLY WHAT THE PARASITES ARE, BUT THEY'VE BEEN PREYING ON INNOCENT PEOPLE SINCE GOD KNOWS WHEN. THEY DRAIN THE LIFE FORCE FROM HUMAN BODIES.
"AND THE SITUATION'S GETTING WORSE. WHEN WE STARTED, A FEW PARASITES WOULD SHOW UP AT NIGHT, AT ACCIDENTS OR HOSPITALS. BUT NOW THERE SEEM TO BE MORE AND MORE OF THEM EVERY WEEK.
"WE DO WHAT WE CAN TO SAVE AS MANY PEOPLE AS WE CAN.
"HERE ENDETH THE LESSON, COSMO. I'VE GOT SOMEWHERE I HAVE TO BE."

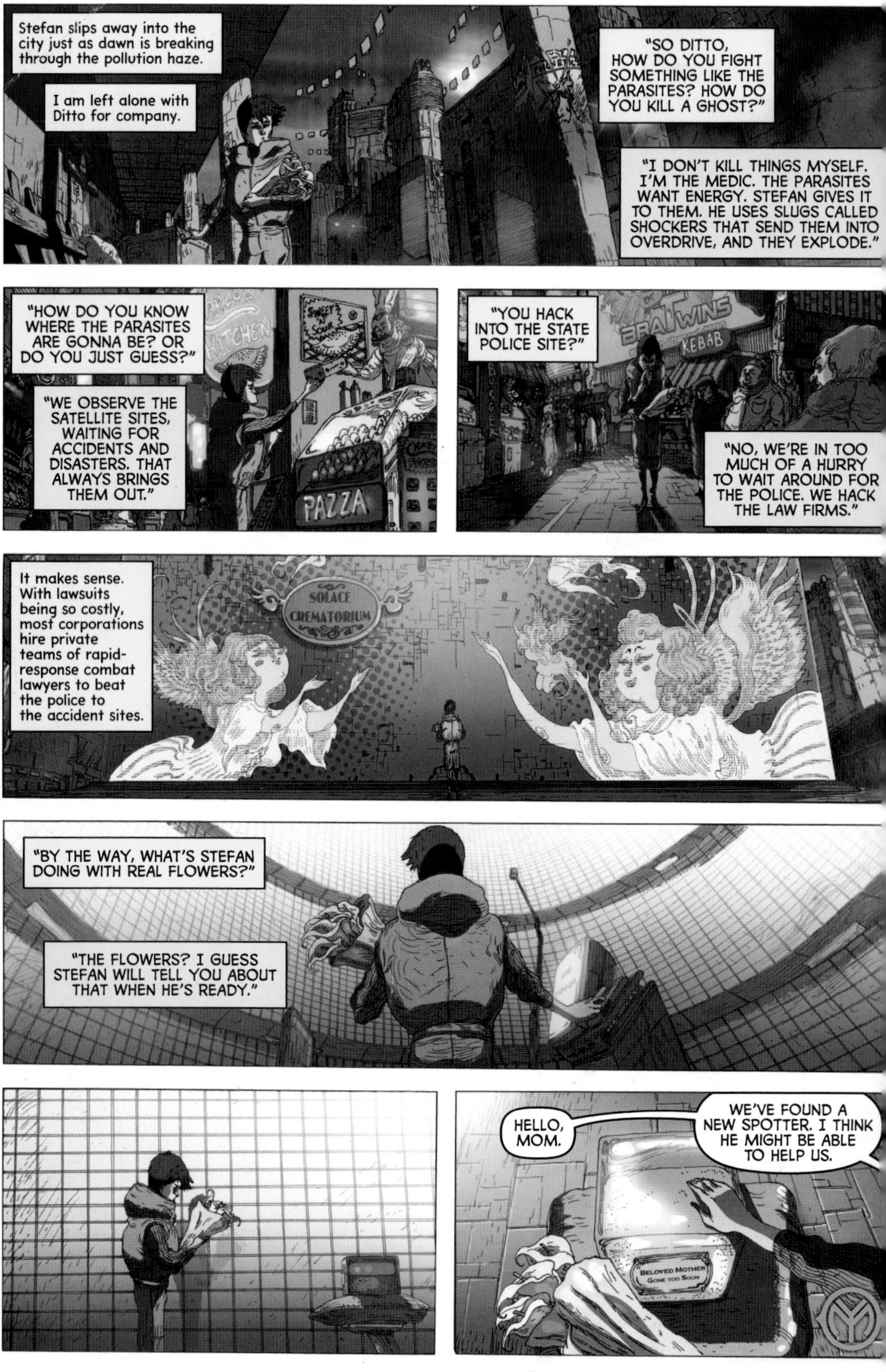
Stefan slips away into the city just as dawn is breaking through the pollution haze.
I am left alone with Ditto for company.
"SO DITTO, HOW DO YOU FIGHT SOMETHING LIKE THE PARASITES? HOW DO YOU KILL A GHOST?"
"I DON'T KILL THINGS MYSELF. I'M THE MEDIC. THE PARASITES WANT ENERGY. STEFAN GIVES IT TO THEM. HE USES SLUGS CALLED SHOCKERS THAT SEND THEM INTO OVERDRIVE, AND THEY EXPLODE."
"HOW DO YOU KNOW WHERE THE PARASITES ARE GONNA BE? OR DO YOU JUST GUESS?"
"WE OBSERVE THE SATELLITE SITES, WAITING FOR ACCIDENTS AND DISASTERS. THAT ALWAYS BRINGS THEM OUT."
PAZZA
"YOU HACK INTO THE STATE POLICE SITE?"
KEBAB
"NO, WE'RE IN TOO MUCH OF A HURRY TO WAIT AROUND FOR THE POLICE. WE HACK THE LAW FIRMS."
It makes sense. With lawsuits being so costly, most corporations hire private teams of rapid-response combat lawyers to beat the police to the accident sites.
SOLACE CREMATORIUM
"BY THE WAY, WHAT'S STEFAN DOING WITH REAL FLOWERS?"
"THE FLOWERS? I GUESS STEFAN WILL TELL YOU ABOUT THAT WHEN HE'S READY."
HELLO, MOM.
WE'VE FOUND A NEW SPOTTER. I THINK HE MIGHT BE ABLE TO HELP US.
Beloved Mother
Gone too Soon

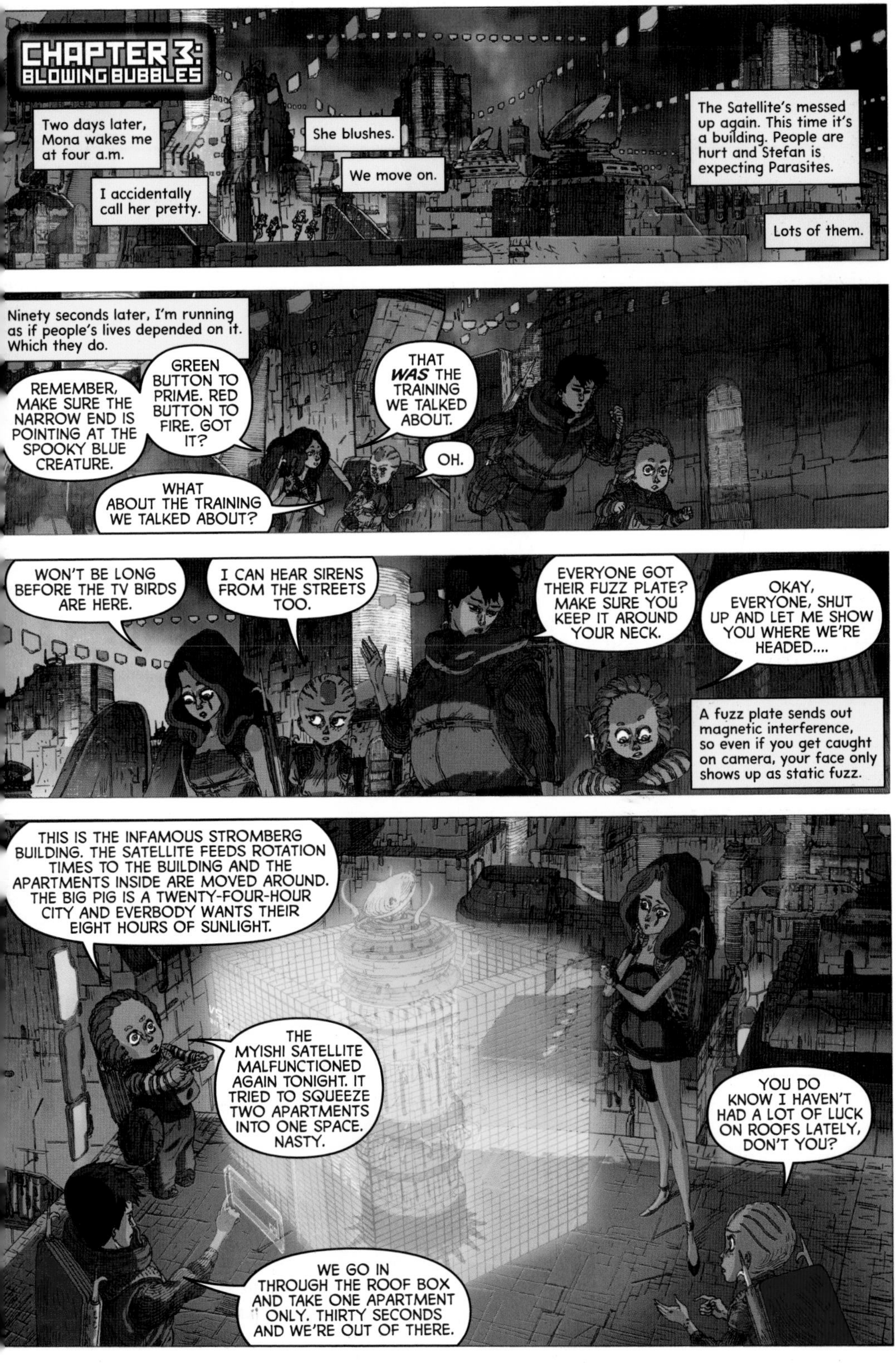
CHAPTER 3:
BLOWING BUBBLES
Two days later, Mona wakes me at four a.m.
I accidentally call her pretty.
She blushes.
We move on.
The Satellite's messed up again. This time it's a building. People are hurt and Stefan is expecting Parasites.
Lots of them.
Ninety seconds later, I'm running as if people's lives depended on it. Which they do.
REMEMBER, MAKE SURE THE NARROW END IS POINTING AT THE SPOOKY BLUE CREATURE.
GREEN BUTTON TO PRIME. RED BUTTON TO FIRE. GOT IT?
WHAT ABOUT THE TRAINING WE TALKED ABOUT?
THAT *WAS* THE TRAINING WE TALKED ABOUT.
OH.
WON'T BE LONG BEFORE THE TV BIRDS ARE HERE.
I CAN HEAR SIRENS FROM THE STREETS TOO.
EVERYONE GOT THEIR FUZZ PLATE? MAKE SURE YOU KEEP IT AROUND YOUR NECK.
OKAY, EVERYONE, SHUT UP AND LET ME SHOW YOU WHERE WE'RE HEADED....
A fuzz plate sends out magnetic interference, so even if you get caught on camera, your face only shows up as static fuzz.
THIS IS THE INFAMOUS STROMBERG BUILDING. THE SATELLITE FEEDS ROTATION TIMES TO THE BUILDING AND THE APARTMENTS INSIDE ARE MOVED AROUND. THE BIG PIG IS A TWENTY-FOUR-HOUR CITY AND EVERBODY WANTS THEIR EIGHT HOURS OF SUNLIGHT.
THE MYISHI SATELLITE MALFUNCTIONED AGAIN TONIGHT. IT TRIED TO SQUEEZE TWO APARTMENTS INTO ONE SPACE. NASTY.
YOU DO KNOW I HAVEN'T HAD A LOT OF LUCK ON ROOFS LATELY, DON'T YOU?
WE GO IN THROUGH THE ROOF BOX AND TAKE ONE APARTMENT ONLY. THIRTY SECONDS AND WE'RE OUT OF THERE.

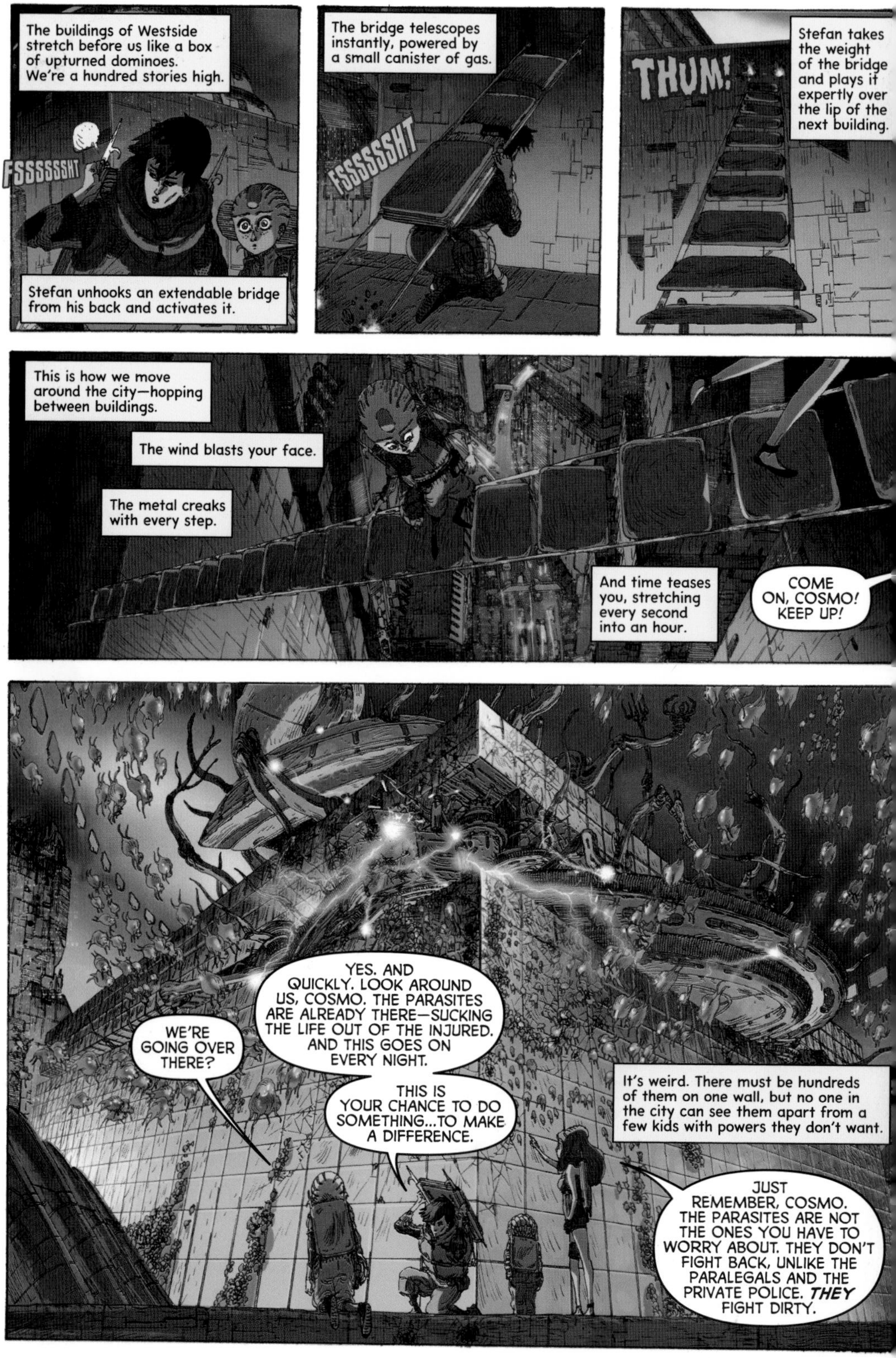
The buildings of Westside stretch before us like a box of upturned dominoes. We're a hundred stories high.
FSSSSSSHT
Stefan unhooks an extendable bridge from his back and activates it.
The bridge telescopes instantly, powered by a small canister of gas.
FSSSSSSHT
THUM!
Stefan takes the weight of the bridge and plays it expertly over the lip of the next building.
This is how we move around the city—hopping between buildings.
The wind blasts your face.
The metal creaks with every step.
And time teases you, stretching every second into an hour.
COME ON, COSMO! KEEP UP!
WE'RE GOING OVER THERE?
YES. AND QUICKLY. LOOK AROUND US, COSMO. THE PARASITES ARE ALREADY THERE—SUCKING THE LIFE OUT OF THE INJURED. AND THIS GOES ON EVERY NIGHT.
THIS IS YOUR CHANCE TO DO SOMETHING...TO MAKE A DIFFERENCE.
It's weird. There must be hundreds of them on one wall, but no one in the city can see them apart from a few kids with powers they don't want.
JUST REMEMBER, COSMO. THE PARASITES ARE NOT THE ONES YOU HAVE TO WORRY ABOUT. THEY DON'T FIGHT BACK, UNLIKE THE PARALEGALS AND THE PRIVATE POLICE. *THEY* FIGHT DIRTY.

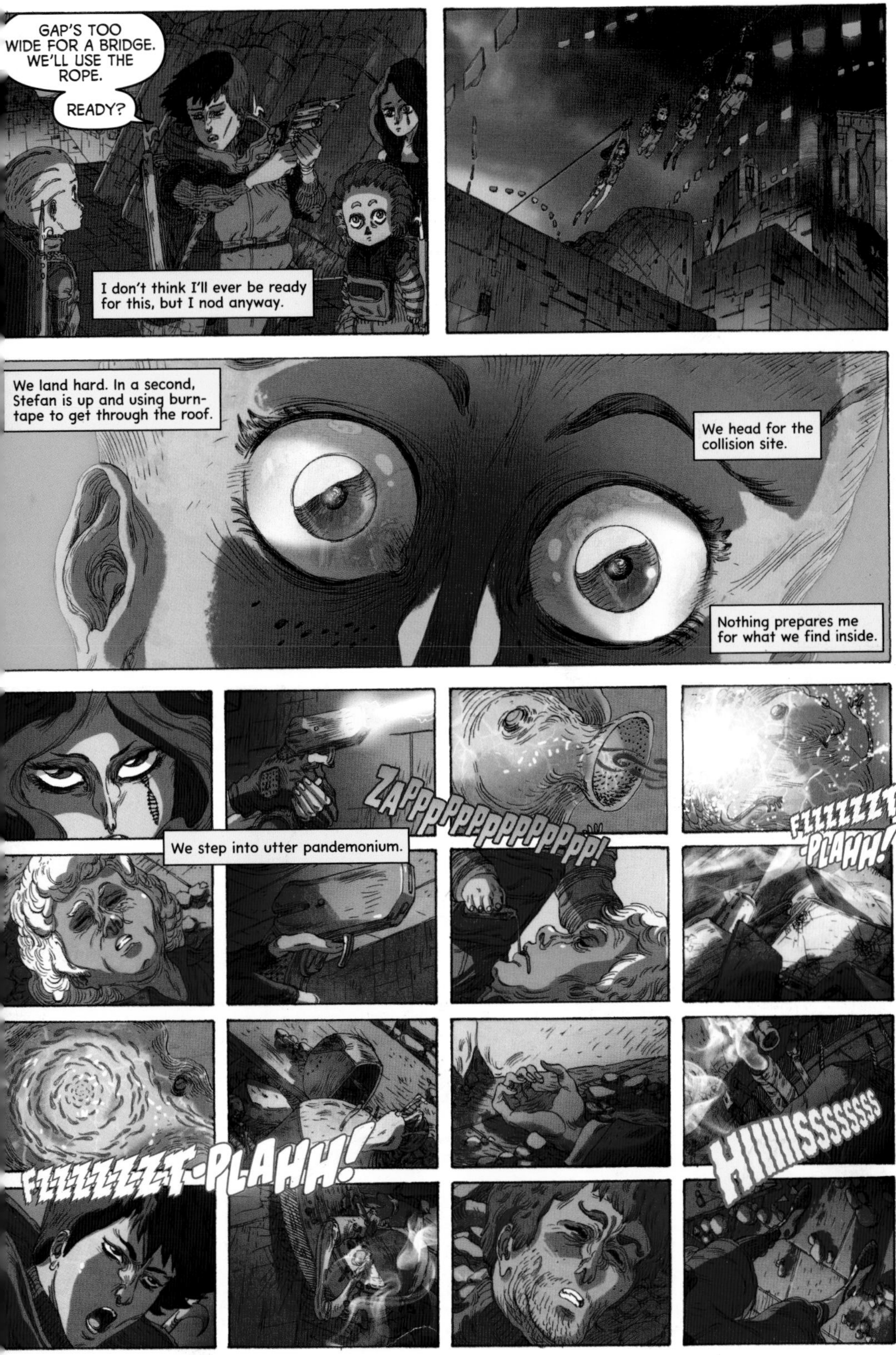
GAP'S TOO WIDE FOR A BRIDGE. WE'LL USE THE ROPE.
READY?
I don't think I'll ever be ready for this, but I nod anyway.
We land hard. In a second, Stefan is up and using burn-tape to get through the roof.
We head for the collision site.
Nothing prepares me for what we find inside.
We step into utter pandemonium.
ZAPPPPPPPPPPPPPPP!
FIZZZZZT-PLAHH!
FIZZZZZZT-PLAHH!
HIIIIISSSSSSS

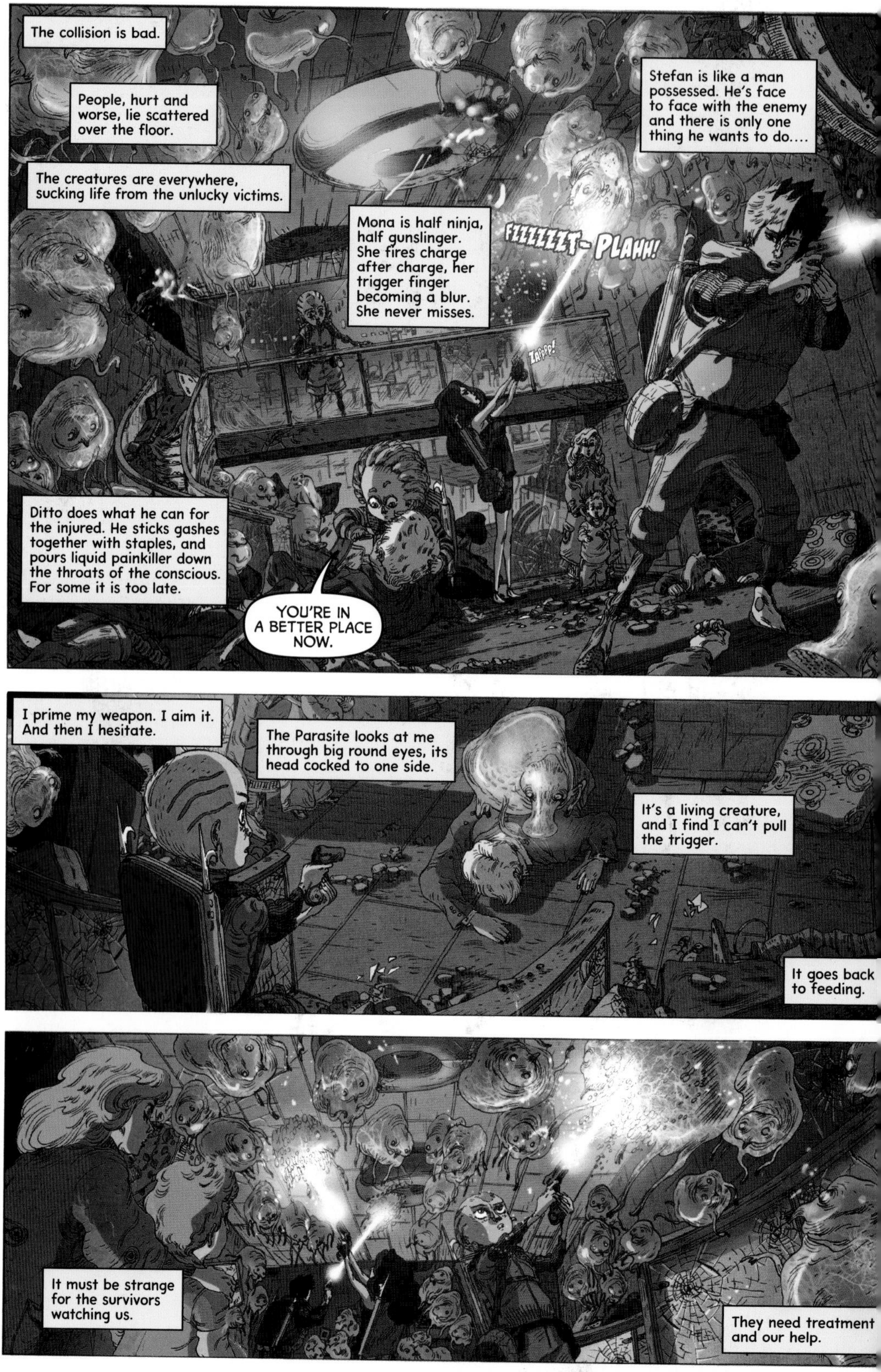
The collision is bad.
People, hurt and worse, lie scattered over the floor.
The creatures are everywhere, sucking life from the unlucky victims.
Mona is half ninja, half gunslinger. She fires charge after charge, her trigger finger becoming a blur. She never misses.
FZZZZZZZT- PLAHH!
Stefan is like a man possessed. He's face to face with the enemy and there is only one thing he wants to do....
ZAPPP!
Ditto does what he can for the injured. He sticks gashes together with staples, and pours liquid painkiller down the throats of the conscious. For some it is too late.
YOU'RE IN A BETTER PLACE NOW.
I prime my weapon. I aim it. And then I hesitate.
The Parasite looks at me through big round eyes, its head cocked to one side.
It's a living creature, and I find I can't pull the trigger.
It goes back to feeding.
It must be strange for the survivors watching us.
They need treatment and our help.

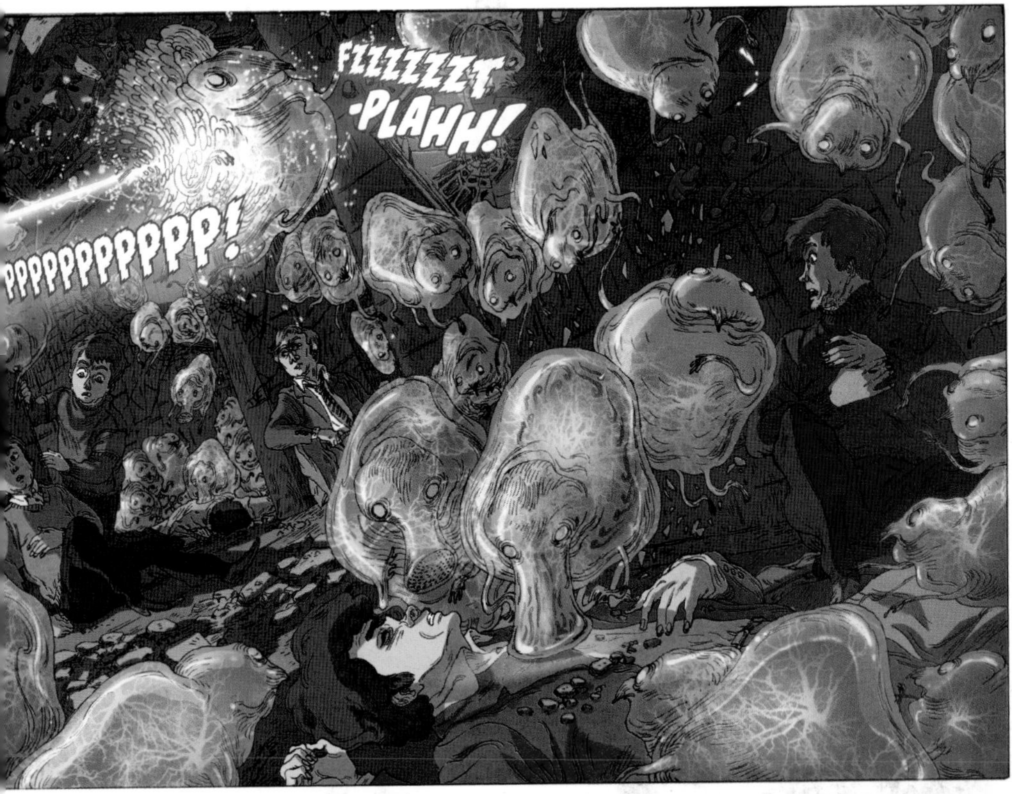
FZZZZZZT
-PLAHH!
PPPPPPPPPPPP!

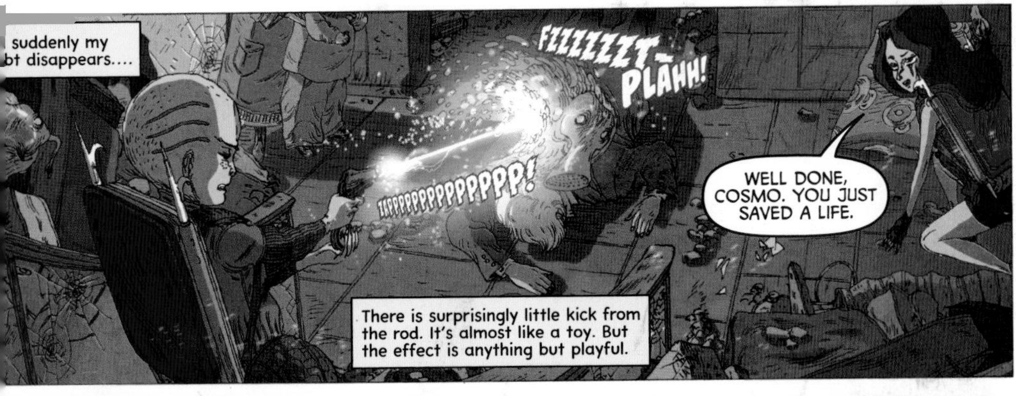
suddenly my
bt disappears....
FZZZZZZT-
PLAHH!
ZZPPPPPPPPPPPPPPP!
WELL DONE, COSMO. YOU JUST SAVED A LIFE.
There is surprisingly little kick from the rod. It's almost like a toy. But the effect is anything but playful.

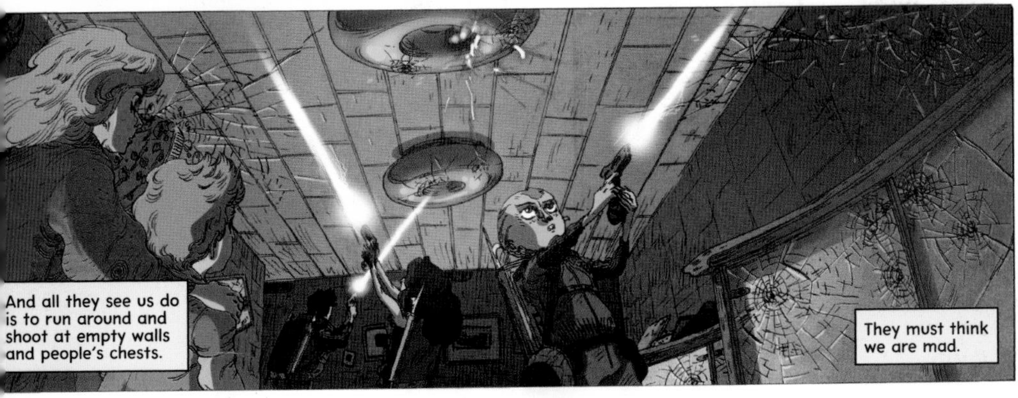
And all they see us do is to run around and shoot at empty walls and people's chests.
They must think we are mad.

I fire again. Then again.

Keep going. Focus. Save one life at a time. Then I see...

HEY, GUYS, THIS WALL IS STARTING TO... TO GLOW.

LAWYERS. THEY'RE COMING THROUGH THE WALL. TIME TO GO!

BUT WE HAVEN'T FINISHED WITH THE PARASITES.

WE'VE DONE WHAT WE CAN HERE.

IF WE GET OURSELVES ARRESTED, THEN WE WON'T BE ABLE TO HELP ANYBODY.

Half a dozen rapid-response lawyers spill into the room and give chase.

MOVE!

YOU THERE!

IT IS ILLEGAL TO FLEE THE SCENE OF AN ACCIDENT.

KA-BOOOM!

FREEZE! OR THE STROMBERG CORPORATION WILL NOT BE RESPONSIBLE FOR YOUR INJURIES!

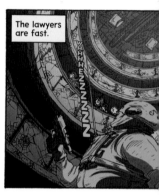

The lawyers are fast.

WHEEENNNNNN

Really fast.

HANDS UP, DEFENDANT.

YOU HAVE THE RIGHT TO GET SERIOUSLY MESSED UP IF YOU ATTEMPT TO FLEE.

MESSED UP? BUT, SIR, I'M JUST AN INNOCENT MINOR.

WELL...

WHACK!

I OBJECT.

I guess Ditto can look after himself.

We head for the roof.

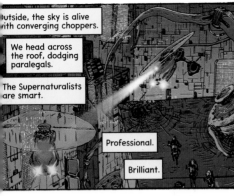

Outside, the sky is alive with converging choppers.

We head across the roof, dodging paralegals.

The Supernaturalists are smart.

Professional.

Brilliant.

"COSMO. BRIDGE. NOW."

FSSSSSHT

"NOT BAD, COSMO.

THUM!

"FOR A FIRST ATTEMPT."

MORE PARALEGALS CLOSING IN, STEFAN.

LET'S USE ONE OF THE RADIOS.

KEEP YOUR HEAD DOWN AND KEEP OUT OF SIGHT.

THOSE PARALEGALS ARE MUCH TOO STUPID TO LOOK FOR US OVER HERE.

Oldest trick in the book—and it works. The lawyers go scampering off chasing no one and leaving the escape route clear for us.

Nearly.

WELL, THAT TAKES CARE OF THAT LITTLE...

CLICK

THEY'RE BEHIND ME, AREN'T THEY?

DO NOT MOVE!

YOU'RE UNDER ARREST.

WATCH AND LEARN, COSMO.

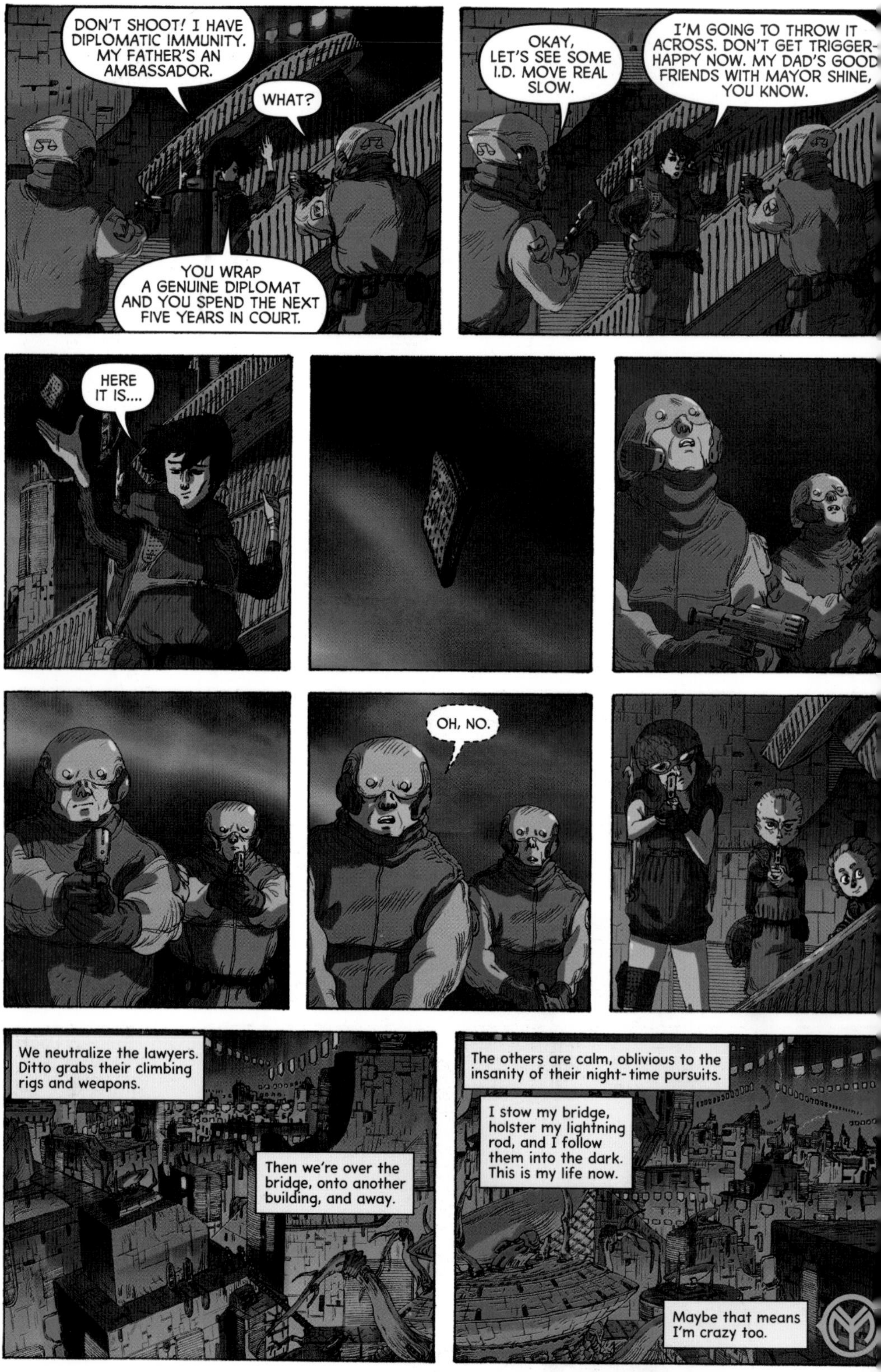
DON'T SHOOT! I HAVE DIPLOMATIC IMMUNITY. MY FATHER'S AN AMBASSADOR.
WHAT?
YOU WRAP A GENUINE DIPLOMAT AND YOU SPEND THE NEXT FIVE YEARS IN COURT.
OKAY, LET'S SEE SOME I.D. MOVE REAL SLOW.
I'M GOING TO THROW IT ACROSS. DON'T GET TRIGGER-HAPPY NOW. MY DAD'S GOOD FRIENDS WITH MAYOR SHINE, YOU KNOW.
HERE IT IS....
OH, NO.
We neutralize the lawyers. Ditto grabs their climbing rigs and weapons.
Then we're over the bridge, onto another building, and away.
The others are calm, oblivious to the insanity of their night-time pursuits.
I stow my bridge, holster my lightning rod, and I follow them into the dark. This is my life now.
Maybe that means I'm crazy too.

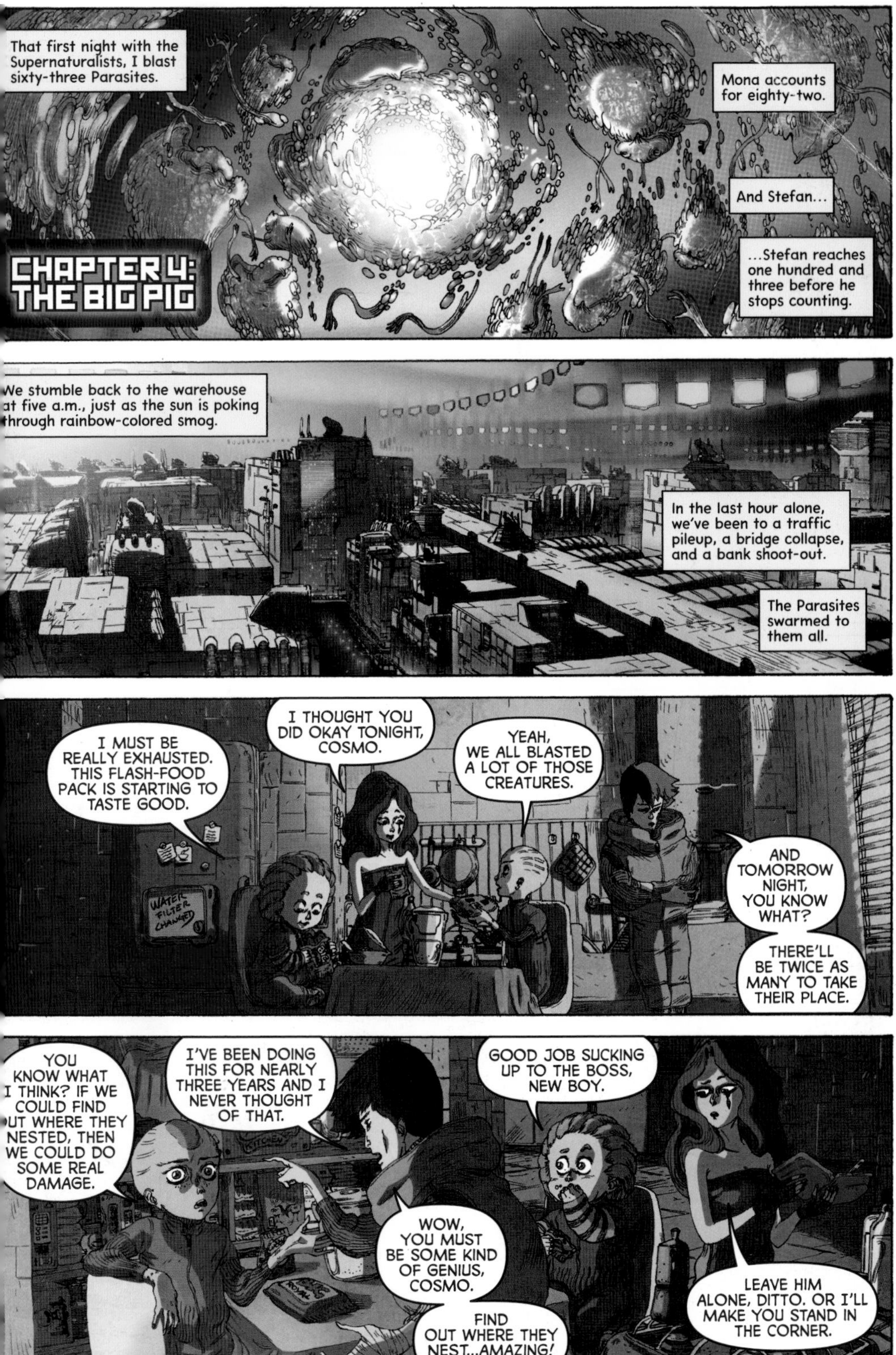

That first night with the Supernaturalists, I blast sixty-three Parasites.
CHAPTER 4: THE BIG PIG
Mona accounts for eighty-two.
And Stefan...
...Stefan reaches one hundred and three before he stops counting.
We stumble back to the warehouse at five a.m., just as the sun is poking through rainbow-colored smog.
In the last hour alone, we've been to a traffic pileup, a bridge collapse, and a bank shoot-out.
The Parasites swarmed to them all.
I MUST BE REALLY EXHAUSTED. THIS FLASH-FOOD PACK IS STARTING TO TASTE GOOD.
I THOUGHT YOU DID OKAY TONIGHT, COSMO.
YEAH, WE ALL BLASTED A LOT OF THOSE CREATURES.
WATER FILTER CHANGED
AND TOMORROW NIGHT, YOU KNOW WHAT?
THERE'LL BE TWICE AS MANY TO TAKE THEIR PLACE.
YOU KNOW WHAT I THINK? IF WE COULD FIND OUT WHERE THEY NESTED, THEN WE COULD DO SOME REAL DAMAGE.
I'VE BEEN DOING THIS FOR NEARLY THREE YEARS AND I NEVER THOUGHT OF THAT.
GOOD JOB SUCKING UP TO THE BOSS, NEW BOY.
WOW, YOU MUST BE SOME KIND OF GENIUS, COSMO.
FIND OUT WHERE THEY NEST...AMAZING!
LEAVE HIM ALONE, DITTO. OR I'LL MAKE YOU STAND IN THE CORNER.

Stefan disappears and we eat the rest of our food in silence. Until...

IT'S NOT YOUR FAULT, COSMO. STEFAN'S WHOLE LIFE IS FIGHTING THE PARASITES. AND EVEN HE CAN SEE WE'RE HARDLY MAKING A DENT.

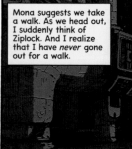

Mona suggests we take a walk. As we head out, I suddenly think of Ziplock. And I realize that I have *never* gone out for a walk.

Booshka—Mona's home turf—is the only neighborhood in the city named after the slang for car theft. Crime is that bad.

Teenage booshka pirates steal cars in the day and refit them for illegal drag racing at night.

FROM THIS POINT, WE'RE ON OUR OWN. NO POLICE EVER RESPOND TO AN ALERT IN BOOSHKA.

I KNOW HOW TO BE INVISIBLE. LEARNED THAT AT THE ORPHANAGE.

DOWN HERE, COSMO, YOU GOTTA WALK TALL. ANY OF THESE VULTURES SMELL WEAKNESS, AND THEY MESS YOU UP FASTER THAN SUGAR IN A GAS TANK.

HOLA, MIGUEL. MAYBE I'LL COME RACE WHEN YOU BUILD SOMETHING WORTH RACING AGAINST.

I COULD WALK FASTER THAN THAT LAST PIECE OF JUNK.

YOU GOT ME, VASQUEZ. BUT SOMEDAY I'LL GET YOU.

"HOW DID YOU GET OUT? I THOUGHT GANG MEMBERSHIP WAS A '*FOR LIFE*' KIND OF THING."

"EIGHTEEN MONTHS AGO I WAS IN A RACE CRASH. A BAD ONE. MY LUNG COLLAPSED AND I WAS BLEEDING TO DEATH. THE PARASITES WERE SETTLING IN TO SUCK ME DRY.

"STEFAN SAVED ME. HE BLASTED THOSE MONSTERS RIGHT OFF MY CHEST. DITTO INFLATED MY LUNG AND THEY DROPPED ME AT GENERAL."

SO STEFAN *BOUGHT* YOU?

NO, COSMO. HE BOUGHT MY *FREEDOM*.

ANYWAY, THAT'S WHY WE'RE RIDING IN THE PIGMOBILE THESE DAYS.

AND THAT'S WHY WE'RE DOWN HERE, DESPERATE TO GET A NEW ENGINE MANIFOLD.

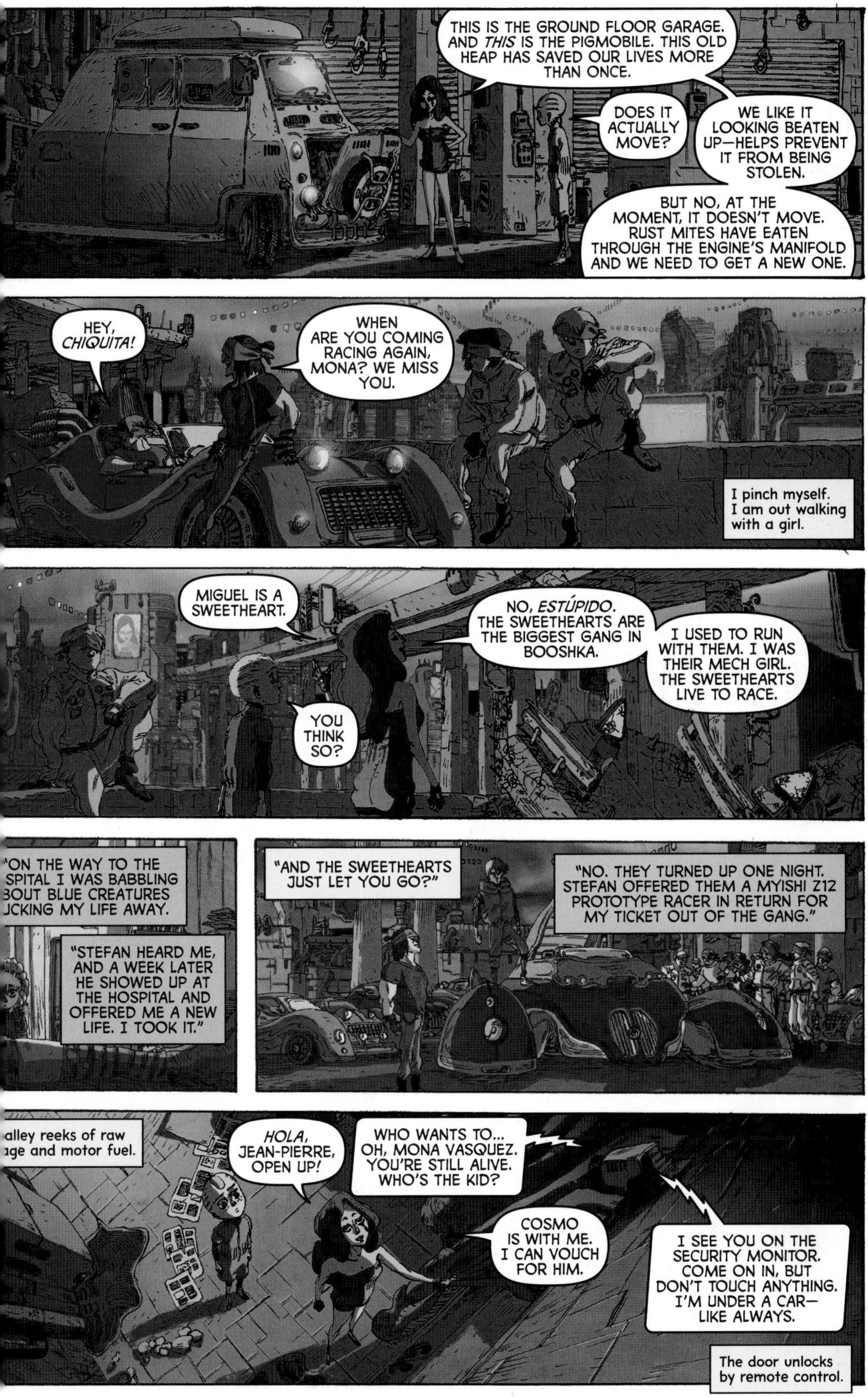
THIS IS THE GROUND FLOOR GARAGE. AND *THIS* IS THE PIGMOBILE. THIS OLD HEAP HAS SAVED OUR LIVES MORE THAN ONCE.
DOES IT ACTUALLY MOVE?
WE LIKE IT LOOKING BEATEN UP—HELPS PREVENT IT FROM BEING STOLEN.
BUT NO, AT THE MOMENT, IT DOESN'T MOVE. RUST MITES HAVE EATEN THROUGH THE ENGINE'S MANIFOLD AND WE NEED TO GET A NEW ONE.
HEY, *CHIQUITA!*
WHEN ARE YOU COMING RACING AGAIN, MONA? WE MISS YOU.
I pinch myself. I am out walking with a girl.
MIGUEL IS A SWEETHEART.
NO, *ESTÚPIDO*. THE SWEETHEARTS ARE THE BIGGEST GANG IN BOOSHKA.
YOU THINK SO?
I USED TO RUN WITH THEM. I WAS THEIR MECH GIRL. THE SWEETHEARTS LIVE TO RACE.
"ON THE WAY TO THE SPITAL I WAS BABBLING BOUT BLUE CREATURES JCKING MY LIFE AWAY.
"STEFAN HEARD ME, AND A WEEK LATER HE SHOWED UP AT THE HOSPITAL AND OFFERED ME A NEW LIFE. I TOOK IT."
"AND THE SWEETHEARTS JUST LET YOU GO?"
"NO. THEY TURNED UP ONE NIGHT. STEFAN OFFERED THEM A MYISHI Z12 PROTOTYPE RACER IN RETURN FOR MY TICKET OUT OF THE GANG."
alley reeks of raw age and motor fuel.
HOLA, JEAN-PIERRE, OPEN UP!
WHO WANTS TO... OH, MONA VASQUEZ. YOU'RE STILL ALIVE. WHO'S THE KID?
COSMO IS WITH ME. I CAN VOUCH FOR HIM.
I SEE YOU ON THE SECURITY MONITOR. COME ON IN, BUT DON'T TOUCH ANYTHING. I'M UNDER A CAR—LIKE ALWAYS.
The door unlocks by remote control.

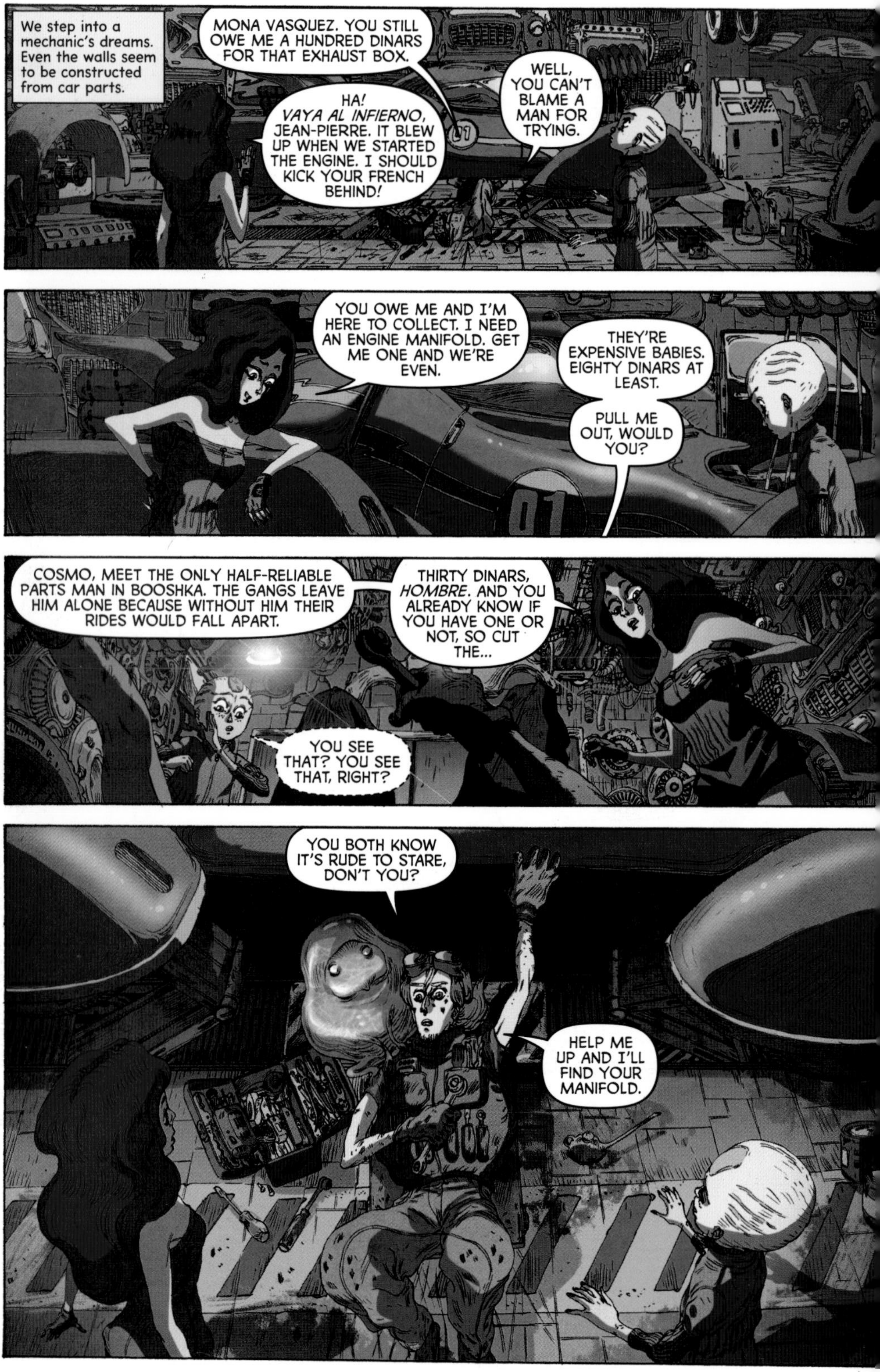
We step into a mechanic's dreams. Even the walls seem to be constructed from car parts.
MONA VASQUEZ. YOU STILL OWE ME A HUNDRED DINARS FOR THAT EXHAUST BOX.
HA! *VAYA AL INFIERNO*, JEAN-PIERRE. IT BLEW UP WHEN WE STARTED THE ENGINE. I SHOULD KICK YOUR FRENCH BEHIND!
WELL, YOU CAN'T BLAME A MAN FOR TRYING.
YOU OWE ME AND I'M HERE TO COLLECT. I NEED AN ENGINE MANIFOLD. GET ME ONE AND WE'RE EVEN.
THEY'RE EXPENSIVE BABIES. EIGHTY DINARS AT LEAST.
PULL ME OUT, WOULD YOU?
COSMO, MEET THE ONLY HALF-RELIABLE PARTS MAN IN BOOSHKA. THE GANGS LEAVE HIM ALONE BECAUSE WITHOUT HIM THEIR RIDES WOULD FALL APART.
THIRTY DINARS, *HOMBRE*. AND YOU ALREADY KNOW IF YOU HAVE ONE OR NOT, SO CUT THE...
YOU SEE THAT? YOU SEE THAT, RIGHT?
YOU BOTH KNOW IT'S RUDE TO STARE, DON'T YOU?
HELP ME UP AND I'LL FIND YOUR MANIFOLD.

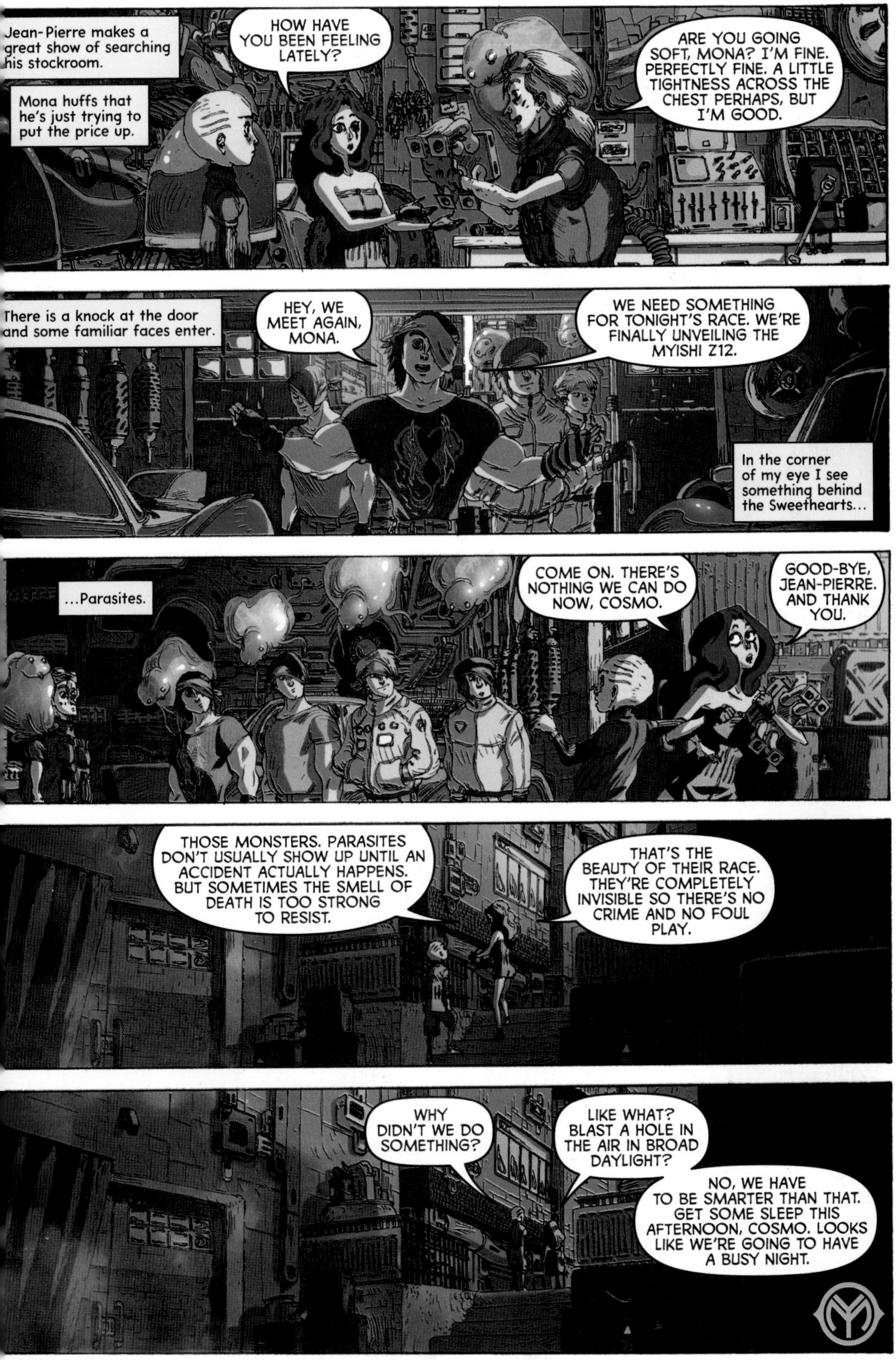
Jean-Pierre makes a great show of searching his stockroom.
Mona huffs that he's just trying to put the price up.
HOW HAVE YOU BEEN FEELING LATELY?
ARE YOU GOING SOFT, MONA? I'M FINE. PERFECTLY FINE. A LITTLE TIGHTNESS ACROSS THE CHEST PERHAPS, BUT I'M GOOD.
There is a knock at the door and some familiar faces enter.
HEY, WE MEET AGAIN, MONA.
WE NEED SOMETHING FOR TONIGHT'S RACE. WE'RE FINALLY UNVEILING THE MYISHI Z12.
In the corner of my eye I see something behind the Sweethearts...
...Parasites.
COME ON. THERE'S NOTHING WE CAN DO NOW, COSMO.
GOOD-BYE, JEAN-PIERRE. AND THANK YOU.
THOSE MONSTERS. PARASITES DON'T USUALLY SHOW UP UNTIL AN ACCIDENT ACTUALLY HAPPENS. BUT SOMETIMES THE SMELL OF DEATH IS TOO STRONG TO RESIST.
THAT'S THE BEAUTY OF THEIR RACE. THEY'RE COMPLETELY INVISIBLE SO THERE'S NO CRIME AND NO FOUL PLAY.
WHY DIDN'T WE DO SOMETHING?
LIKE WHAT? BLAST A HOLE IN THE AIR IN BROAD DAYLIGHT?
NO, WE HAVE TO BE SMARTER THAN THAT. GET SOME SLEEP THIS AFTERNOON, COSMO. LOOKS LIKE WE'RE GOING TO HAVE A BUSY NIGHT.

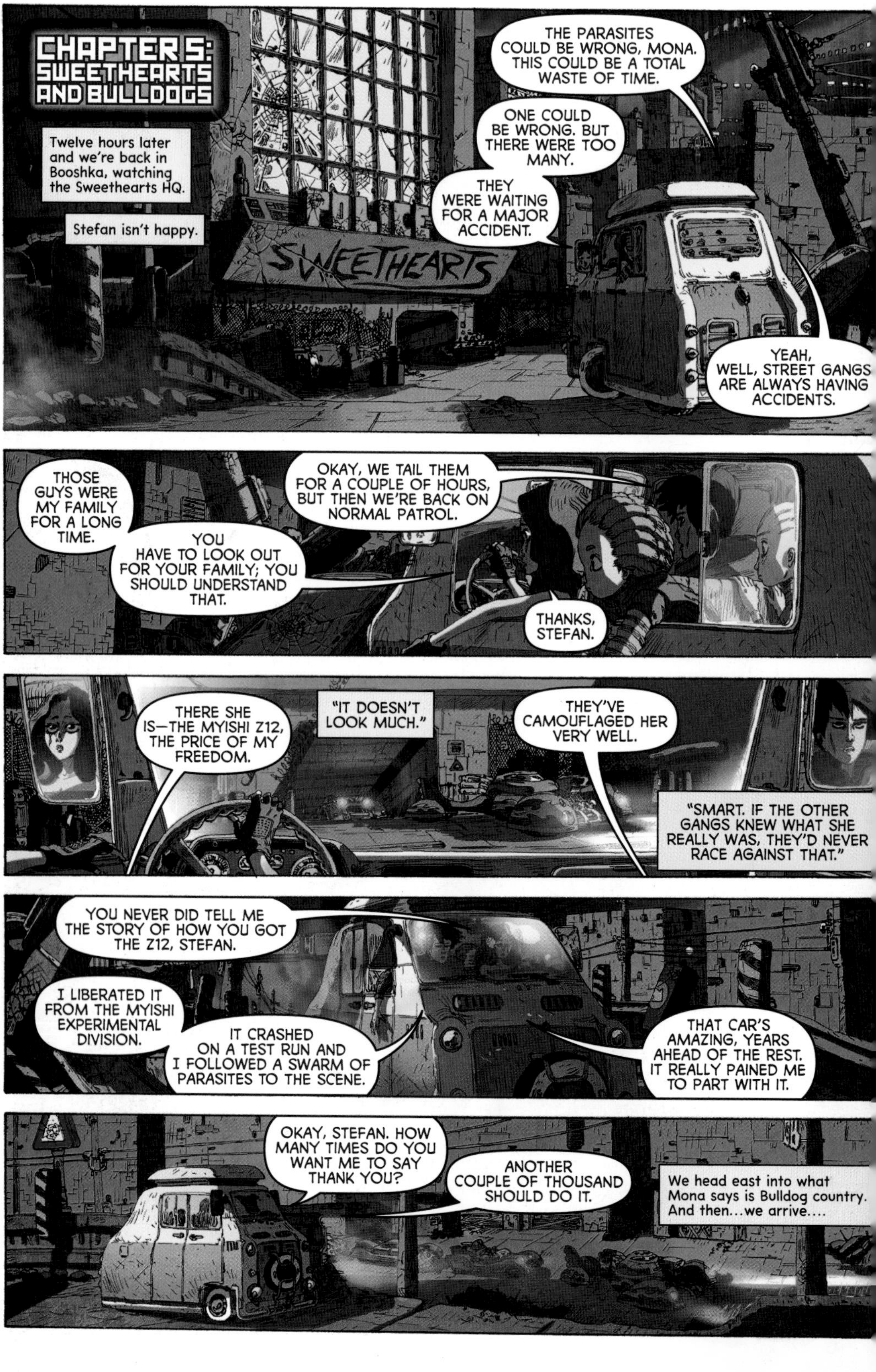
CHAPTER 5: SWEETHEARTS AND BULLDOGS
Twelve hours later and we're back in Booshka, watching the Sweethearts HQ.
Stefan isn't happy.
SWEETHEARTS
THE PARASITES COULD BE WRONG, MONA. THIS COULD BE A TOTAL WASTE OF TIME.
ONE COULD BE WRONG. BUT THERE WERE TOO MANY.
THEY WERE WAITING FOR A MAJOR ACCIDENT.
YEAH, WELL, STREET GANGS ARE ALWAYS HAVING ACCIDENTS.
THOSE GUYS WERE MY FAMILY FOR A LONG TIME.
YOU HAVE TO LOOK OUT FOR YOUR FAMILY; YOU SHOULD UNDERSTAND THAT.
OKAY, WE TAIL THEM FOR A COUPLE OF HOURS, BUT THEN WE'RE BACK ON NORMAL PATROL.
THANKS, STEFAN.
THERE SHE IS—THE MYISHI Z12, THE PRICE OF MY FREEDOM.
"IT DOESN'T LOOK MUCH."
THEY'VE CAMOUFLAGED HER VERY WELL.
"SMART. IF THE OTHER GANGS KNEW WHAT SHE REALLY WAS, THEY'D NEVER RACE AGAINST THAT."
YOU NEVER DID TELL ME THE STORY OF HOW YOU GOT THE Z12, STEFAN.
I LIBERATED IT FROM THE MYISHI EXPERIMENTAL DIVISION.
IT CRASHED ON A TEST RUN AND I FOLLOWED A SWARM OF PARASITES TO THE SCENE.
THAT CAR'S AMAZING, YEARS AHEAD OF THE REST. IT REALLY PAINED ME TO PART WITH IT.
OKAY, STEFAN. HOW MANY TIMES DO YOU WANT ME TO SAY THANK YOU?
ANOTHER COUPLE OF THOUSAND SHOULD DO IT.
We head east into what Mona says is Bulldog country. And then...we arrive....

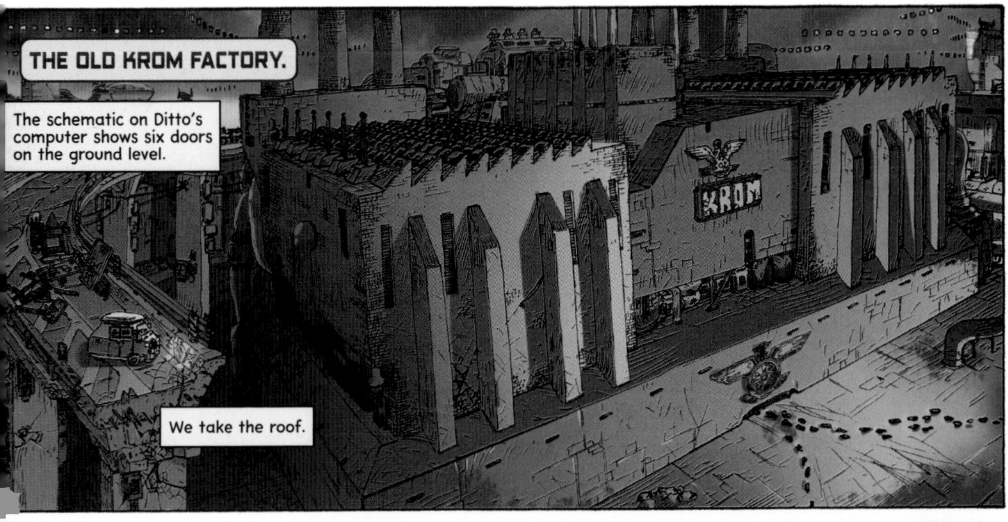
THE OLD KROM FACTORY.
The schematic on Ditto's computer shows six doors on the ground level.
KROM
We take the roof.

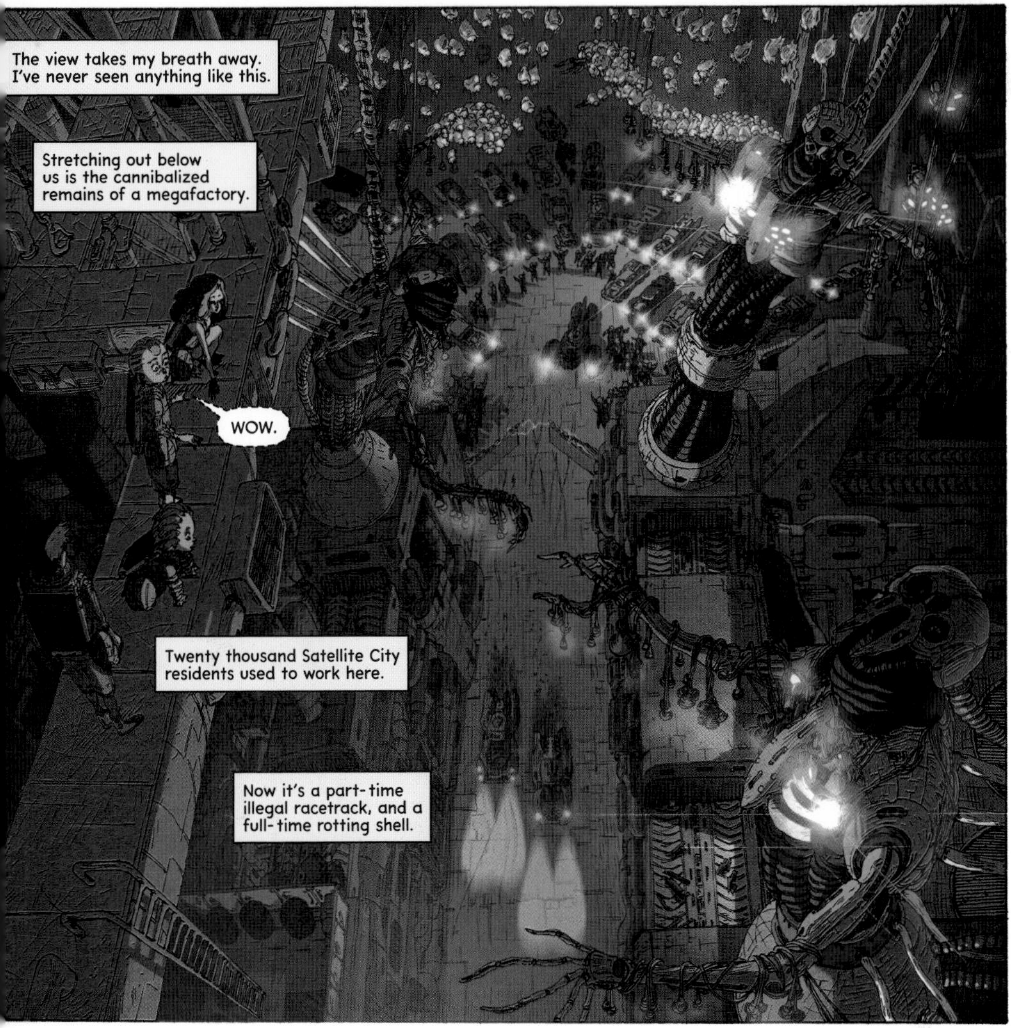
The view takes my breath away. I've never seen anything like this.
Stretching out below us is the cannibalized remains of a megafactory.
WOW.
Twenty thousand Satellite City residents used to work here.
Now it's a part-time illegal racetrack, and a full-time rotting shell.

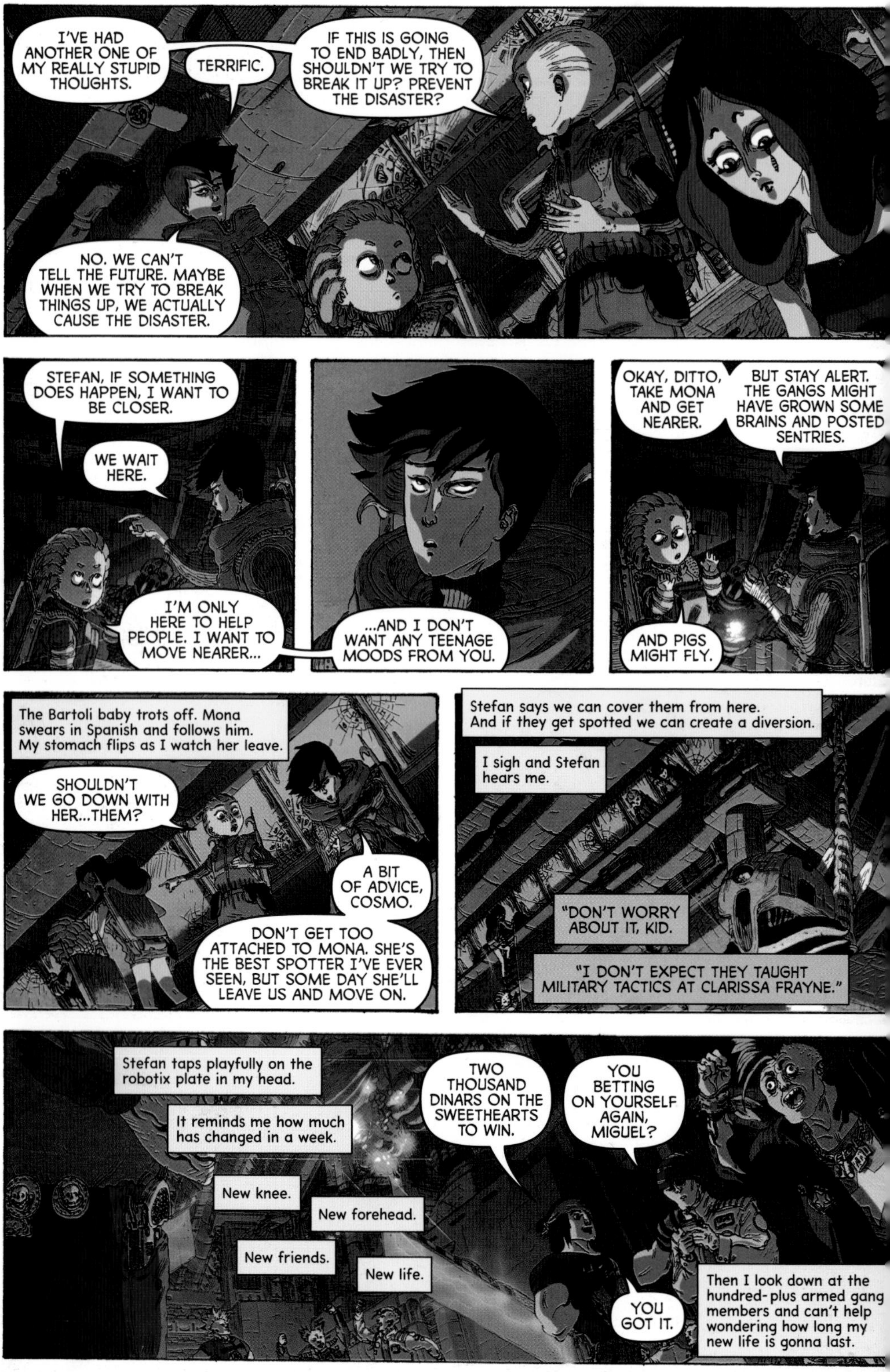
I'VE HAD ANOTHER ONE OF MY REALLY STUPID THOUGHTS.
TERRIFIC.
IF THIS IS GOING TO END BADLY, THEN SHOULDN'T WE TRY TO BREAK IT UP? PREVENT THE DISASTER?
NO. WE CAN'T TELL THE FUTURE. MAYBE WHEN WE TRY TO BREAK THINGS UP, WE ACTUALLY CAUSE THE DISASTER.
STEFAN, IF SOMETHING DOES HAPPEN, I WANT TO BE CLOSER.
WE WAIT HERE.
I'M ONLY HERE TO HELP PEOPLE. I WANT TO MOVE NEARER...
...AND I DON'T WANT ANY TEENAGE MOODS FROM YOU.
OKAY, DITTO, TAKE MONA AND GET NEARER.
BUT STAY ALERT. THE GANGS MIGHT HAVE GROWN SOME BRAINS AND POSTED SENTRIES.
AND PIGS MIGHT FLY.
The Bartoli baby trots off. Mona swears in Spanish and follows him. My stomach flips as I watch her leave.
SHOULDN'T WE GO DOWN WITH HER...THEM?
A BIT OF ADVICE, COSMO.
DON'T GET TOO ATTACHED TO MONA. SHE'S THE BEST SPOTTER I'VE EVER SEEN, BUT SOME DAY SHE'LL LEAVE US AND MOVE ON.
Stefan says we can cover them from here. And if they get spotted we can create a diversion.
I sigh and Stefan hears me.
"DON'T WORRY ABOUT IT, KID.
"I DON'T EXPECT THEY TAUGHT MILITARY TACTICS AT CLARISSA FRAYNE."
Stefan taps playfully on the robotix plate in my head.
It reminds me how much has changed in a week.
New knee.
New forehead.
New friends.
New life.
TWO THOUSAND DINARS ON THE SWEETHEARTS TO WIN.
YOU BETTING ON YOURSELF AGAIN, MIGUEL?
YOU GOT IT.
Then I look down at the hundred-plus armed gang members and can't help wondering how long my new life is gonna last.

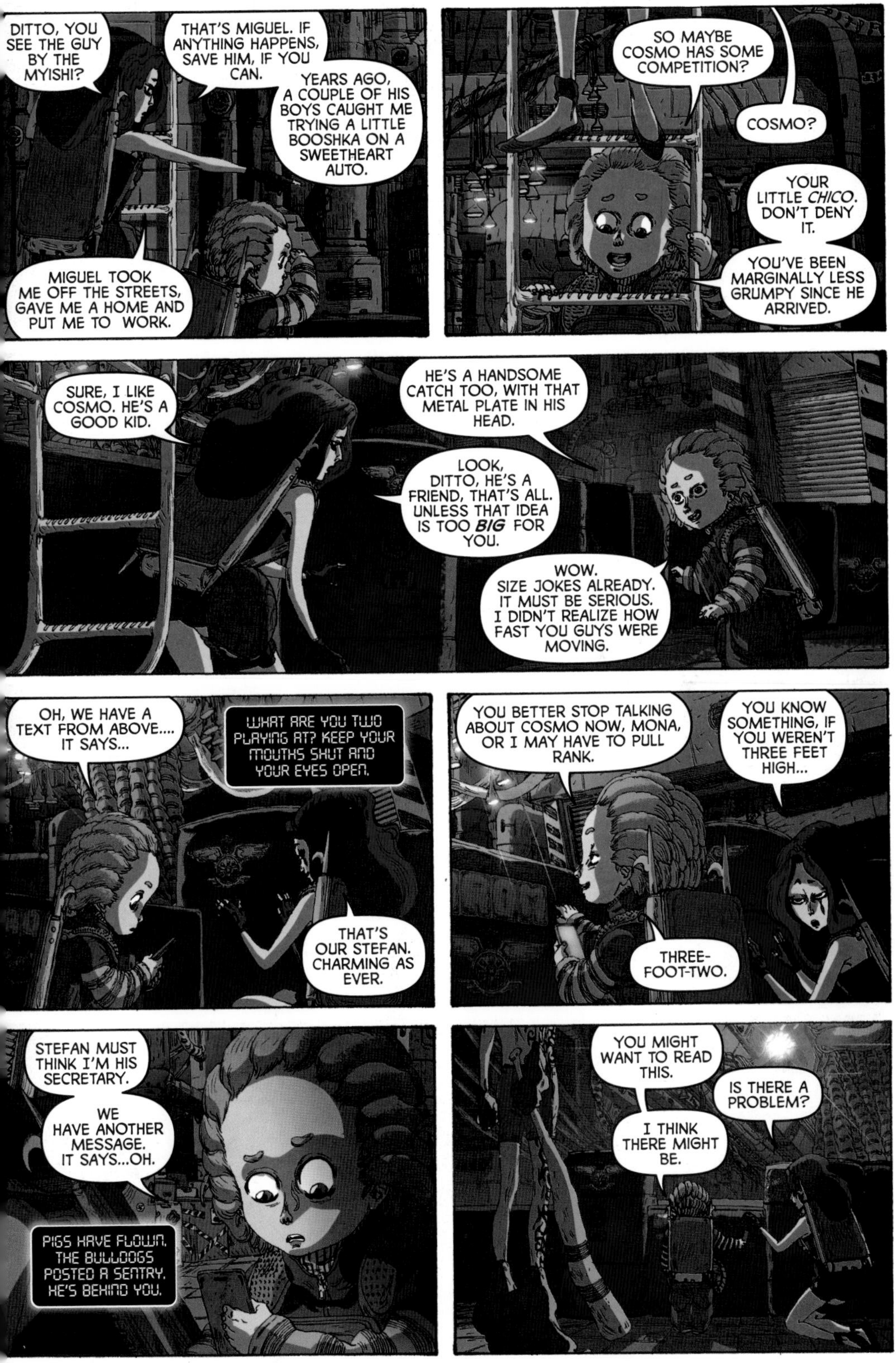

DITTO, YOU SEE THE GUY BY THE MYISHI?
THAT'S MIGUEL. IF ANYTHING HAPPENS, SAVE HIM, IF YOU CAN.
YEARS AGO, A COUPLE OF HIS BOYS CAUGHT ME TRYING A LITTLE BOOSHKA ON A SWEETHEART AUTO.
MIGUEL TOOK ME OFF THE STREETS, GAVE ME A HOME AND PUT ME TO WORK.
SO MAYBE COSMO HAS SOME COMPETITION?
COSMO?
YOUR LITTLE *CHICO*. DON'T DENY IT.
YOU'VE BEEN MARGINALLY LESS GRUMPY SINCE HE ARRIVED.
SURE, I LIKE COSMO. HE'S A GOOD KID.
HE'S A HANDSOME CATCH TOO, WITH THAT METAL PLATE IN HIS HEAD.
LOOK, DITTO, HE'S A FRIEND, THAT'S ALL. UNLESS THAT IDEA IS TOO ***BIG*** FOR YOU.
WOW. SIZE JOKES ALREADY. IT MUST BE SERIOUS. I DIDN'T REALIZE HOW FAST YOU GUYS WERE MOVING.
OH, WE HAVE A TEXT FROM ABOVE.... IT SAYS...
WHAT ARE YOU TWO PLAYING AT? KEEP YOUR MOUTHS SHUT AND YOUR EYES OPEN.
THAT'S OUR STEFAN. CHARMING AS EVER.
YOU BETTER STOP TALKING ABOUT COSMO NOW, MONA, OR I MAY HAVE TO PULL RANK.
YOU KNOW SOMETHING, IF YOU WEREN'T THREE FEET HIGH...
THREE-FOOT-TWO.
STEFAN MUST THINK I'M HIS SECRETARY.
WE HAVE ANOTHER MESSAGE. IT SAYS...OH.
PIGS HAVE FLOWN. THE BULLDOGS POSTED A SENTRY. HE'S BEHIND YOU.
YOU MIGHT WANT TO READ THIS.
IS THERE A PROBLEM?
I THINK THERE MIGHT BE.

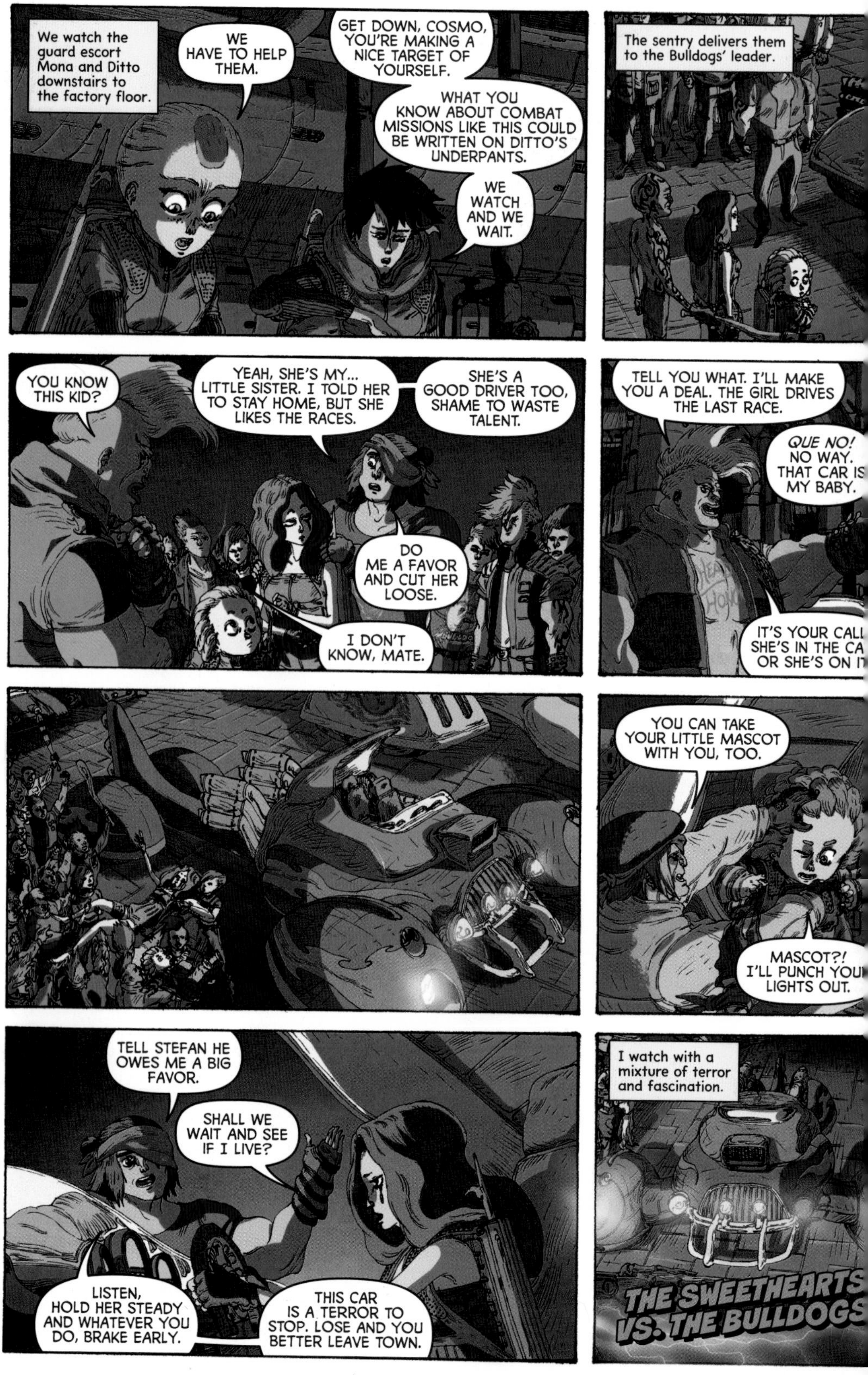
We watch the guard escort Mona and Ditto downstairs to the factory floor.
WE HAVE TO HELP THEM.
GET DOWN, COSMO, YOU'RE MAKING A NICE TARGET OF YOURSELF.
WHAT YOU KNOW ABOUT COMBAT MISSIONS LIKE THIS COULD BE WRITTEN ON DITTO'S UNDERPANTS.
WE WATCH AND WE WAIT.
The sentry delivers them to the Bulldogs' leader.
YOU KNOW THIS KID?
YEAH, SHE'S MY... LITTLE SISTER. I TOLD HER TO STAY HOME, BUT SHE LIKES THE RACES.
SHE'S A GOOD DRIVER TOO, SHAME TO WASTE TALENT.
DO ME A FAVOR AND CUT HER LOOSE.
I DON'T KNOW, MATE.
TELL YOU WHAT. I'LL MAKE YOU A DEAL. THE GIRL DRIVES THE LAST RACE.
QUE NO! NO WAY. THAT CAR IS MY BABY.
IT'S YOUR CALL. SHE'S IN THE CA OR SHE'S ON I
YOU CAN TAKE YOUR LITTLE MASCOT WITH YOU, TOO.
MASCOT?! I'LL PUNCH YOU LIGHTS OUT.
TELL STEFAN HE OWES ME A BIG FAVOR.
SHALL WE WAIT AND SEE IF I LIVE?
LISTEN, HOLD HER STEADY AND WHATEVER YOU DO, BRAKE EARLY.
THIS CAR IS A TERROR TO STOP. LOSE AND YOU BETTER LEAVE TOWN.
I watch with a mixture of terror and fascination.
THE SWEETHEARTS VS. THE BULLDOGS

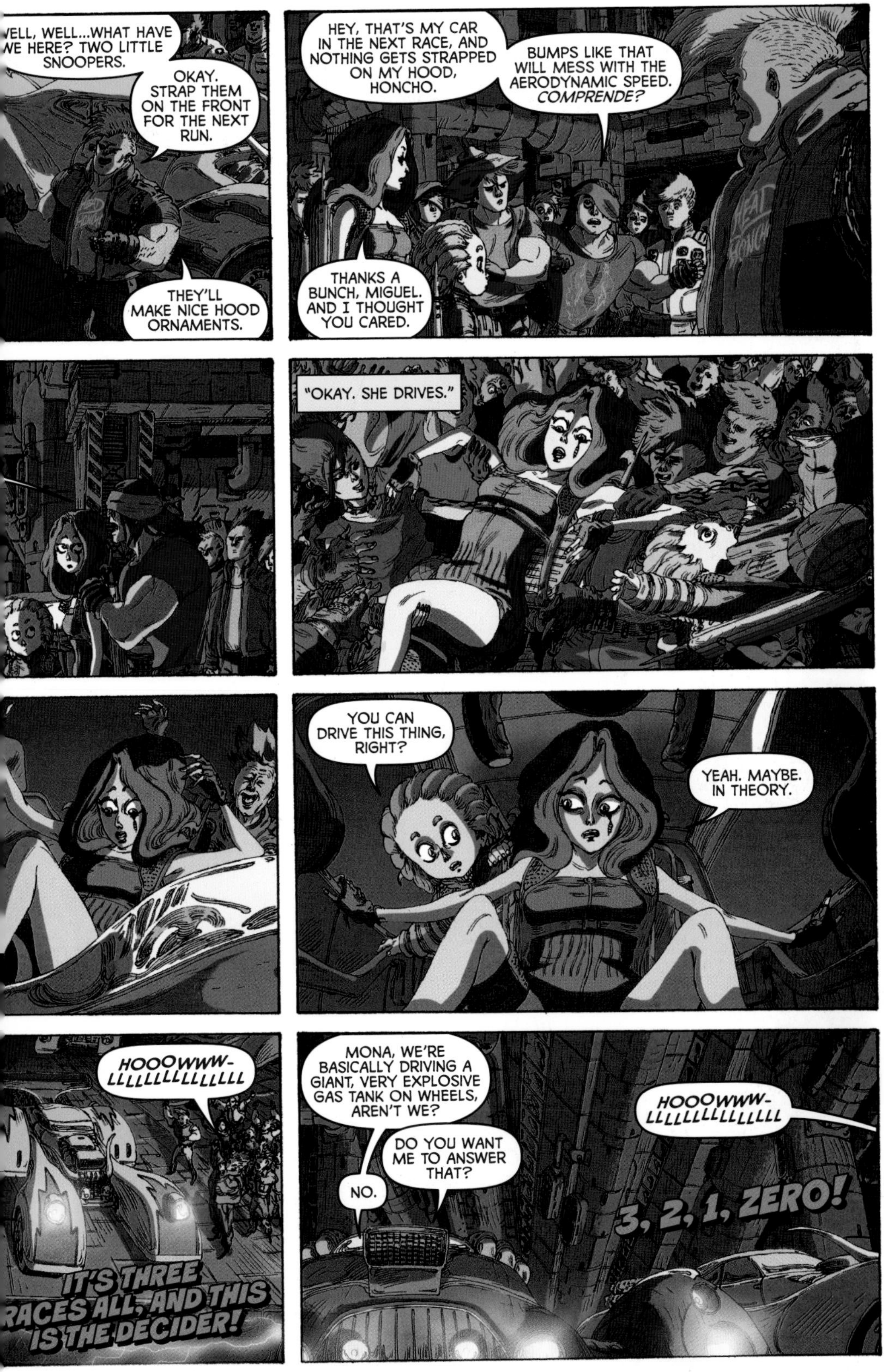
WELL, WELL...WHAT HAVE WE HERE? TWO LITTLE SNOOPERS.
OKAY. STRAP THEM ON THE FRONT FOR THE NEXT RUN.
THEY'LL MAKE NICE HOOD ORNAMENTS.
HEY, THAT'S MY CAR IN THE NEXT RACE, AND NOTHING GETS STRAPPED ON MY HOOD, HONCHO.
BUMPS LIKE THAT WILL MESS WITH THE AERODYNAMIC SPEED. *COMPRENDE?*
THANKS A BUNCH, MIGUEL. AND I THOUGHT YOU CARED.
"OKAY. SHE DRIVES."
YOU CAN DRIVE THIS THING, RIGHT?
YEAH. MAYBE. IN THEORY.
HOOOWWW-LLLLLLLLLLLLLL
IT'S THREE RACES ALL, AND THIS IS THE DECIDER!
MONA, WE'RE BASICALLY DRIVING A GIANT, VERY EXPLOSIVE GAS TANK ON WHEELS, AREN'T WE?
DO YOU WANT ME TO ANSWER THAT?
NO.
HOOOWWW-LLLLLLLLLLLLLL
3, 2, 1, ZERO!

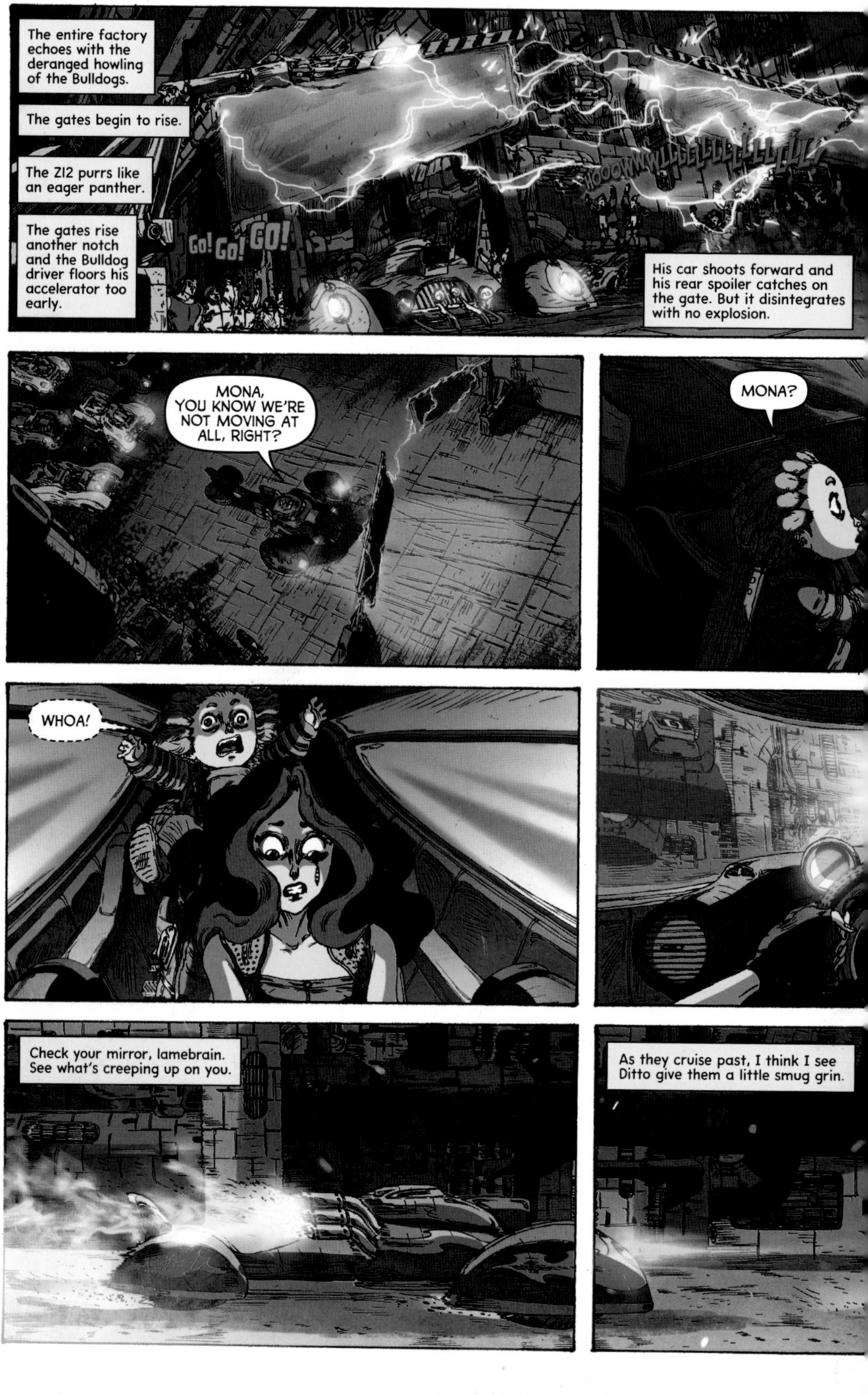
The entire factory echoes with the deranged howling of the Bulldogs.
The gates begin to rise.
The Z12 purrs like an eager panther.
The gates rise another notch and the Bulldog driver floors his accelerator too early.
GO! GO! GO!
His car shoots forward and his rear spoiler catches on the gate. But it disintegrates with no explosion.
MONA, YOU KNOW WE'RE NOT MOVING AT ALL, RIGHT?
MONA?
WHOA!
Check your mirror, lamebrain. See what's creeping up on you.
As they cruise past, I think I see Ditto give them a little smug grin.

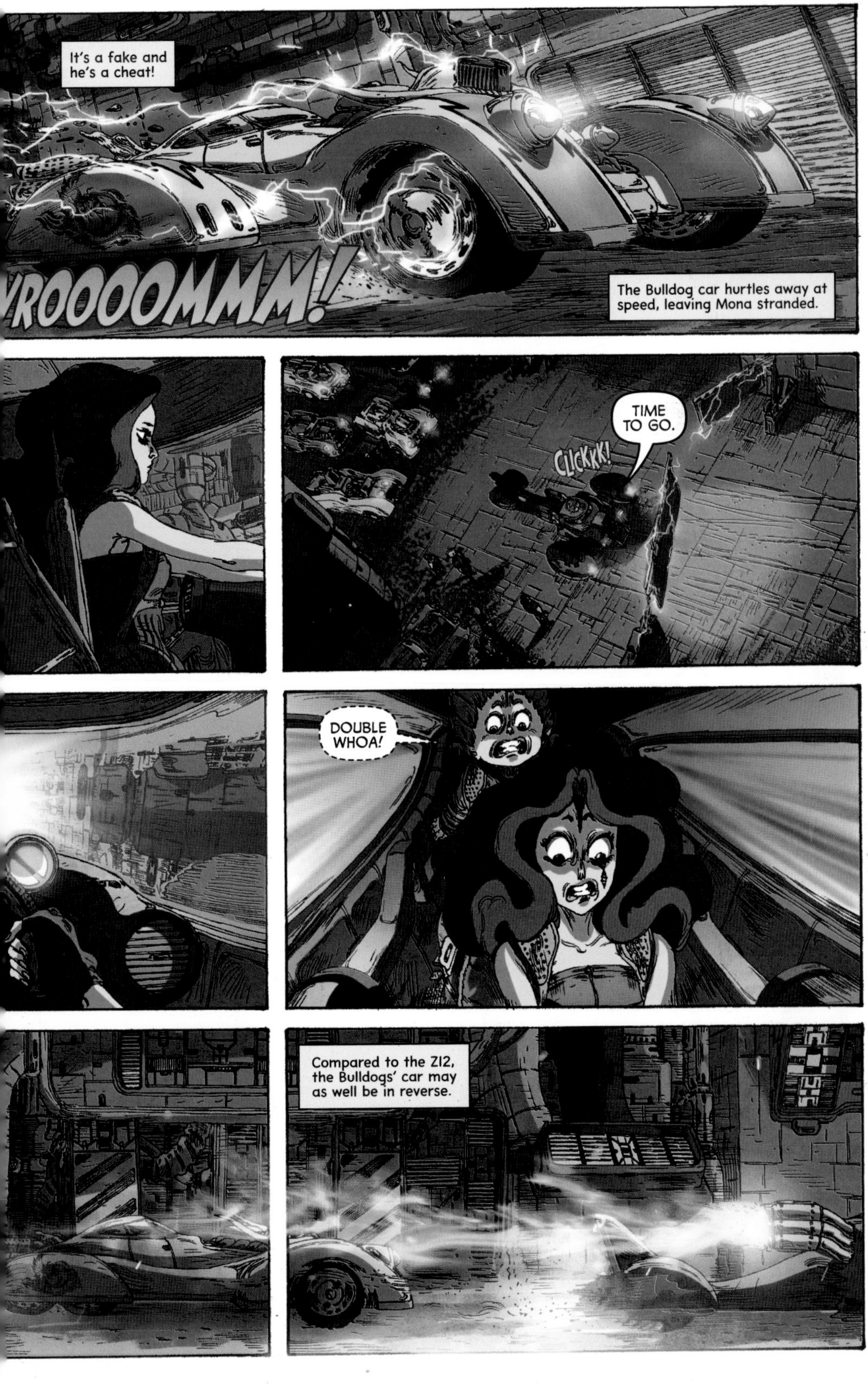
It's a fake and he's a cheat!
VROOOOMMM!
The Bulldog car hurtles away at speed, leaving Mona stranded.
CLICKKK!
TIME TO GO.
DOUBLE WHOA!
Compared to the ZI2, the Bulldogs' car may as well be in reverse.

AND CROSSING THE LINE FIRST...
THE SWEETHEARTS ARE THE WINNERS!

Mona had won the race. Stefan and I wanted to see what she would do next.

YOU FORGOT TO BRAKE.

YOUR OLD BOYFRIEND SAID TO BRAKE EARLY REMEMBER?

MONA?

OH, GREAT.

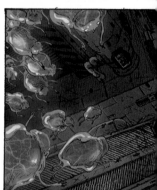

OH, NO.

YOU SE THEM?

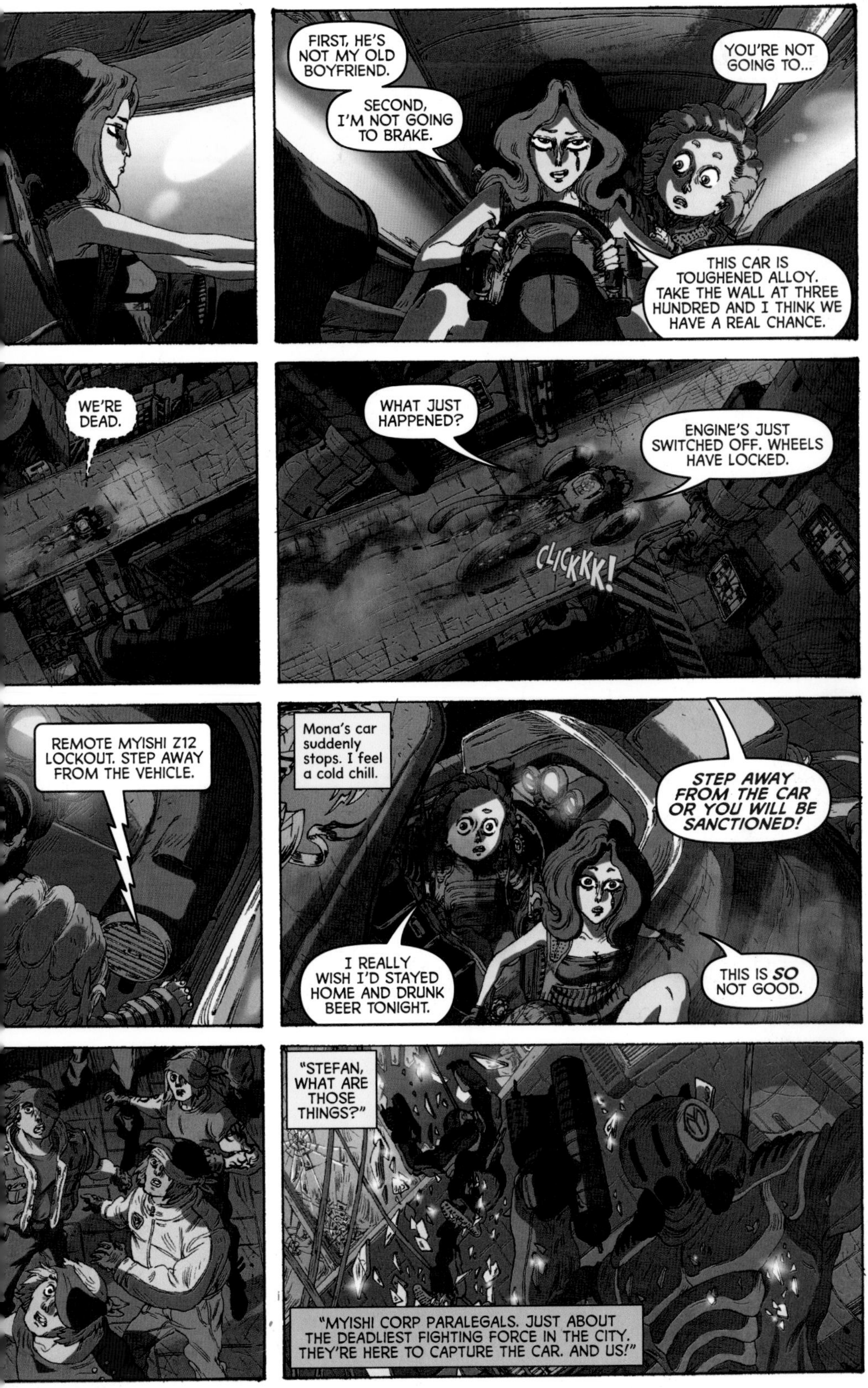
FIRST, HE'S NOT MY OLD BOYFRIEND.
SECOND, I'M NOT GOING TO BRAKE.
YOU'RE NOT GOING TO...
THIS CAR IS TOUGHENED ALLOY. TAKE THE WALL AT THREE HUNDRED AND I THINK WE HAVE A REAL CHANCE.
WE'RE DEAD.
WHAT JUST HAPPENED?
ENGINE'S JUST SWITCHED OFF. WHEELS HAVE LOCKED.
CLICKKK!
REMOTE MYISHI Z12 LOCKOUT. STEP AWAY FROM THE VEHICLE.
Mona's car suddenly stops. I feel a cold chill.
STEP AWAY FROM THE CAR OR YOU WILL BE SANCTIONED!
I REALLY WISH I'D STAYED HOME AND DRUNK BEER TONIGHT.
THIS IS SO NOT GOOD.
"STEFAN, WHAT ARE THOSE THINGS?"
"MYISHI CORP PARALEGALS. JUST ABOUT THE DEADLIEST FIGHTING FORCE IN THE CITY. THEY'RE HERE TO CAPTURE THE CAR. AND US!"

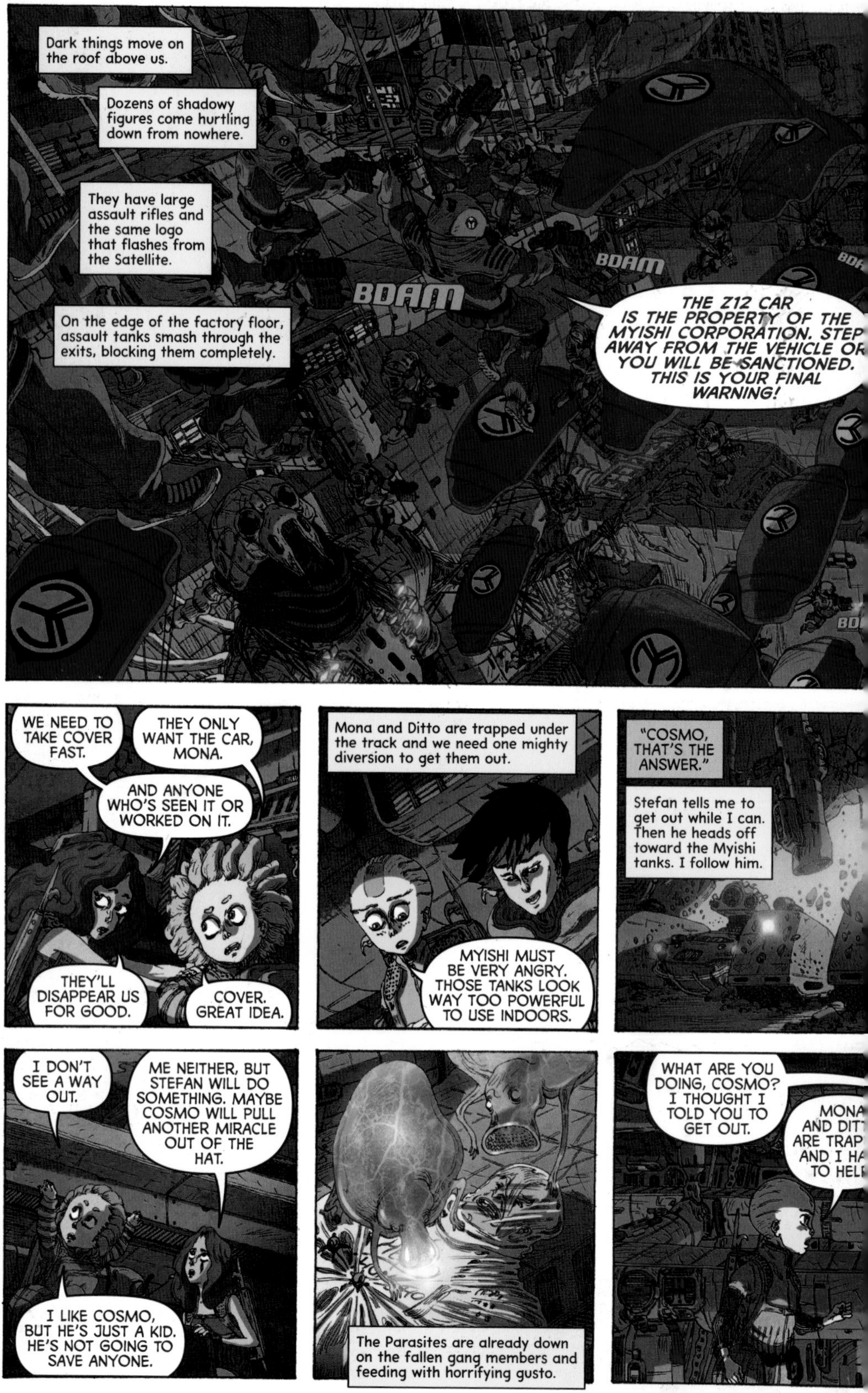

Dark things move on the roof above us.
Dozens of shadowy figures come hurtling down from nowhere.
They have large assault rifles and the same logo that flashes from the Satellite.
BDAM
BDAM
On the edge of the factory floor, assault tanks smash through the exits, blocking them completely.
THE Z12 CAR IS THE PROPERTY OF THE MYISHI CORPORATION. STEP AWAY FROM THE VEHICLE OR YOU WILL BE SANCTIONED. THIS IS YOUR FINAL WARNING!
WE NEED TO TAKE COVER FAST.
THEY ONLY WANT THE CAR, MONA.
AND ANYONE WHO'S SEEN IT OR WORKED ON IT.
THEY'LL DISAPPEAR US FOR GOOD.
COVER. GREAT IDEA.
Mona and Ditto are trapped under the track and we need one mighty diversion to get them out.
MYISHI MUST BE VERY ANGRY. THOSE TANKS LOOK WAY TOO POWERFUL TO USE INDOORS.
"COSMO, THAT'S THE ANSWER."
Stefan tells me to get out while I can. Then he heads off toward the Myishi tanks. I follow him.
I DON'T SEE A WAY OUT.
ME NEITHER, BUT STEFAN WILL DO SOMETHING. MAYBE COSMO WILL PULL ANOTHER MIRACLE OUT OF THE HAT.
I LIKE COSMO, BUT HE'S JUST A KID. HE'S NOT GOING TO SAVE ANYONE.
The Parasites are already down on the fallen gang members and feeding with horrifying gusto.
WHAT ARE YOU DOING, COSMO? I THOUGHT I TOLD YOU TO GET OUT.
MONA AND DITT ARE TRAP AND I HA TO HEL

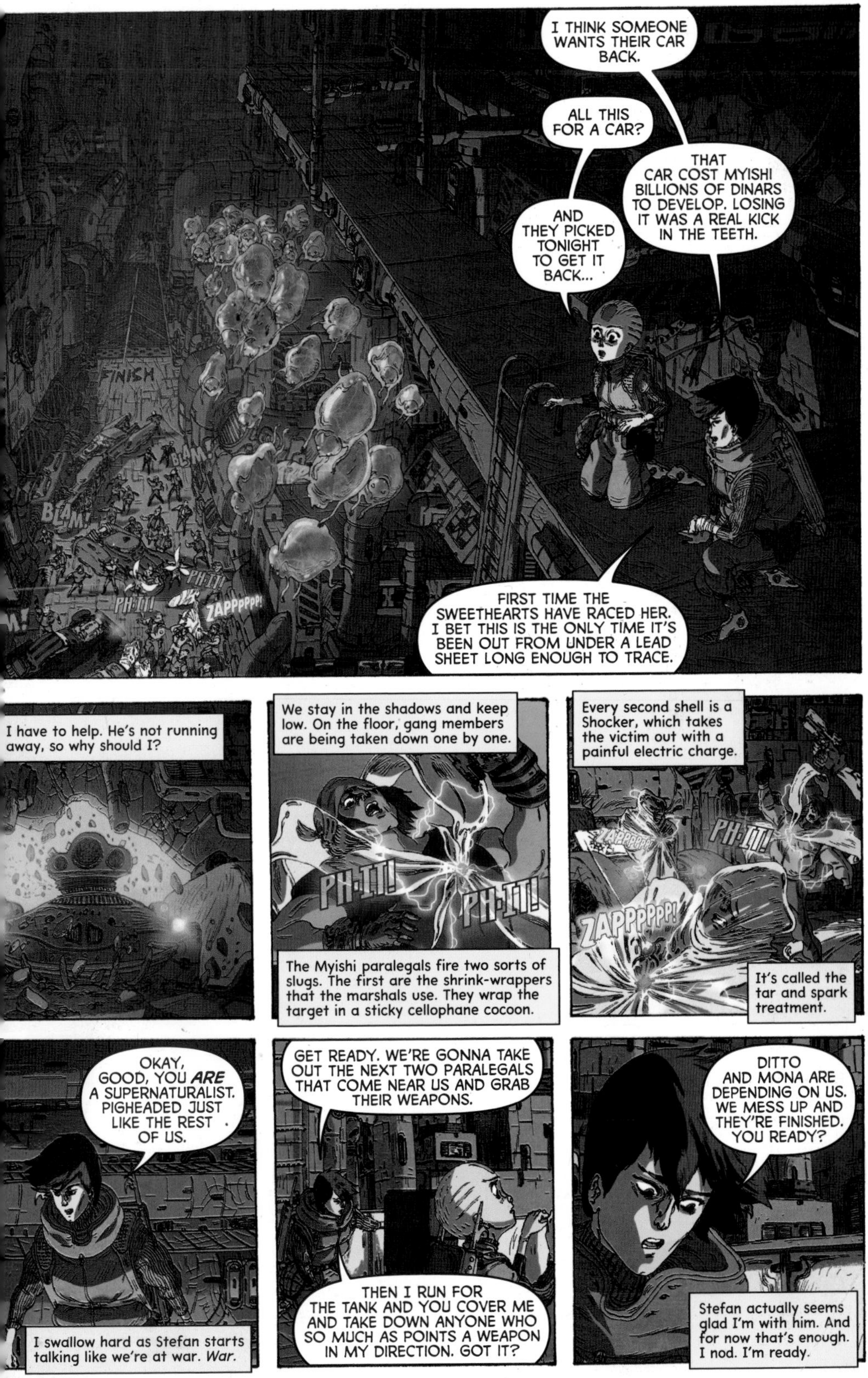
I THINK SOMEONE WANTS THEIR CAR BACK.
ALL THIS FOR A CAR?
THAT CAR COST MYISHI BILLIONS OF DINARS TO DEVELOP. LOSING IT WAS A REAL KICK IN THE TEETH.
AND THEY PICKED TONIGHT TO GET IT BACK...
FINISH
BLAM!
BLAM!
PH-IT!
PH-IT!
ZAPPPPPP!
FIRST TIME THE SWEETHEARTS HAVE RACED HER. I BET THIS IS THE ONLY TIME IT'S BEEN OUT FROM UNDER A LEAD SHEET LONG ENOUGH TO TRACE.
I have to help. He's not running away, so why should I?
We stay in the shadows and keep low. On the floor, gang members are being taken down one by one.
PH-IT!
PH-IT!
The Myishi paralegals fire two sorts of slugs. The first are the shrink-wrappers that the marshals use. They wrap the target in a sticky cellophane cocoon.
Every second shell is a Shocker, which takes the victim out with a painful electric charge.
PH-IT!
ZAPPPPPP!
It's called the tar and spark treatment.
OKAY, GOOD, YOU *ARE* A SUPERNATURALIST. PIGHEADED JUST LIKE THE REST OF US.
I swallow hard as Stefan starts talking like we're at war. *War.*
GET READY. WE'RE GONNA TAKE OUT THE NEXT TWO PARALEGALS THAT COME NEAR US AND GRAB THEIR WEAPONS.
THEN I RUN FOR THE TANK AND YOU COVER ME AND TAKE DOWN ANYONE WHO SO MUCH AS POINTS A WEAPON IN MY DIRECTION. GOT IT?
DITTO AND MONA ARE DEPENDING ON US. WE MESS UP AND THEY'RE FINISHED. YOU READY?
Stefan actually seems glad I'm with him. And for now that's enough. I nod. I'm ready.

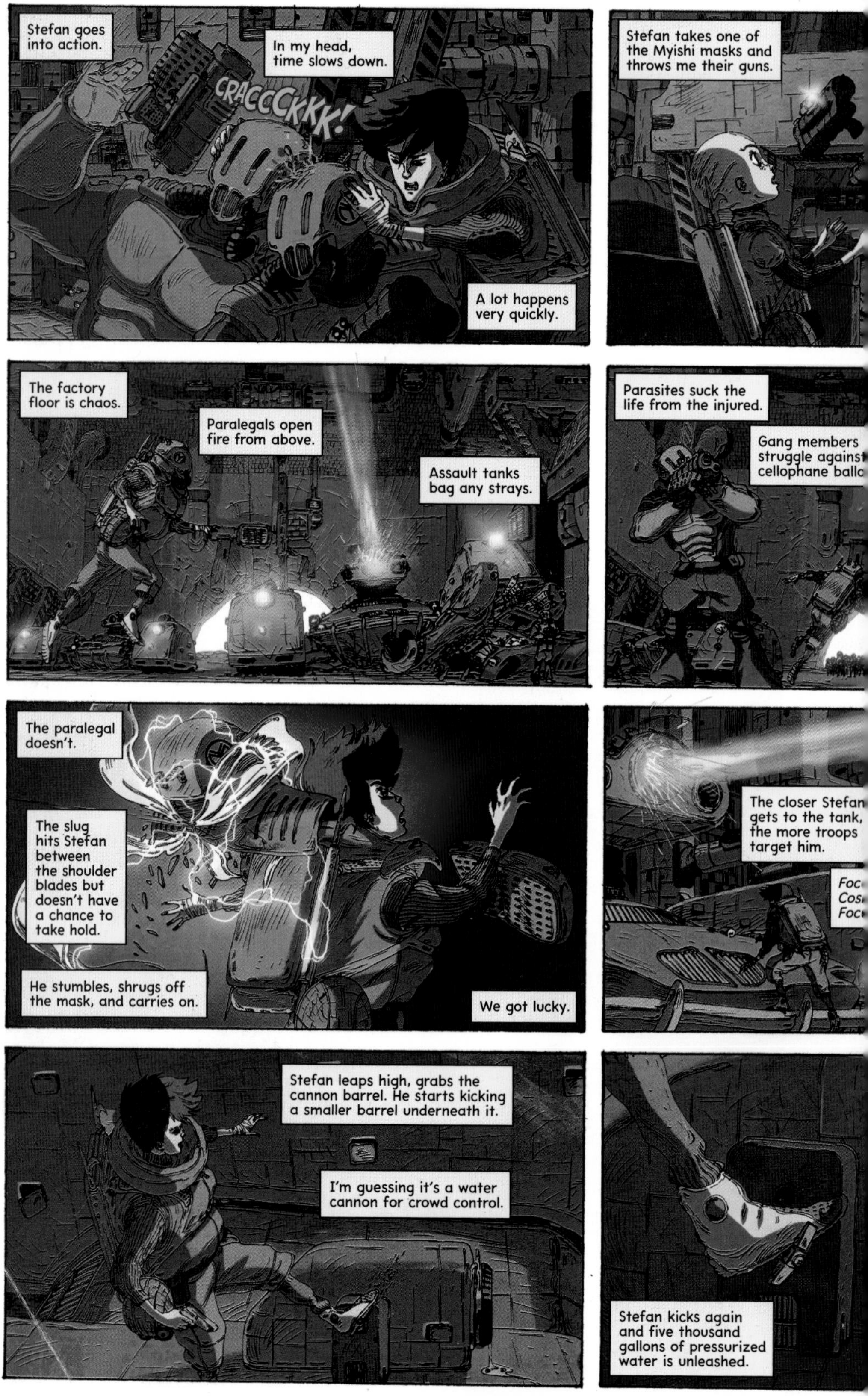

Stefan goes into action.
In my head, time slows down.
CRACCCKKK!
A lot happens very quickly.
Stefan takes one of the Myishi masks and throws me their guns.
The factory floor is chaos.
Paralegals open fire from above.
Assault tanks bag any strays.
Parasites suck the life from the injured.
Gang members struggle agains cellophane ballo
The paralegal doesn't.
The slug hits Stefan between the shoulder blades but doesn't have a chance to take hold.
He stumbles, shrugs off the mask, and carries on.
We got lucky.
The closer Stefan gets to the tank, the more troops target him.
Stefan leaps high, grabs the cannon barrel. He starts kicking a smaller barrel underneath it.
I'm guessing it's a water cannon for crowd control.
Stefan kicks again and five thousand gallons of pressurized water is unleashed.

LAWYERS. LIKED THEM BETTER WHEN THEY FOUGHT WITH THEIR BRIEFCASES.

THESE GUNS ARE SET ON CELLOPHANE SLUGS. AIM ABOUT TWO FEET HIGHER THAN THE TARGET.

I look at the confusing array of barrels and buttons, but before I can tell Stefan I can't work it, his mask is on and he's running toward the tank.

BUT...

Running toward the tank and relying on me.

And in the middle of all this I have to watch Stefan's back. And front. And both sides.

I see a paralegal spot Stefan's run.

He takes aim. So do I.

I fire... and miss.

I take out a cluster of troops one floor up.

Stefan gets close enough to fire a Shocker slug down the main barrel.

Focus, Cosmo. Focus.

No point being delicate about it. I fire everything in the clip to buy him time.

AABLOOOSSHHH!

Troops, vehicles, and gang members are scattered by the deluge.

The Parasites abandon their prizes and flee.

Mona and Ditto slip away. We've done it.

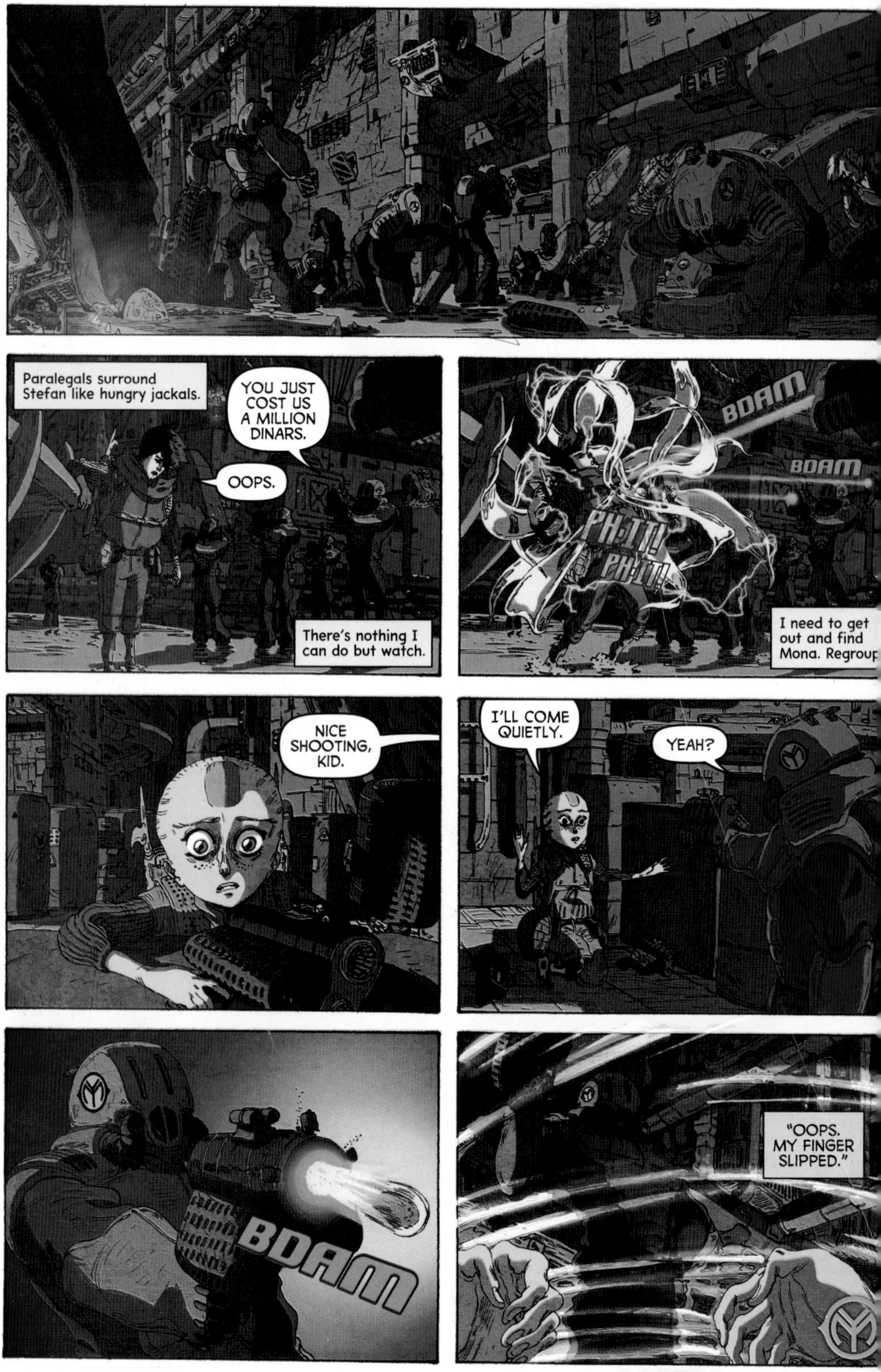
Paralegals surround Stefan like hungry jackals.
YOU JUST COST US A MILLION DINARS.
OOPS.
There's nothing I can do but watch.
BDAM
BDAM
PH-IT!
PH-IT!
I need to get out and find Mona. Regroup
NICE SHOOTING, KID.
I'LL COME QUIETLY.
YEAH?
BDAM
"OOPS. MY FINGER SLIPPED."

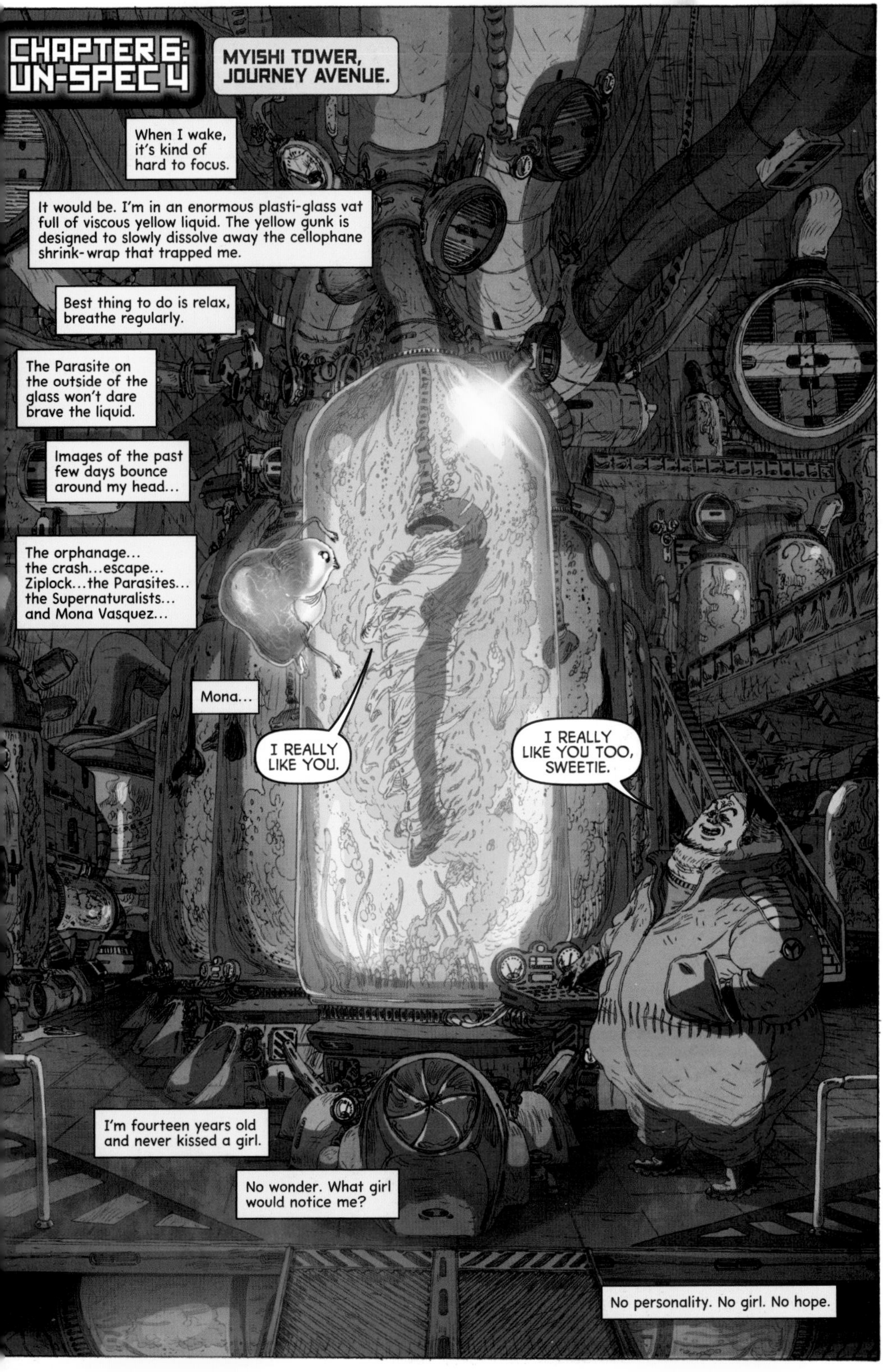
CHAPTER 6: UN-SPEC 4
MYISHI TOWER, JOURNEY AVENUE.
When I wake, it's kind of hard to focus.
It would be. I'm in an enormous plasti-glass vat full of viscous yellow liquid. The yellow gunk is designed to slowly dissolve away the cellophane shrink-wrap that trapped me.
Best thing to do is relax, breathe regularly.
The Parasite on the outside of the glass won't dare brave the liquid.
Images of the past few days bounce around my head...
The orphanage... the crash...escape... Ziplock...the Parasites... the Supernaturalists... and Mona Vasquez...
Mona...
I REALLY LIKE YOU.
I REALLY LIKE YOU TOO, SWEETIE.
I'm fourteen years old and never kissed a girl.
No wonder. What girl would notice me?
No personality. No girl. No hope.

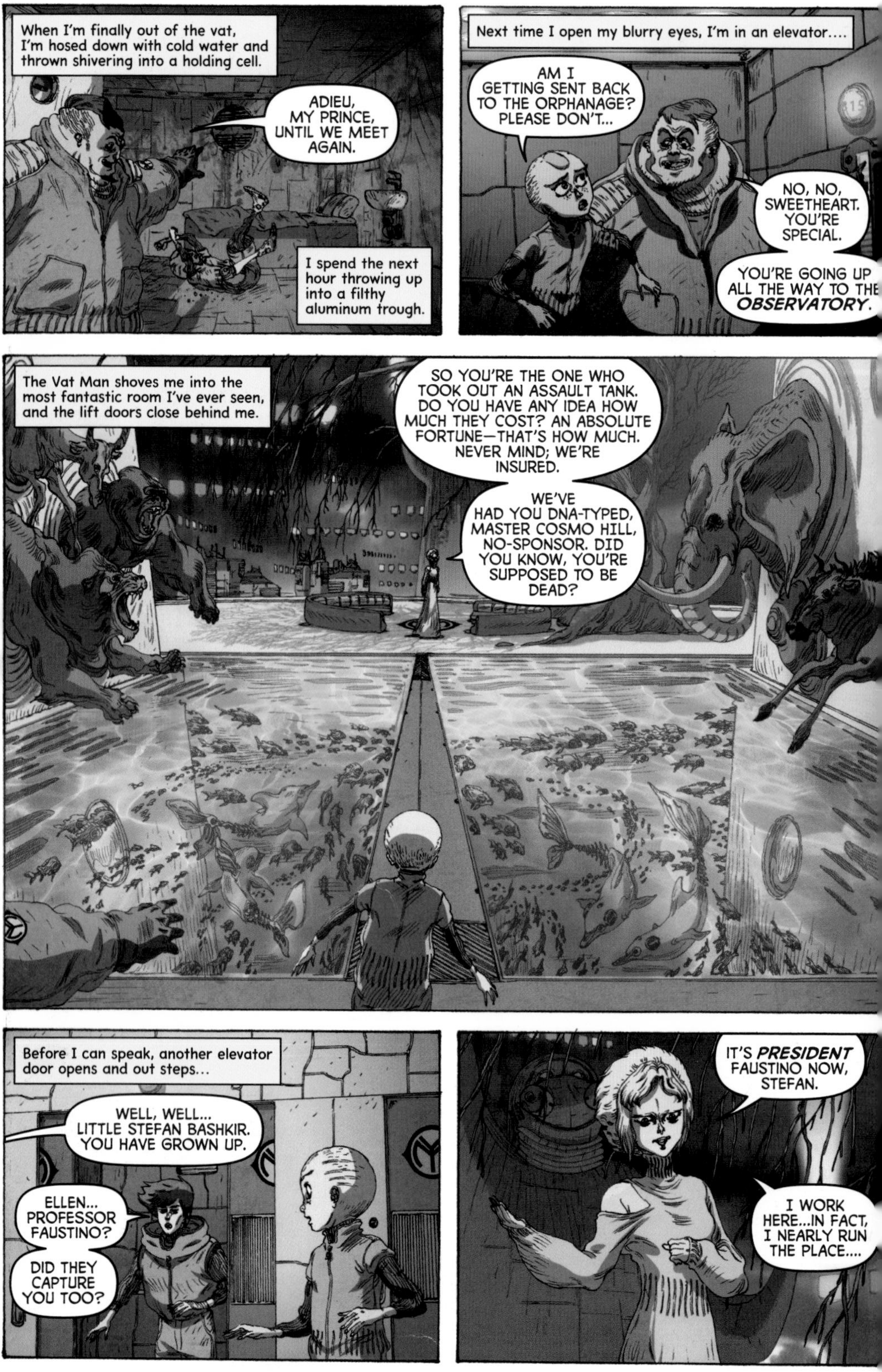
When I'm finally out of the vat, I'm hosed down with cold water and thrown shivering into a holding cell.
ADIEU, MY PRINCE, UNTIL WE MEET AGAIN.
I spend the next hour throwing up into a filthy aluminum trough.
Next time I open my blurry eyes, I'm in an elevator....
AM I GETTING SENT BACK TO THE ORPHANAGE? PLEASE DON'T...
NO, NO, SWEETHEART. YOU'RE SPECIAL.
YOU'RE GOING UP ALL THE WAY TO THE *OBSERVATORY*.
The Vat Man shoves me into the most fantastic room I've ever seen, and the lift doors close behind me.
SO YOU'RE THE ONE WHO TOOK OUT AN ASSAULT TANK. DO YOU HAVE ANY IDEA HOW MUCH THEY COST? AN ABSOLUTE FORTUNE—THAT'S HOW MUCH. NEVER MIND; WE'RE INSURED.
WE'VE HAD YOU DNA-TYPED, MASTER COSMO HILL, NO-SPONSOR. DID YOU KNOW, YOU'RE SUPPOSED TO BE DEAD?
Before I can speak, another elevator door opens and out steps...
WELL, WELL... LITTLE STEFAN BASHKIR. YOU HAVE GROWN UP.
ELLEN... PROFESSOR FAUSTINO?
DID THEY CAPTURE YOU TOO?
IT'S *PRESIDENT* FAUSTINO NOW, STEFAN.
I WORK HERE...IN FACT, I NEARLY RUN THE PLACE....

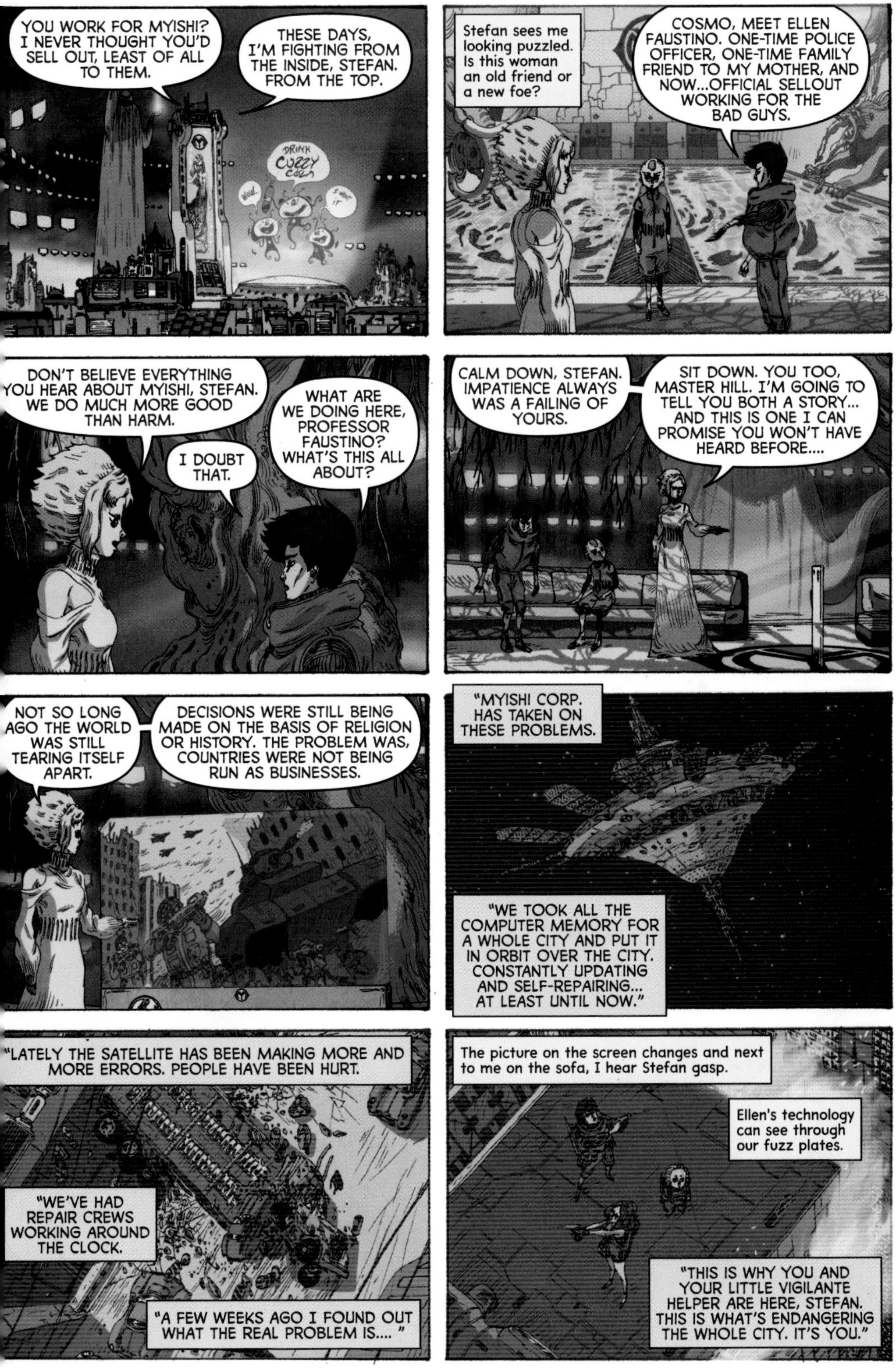
YOU WORK FOR MYISHI? I NEVER THOUGHT YOU'D SELL OUT, LEAST OF ALL TO THEM.
THESE DAYS, I'M FIGHTING FROM THE INSIDE, STEFAN. FROM THE TOP.
DRINK CUZZY COLA
Stefan sees me looking puzzled. Is this woman an old friend or a new foe?
COSMO, MEET ELLEN FAUSTINO. ONE-TIME POLICE OFFICER, ONE-TIME FAMILY FRIEND TO MY MOTHER, AND NOW...OFFICIAL SELLOUT WORKING FOR THE BAD GUYS.
DON'T BELIEVE EVERYTHING YOU HEAR ABOUT MYISHI, STEFAN. WE DO MUCH MORE GOOD THAN HARM.
I DOUBT THAT.
WHAT ARE WE DOING HERE, PROFESSOR FAUSTINO? WHAT'S THIS ALL ABOUT?
CALM DOWN, STEFAN. IMPATIENCE ALWAYS WAS A FAILING OF YOURS.
SIT DOWN. YOU TOO, MASTER HILL. I'M GOING TO TELL YOU BOTH A STORY... AND THIS IS ONE I CAN PROMISE YOU WON'T HAVE HEARD BEFORE....
NOT SO LONG AGO THE WORLD WAS STILL TEARING ITSELF APART.
DECISIONS WERE STILL BEING MADE ON THE BASIS OF RELIGION OR HISTORY. THE PROBLEM WAS, COUNTRIES WERE NOT BEING RUN AS BUSINESSES.
"MYISHI CORP. HAS TAKEN ON THESE PROBLEMS.
"WE TOOK ALL THE COMPUTER MEMORY FOR A WHOLE CITY AND PUT IT IN ORBIT OVER THE CITY. CONSTANTLY UPDATING AND SELF-REPAIRING... AT LEAST UNTIL NOW."
"LATELY THE SATELLITE HAS BEEN MAKING MORE AND MORE ERRORS. PEOPLE HAVE BEEN HURT.
"WE'VE HAD REPAIR CREWS WORKING AROUND THE CLOCK.
"A FEW WEEKS AGO I FOUND OUT WHAT THE REAL PROBLEM IS.... "
The picture on the screen changes and next to me on the sofa, I hear Stefan gasp.
Ellen's technology can see through our fuzz plates.
"THIS IS WHY YOU AND YOUR LITTLE VIGILANTE HELPER ARE HERE, STEFAN. THIS IS WHAT'S ENDANGERING THE WHOLE CITY. IT'S YOU."

Cameras don't pick up the Parasites, so Stefan shrugs off the fight footage as kids messing around. But our host has a lot more....

STEFAN BASHKIR   MONA VASQUEZ   Z

COSMO HILL   LUCIEN "DITTO" BONN

"I'VE HAD MY ELECTRONIC EYE ON YOU AND YOUR GANG FOR A LONG TIME NOW, STEFAN. A SPECIAL SCOPE ON THE SATELLITE, DEDICATED TO YOUR NIGHTLY ACTIVITIES ON THE CITY'S ROOFTOPS. YOU SHOULD FEEL HONORED."

AND LAST NIGHT YOU DECIDED TO PULL US IN? WHY?

NO, LAST NIGHT WAS A HAPPY ACCIDENT. YOU GOT MIXED UP IN ANOTHER DEPARTMENT'S OPERATION.

I SAY "HAPPY" BECAUSE I'VE BEEN TRYING TO GET TO YOU FOR WEEKS NOW.

YOU SEE, WE URGENTLY NEED TO TALK ABOUT WHAT YOU'VE BEEN DOING WITH THE CITY'S INFESTATION PROBLEM.

Stefan gasps for the second time in as many minutes.

"I SEE THEM, STEFAN. UN-SPEC 4. THE LIFE-EATERS."

"THE FIRST THING I DID WHEN I ARRIVED HERE WAS DEVELOP A CAMERA LENS THAT COULD CAPTURE UN-SPEC 4 ON FILM."

"AT LEAST IT DID IF YOU WERE ALREADY ABLE TO PERCEIVE THE CREATURES. TO A NORMAL PERSON WE'RE SITTING HERE LOOKING AT AN EMPTY SCREEN RIGHT NOW."

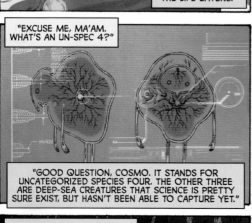

"EXCUSE ME, MA'AM. WHAT'S AN UN-SPEC 4?"

"GOOD QUESTION, COSMO. IT STANDS FOR UNCATEGORIZED SPECIES FOUR. THE OTHER THREE ARE DEEP-SEA CREATURES THAT SCIENCE IS PRETTY SURE EXIST, BUT HASN'T BEEN ABLE TO CAPTURE YET."

YEARS AGO, WHEN I FIRST JOINED THE POLICE FORCE, I WAS ON THE BEAT.

ONE NIGHT, BREAKING UP A DOMESTIC, I TOOK A KNIFE IN THE RIBS.

I NEARLY DIED: OUT OF THE BODY, INTO THE LIGHT, THE WHOLE THING. PARAMEDICS BROUGHT ME BACK.

"I SAW SOMETHING THAT NIGHT, SOMETHING I'VE BEEN ABLE TO SEE EVER SINCE."

YOU'RE A SPOTTER. LIKE ME!

"AT FIRST I THOUGHT I WAS GOING CRAZY, BUT THEN I HEARD ABOUT SOMEONE ELSE WHO'D HAD AN ACCIDENT AND STARTED BABBLING ON ABOUT BLUE CREATURES...YOU... STEFAN."

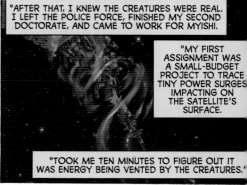

"AFTER THAT, I KNEW THE CREATURES WERE REAL. I LEFT THE POLICE FORCE, FINISHED MY SECOND DOCTORATE, AND CAME TO WORK FOR MYISHI.

"MY FIRST ASSIGNMENT WAS A SMALL-BUDGET PROJECT TO TRACE TINY POWER SURGES IMPACTING ON THE SATELLITE'S SURFACE.

"TOOK ME TEN MINUTES TO FIGURE OUT IT WAS ENERGY BEING VENTED BY THE CREATURES."

"OF COURSE, I COULDN'T SAY ANYTHING. IT WOULD HAVE ENDED MY CAREER. SO I KEPT QUIET."

"BUT THEN THE CHARGES STARTED TO INCREASE. SLOWLY AT FIRST, BUT THEN AT AN ALARMING RATE THAT DID REAL DAMAGE TO THE SATELLITE."

"WE WERE SOON LOSING LINKS TO THE SURFACE. PEOPLE WERE DYING."

"I PUT TOGETHER A TEAM TO TRY TO FIND OUT WHY THE PARASITES WERE GROWING IN NUMBER."

"I RAN TESTS ON MYISHI EMPLOYEES AND FOUND THREE OTHER SPOTTERS, ALL WITH NEAR-DEATH EXPERIENCES."

"WE LEARNED THAT THE CREATURES ARE MADE OF PURE ENERGY."

"WE PREFER THE TERM PARASITES."

"THAT'S GOOD, STEFAN. I'LL USE IT."

"AFTER FEEDING, THE PARASITE'S ABSORBED ENERGY RUNS THROUGH ITS ORGANS UNTIL IT'S DISCHARGED IN A SINGLE BURST.

"THOSE ENERGY DISCHARGES ARE WHAT'S DAMAGING THE SATELLITE."

"PARASITE POOP?"

"EXACTLY, COSMO. PARASITE POOP."

"THESE SHIMMERING SPHERES ARE WHAT'S LEFT AFTER YOU BLAST A PARASITE, RIGHT?

"WATCH...

"THIS ONE FLOATED UP TO A HEIGHT OF A KILOMETER."

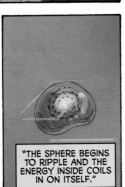

"THE SPHERE BEGINS TO RIPPLE AND THE ENERGY INSIDE COILS IN ON ITSELF."

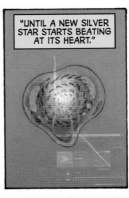

"UNTIL A NEW SILVER STAR STARTS BEATING AT ITS HEART."

"THEN THE EYES AND FINGERS APPEAR...."

"OH NO...NO...NO..."

"IT'S NOT YOUR FAULT, STEFAN. YOU COULDN'T HAVE KNOWN."

ALL THIS TIME. I'VE BEEN *HELPING* THEM. NOT DESTROYING THEM. HELPING THEM TO REPRODUCE.

EVERY PARASITE WE'VE BLASTED MUST HAVE MADE A HUNDRED MORE....

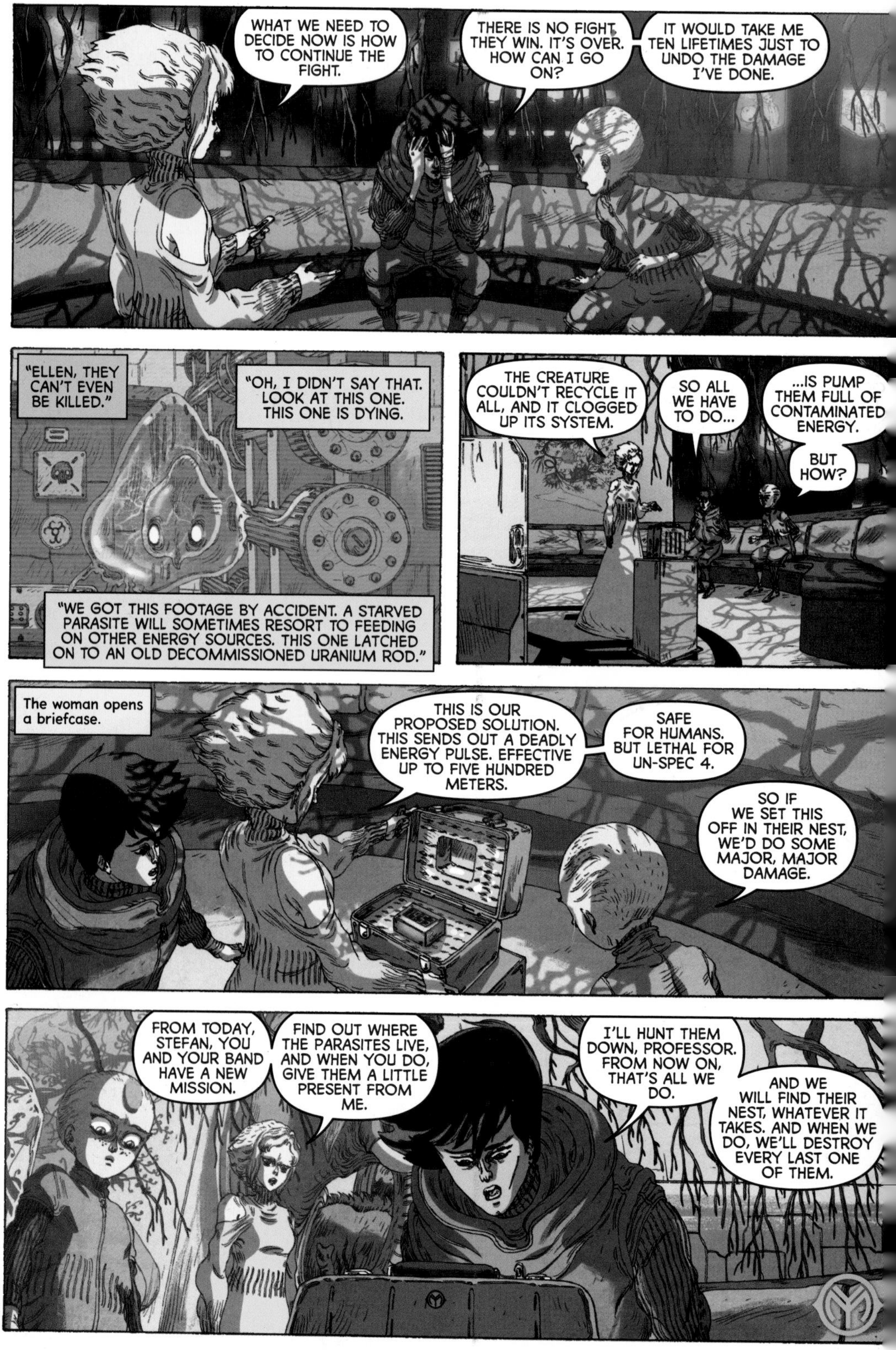
WHAT WE NEED TO DECIDE NOW IS HOW TO CONTINUE THE FIGHT.
THERE IS NO FIGHT. THEY WIN. IT'S OVER. HOW CAN I GO ON?
IT WOULD TAKE ME TEN LIFETIMES JUST TO UNDO THE DAMAGE I'VE DONE.
"ELLEN, THEY CAN'T EVEN BE KILLED."
"OH, I DIDN'T SAY THAT. LOOK AT THIS ONE. THIS ONE IS DYING.
"WE GOT THIS FOOTAGE BY ACCIDENT. A STARVED PARASITE WILL SOMETIMES RESORT TO FEEDING ON OTHER ENERGY SOURCES. THIS ONE LATCHED ON TO AN OLD DECOMMISSIONED URANIUM ROD."
THE CREATURE COULDN'T RECYCLE IT ALL, AND IT CLOGGED UP ITS SYSTEM.
SO ALL WE HAVE TO DO...
...IS PUMP THEM FULL OF CONTAMINATED ENERGY.
BUT HOW?
The woman opens a briefcase.
THIS IS OUR PROPOSED SOLUTION. THIS SENDS OUT A DEADLY ENERGY PULSE. EFFECTIVE UP TO FIVE HUNDRED METERS.
SAFE FOR HUMANS. BUT LETHAL FOR UN-SPEC 4.
SO IF WE SET THIS OFF IN THEIR NEST, WE'D DO SOME MAJOR, MAJOR DAMAGE.
FROM TODAY, STEFAN, YOU AND YOUR BAND HAVE A NEW MISSION.
FIND OUT WHERE THE PARASITES LIVE, AND WHEN YOU DO, GIVE THEM A LITTLE PRESENT FROM ME.
I'LL HUNT THEM DOWN, PROFESSOR. FROM NOW ON, THAT'S ALL WE DO.
AND WE WILL FIND THEIR NEST, WHATEVER IT TAKES. AND WHEN WE DO, WE'LL DESTROY EVERY LAST ONE OF THEM.

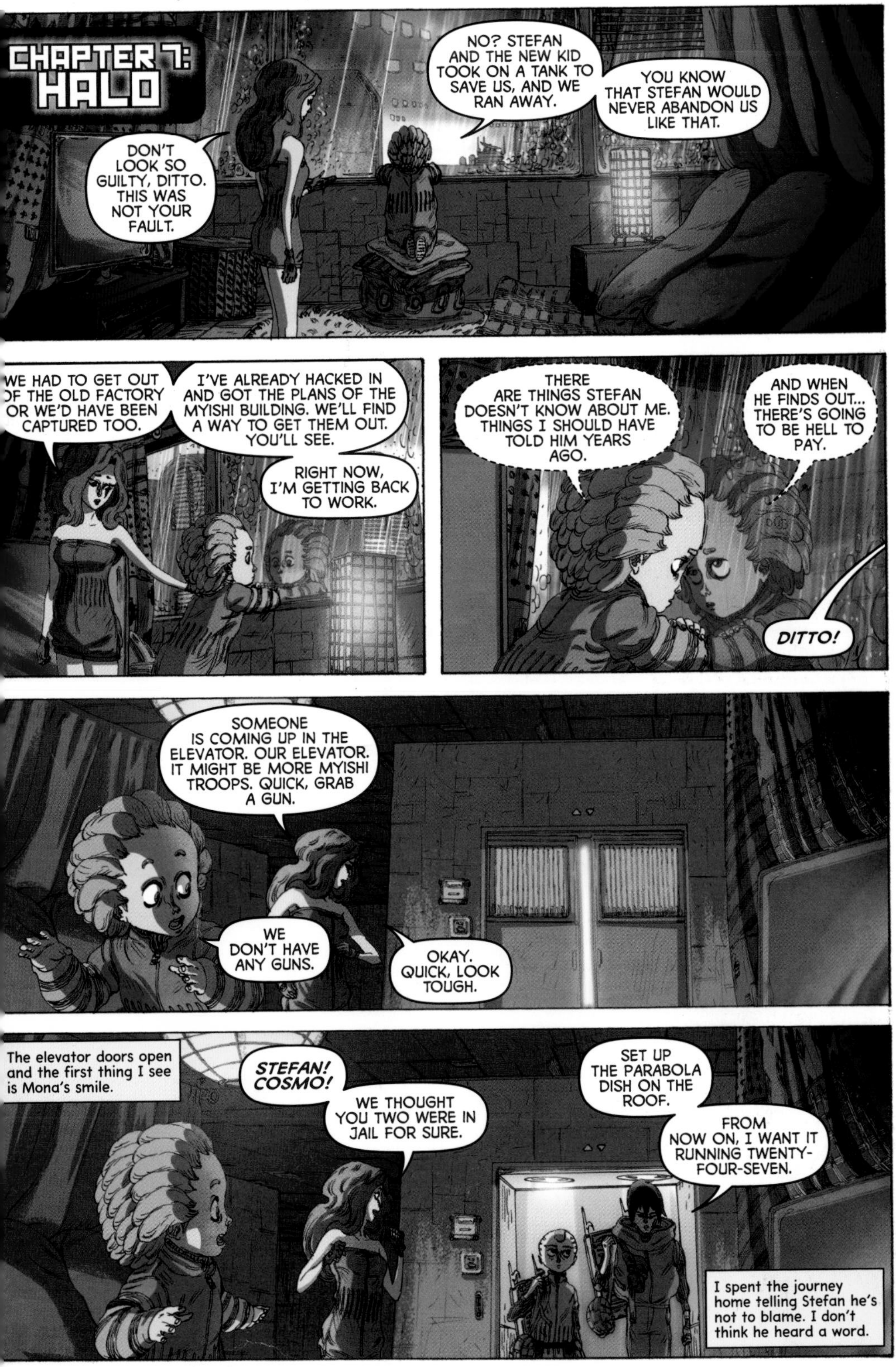
CHAPTER 7: HALO
DON'T LOOK SO GUILTY, DITTO. THIS WAS NOT YOUR FAULT.
NO? STEFAN AND THE NEW KID TOOK ON A TANK TO SAVE US, AND WE RAN AWAY.
YOU KNOW THAT STEFAN WOULD NEVER ABANDON US LIKE THAT.
WE HAD TO GET OUT OF THE OLD FACTORY OR WE'D HAVE BEEN CAPTURED TOO.
I'VE ALREADY HACKED IN AND GOT THE PLANS OF THE MYISHI BUILDING. WE'LL FIND A WAY TO GET THEM OUT. YOU'LL SEE.
RIGHT NOW, I'M GETTING BACK TO WORK.
THERE ARE THINGS STEFAN DOESN'T KNOW ABOUT ME. THINGS I SHOULD HAVE TOLD HIM YEARS AGO.
AND WHEN HE FINDS OUT... THERE'S GOING TO BE HELL TO PAY.
DITTO!
SOMEONE IS COMING UP IN THE ELEVATOR. OUR ELEVATOR. IT MIGHT BE MORE MYISHI TROOPS. QUICK, GRAB A GUN.
WE DON'T HAVE ANY GUNS.
OKAY. QUICK, LOOK TOUGH.
The elevator doors open and the first thing I see is Mona's smile.
STEFAN! COSMO!
WE THOUGHT YOU TWO WERE IN JAIL FOR SURE.
SET UP THE PARABOLA DISH ON THE ROOF.
FROM NOW ON, I WANT IT RUNNING TWENTY-FOUR-SEVEN.
I spent the journey home telling Stefan he's not to blame. I don't think he heard a word.

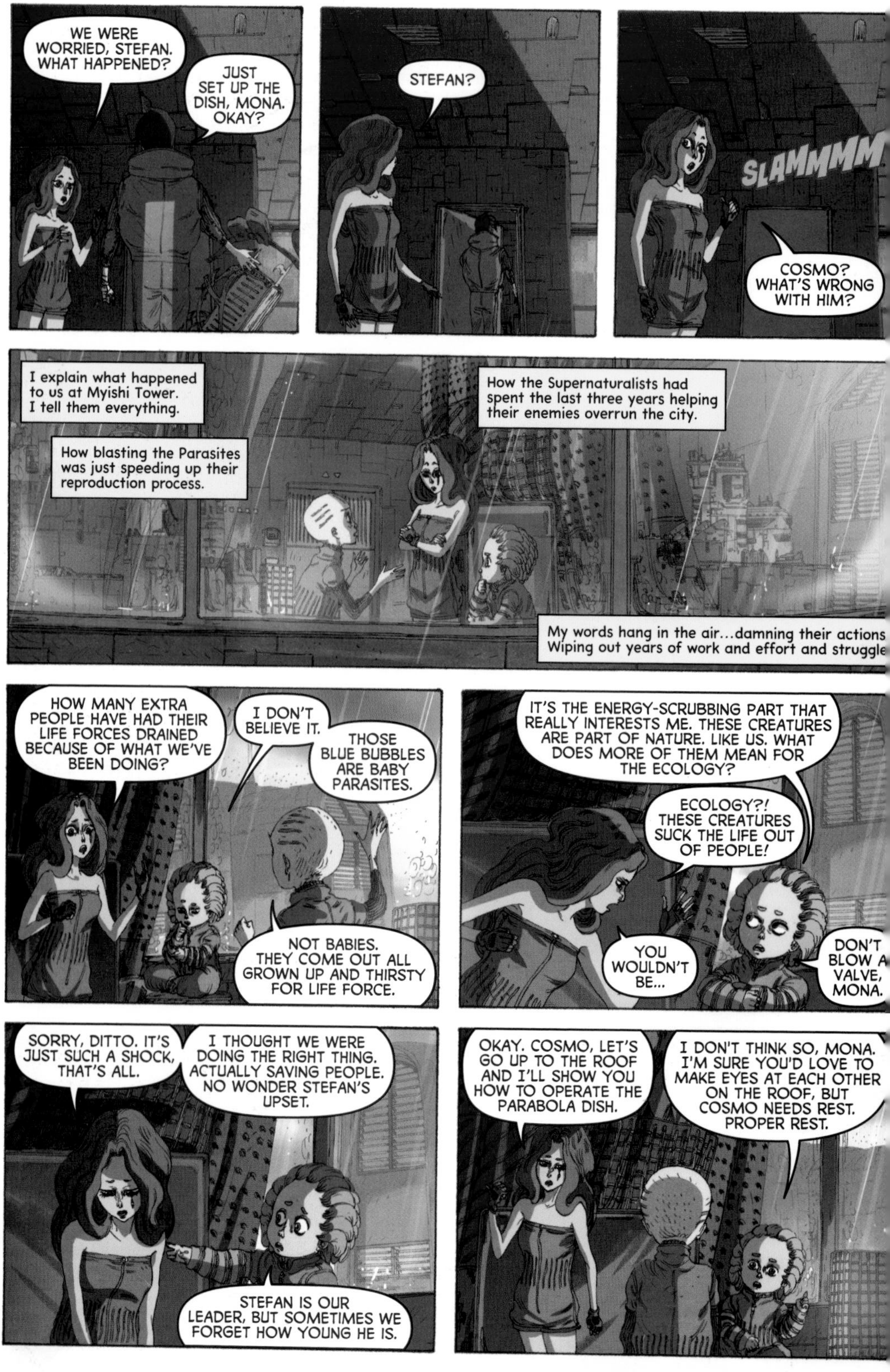
WE WERE WORRIED, STEFAN. WHAT HAPPENED?
JUST SET UP THE DISH, MONA. OKAY?
STEFAN?
SLAMMMM
COSMO? WHAT'S WRONG WITH HIM?
I explain what happened to us at Myishi Tower. I tell them everything.
How blasting the Parasites was just speeding up their reproduction process.
How the Supernaturalists had spent the last three years helping their enemies overrun the city.
My words hang in the air...damning their actions. Wiping out years of work and effort and struggle
HOW MANY EXTRA PEOPLE HAVE HAD THEIR LIFE FORCES DRAINED BECAUSE OF WHAT WE'VE BEEN DOING?
I DON'T BELIEVE IT.
THOSE BLUE BUBBLES ARE BABY PARASITES.
NOT BABIES. THEY COME OUT ALL GROWN UP AND THIRSTY FOR LIFE FORCE.
IT'S THE ENERGY-SCRUBBING PART THAT REALLY INTERESTS ME. THESE CREATURES ARE PART OF NATURE. LIKE US. WHAT DOES MORE OF THEM MEAN FOR THE ECOLOGY?
ECOLOGY?! THESE CREATURES SUCK THE LIFE OUT OF PEOPLE!
YOU WOULDN'T BE...
DON'T BLOW A VALVE, MONA.
SORRY, DITTO. IT'S JUST SUCH A SHOCK, THAT'S ALL.
I THOUGHT WE WERE DOING THE RIGHT THING. ACTUALLY SAVING PEOPLE. NO WONDER STEFAN'S UPSET.
STEFAN IS OUR LEADER, BUT SOMETIMES WE FORGET HOW YOUNG HE IS.
OKAY. COSMO, LET'S GO UP TO THE ROOF AND I'LL SHOW YOU HOW TO OPERATE THE PARABOLA DISH.
I DON'T THINK SO, MONA. I'M SURE YOU'D LOVE TO MAKE EYES AT EACH OTHER ON THE ROOF, BUT COSMO NEEDS REST. PROPER REST.

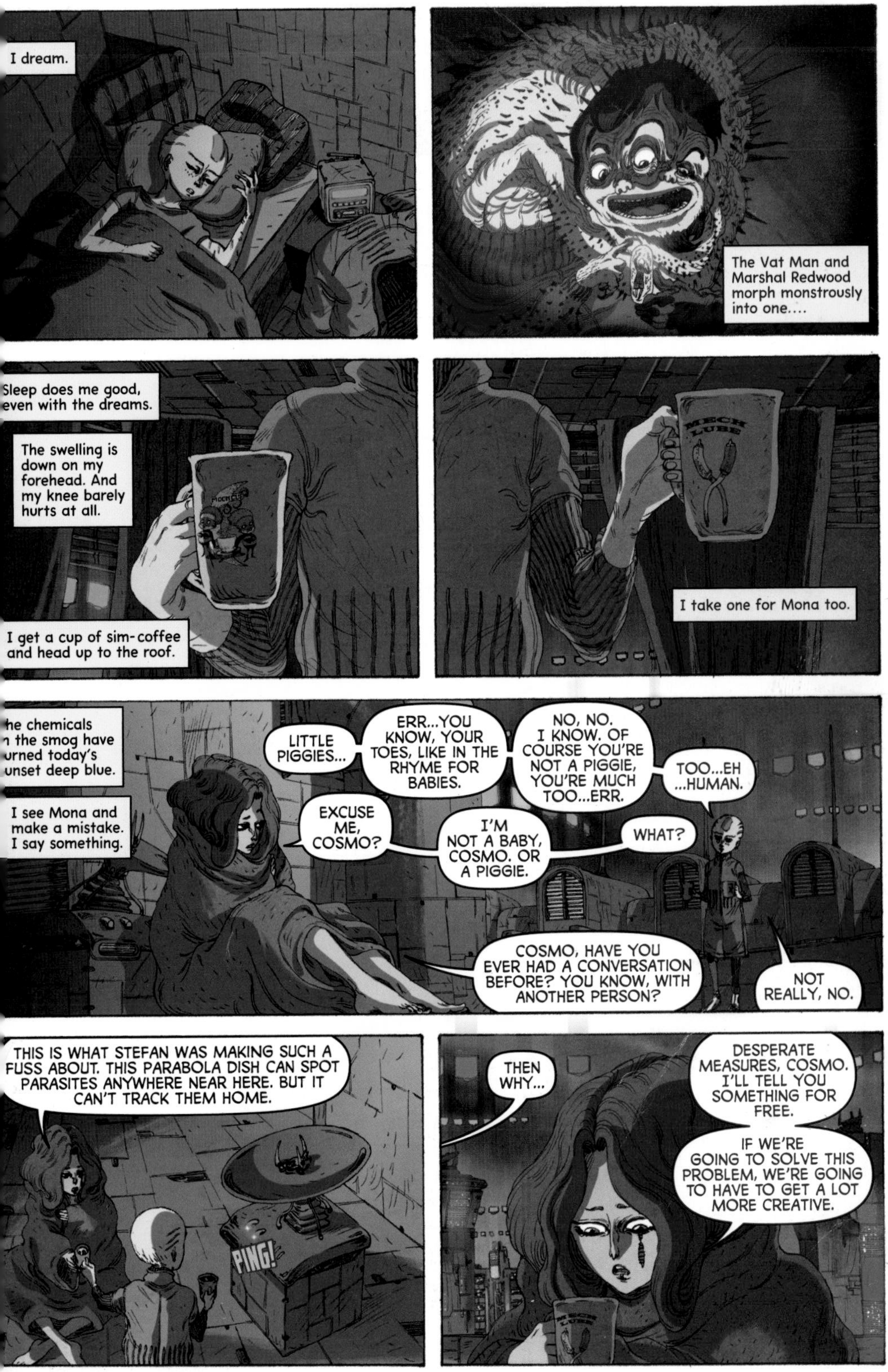

I dream.
The Vat Man and Marshal Redwood morph monstrously into one....
Sleep does me good, even with the dreams.
The swelling is down on my forehead. And my knee barely hurts at all.
I get a cup of sim-coffee and head up to the roof.
MECH LUBE
I take one for Mona too.
he chemicals n the smog have urned today's unset deep blue.
I see Mona and make a mistake. I say something.
LITTLE PIGGIES...
EXCUSE ME, COSMO?
ERR...YOU KNOW, YOUR TOES, LIKE IN THE RHYME FOR BABIES.
I'M NOT A BABY, COSMO. OR A PIGGIE.
NO, NO. I KNOW. OF COURSE YOU'RE NOT A PIGGIE, YOU'RE MUCH TOO...ERR.
WHAT?
TOO...EH ...HUMAN.
COSMO, HAVE YOU EVER HAD A CONVERSATION BEFORE? YOU KNOW, WITH ANOTHER PERSON?
NOT REALLY, NO.
THIS IS WHAT STEFAN WAS MAKING SUCH A FUSS ABOUT. THIS PARABOLA DISH CAN SPOT PARASITES ANYWHERE NEAR HERE. BUT IT CAN'T TRACK THEM HOME.
PING!
THEN WHY...
DESPERATE MEASURES, COSMO. I'LL TELL YOU SOMETHING FOR FREE.
IF WE'RE GOING TO SOLVE THIS PROBLEM, WE'RE GOING TO HAVE TO GET A LOT MORE CREATIVE.

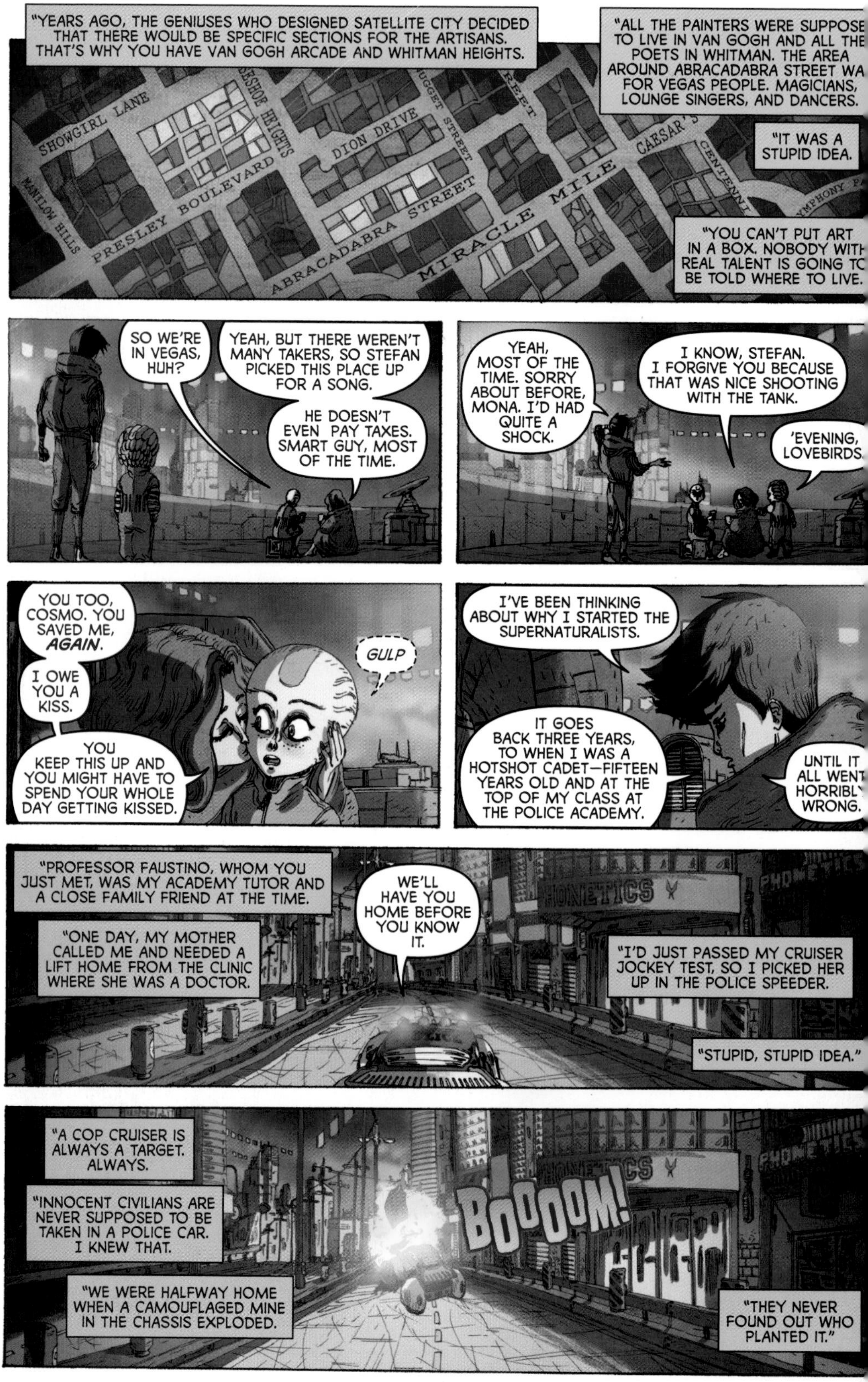

"YEARS AGO, THE GENIUSES WHO DESIGNED SATELLITE CITY DECIDED THAT THERE WOULD BE SPECIFIC SECTIONS FOR THE ARTISANS. THAT'S WHY YOU HAVE VAN GOGH ARCADE AND WHITMAN HEIGHTS.
"ALL THE PAINTERS WERE SUPPOSE TO LIVE IN VAN GOGH AND ALL THE POETS IN WHITMAN. THE AREA AROUND ABRACADABRA STREET WA FOR VEGAS PEOPLE. MAGICIANS, LOUNGE SINGERS, AND DANCERS.
SHOWGIRL LANE
MANILOW HILLS
PRESLEY BOULEVARD
DION DRIVE
ABRACADABRA STREET
MIRACLE MILE
CAESAR'S
"IT WAS A STUPID IDEA.
"YOU CAN'T PUT ART IN A BOX. NOBODY WITH REAL TALENT IS GOING TO BE TOLD WHERE TO LIVE.
SO WE'RE IN VEGAS, HUH?
YEAH, BUT THERE WEREN'T MANY TAKERS, SO STEFAN PICKED THIS PLACE UP FOR A SONG.
HE DOESN'T EVEN PAY TAXES. SMART GUY, MOST OF THE TIME.
YEAH, MOST OF THE TIME. SORRY ABOUT BEFORE, MONA. I'D HAD QUITE A SHOCK.
I KNOW, STEFAN. I FORGIVE YOU BECAUSE THAT WAS NICE SHOOTING WITH THE TANK.
'EVENING, LOVEBIRDS.
YOU TOO, COSMO. YOU SAVED ME, AGAIN.
I OWE YOU A KISS.
GULP
YOU KEEP THIS UP AND YOU MIGHT HAVE TO SPEND YOUR WHOLE DAY GETTING KISSED.
I'VE BEEN THINKING ABOUT WHY I STARTED THE SUPERNATURALISTS.
IT GOES BACK THREE YEARS, TO WHEN I WAS A HOTSHOT CADET—FIFTEEN YEARS OLD AND AT THE TOP OF MY CLASS AT THE POLICE ACADEMY.
UNTIL IT ALL WENT HORRIBLY WRONG.
"PROFESSOR FAUSTINO, WHOM YOU JUST MET, WAS MY ACADEMY TUTOR AND A CLOSE FAMILY FRIEND AT THE TIME.
"ONE DAY, MY MOTHER CALLED ME AND NEEDED A LIFT HOME FROM THE CLINIC WHERE SHE WAS A DOCTOR.
WE'LL HAVE YOU HOME BEFORE YOU KNOW IT.
"I'D JUST PASSED MY CRUISER JOCKEY TEST, SO I PICKED HER UP IN THE POLICE SPEEDER.
"STUPID, STUPID IDEA."
"A COP CRUISER IS ALWAYS A TARGET. ALWAYS.
"INNOCENT CIVILIANS ARE NEVER SUPPOSED TO BE TAKEN IN A POLICE CAR. I KNEW THAT.
"WE WERE HALFWAY HOME WHEN A CAMOUFLAGED MINE IN THE CHASSIS EXPLODED.
BOOOOM!
"THEY NEVER FOUND OUT WHO PLANTED IT."

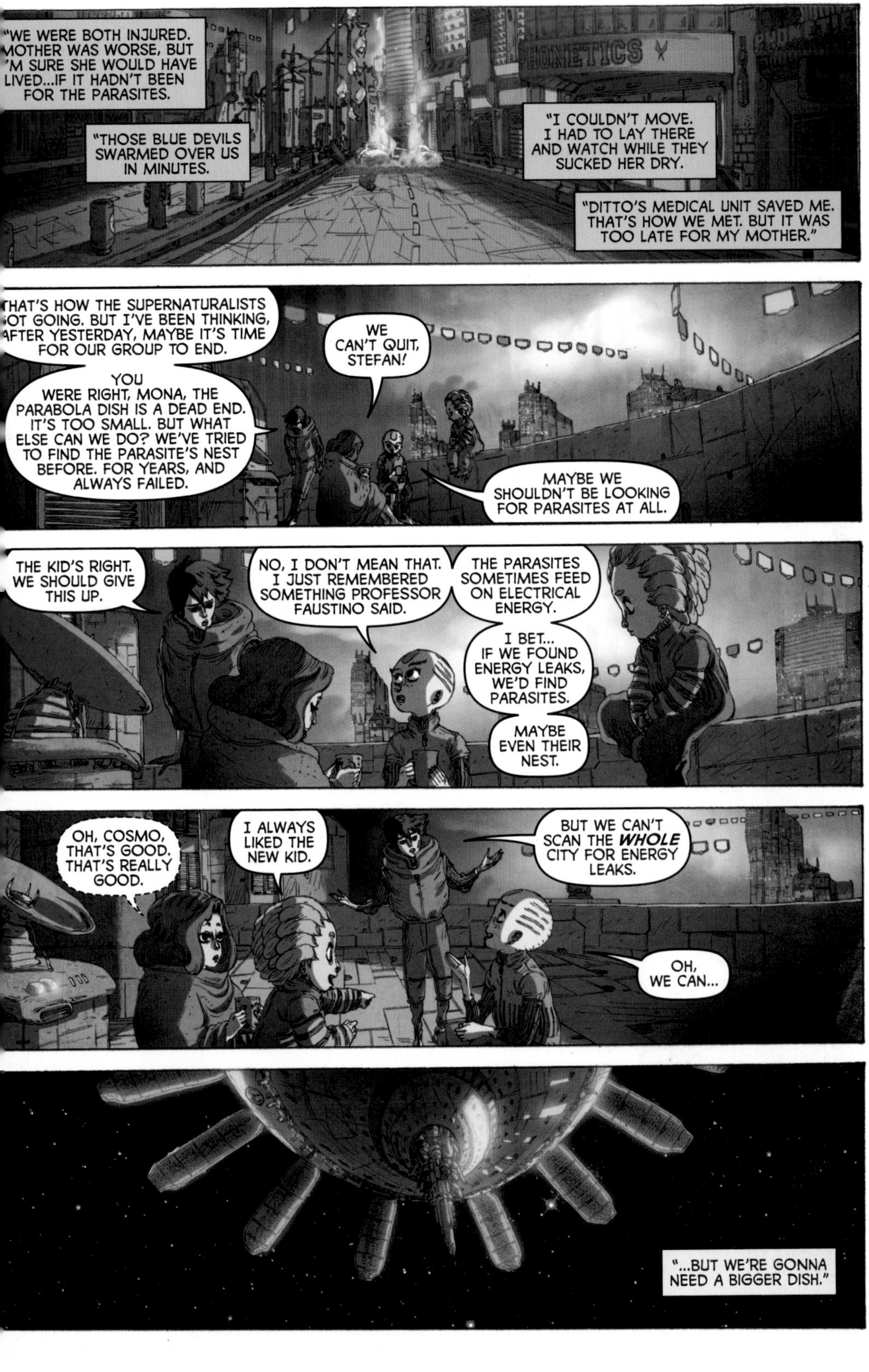
"WE WERE BOTH INJURED. MOTHER WAS WORSE, BUT I'M SURE SHE WOULD HAVE LIVED...IF IT HADN'T BEEN FOR THE PARASITES.
"THOSE BLUE DEVILS SWARMED OVER US IN MINUTES.
PHONETICS
"I COULDN'T MOVE. I HAD TO LAY THERE AND WATCH WHILE THEY SUCKED HER DRY.
"DITTO'S MEDICAL UNIT SAVED ME. THAT'S HOW WE MET. BUT IT WAS TOO LATE FOR MY MOTHER."
THAT'S HOW THE SUPERNATURALISTS GOT GOING. BUT I'VE BEEN THINKING, AFTER YESTERDAY, MAYBE IT'S TIME FOR OUR GROUP TO END.
WE CAN'T QUIT, STEFAN!
YOU WERE RIGHT, MONA, THE PARABOLA DISH IS A DEAD END. IT'S TOO SMALL. BUT WHAT ELSE CAN WE DO? WE'VE TRIED TO FIND THE PARASITE'S NEST BEFORE. FOR YEARS, AND ALWAYS FAILED.
MAYBE WE SHOULDN'T BE LOOKING FOR PARASITES AT ALL.
THE KID'S RIGHT. WE SHOULD GIVE THIS UP.
NO, I DON'T MEAN THAT. I JUST REMEMBERED SOMETHING PROFESSOR FAUSTINO SAID.
THE PARASITES SOMETIMES FEED ON ELECTRICAL ENERGY.
I BET... IF WE FOUND ENERGY LEAKS, WE'D FIND PARASITES.
MAYBE EVEN THEIR NEST.
OH, COSMO, THAT'S GOOD. THAT'S REALLY GOOD.
I ALWAYS LIKED THE NEW KID.
BUT WE CAN'T SCAN THE *WHOLE* CITY FOR ENERGY LEAKS.
OH, WE CAN...
"...BUT WE'RE GONNA NEED A BIGGER DISH."

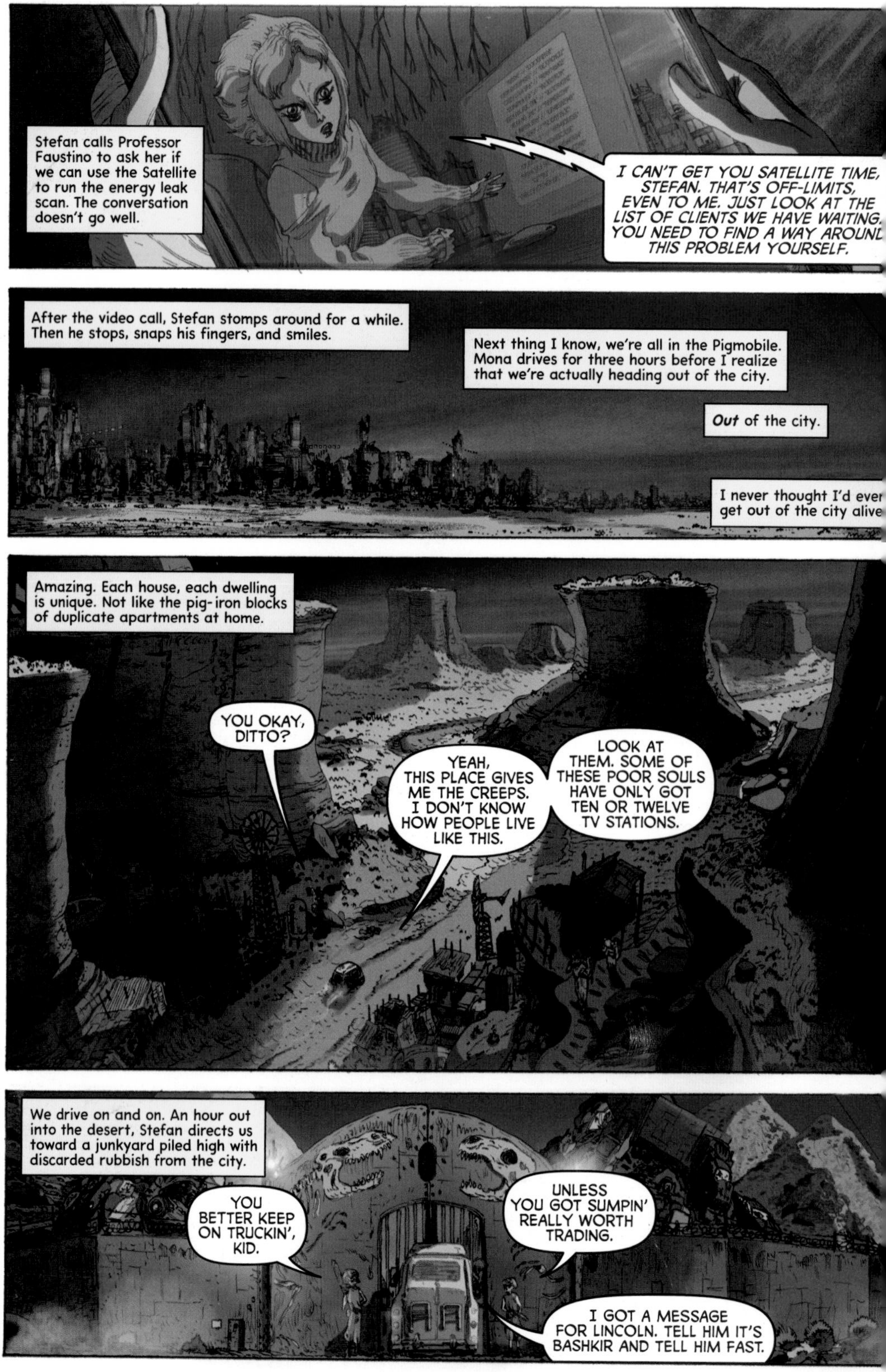

Stefan calls Professor Faustino to ask her if we can use the Satellite to run the energy leak scan. The conversation doesn't go well.
I CAN'T GET YOU SATELLITE TIME, STEFAN. THAT'S OFF-LIMITS, EVEN TO ME. JUST LOOK AT THE LIST OF CLIENTS WE HAVE WAITING. YOU NEED TO FIND A WAY AROUND THIS PROBLEM YOURSELF.
After the video call, Stefan stomps around for a while. Then he stops, snaps his fingers, and smiles.
Next thing I know, we're all in the Pigmobile. Mona drives for three hours before I realize that we're actually heading out of the city.
Out of the city.
I never thought I'd ever get out of the city alive
Amazing. Each house, each dwelling is unique. Not like the pig-iron blocks of duplicate apartments at home.
YOU OKAY, DITTO?
YEAH, THIS PLACE GIVES ME THE CREEPS. I DON'T KNOW HOW PEOPLE LIVE LIKE THIS.
LOOK AT THEM. SOME OF THESE POOR SOULS HAVE ONLY GOT TEN OR TWELVE TV STATIONS.
We drive on and on. An hour out into the desert, Stefan directs us toward a junkyard piled high with discarded rubbish from the city.
YOU BETTER KEEP ON TRUCKIN', KID.
UNLESS YOU GOT SUMPIN' REALLY WORTH TRADING.
I GOT A MESSAGE FOR LINCOLN. TELL HIM IT'S BASHKIR AND TELL HIM FAST.

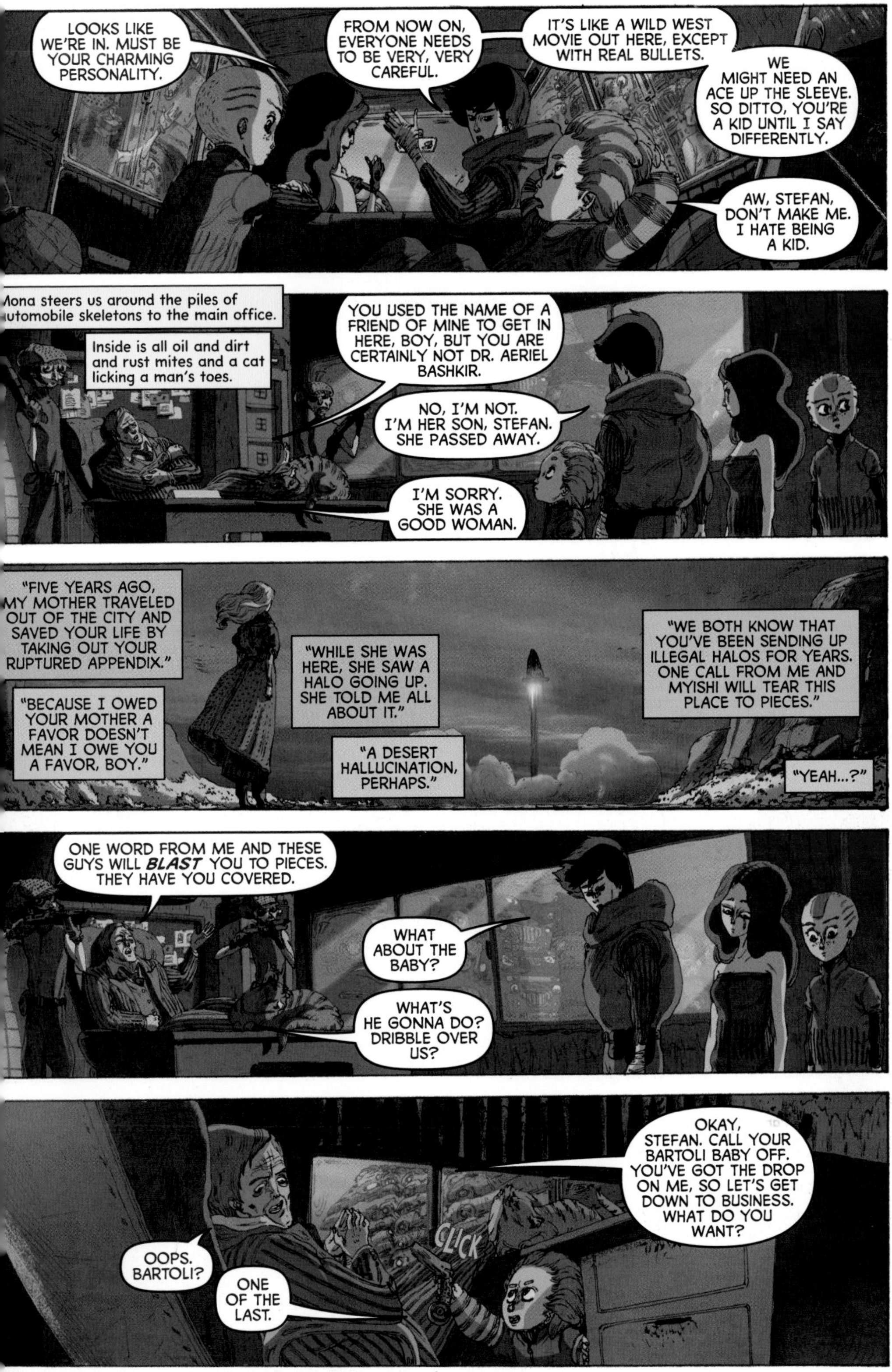
LOOKS LIKE WE'RE IN. MUST BE YOUR CHARMING PERSONALITY.
FROM NOW ON, EVERYONE NEEDS TO BE VERY, VERY CAREFUL.
IT'S LIKE A WILD WEST MOVIE OUT HERE, EXCEPT WITH REAL BULLETS.
WE MIGHT NEED AN ACE UP THE SLEEVE. SO DITTO, YOU'RE A KID UNTIL I SAY DIFFERENTLY.
AW, STEFAN, DON'T MAKE ME. I HATE BEING A KID.
Mona steers us around the piles of automobile skeletons to the main office.
Inside is all oil and dirt and rust mites and a cat licking a man's toes.
YOU USED THE NAME OF A FRIEND OF MINE TO GET IN HERE, BOY, BUT YOU ARE CERTAINLY NOT DR. AERIEL BASHKIR.
NO, I'M NOT. I'M HER SON, STEFAN. SHE PASSED AWAY.
I'M SORRY. SHE WAS A GOOD WOMAN.
"FIVE YEARS AGO, MY MOTHER TRAVELED OUT OF THE CITY AND SAVED YOUR LIFE BY TAKING OUT YOUR RUPTURED APPENDIX."
"BECAUSE I OWED YOUR MOTHER A FAVOR DOESN'T MEAN I OWE YOU A FAVOR, BOY."
"WHILE SHE WAS HERE, SHE SAW A HALO GOING UP. SHE TOLD ME ALL ABOUT IT."
"A DESERT HALLUCINATION, PERHAPS."
"WE BOTH KNOW THAT YOU'VE BEEN SENDING UP ILLEGAL HALOS FOR YEARS. ONE CALL FROM ME AND MYISHI WILL TEAR THIS PLACE TO PIECES."
"YEAH...?"
ONE WORD FROM ME AND THESE GUYS WILL *BLAST* YOU TO PIECES. THEY HAVE YOU COVERED.
WHAT ABOUT THE BABY?
WHAT'S HE GONNA DO? DRIBBLE OVER US?
OKAY, STEFAN. CALL YOUR BARTOLI BABY OFF. YOU'VE GOT THE DROP ON ME, SO LET'S GET DOWN TO BUSINESS. WHAT DO YOU WANT?
CLICK
OOPS. BARTOLI?
ONE OF THE LAST.

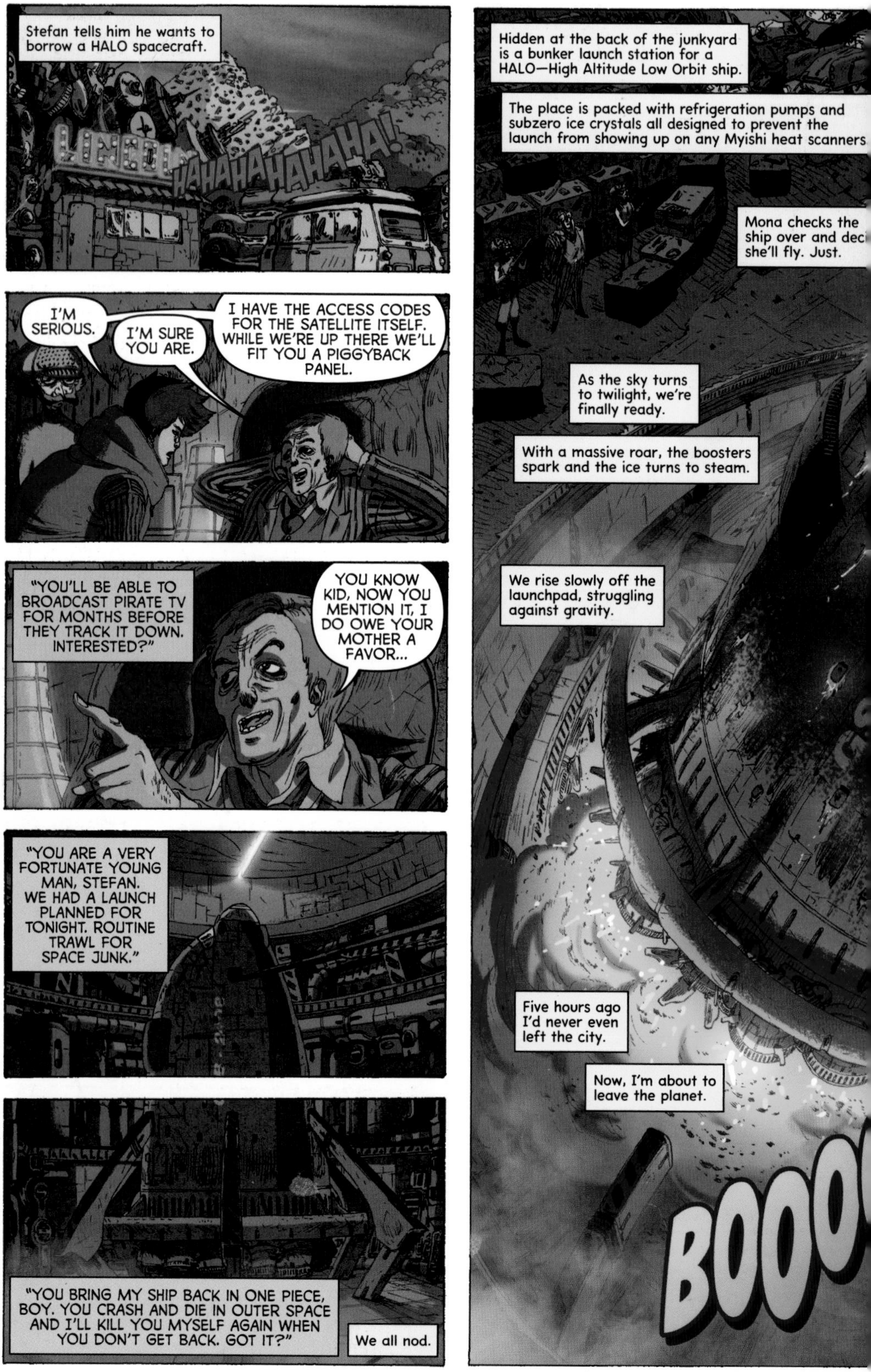
Stefan tells him he wants to borrow a HALO spacecraft.
HAHAHAHAHAHA!
I'M SERIOUS.
I'M SURE YOU ARE.
I HAVE THE ACCESS CODES FOR THE SATELLITE ITSELF. WHILE WE'RE UP THERE WE'LL FIT YOU A PIGGYBACK PANEL.
"YOU'LL BE ABLE TO BROADCAST PIRATE TV FOR MONTHS BEFORE THEY TRACK IT DOWN. INTERESTED?"
YOU KNOW KID, NOW YOU MENTION IT, I DO OWE YOUR MOTHER A FAVOR...
"YOU ARE A VERY FORTUNATE YOUNG MAN, STEFAN. WE HAD A LAUNCH PLANNED FOR TONIGHT. ROUTINE TRAWL FOR SPACE JUNK."
"YOU BRING MY SHIP BACK IN ONE PIECE, BOY. YOU CRASH AND DIE IN OUTER SPACE AND I'LL KILL YOU MYSELF AGAIN WHEN YOU DON'T GET BACK. GOT IT?"
We all nod.
Hidden at the back of the junkyard is a bunker launch station for a HALO—High Altitude Low Orbit ship.
The place is packed with refrigeration pumps and subzero ice crystals all designed to prevent the launch from showing up on any Myishi heat scanners
Mona checks the ship over and dec she'll fly. Just.
As the sky turns to twilight, we're finally ready.
With a massive roar, the boosters spark and the ice turns to steam.
We rise slowly off the launchpad, struggling against gravity.
Five hours ago I'd never even left the city.
Now, I'm about to leave the planet.
BOOO

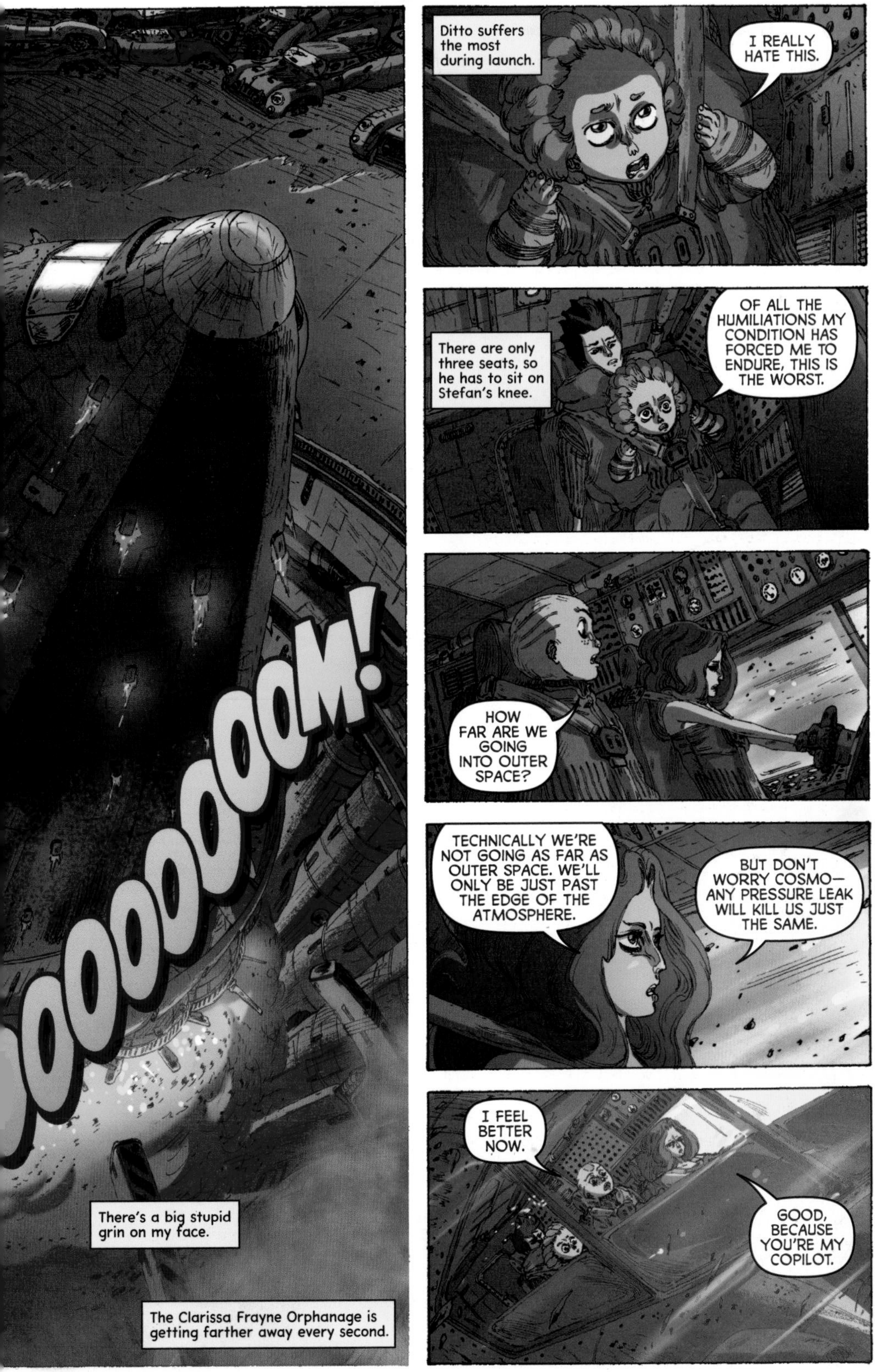
OOOOOOOOOM!
There's a big stupid grin on my face.
The Clarissa Frayne Orphanage is getting farther away every second.
Ditto suffers the most during launch.
I REALLY HATE THIS.
There are only three seats, so he has to sit on Stefan's knee.
OF ALL THE HUMILIATIONS MY CONDITION HAS FORCED ME TO ENDURE, THIS IS THE WORST.
HOW FAR ARE WE GOING INTO OUTER SPACE?
TECHNICALLY WE'RE NOT GOING AS FAR AS OUTER SPACE. WE'LL ONLY BE JUST PAST THE EDGE OF THE ATMOSPHERE.
BUT DON'T WORRY COSMO— ANY PRESSURE LEAK WILL KILL US JUST THE SAME.
I FEEL BETTER NOW.
GOOD, BECAUSE YOU'RE MY COPILOT.

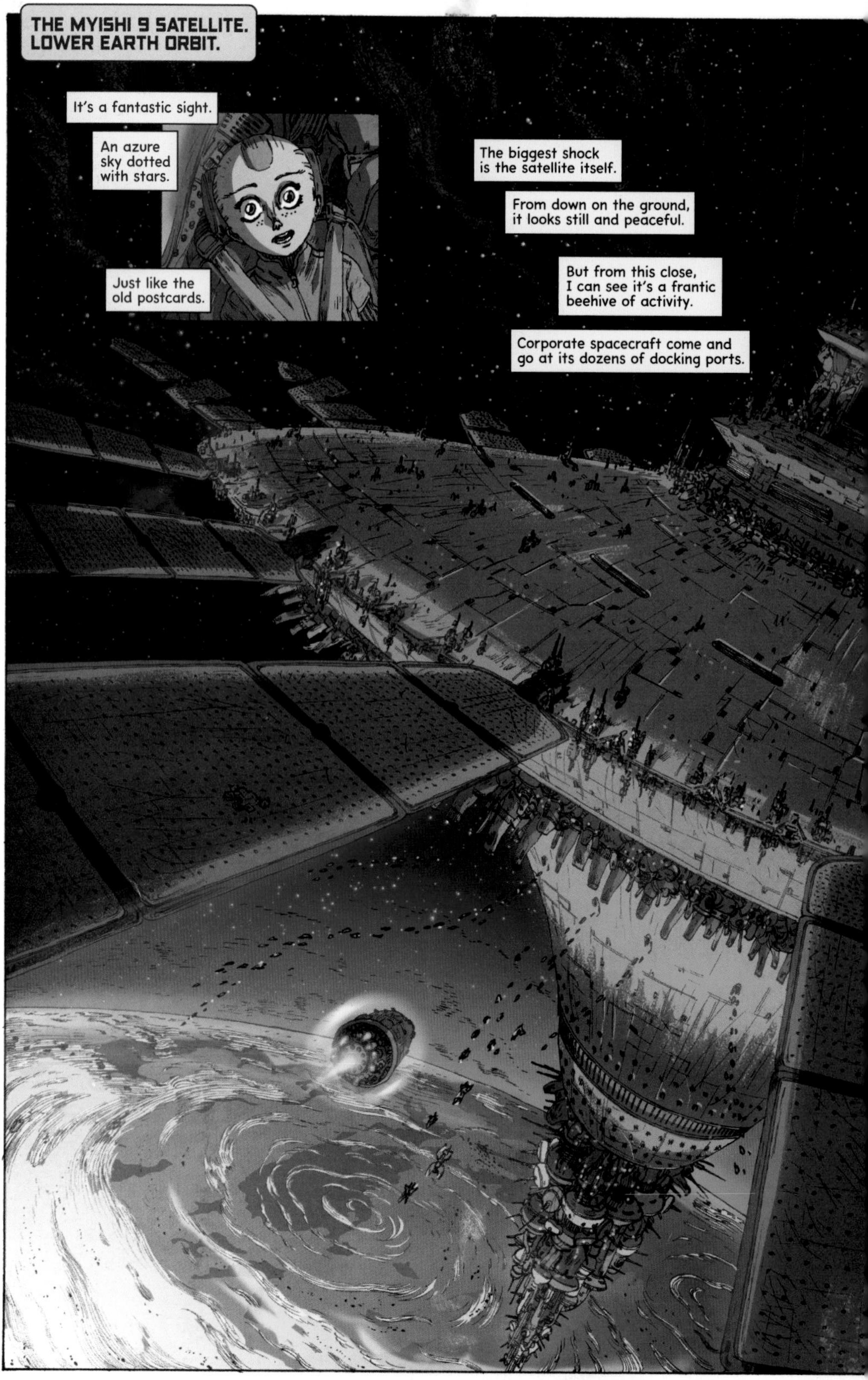
THE MYISHI 9 SATELLITE. LOWER EARTH ORBIT.
It's a fantastic sight.
An azure sky dotted with stars.
Just like the old postcards.
The biggest shock is the satellite itself.
From down on the ground, it looks still and peaceful.
But from this close, I can see it's a frantic beehive of activity.
Corporate spacecraft come and go at its dozens of docking ports.

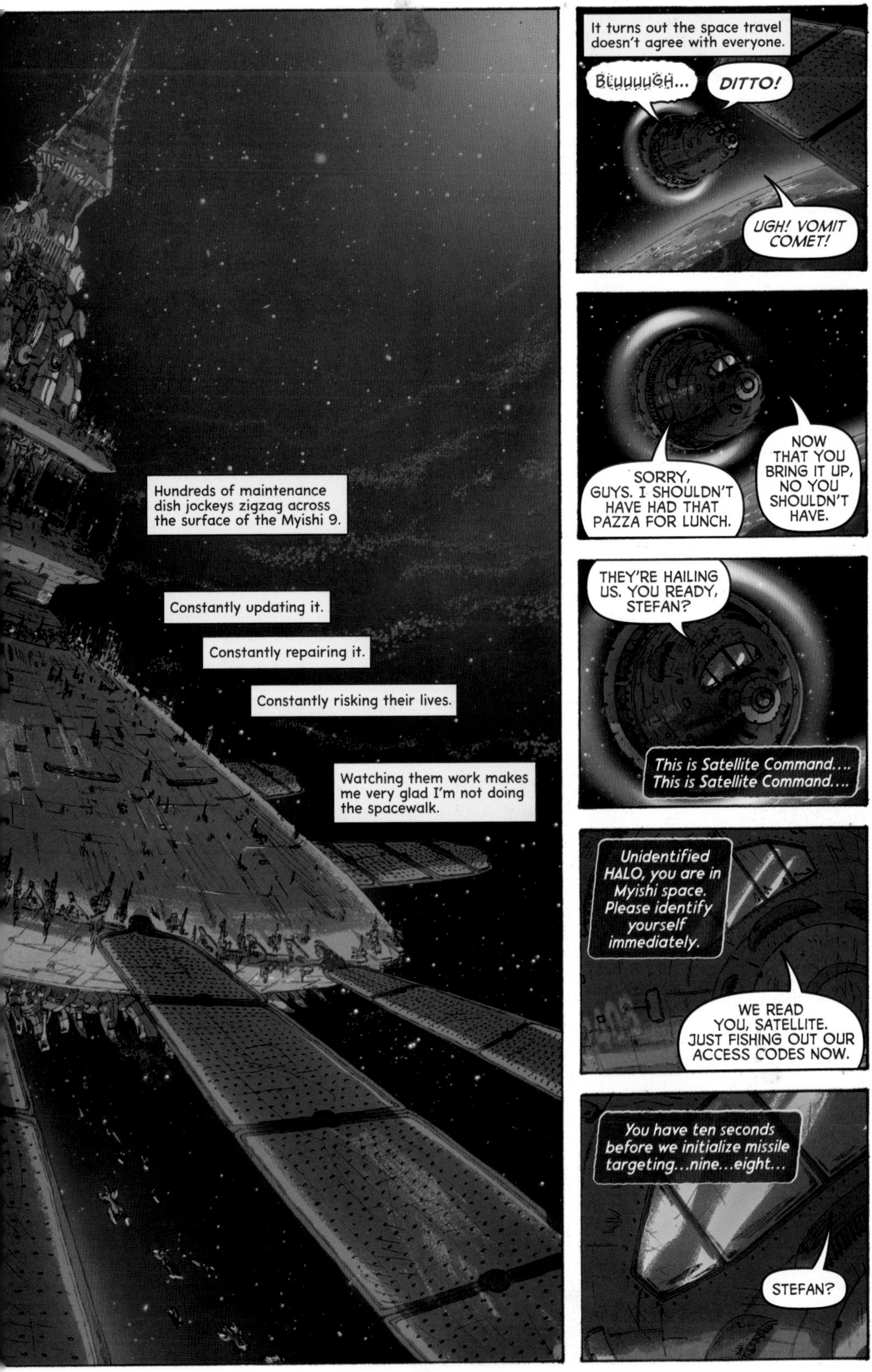
Hundreds of maintenance dish jockeys zigzag across the surface of the Myishi 9.
Constantly updating it.
Constantly repairing it.
Constantly risking their lives.
Watching them work makes me very glad I'm not doing the spacewalk.
It turns out the space travel doesn't agree with everyone.
BLUUUUGH...
DITTO!
UGH! VOMIT COMET!
SORRY, GUYS. I SHOULDN'T HAVE HAD THAT PAZZA FOR LUNCH.
NOW THAT YOU BRING IT UP, NO YOU SHOULDN'T HAVE.
THEY'RE HAILING US. YOU READY, STEFAN?
This is Satellite Command.... This is Satellite Command....
Unidentified HALO, you are in Myishi space. Please identify yourself immediately.
WE READ YOU, SATELLITE. JUST FISHING OUT OUR ACCESS CODES NOW.
You have ten seconds before we initialize missile targeting...nine...eight...
STEFAN?

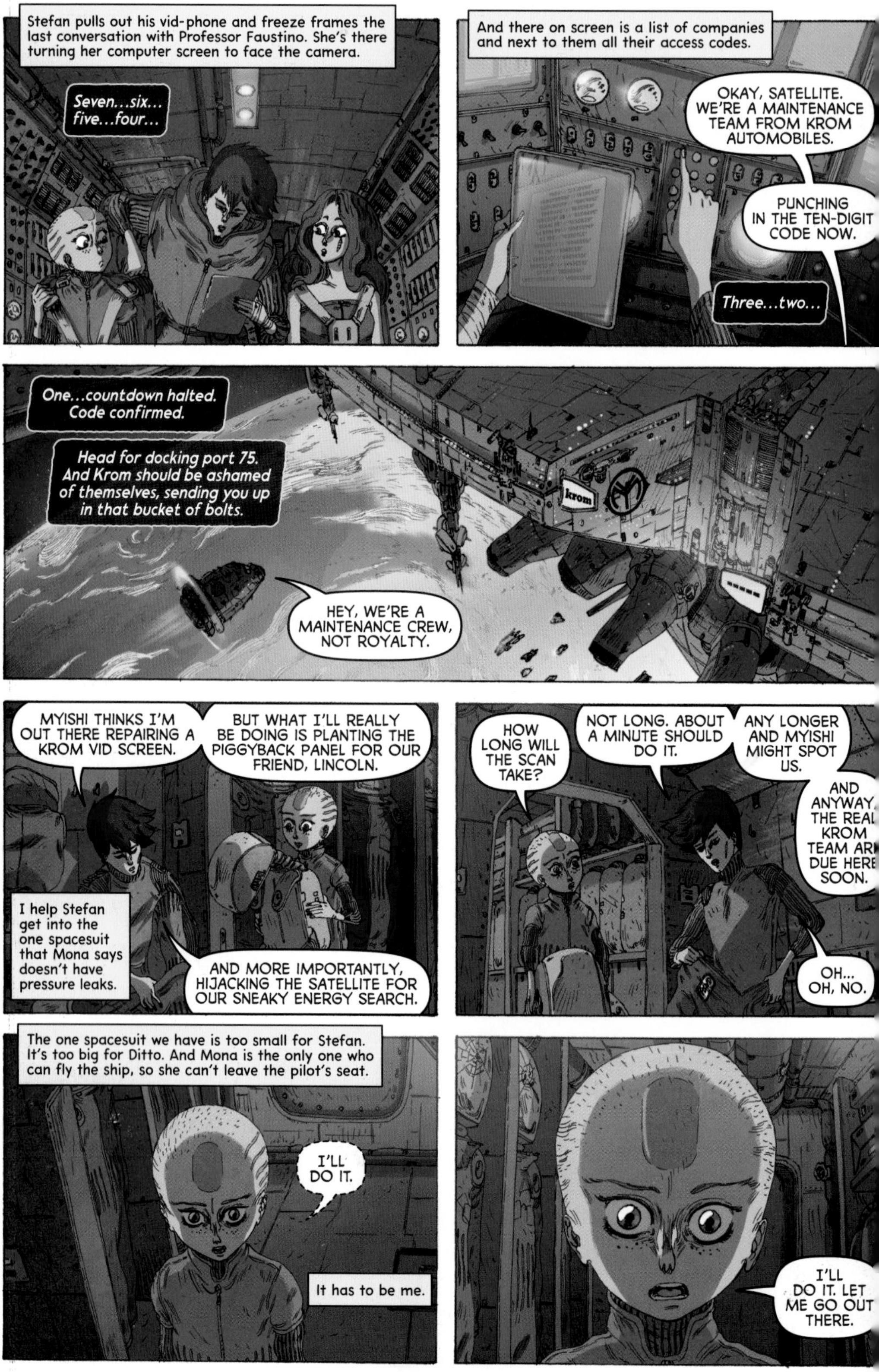
Stefan pulls out his vid-phone and freeze frames the last conversation with Professor Faustino. She's there turning her computer screen to face the camera.
Seven...six... five...four...
And there on screen is a list of companies and next to them all their access codes.
OKAY, SATELLITE. WE'RE A MAINTENANCE TEAM FROM KROM AUTOMOBILES.
PUNCHING IN THE TEN-DIGIT CODE NOW.
Three...two...
One...countdown halted. Code confirmed.
Head for docking port 75. And Krom should be ashamed of themselves, sending you up in that bucket of bolts.
krom
HEY, WE'RE A MAINTENANCE CREW, NOT ROYALTY.
MYISHI THINKS I'M OUT THERE REPAIRING A KROM VID SCREEN.
BUT WHAT I'LL REALLY BE DOING IS PLANTING THE PIGGYBACK PANEL FOR OUR FRIEND, LINCOLN.
I help Stefan get into the one spacesuit that Mona says doesn't have pressure leaks.
AND MORE IMPORTANTLY, HIJACKING THE SATELLITE FOR OUR SNEAKY ENERGY SEARCH.
HOW LONG WILL THE SCAN TAKE?
NOT LONG. ABOUT A MINUTE SHOULD DO IT.
ANY LONGER AND MYISHI MIGHT SPOT US.
AND ANYWAY, THE REAL KROM TEAM AR DUE HERE SOON.
OH... OH, NO.
The one spacesuit we have is too small for Stefan. It's too big for Ditto. And Mona is the only one who can fly the ship, so she can't leave the pilot's seat.
I'LL DO IT.
It has to be me.
I'LL DO IT. LET ME GO OUT THERE.

There's a lot of arguing about how dangerous it is. But everyone knows this is our only chance to get the scan.

I look down and I can see the whole world. There's no radio in the spacesuit. So I am very much on my own.

All I have to do is edge along the walkway and climb up the aerial rigging.

Then I plug in Lincoln's pirate plate and the data lead from the ship.

I wait sixty seconds while Stefan runs the energy scan, then I turn around and go back to the ship.

And the whole way I have a safety cord connecting me to the ship.

What could possibly go wrong?

My shoes are not magnetic, so I have to pull myself along the walkway inch by inch.

Halfway along, I think I see something blue flash past. For a second I think it's a Parasite. But of course it's not. It's my mind playing tricks.

Keep moving, Cosmo.

MONA? YOU OKAY

I'M A GREASE MONKEY FROM BOOSHKA.

AND LOOK AT ME, I'M FLYING A SPACESHIP AROUND THE EARTH SO THAT WE CAN SAVE THE WHOLE CITY.

IF COSMO MAKES IT BACK ALIVE, I THINK TODAY WILL BE THE BEST DAY OF MY LIFE. *IF....*

I'm starting the climb up the aerial rigging and I run out of bungee cord.

It's three yards short.

I can see where I need to be, but I can't get there.

There's no other way.

I have to untie the bungee cord.

Just for one minute. Just for sixty seconds.

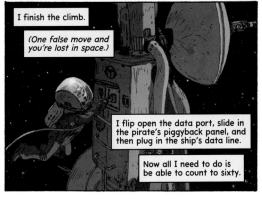

I finish the climb.

(One false move and you're lost in space.)

I flip open the data port, slide in the pirate's piggyback panel, and then plug in the ship's data line.

Now all I need to do is be able to count to sixty.

I CAN'T BELIEVE HE ACTUALLY UNTIED HIMSELF. *ESTÚPIDO!* I HOPE HE DOESN'T THINK THIS WILL IMPRESS ME, BECAUSE IT WON'T. IS IT RUNNING?

IT'S RUNNING. NOW ALL WE NEED ARE SIXTY SECONDS.

THERE GOES ANOTHER SPOTTER. WE'RE GOING TO HAVE TO TAKE OUT AN ADVERTISEMENT ON TV. WANTED: CRAZY KID WITH A DEATH WISH. ROBOTIX PLATES SUPPLIED.

ALL HE HAS TO DO IS HOLD ON FOR SIXTY SECONDS.

THE WAY HIS LUCK'S BEEN GOING LATELY, THAT MAY AS WELL BE A LIFETIME.

I'm counting seconds and I'm up to fifty-five elephants, when a spiral of swirling blue energy strikes the walkway, causing a tremor.

I know that color. That's discharged Parasite energy. Exactly what's been damaging the dish.

Only we can see the Parasites, and I bet only we can see their energy bursts.

And even as I've finished that thought, I look down and see another cloud of Parasite energy heading straight for m[e]

This one is much bigger

The impact wrenches my fingers from the handr[o]

I'm floating away from the Satellite, and there's nothing I can do about it.

Overhead, a residential unit full of off-duty dish jockeys breaks free and starts to drift off.

I'm floating away in space with no radio and no emergency lights.

I am an idio[t]

Dozens of dish jockeys hurl themselves at the unit.

They spin it around so that the venting gas pipes propel it back toward the dish.

All I can do is watch as I fall away into the darkness.

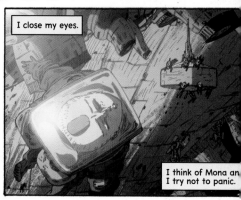

I close my eyes.

I think of Mona an[d] I try not to panic.

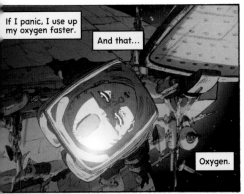

If I panic, I use up my oxygen faster.

And that...

Oxygen.

I have my own gas supply on my back.

Could I vent half my oxygen and push myself back toward the Satellite?

I have two tanks on my back.

If they're separate then I have a chance.

I seal the helmet connection and get ready to pull.

If they're linked then I'll die a few minutes sooner than if I do nothing.

I grab hold of one of the supply lines. I think of Mona and yank the pipe from its connection.

Suddenly I'm going fast.

Much too fast.

I'm about to die horribly in a crash as opposed to dying horribly of suffocation when something grabs my waist.

WHERE THE HECK DID YOU COME FROM, BOY?

YOU'RE VENTING GAS EVERYWHERE!

He sticks a little speaker on my helmet and starts shouting at me. (I don't care, he's saving my life.)

He asks who I'm working for.

KROM? TYPICAL. I BET YOU HAVEN'T HAD MORE THAN A COUPLE OF HOURS' SPACE TIME.

EMPLOY AMATEURS, SAVE MONEY, THAT'S THE KROM WAY. NO OFFENSE.

He shouts at me some more. (I don't care, he's saving my life.)

YOU CAN'T BE MUCH MORE THAN A BOY.

HOW OLD ARE YOU?

TWENTY-TWO. I DRINK A LOT OF WATER. KEEPS ME LOOKING YOUNG.

MORON.

I KNOW.

It takes about thirty minutes for my legs to stop shaking.

CAN WE PLEASE GO BACK TO EARTH?

I'M NOT SURE YOU'LL WANT TO WHEN YOU SEE THE RESULTS OF THE ENERGY SCAN.

WHY? IT'S NOT AS IF THE PARASITE NEST IS UNDER CLARISSA FRAYNE, IS IT?

I make a joke. No one else laughs

OH.

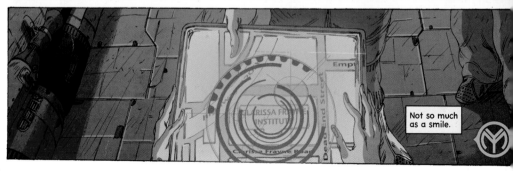

Not so much as a smile.

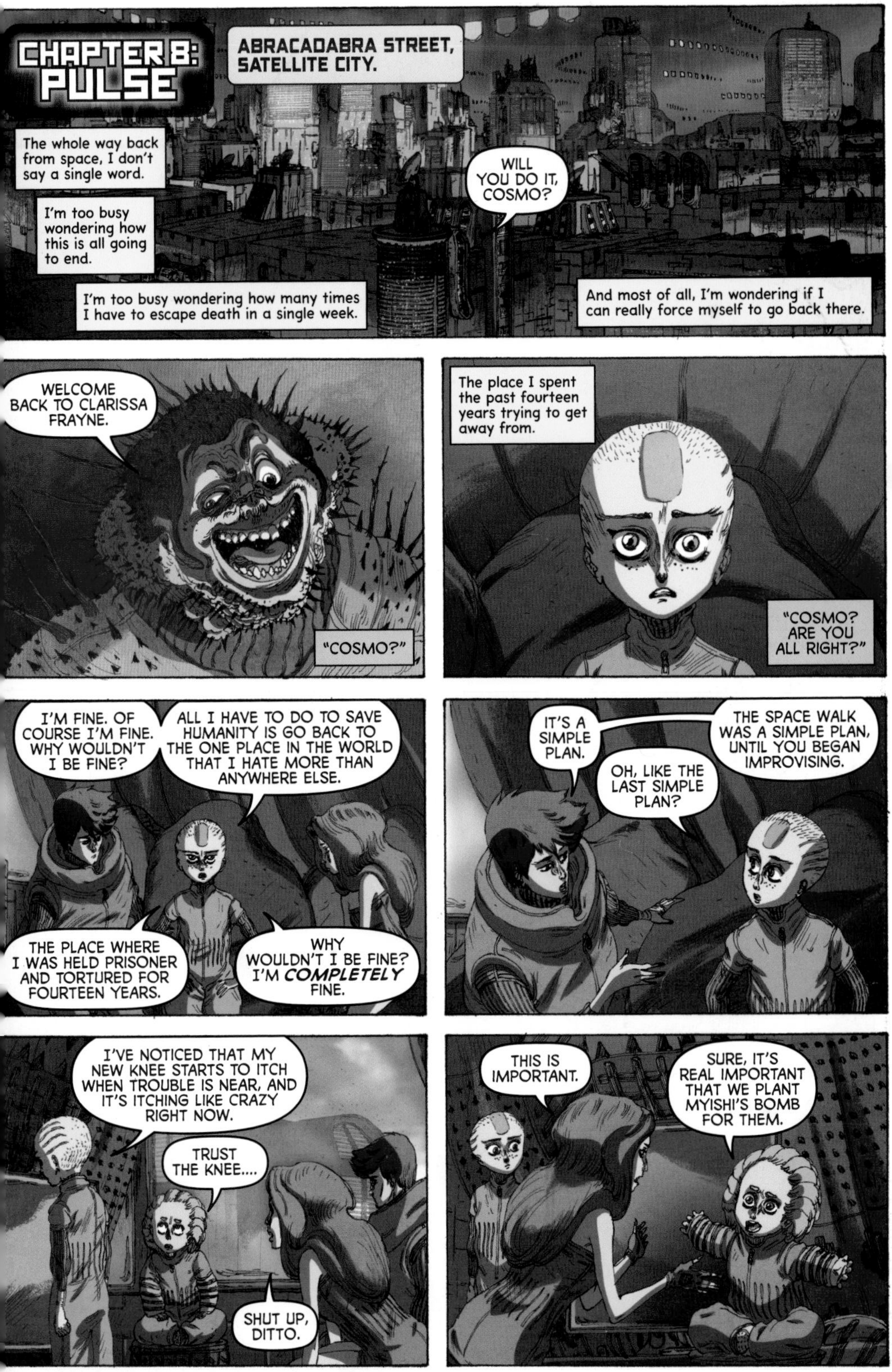

CHAPTER 8: PULSE
ABRACADABRA STREET, SATELLITE CITY.
The whole way back from space, I don't say a single word.
I'm too busy wondering how this is all going to end.
WILL YOU DO IT, COSMO?
I'm too busy wondering how many times I have to escape death in a single week.
And most of all, I'm wondering if I can really force myself to go back there.
WELCOME BACK TO CLARISSA FRAYNE.
"COSMO?"
The place I spent the past fourteen years trying to get away from.
"COSMO? ARE YOU ALL RIGHT?"
I'M FINE. OF COURSE I'M FINE. WHY WOULDN'T I BE FINE?
ALL I HAVE TO DO TO SAVE HUMANITY IS GO BACK TO THE ONE PLACE IN THE WORLD THAT I HATE MORE THAN ANYWHERE ELSE.
THE PLACE WHERE I WAS HELD PRISONER AND TORTURED FOR FOURTEEN YEARS.
WHY WOULDN'T I BE FINE? I'M *COMPLETELY* FINE.
IT'S A SIMPLE PLAN.
THE SPACE WALK WAS A SIMPLE PLAN, UNTIL YOU BEGAN IMPROVISING.
OH, LIKE THE LAST SIMPLE PLAN?
I'VE NOTICED THAT MY NEW KNEE STARTS TO ITCH WHEN TROUBLE IS NEAR, AND IT'S ITCHING LIKE CRAZY RIGHT NOW.
TRUST THE KNEE....
SHUT UP, DITTO.
THIS IS IMPORTANT.
SURE, IT'S REAL IMPORTANT THAT WE PLANT MYISHI'S BOMB FOR THEM.

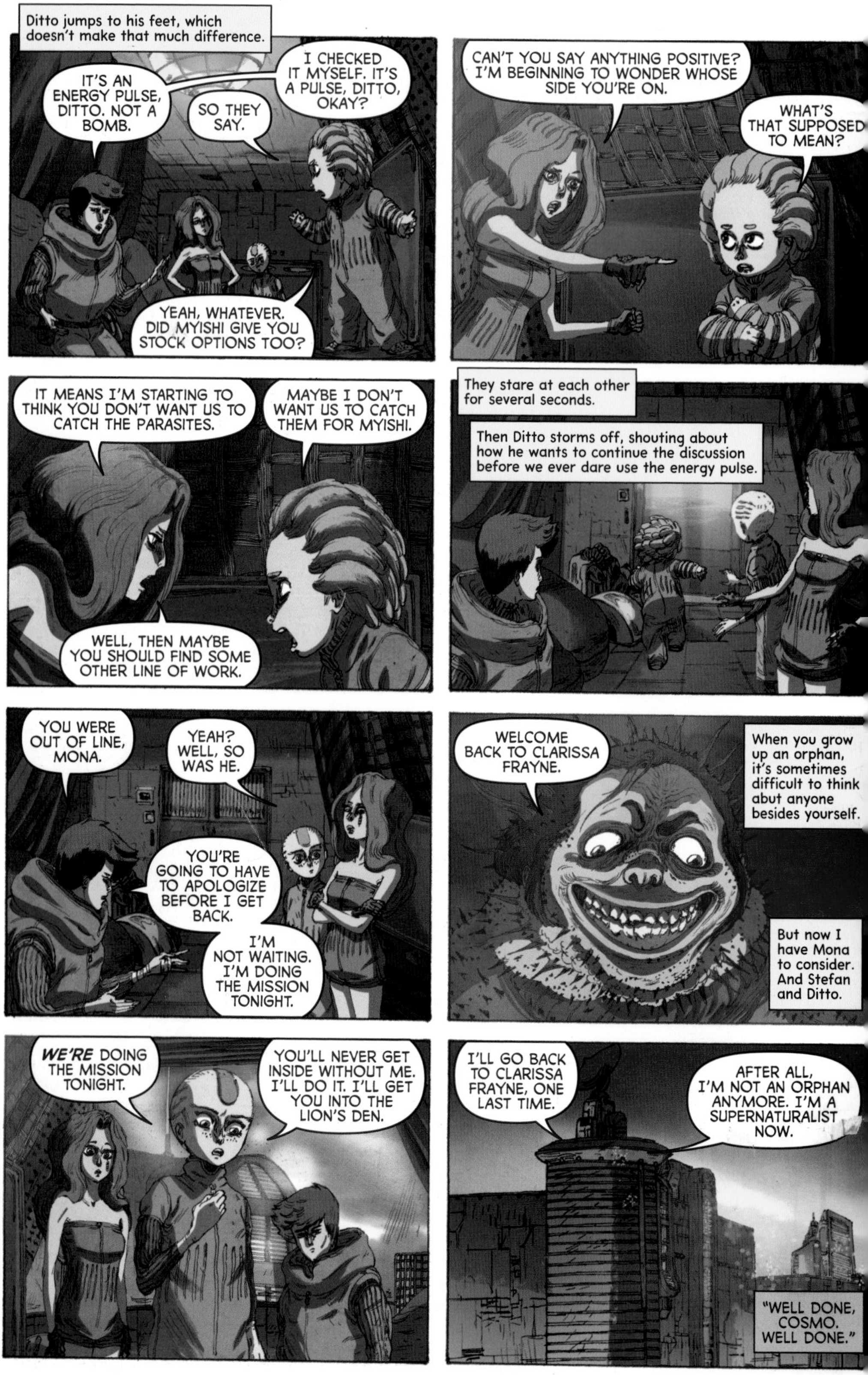
Ditto jumps to his feet, which doesn't make that much difference.
IT'S AN ENERGY PULSE, DITTO. NOT A BOMB.
SO THEY SAY.
I CHECKED IT MYSELF. IT'S A PULSE, DITTO, OKAY?
YEAH, WHATEVER. DID MYISHI GIVE YOU STOCK OPTIONS TOO?
CAN'T YOU SAY ANYTHING POSITIVE? I'M BEGINNING TO WONDER WHOSE SIDE YOU'RE ON.
WHAT'S THAT SUPPOSED TO MEAN?
IT MEANS I'M STARTING TO THINK YOU DON'T WANT US TO CATCH THE PARASITES.
MAYBE I DON'T WANT US TO CATCH THEM FOR MYISHI.
WELL, THEN MAYBE YOU SHOULD FIND SOME OTHER LINE OF WORK.
They stare at each other for several seconds.
Then Ditto storms off, shouting about how he wants to continue the discussion before we ever dare use the energy pulse.
YOU WERE OUT OF LINE, MONA.
YEAH? WELL, SO WAS HE.
YOU'RE GOING TO HAVE TO APOLOGIZE BEFORE I GET BACK.
I'M NOT WAITING. I'M DOING THE MISSION TONIGHT.
WELCOME BACK TO CLARISSA FRAYNE.
When you grow up an orphan, it's sometimes difficult to think abut anyone besides yourself.
But now I have Mona to consider. And Stefan and Ditto.
WE'RE DOING THE MISSION TONIGHT.
YOU'LL NEVER GET INSIDE WITHOUT ME. I'LL DO IT. I'LL GET YOU INTO THE LION'S DEN.
I'LL GO BACK TO CLARISSA FRAYNE, ONE LAST TIME.
AFTER ALL, I'M NOT AN ORPHAN ANYMORE. I'M A SUPERNATURALIST NOW.
"WELL DONE, COSMO. WELL DONE."

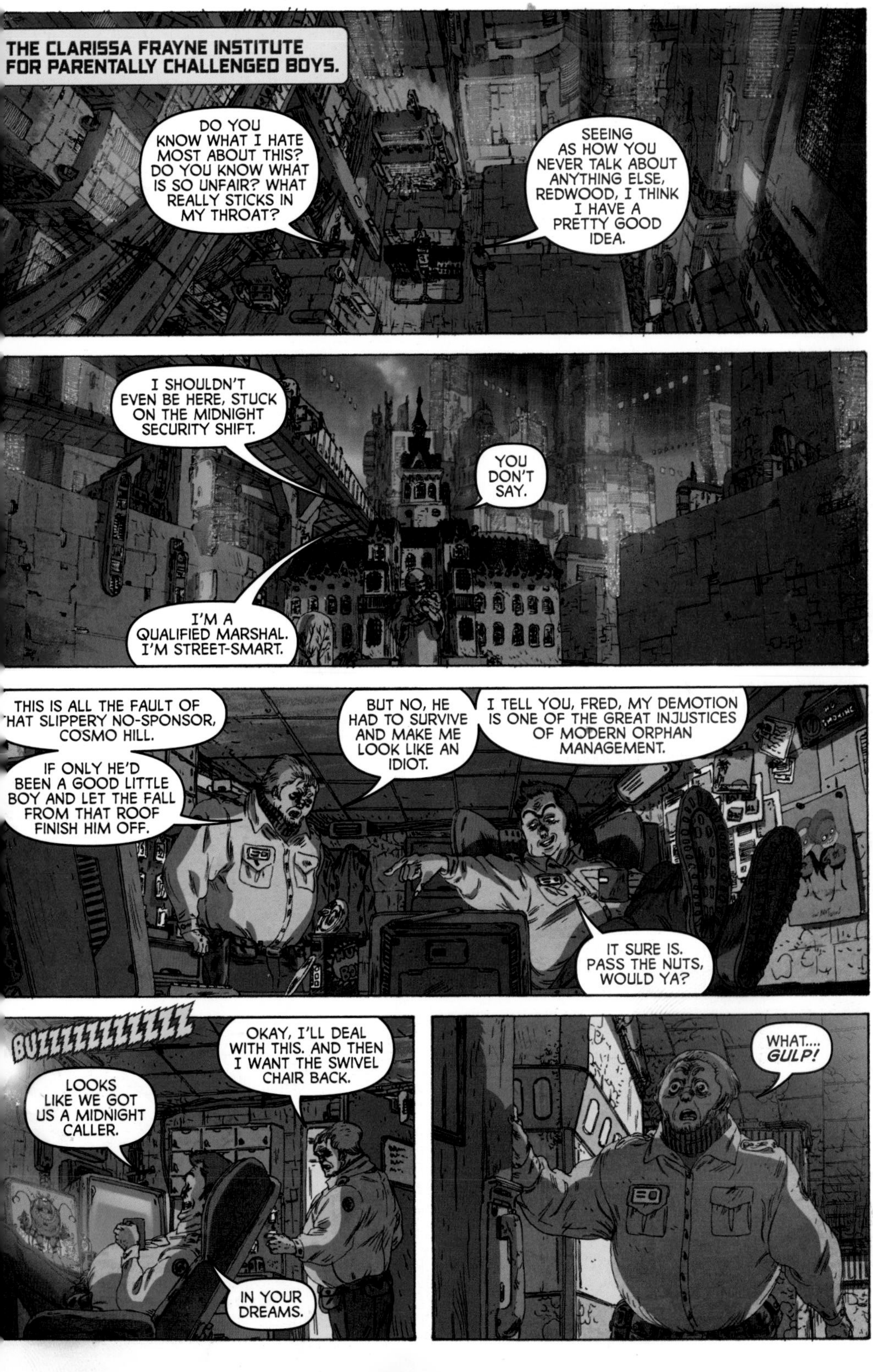
THE CLARISSA FRAYNE INSTITUTE FOR PARENTALLY CHALLENGED BOYS.
DO YOU KNOW WHAT I HATE MOST ABOUT THIS? DO YOU KNOW WHAT IS SO UNFAIR? WHAT REALLY STICKS IN MY THROAT?
SEEING AS HOW YOU NEVER TALK ABOUT ANYTHING ELSE, REDWOOD, I THINK I HAVE A PRETTY GOOD IDEA.
I SHOULDN'T EVEN BE HERE, STUCK ON THE MIDNIGHT SECURITY SHIFT.
YOU DON'T SAY.
I'M A QUALIFIED MARSHAL. I'M STREET-SMART.
THIS IS ALL THE FAULT OF THAT SLIPPERY NO-SPONSOR, COSMO HILL.
IF ONLY HE'D BEEN A GOOD LITTLE BOY AND LET THE FALL FROM THAT ROOF FINISH HIM OFF.
BUT NO, HE HAD TO SURVIVE AND MAKE ME LOOK LIKE AN IDIOT.
I TELL YOU, FRED, MY DEMOTION IS ONE OF THE GREAT INJUSTICES OF MODERN ORPHAN MANAGEMENT.
IT SURE IS. PASS THE NUTS, WOULD YA?
BUZZZZZZZZZZZ
LOOKS LIKE WE GOT US A MIDNIGHT CALLER.
OKAY, I'LL DEAL WITH THIS. AND THEN I WANT THE SWIVEL CHAIR BACK.
IN YOUR DREAMS.
WHAT.... *GULP!*

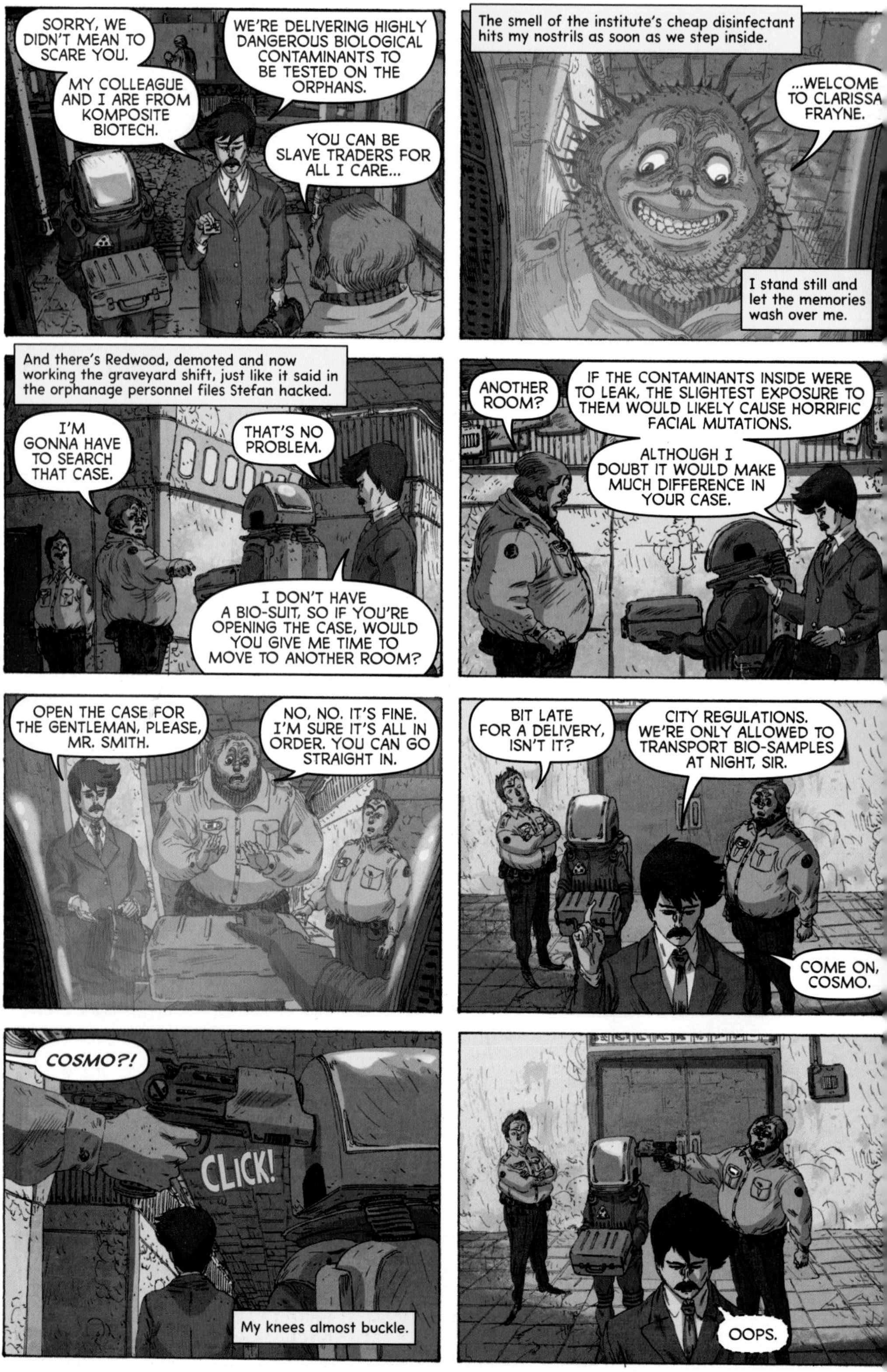
SORRY, WE DIDN'T MEAN TO SCARE YOU.
MY COLLEAGUE AND I ARE FROM KOMPOSITE BIOTECH.
WE'RE DELIVERING HIGHLY DANGEROUS BIOLOGICAL CONTAMINANTS TO BE TESTED ON THE ORPHANS.
YOU CAN BE SLAVE TRADERS FOR ALL I CARE...
The smell of the institute's cheap disinfectant hits my nostrils as soon as we step inside.
...WELCOME TO CLARISSA FRAYNE.
I stand still and let the memories wash over me.
And there's Redwood, demoted and now working the graveyard shift, just like it said in the orphanage personnel files Stefan hacked.
I'M GONNA HAVE TO SEARCH THAT CASE.
THAT'S NO PROBLEM.
I DON'T HAVE A BIO-SUIT, SO IF YOU'RE OPENING THE CASE, WOULD YOU GIVE ME TIME TO MOVE TO ANOTHER ROOM?
ANOTHER ROOM?
IF THE CONTAMINANTS INSIDE WERE TO LEAK, THE SLIGHTEST EXPOSURE TO THEM WOULD LIKELY CAUSE HORRIFIC FACIAL MUTATIONS.
ALTHOUGH I DOUBT IT WOULD MAKE MUCH DIFFERENCE IN YOUR CASE.
OPEN THE CASE FOR THE GENTLEMAN, PLEASE, MR. SMITH.
NO, NO. IT'S FINE. I'M SURE IT'S ALL IN ORDER. YOU CAN GO STRAIGHT IN.
BIT LATE FOR A DELIVERY, ISN'T IT?
CITY REGULATIONS. WE'RE ONLY ALLOWED TO TRANSPORT BIO-SAMPLES AT NIGHT, SIR.
COME ON, COSMO.
COSMO?!
CLICK!
My knees almost buckle.
OOPS.

YEAH, EVERYONE WHO WEARS THAT SUIT GETS CALLED COSMO BECAUSE IT LOOKS LIKE THE SUITS THE OLD COSMONAUTS USED TO WEAR.

IS THERE A PROBLEM? YOU WANNA GET THE GUN OUT OF MY FRIEND'S FACE? OR DO YOU WANT ANOTHER DEMOTION?

COME ON, REDWOOD. YOU GOTTA RELAX AND FORGET ABOUT THAT COSMO KID. YOU'RE NEVER GONNA SEE HIM AGAIN. LET IT GO.

YOU'RE RIGHT. I'M SORRY, SIR. I GUESS I'M A LITTLE JUMPY.

HEY, NO PROBLEM.

lead Stefan though the vaulted reception area.

KEEP WALKING. NEXT LEFT, THEN SHARP RIGHT.

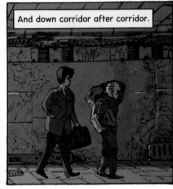

And down corridor after corridor.

IN HERE.

THIS IS CHARMING.

YOU SHOULD SEE THE DORMITORIES. HELP ME OUT OF THE SUIT AND LET'S GO.

I'M ONLY GIVING YOU THE SWIVEL CHAIR FOR TWENTY MINUTES, BECAUSE YOU'RE NOT A WELL MAN. IS THAT CLEAR?

SURE. I NEED TO RELAX.

THE LAST THING I WANT IS TO GET DEMOTED AG...

SAY, HOW DID THAT BIOTECH GUY KNOW I'D BEEN DEMOTED?

MAYBE HE OVERHEARD US TALKING? WHO KNOWS?

HE DIDN'T OVERHEAR ANYTHING. I'M RUNNING A FULL SCAN.

BEEP. BEEP. BEEP.

OH NO... IT'S FAINT, VERY FAINT, BUT THE SCANNER'S PICKING UP THE TRACKER-PATTERN OF COSMO HILL. HE'S BACK.

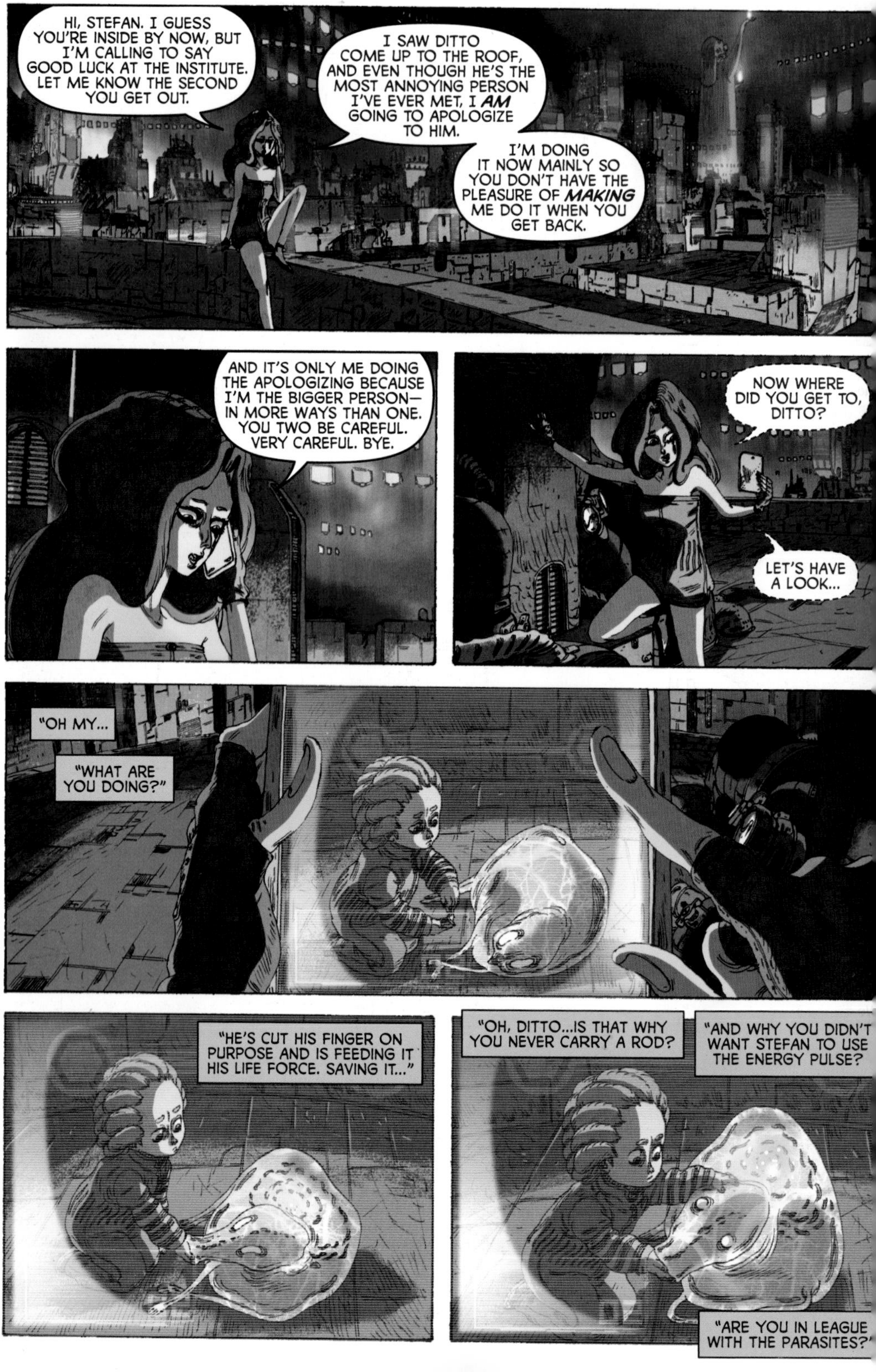
HI, STEFAN. I GUESS YOU'RE INSIDE BY NOW, BUT I'M CALLING TO SAY GOOD LUCK AT THE INSTITUTE. LET ME KNOW THE SECOND YOU GET OUT.
I SAW DITTO COME UP TO THE ROOF, AND EVEN THOUGH HE'S THE MOST ANNOYING PERSON I'VE EVER MET, I *AM* GOING TO APOLOGIZE TO HIM.
I'M DOING IT NOW MAINLY SO YOU DON'T HAVE THE PLEASURE OF *MAKING* ME DO IT WHEN YOU GET BACK.
AND IT'S ONLY ME DOING THE APOLOGIZING BECAUSE I'M THE BIGGER PERSON—IN MORE WAYS THAN ONE. YOU TWO BE CAREFUL. VERY CAREFUL. BYE.
NOW WHERE DID YOU GET TO, DITTO?
LET'S HAVE A LOOK...
"OH MY...
"WHAT ARE YOU DOING?"
"HE'S CUT HIS FINGER ON PURPOSE AND IS FEEDING IT HIS LIFE FORCE. SAVING IT..."
"OH, DITTO...IS THAT WHY YOU NEVER CARRY A ROD?
"AND WHY YOU DIDN'T WANT STEFAN TO USE THE ENERGY PULSE?
"ARE YOU IN LEAGUE WITH THE PARASITES?"

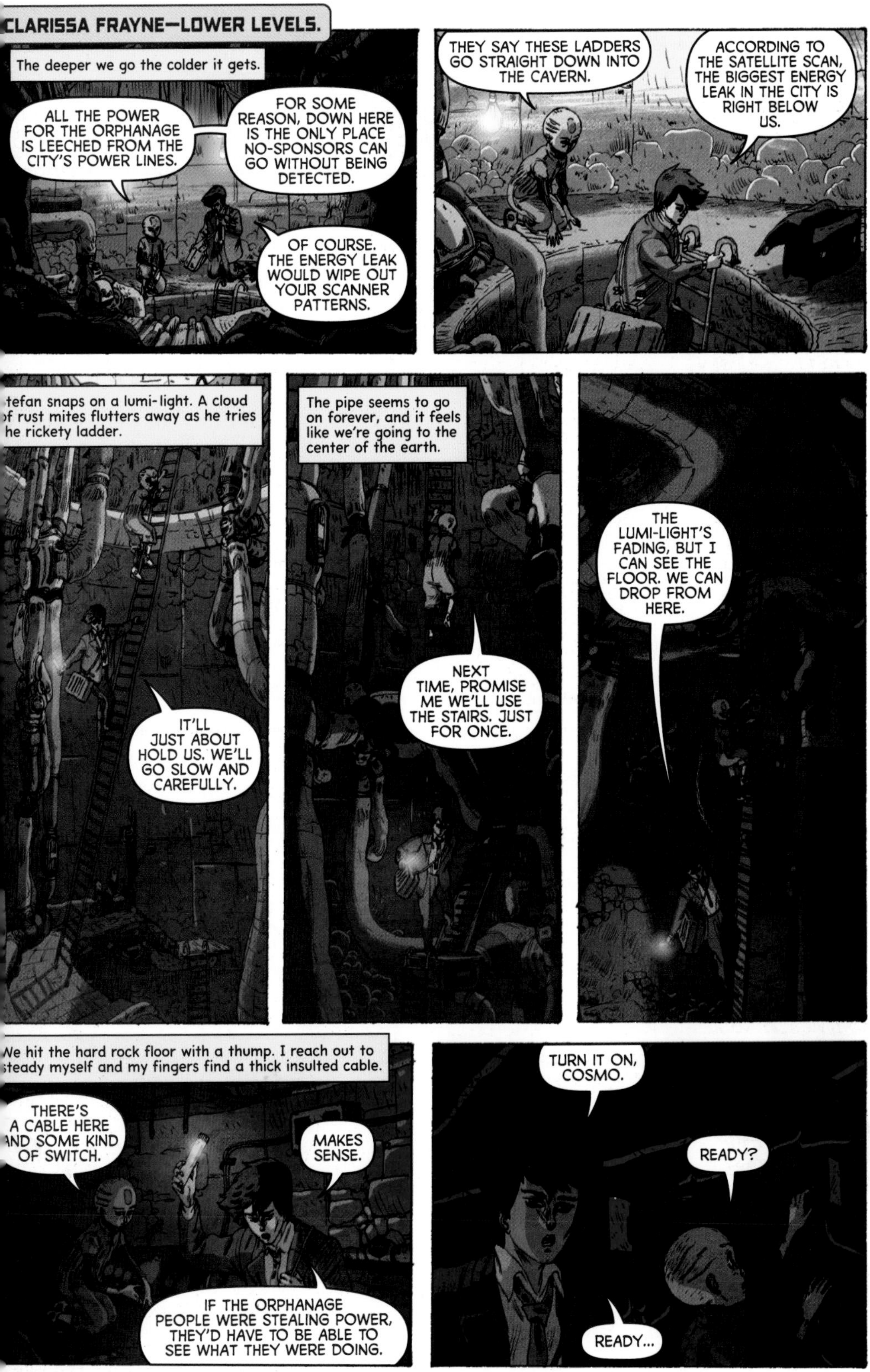
CLARISSA FRAYNE—LOWER LEVELS.
The deeper we go the colder it gets.
ALL THE POWER FOR THE ORPHANAGE IS LEECHED FROM THE CITY'S POWER LINES.
FOR SOME REASON, DOWN HERE IS THE ONLY PLACE NO-SPONSORS CAN GO WITHOUT BEING DETECTED.
OF COURSE. THE ENERGY LEAK WOULD WIPE OUT YOUR SCANNER PATTERNS.
THEY SAY THESE LADDERS GO STRAIGHT DOWN INTO THE CAVERN.
ACCORDING TO THE SATELLITE SCAN, THE BIGGEST ENERGY LEAK IN THE CITY IS RIGHT BELOW US.
tefan snaps on a lumi-light. A cloud f rust mites flutters away as he tries he rickety ladder.
IT'LL JUST ABOUT HOLD US. WE'LL GO SLOW AND CAREFULLY.
The pipe seems to go on forever, and it feels like we're going to the center of the earth.
NEXT TIME, PROMISE ME WE'LL USE THE STAIRS. JUST FOR ONCE.
THE LUMI-LIGHT'S FADING, BUT I CAN SEE THE FLOOR. WE CAN DROP FROM HERE.
Ve hit the hard rock floor with a thump. I reach out to teady myself and my fingers find a thick insulted cable.
THERE'S A CABLE HERE ND SOME KIND OF SWITCH.
MAKES SENSE.
IF THE ORPHANAGE PEOPLE WERE STEALING POWER, THEY'D HAVE TO BE ABLE TO SEE WHAT THEY WERE DOING.
TURN IT ON, COSMO.
READY?
READY...

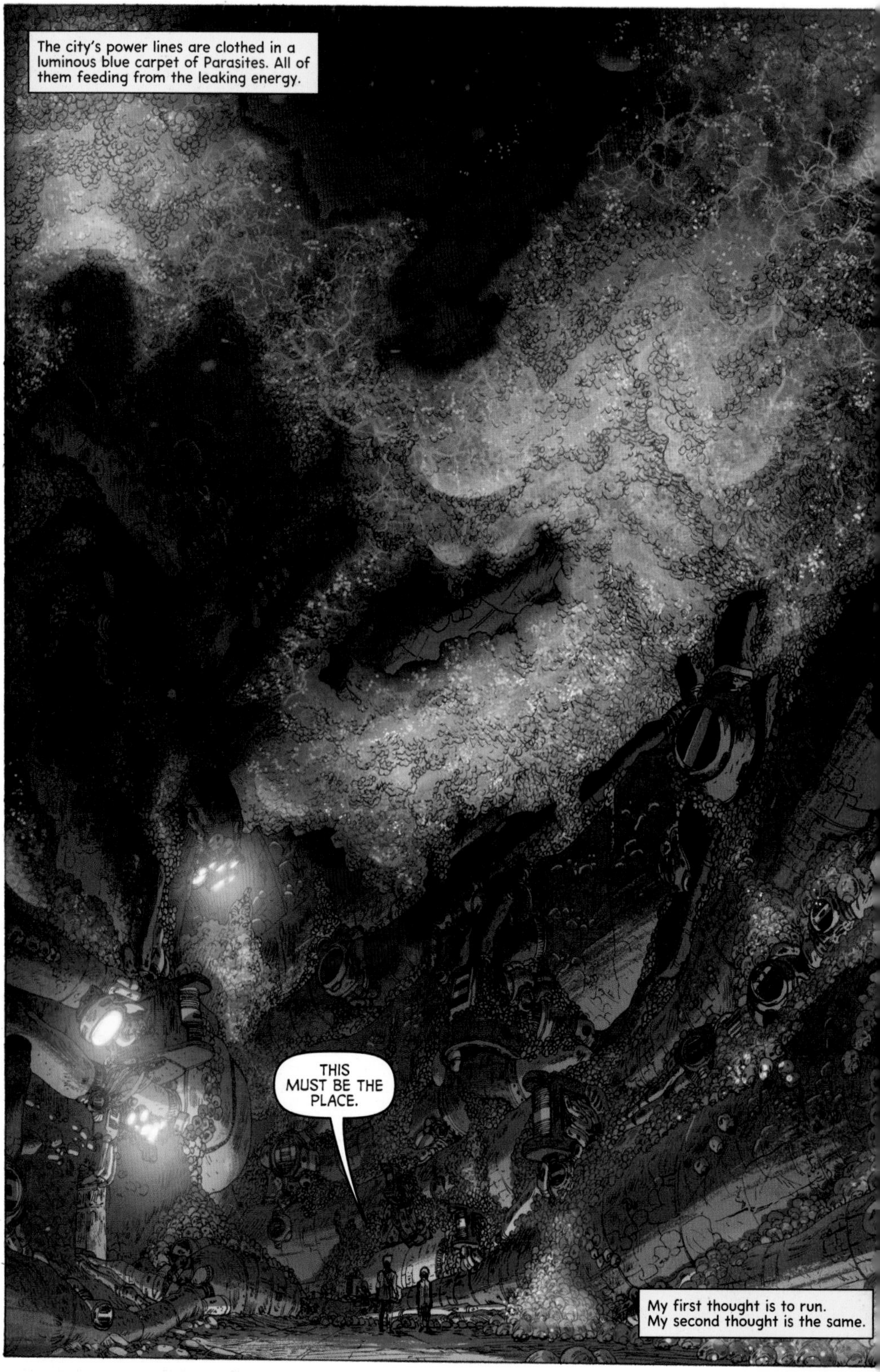
The city's power lines are clothed in a luminous blue carpet of Parasites. All of them feeding from the leaking energy.
THIS MUST BE THE PLACE.
My first thought is to run. My second thought is the same.

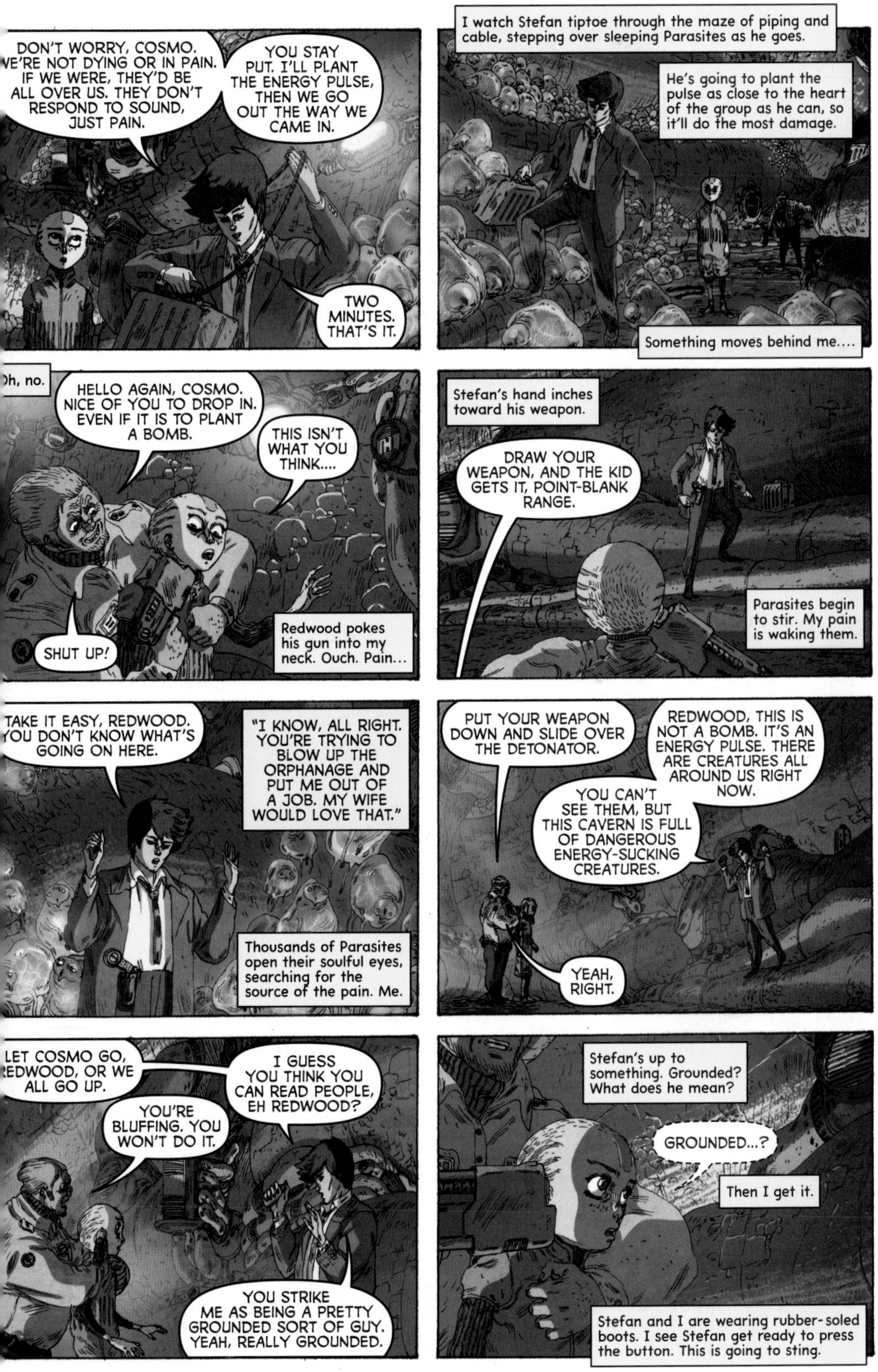
DON'T WORRY, COSMO. WE'RE NOT DYING OR IN PAIN. IF WE WERE, THEY'D BE ALL OVER US. THEY DON'T RESPOND TO SOUND, JUST PAIN.
YOU STAY PUT. I'LL PLANT THE ENERGY PULSE, THEN WE GO OUT THE WAY WE CAME IN.
TWO MINUTES. THAT'S IT.
I watch Stefan tiptoe through the maze of piping and cable, stepping over sleeping Parasites as he goes.
He's going to plant the pulse as close to the heart of the group as he can, so it'll do the most damage.
Something moves behind me....
Oh, no.
HELLO AGAIN, COSMO. NICE OF YOU TO DROP IN. EVEN IF IT IS TO PLANT A BOMB.
THIS ISN'T WHAT YOU THINK....
SHUT UP!
Redwood pokes his gun into my neck. Ouch. Pain...
Stefan's hand inches toward his weapon.
DRAW YOUR WEAPON, AND THE KID GETS IT, POINT-BLANK RANGE.
Parasites begin to stir. My pain is waking them.
TAKE IT EASY, REDWOOD. YOU DON'T KNOW WHAT'S GOING ON HERE.
"I KNOW, ALL RIGHT. YOU'RE TRYING TO BLOW UP THE ORPHANAGE AND PUT ME OUT OF A JOB. MY WIFE WOULD LOVE THAT."
Thousands of Parasites open their soulful eyes, searching for the source of the pain. Me.
PUT YOUR WEAPON DOWN AND SLIDE OVER THE DETONATOR.
REDWOOD, THIS IS NOT A BOMB. IT'S AN ENERGY PULSE. THERE ARE CREATURES ALL AROUND US RIGHT NOW.
YOU CAN'T SEE THEM, BUT THIS CAVERN IS FULL OF DANGEROUS ENERGY-SUCKING CREATURES.
YEAH, RIGHT.
LET COSMO GO, REDWOOD, OR WE ALL GO UP.
YOU'RE BLUFFING. YOU WON'T DO IT.
I GUESS YOU THINK YOU CAN READ PEOPLE, EH REDWOOD?
YOU STRIKE ME AS BEING A PRETTY GROUNDED SORT OF GUY. YEAH, REALLY GROUNDED.
Stefan's up to something. Grounded? What does he mean?
GROUNDED...?
Then I get it.
Stefan and I are wearing rubber-soled boots. I see Stefan get ready to press the button. This is going to sting.

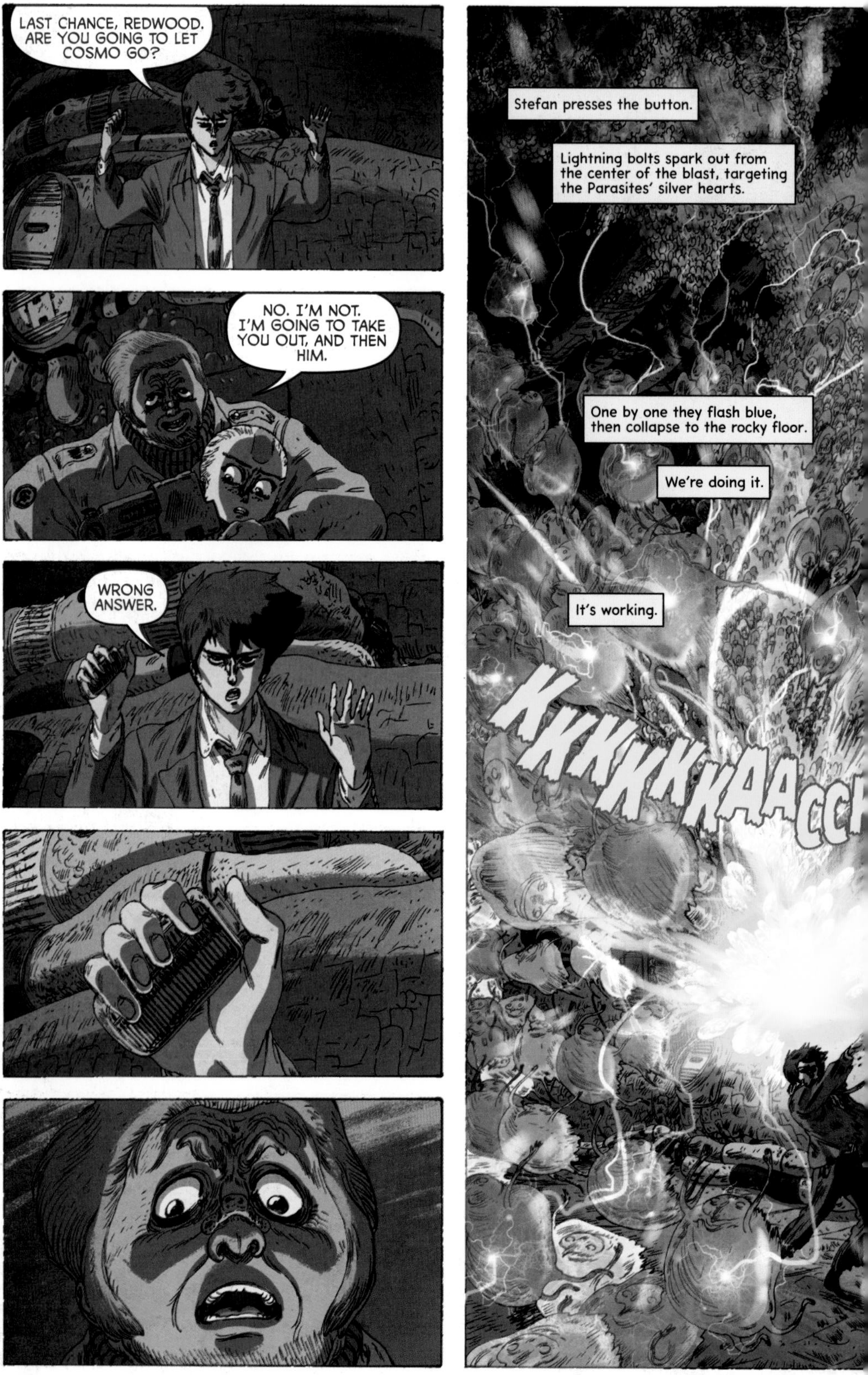

LAST CHANCE, REDWOOD. ARE YOU GOING TO LET COSMO GO?
NO. I'M NOT. I'M GOING TO TAKE YOU OUT, AND THEN HIM.
WRONG ANSWER.
Stefan presses the button.
Lightning bolts spark out from the center of the blast, targeting the Parasites' silver hearts.
One by one they flash blue, then collapse to the rocky floor.
We're doing it.
It's working.
KKKKKKAACC

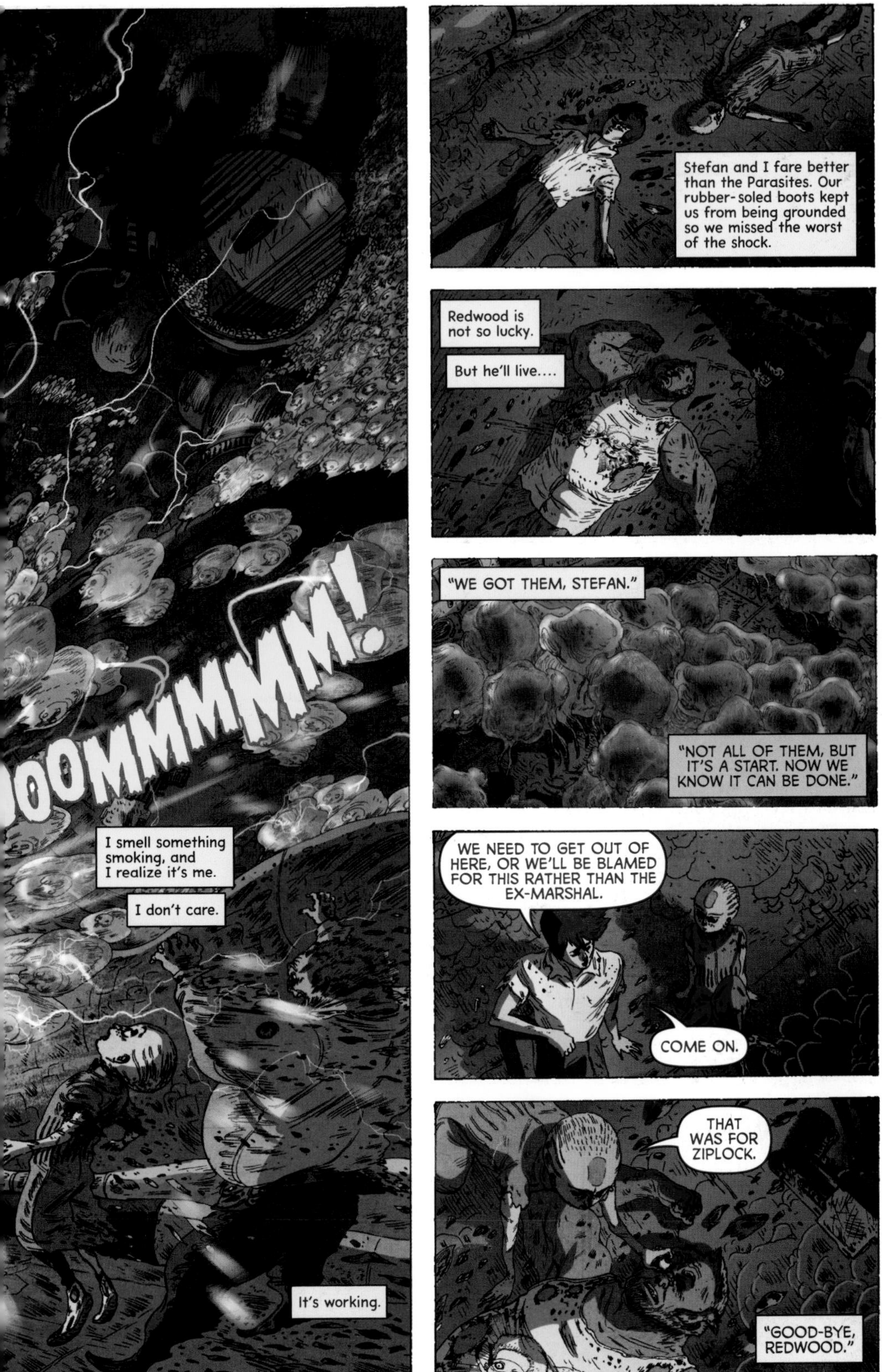
OOMMMMMM!
I smell something smoking, and I realize it's me.
I don't care.
It's working.
Stefan and I fare better than the Parasites. Our rubber-soled boots kept us from being grounded so we missed the worst of the shock.
Redwood is not so lucky.
But he'll live....
"WE GOT THEM, STEFAN."
"NOT ALL OF THEM, BUT IT'S A START. NOW WE KNOW IT CAN BE DONE."
WE NEED TO GET OUT OF HERE, OR WE'LL BE BLAMED FOR THIS RATHER THAN THE EX-MARSHAL.
COME ON.
THAT WAS FOR ZIPLOCK.
"GOOD-BYE, REDWOOD."

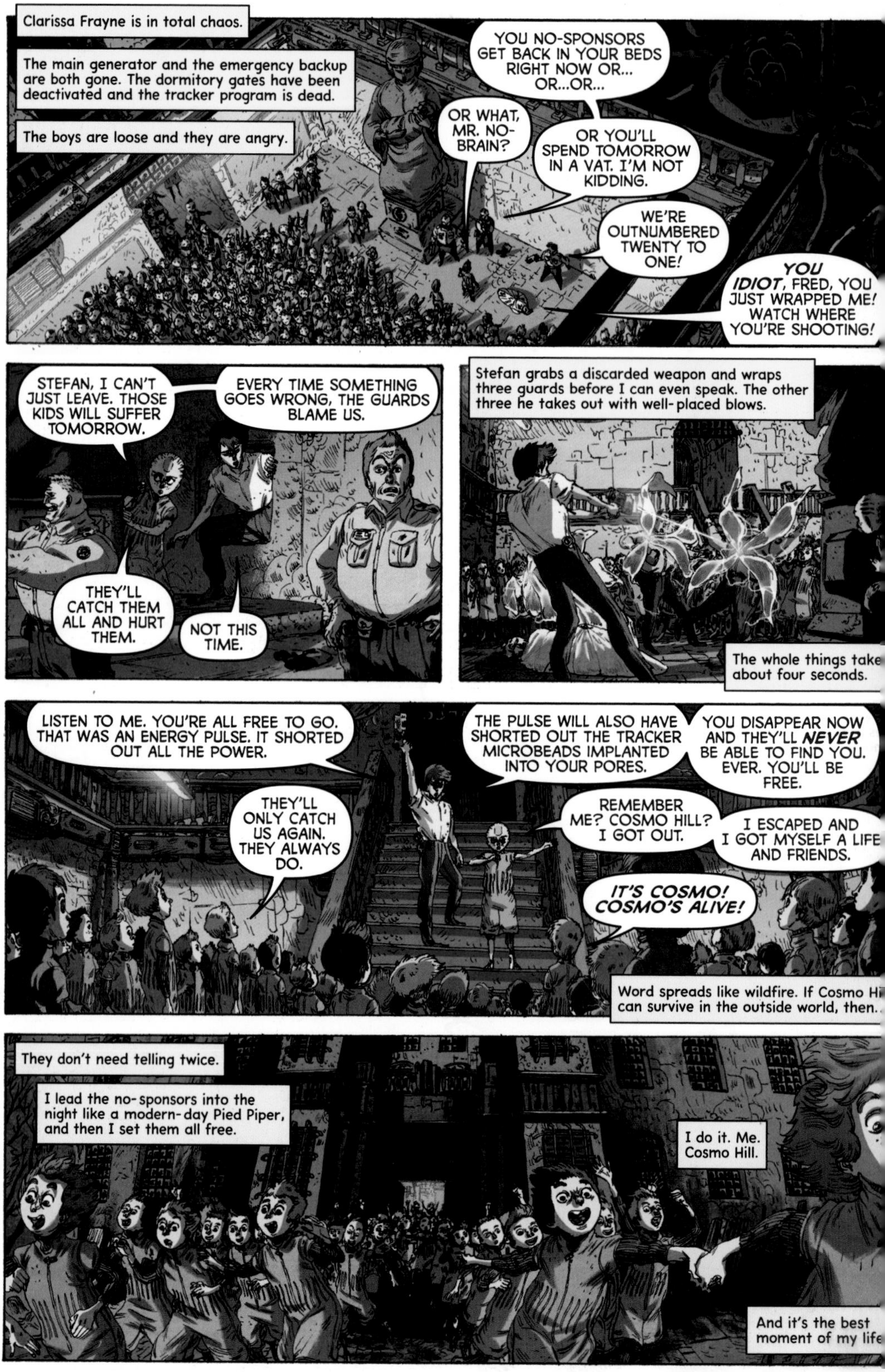

Clarissa Frayne is in total chaos.
The main generator and the emergency backup are both gone. The dormitory gates have been deactivated and the tracker program is dead.
The boys are loose and they are angry.
YOU NO-SPONSORS GET BACK IN YOUR BEDS RIGHT NOW OR... OR...OR...
OR WHAT, MR. NO-BRAIN?
OR YOU'LL SPEND TOMORROW IN A VAT. I'M NOT KIDDING.
WE'RE OUTNUMBERED TWENTY TO ONE!
YOU IDIOT, FRED, YOU JUST WRAPPED ME! WATCH WHERE YOU'RE SHOOTING!
STEFAN, I CAN'T JUST LEAVE. THOSE KIDS WILL SUFFER TOMORROW.
EVERY TIME SOMETHING GOES WRONG, THE GUARDS BLAME US.
THEY'LL CATCH THEM ALL AND HURT THEM.
NOT THIS TIME.
Stefan grabs a discarded weapon and wraps three guards before I can even speak. The other three he takes out with well-placed blows.
The whole things take about four seconds.
LISTEN TO ME. YOU'RE ALL FREE TO GO. THAT WAS AN ENERGY PULSE. IT SHORTED OUT ALL THE POWER.
THE PULSE WILL ALSO HAVE SHORTED OUT THE TRACKER MICROBEADS IMPLANTED INTO YOUR PORES.
YOU DISAPPEAR NOW AND THEY'LL NEVER BE ABLE TO FIND YOU. EVER. YOU'LL BE FREE.
THEY'LL ONLY CATCH US AGAIN. THEY ALWAYS DO.
REMEMBER ME? COSMO HILL? I GOT OUT.
I ESCAPED AND I GOT MYSELF A LIFE AND FRIENDS.
IT'S COSMO! COSMO'S ALIVE!
Word spreads like wildfire. If Cosmo Hi can survive in the outside world, then...
They don't need telling twice.
I lead the no-sponsors into the night like a modern-day Pied Piper, and then I set them all free.
I do it. Me. Cosmo Hill.
And it's the best moment of my life

Stefan and I walk home through the darkened city streets.

Every now and then we catch a glimpse of a happy no-sponsor making his escape.

ANYTHING?

NO. THE ENERGY PULSE HAS KNOCKED OUT OUR PHONES. HECK, IT'S KNOCKED OUT EVERYTHING ELECTRONIC FOR ABOUT TEN BLOCKS.

BY THE TIME CLARRISA FRAYNE CAN EVEN *REPORT* THE BREAKOUT, THOSE ORPHANS WILL BE LONG GONE.

We walk and we talk.

Stefan is full of plans for the future. And I'm right at the center of them.

WE NEED TO GET MORE OF THE ENERGY PULSES FROM ELLEN. FIND A WAY TO MONITOR HOW MANY PARASITES WE TAKE OUT WITH EACH ONE. AND FIND OUT WHERE ELSE THEY'RE HIDING.

WE'RE A GREAT TEAM, COSMO.

YOU, ME, MONA, AND DITTO. TONIGHT WAS A REAL TURNING POINT IN OUR FIGHT. I KNOW IT.

HA—I STILL CAN'T BELIEVE WE GOT ONE OVER ON REDWOOD.

We're back at Abracadabra Street for less than two seconds and our good mood vanishes like it was never there.

At first I think Mona is angry because we couldn't call her after the blast. But it's not that.

It's not that at all.

Stefan is making Mona explain it all for the third time when Ditto comes in looking like he's the one who should be angry.

YOU HAD TO DO IT, DIDN'T YOU?

I SAID TO TALK TO ME BEFORE YOU USED THAT MYISHI BOMB, BUT NO, YOU COULDN'T WAIT.

I REALLY THINK YOU NEED TO HAVE A LOOK AT THIS.

IF THAT'S ONE OF THOSE COMEDY E-MAILS, I'M NOT IN THE MOOD.

YOU'RE NOT IN THE MOOD?

HAVE A LOOK AT THIS, DITTO. BECAUSE WE'RE NOT IN THE MOOD EITHER.

The color drains from Ditto's cheeks as he realizes he's been caught.

OKAY, I KNOW THIS LOOKS BAD, BUT I CAN EXPLAIN.

ALL THIS TIME, WHY DIDN'T I SEE IT? NO WONDER YOU WOULDN'T SHOOT THE PARASITES. NO WONDER YOU DIDN'T WANT US TO USE THE ENERGY PULSE ON YOUR "FRIENDS."

PACK UP YOUR GEAR AND GET OUT. I WANT YOU GONE BY MORNING.

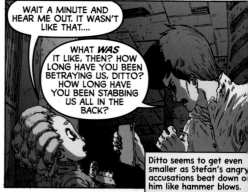

WAIT A MINUTE AND HEAR ME OUT. IT WASN'T LIKE THAT....

WHAT *WAS* IT LIKE, THEN? HOW LONG HAVE YOU BEEN BETRAYING US, DITTO? HOW LONG HAVE YOU BEEN STABBING US ALL IN THE BACK?

Ditto seems to get even smaller as Stefan's angry accusations beat down on him like hammer blows.

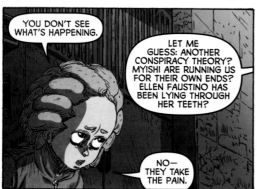

YOU DON'T SEE WHAT'S HAPPENING.

LET ME GUESS: ANOTHER CONSPIRACY THEORY? MYISHI ARE RUNNING US FOR THEIR OWN ENDS? ELLEN FAUSTINO HAS BEEN LYING THROUGH HER TEETH?

NO— THEY TAKE THE PAIN.

"I THINK THE PARASITES HELP PEOPLE. I THINK THEY TAKE AWAY SUFFERING. NOT LIFE FORCE, JUST PAIN.

"THEY HELP US. THEY HAVE ALWAYS HELPED US."

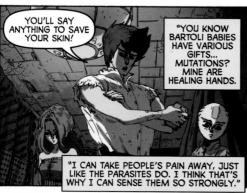

YOU'LL SAY ANYTHING TO SAVE YOUR SKIN!

"YOU KNOW BARTOLI BABIES HAVE VARIOUS GIFTS... MUTATIONS? MINE ARE HEALING HANDS.

"I CAN TAKE PEOPLE'S PAIN AWAY, JUST LIKE THE PARASITES DO. I THINK THAT'S WHY I CAN SENSE THEM SO STRONGLY."

ALL MY LIFE I'VE BEEN ABLE TO SEE THEM.

I FEEL THE SUPERNATURAL AND THEY FEEL ME.

PEOPLE CALL IT SECOND SIGHT.

I SHOULD HAVE TOLD YOU ABOUT THIS YEARS AGO. I KNOW THAT.

I GUESS I GOT TOO ACCUSTOMED TO KEEPING MY OWN GIFTS A SECRET.

"IN MOVIES, PEOPLE WITH GIFTS BECOME SUPERHEROES; IN REAL LIFE THEY GET LOCKED UP IN DR. BARTOLI'S SCIENCE LAB, WHERE THEY'RE EXPERIMENTED ON TWENTY-FOUR HOURS A DAY."

NOW, LUCIEN. DO YOU HAVE ANY OTHER GIFTS YOU WANT TO TELL NICE KINDLY DR. BARTOLI ABOUT? SOME OF THE OTHER CHILDREN CLAIM TO SEE STRANGE BLUE BEINGS. DO YOU SEE STRANGE CREATURES?

I THOUGHT I SAW A WEREWOLF ONCE, JUST OUTSIDE MY WINDOW.

"I LIED AND CONVINCED THEM THAT THERE WAS NOTHING EXTRAORDINARY ABOUT ME."

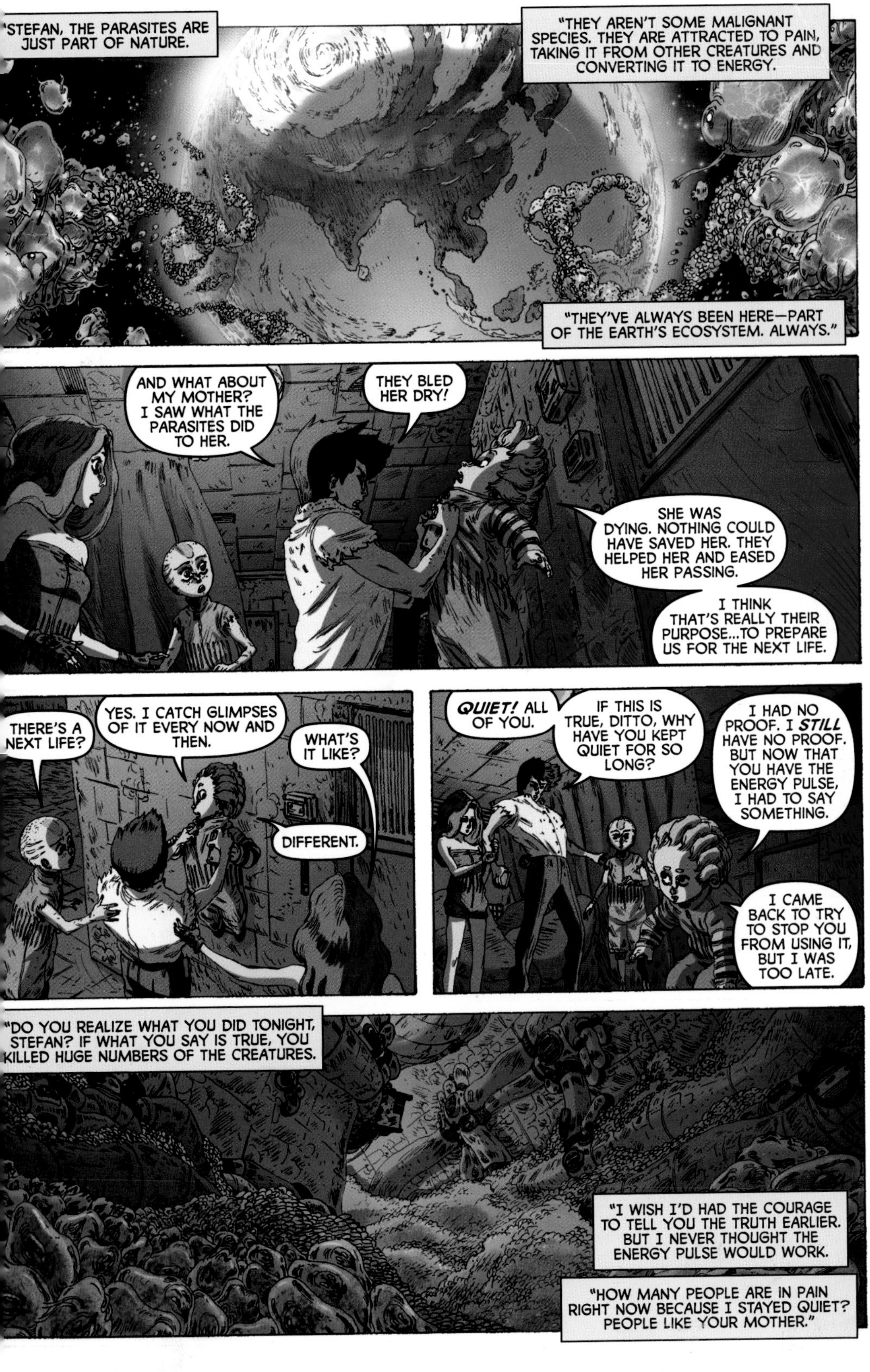

"STEFAN, THE PARASITES ARE JUST PART OF NATURE.
"THEY AREN'T SOME MALIGNANT SPECIES. THEY ARE ATTRACTED TO PAIN, TAKING IT FROM OTHER CREATURES AND CONVERTING IT TO ENERGY.
"THEY'VE ALWAYS BEEN HERE—PART OF THE EARTH'S ECOSYSTEM. ALWAYS."
AND WHAT ABOUT MY MOTHER? I SAW WHAT THE PARASITES DID TO HER.
THEY BLED HER DRY!
SHE WAS DYING. NOTHING COULD HAVE SAVED HER. THEY HELPED HER AND EASED HER PASSING.
I THINK THAT'S REALLY THEIR PURPOSE...TO PREPARE US FOR THE NEXT LIFE.
THERE'S A NEXT LIFE?
YES. I CATCH GLIMPSES OF IT EVERY NOW AND THEN.
WHAT'S IT LIKE?
DIFFERENT.
QUIET! ALL OF YOU.
IF THIS IS TRUE, DITTO, WHY HAVE YOU KEPT QUIET FOR SO LONG?
I HAD NO PROOF. I *STILL* HAVE NO PROOF. BUT NOW THAT YOU HAVE THE ENERGY PULSE, I HAD TO SAY SOMETHING.
I CAME BACK TO TRY TO STOP YOU FROM USING IT, BUT I WAS TOO LATE.
"DO YOU REALIZE WHAT YOU DID TONIGHT, STEFAN? IF WHAT YOU SAY IS TRUE, YOU KILLED HUGE NUMBERS OF THE CREATURES.
"I WISH I'D HAD THE COURAGE TO TELL YOU THE TRUTH EARLIER. BUT I NEVER THOUGHT THE ENERGY PULSE WOULD WORK.
"HOW MANY PEOPLE ARE IN PAIN RIGHT NOW BECAUSE I STAYED QUIET? PEOPLE LIKE YOUR MOTHER."

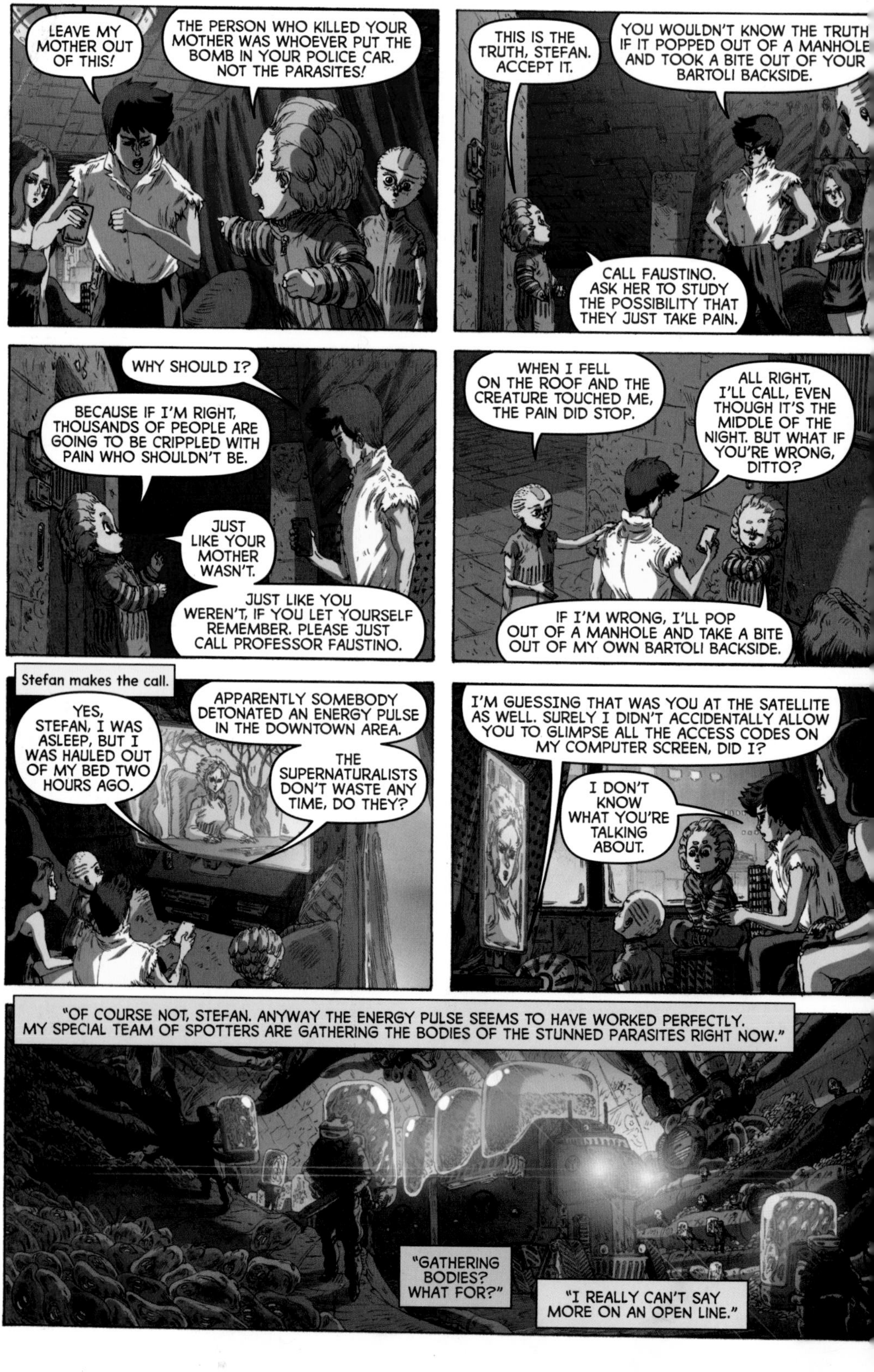
LEAVE MY MOTHER OUT OF THIS!
THE PERSON WHO KILLED YOUR MOTHER WAS WHOEVER PUT THE BOMB IN YOUR POLICE CAR. NOT THE PARASITES!
THIS IS THE TRUTH, STEFAN. ACCEPT IT.
YOU WOULDN'T KNOW THE TRUTH IF IT POPPED OUT OF A MANHOLE AND TOOK A BITE OUT OF YOUR BARTOLI BACKSIDE.
CALL FAUSTINO. ASK HER TO STUDY THE POSSIBILITY THAT THEY JUST TAKE PAIN.
WHY SHOULD I?
BECAUSE IF I'M RIGHT, THOUSANDS OF PEOPLE ARE GOING TO BE CRIPPLED WITH PAIN WHO SHOULDN'T BE.
JUST LIKE YOUR MOTHER WASN'T.
JUST LIKE YOU WEREN'T, IF YOU LET YOURSELF REMEMBER. PLEASE JUST CALL PROFESSOR FAUSTINO.
WHEN I FELL ON THE ROOF AND THE CREATURE TOUCHED ME, THE PAIN DID STOP.
ALL RIGHT, I'LL CALL, EVEN THOUGH IT'S THE MIDDLE OF THE NIGHT. BUT WHAT IF YOU'RE WRONG, DITTO?
IF I'M WRONG, I'LL POP OUT OF A MANHOLE AND TAKE A BITE OUT OF MY OWN BARTOLI BACKSIDE.
Stefan makes the call.
YES, STEFAN, I WAS ASLEEP, BUT I WAS HAULED OUT OF MY BED TWO HOURS AGO.
APPARENTLY SOMEBODY DETONATED AN ENERGY PULSE IN THE DOWNTOWN AREA.
THE SUPERNATURALISTS DON'T WASTE ANY TIME, DO THEY?
I'M GUESSING THAT WAS YOU AT THE SATELLITE AS WELL. SURELY I DIDN'T ACCIDENTALLY ALLOW YOU TO GLIMPSE ALL THE ACCESS CODES ON MY COMPUTER SCREEN, DID I?
I DON'T KNOW WHAT YOU'RE TALKING ABOUT.
"OF COURSE NOT, STEFAN. ANYWAY THE ENERGY PULSE SEEMS TO HAVE WORKED PERFECTLY. MY SPECIAL TEAM OF SPOTTERS ARE GATHERING THE BODIES OF THE STUNNED PARASITES RIGHT NOW."
"GATHERING BODIES? WHAT FOR?"
"I REALLY CAN'T SAY MORE ON AN OPEN LINE."

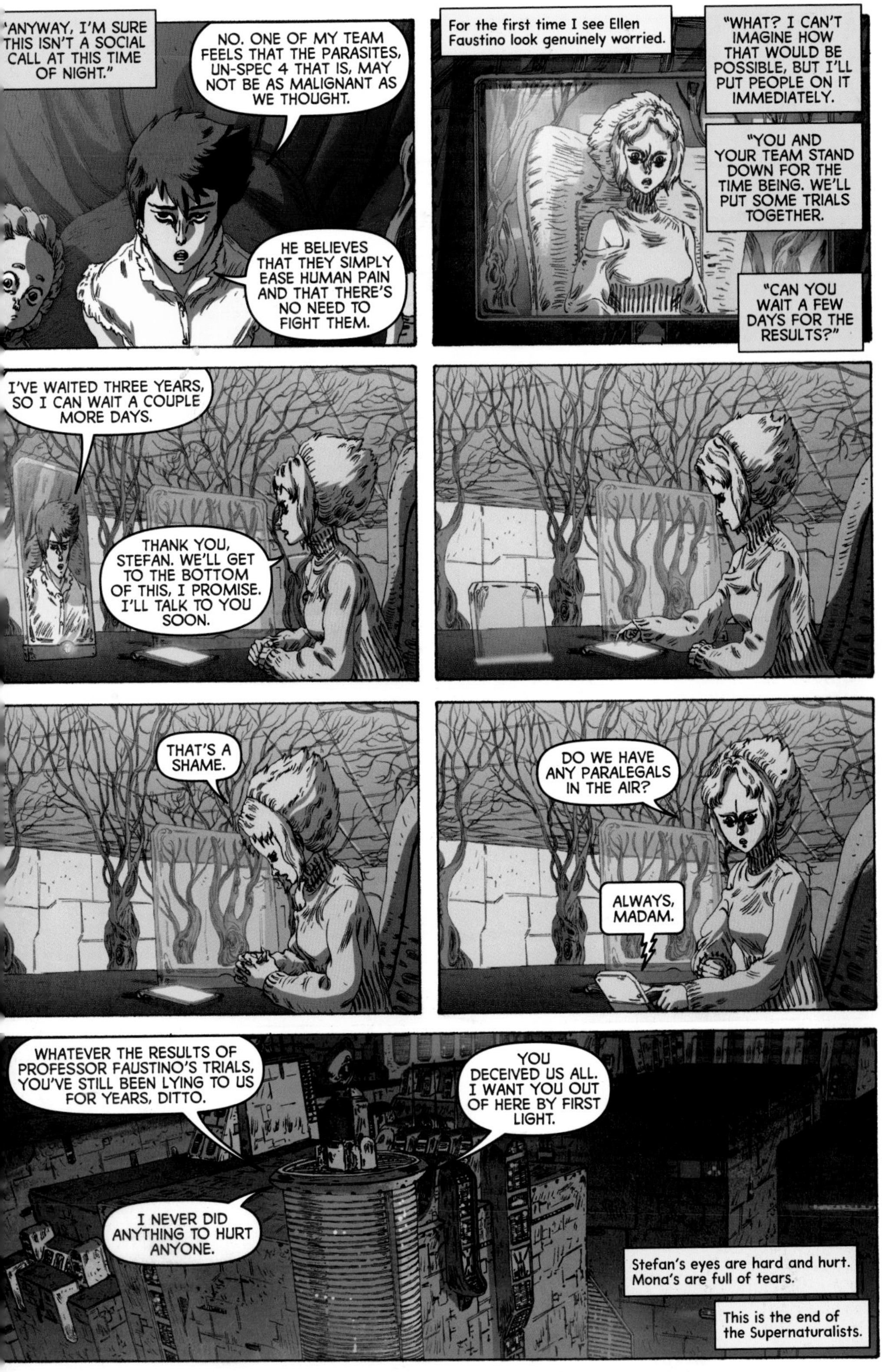
"ANYWAY, I'M SURE THIS ISN'T A SOCIAL CALL AT THIS TIME OF NIGHT."
NO. ONE OF MY TEAM FEELS THAT THE PARASITES, UN-SPEC 4 THAT IS, MAY NOT BE AS MALIGNANT AS WE THOUGHT.
HE BELIEVES THAT THEY SIMPLY EASE HUMAN PAIN AND THAT THERE'S NO NEED TO FIGHT THEM.
For the first time I see Ellen Faustino look genuinely worried.
"WHAT? I CAN'T IMAGINE HOW THAT WOULD BE POSSIBLE, BUT I'LL PUT PEOPLE ON IT IMMEDIATELY.
"YOU AND YOUR TEAM STAND DOWN FOR THE TIME BEING. WE'LL PUT SOME TRIALS TOGETHER.
"CAN YOU WAIT A FEW DAYS FOR THE RESULTS?"
I'VE WAITED THREE YEARS, SO I CAN WAIT A COUPLE MORE DAYS.
THANK YOU, STEFAN. WE'LL GET TO THE BOTTOM OF THIS, I PROMISE. I'LL TALK TO YOU SOON.
THAT'S A SHAME.
DO WE HAVE ANY PARALEGALS IN THE AIR?
ALWAYS, MADAM.
WHATEVER THE RESULTS OF PROFESSOR FAUSTINO'S TRIALS, YOU'VE STILL BEEN LYING TO US FOR YEARS, DITTO.
YOU DECEIVED US ALL. I WANT YOU OUT OF HERE BY FIRST LIGHT.
I NEVER DID ANYTHING TO HURT ANYONE.
Stefan's eyes are hard and hurt. Mona's are full of tears.
This is the end of the Supernaturalists.

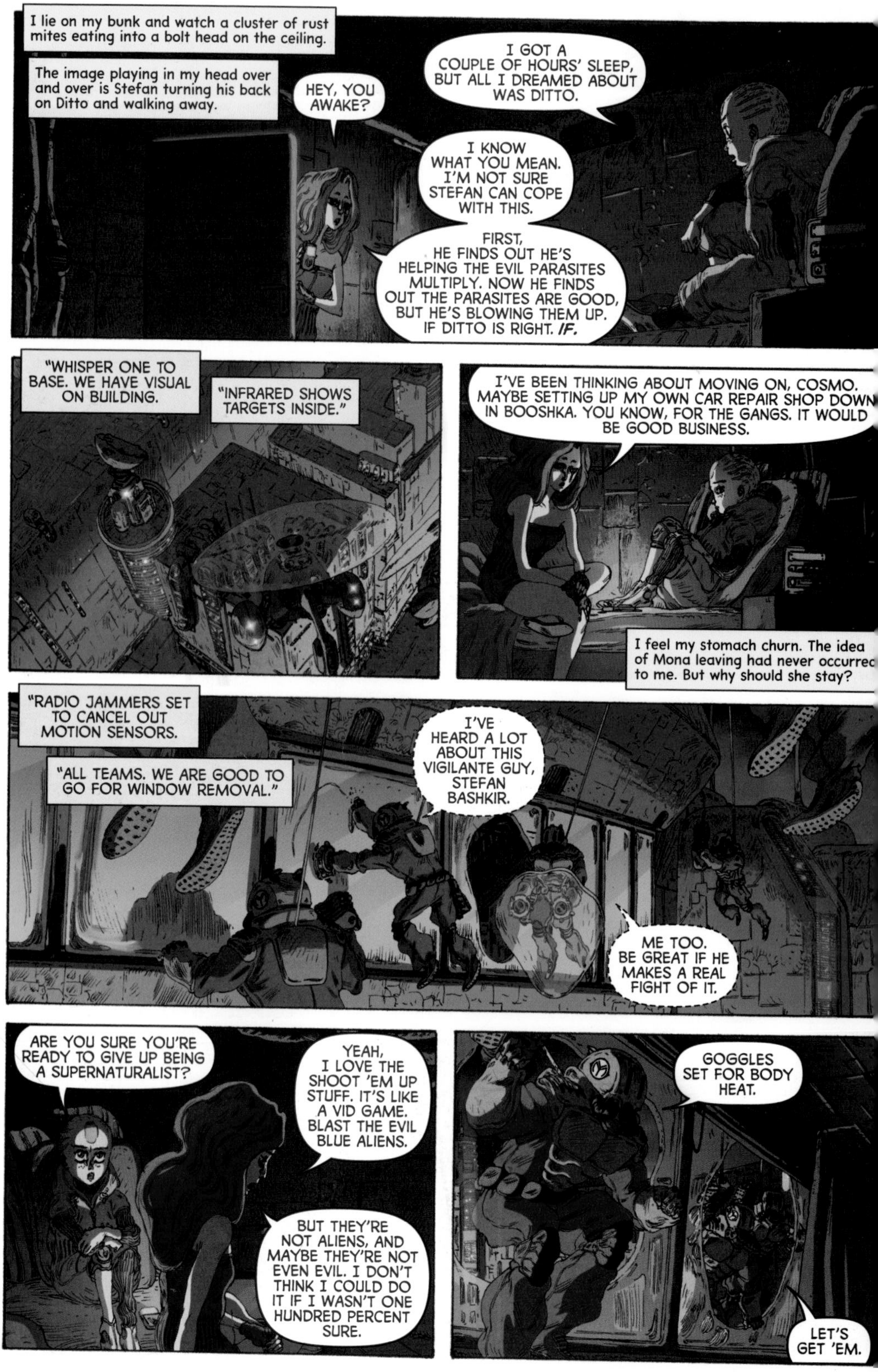
I lie on my bunk and watch a cluster of rust mites eating into a bolt head on the ceiling.
The image playing in my head over and over is Stefan turning his back on Ditto and walking away.
HEY, YOU AWAKE?
I GOT A COUPLE OF HOURS' SLEEP, BUT ALL I DREAMED ABOUT WAS DITTO.
I KNOW WHAT YOU MEAN. I'M NOT SURE STEFAN CAN COPE WITH THIS.
FIRST, HE FINDS OUT HE'S HELPING THE EVIL PARASITES MULTIPLY. NOW HE FINDS OUT THE PARASITES ARE GOOD, BUT HE'S BLOWING THEM UP. IF DITTO IS RIGHT. *IF.*
"WHISPER ONE TO BASE. WE HAVE VISUAL ON BUILDING.
"INFRARED SHOWS TARGETS INSIDE."
I'VE BEEN THINKING ABOUT MOVING ON, COSMO. MAYBE SETTING UP MY OWN CAR REPAIR SHOP DOWN IN BOOSHKA. YOU KNOW, FOR THE GANGS. IT WOULD BE GOOD BUSINESS.
I feel my stomach churn. The idea of Mona leaving had never occurred to me. But why should she stay?
"RADIO JAMMERS SET TO CANCEL OUT MOTION SENSORS.
"ALL TEAMS. WE ARE GOOD TO GO FOR WINDOW REMOVAL."
I'VE HEARD A LOT ABOUT THIS VIGILANTE GUY, STEFAN BASHKIR.
ME TOO. BE GREAT IF HE MAKES A REAL FIGHT OF IT.
ARE YOU SURE YOU'RE READY TO GIVE UP BEING A SUPERNATURALIST?
YEAH, I LOVE THE SHOOT 'EM UP STUFF. IT'S LIKE A VID GAME. BLAST THE EVIL BLUE ALIENS.
BUT THEY'RE NOT ALIENS, AND MAYBE THEY'RE NOT EVEN EVIL. I DON'T THINK I COULD DO IT IF I WASN'T ONE HUNDRED PERCENT SURE.
GOGGLES SET FOR BODY HEAT.
LET'S GET 'EM.

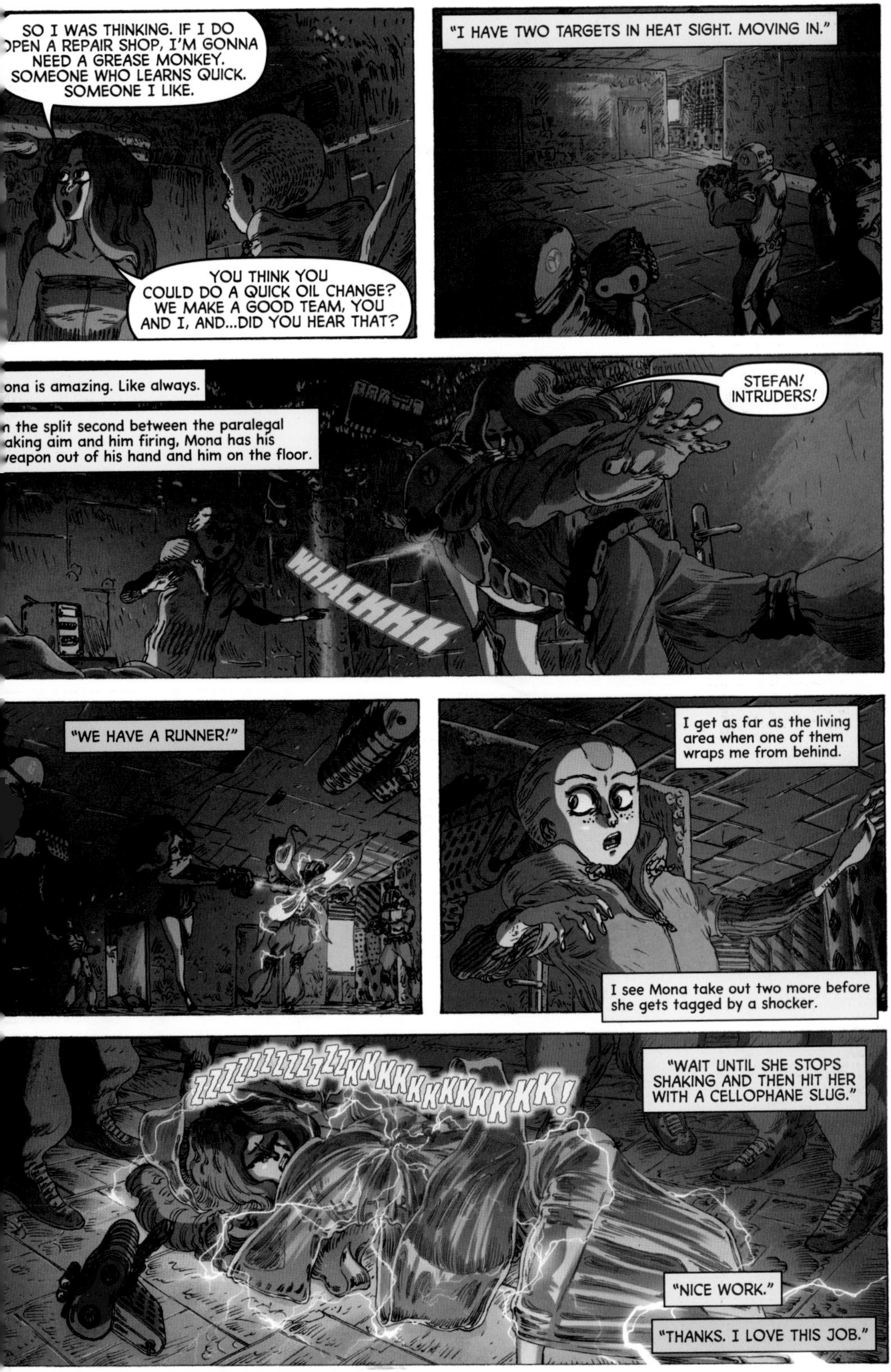

SO I WAS THINKING. IF I DO OPEN A REPAIR SHOP, I'M GONNA NEED A GREASE MONKEY. SOMEONE WHO LEARNS QUICK. SOMEONE I LIKE.
YOU THINK YOU COULD DO A QUICK OIL CHANGE? WE MAKE A GOOD TEAM, YOU AND I, AND...DID YOU HEAR THAT?
"I HAVE TWO TARGETS IN HEAT SIGHT. MOVING IN."
ona is amazing. Like always.
n the split second between the paralegal aking aim and him firing, Mona has his weapon out of his hand and him on the floor.
STEFAN! INTRUDERS!
WHACKKKK
"WE HAVE A RUNNER!"
I get as far as the living area when one of them wraps me from behind.
I see Mona take out two more before she gets tagged by a shocker.
ZZZZZZZZZZZZKKKKKKKKKKKK!
"WAIT UNTIL SHE STOPS SHAKING AND THEN HIT HER WITH A CELLOPHANE SLUG."
"NICE WORK."
"THANKS. I LOVE THIS JOB."

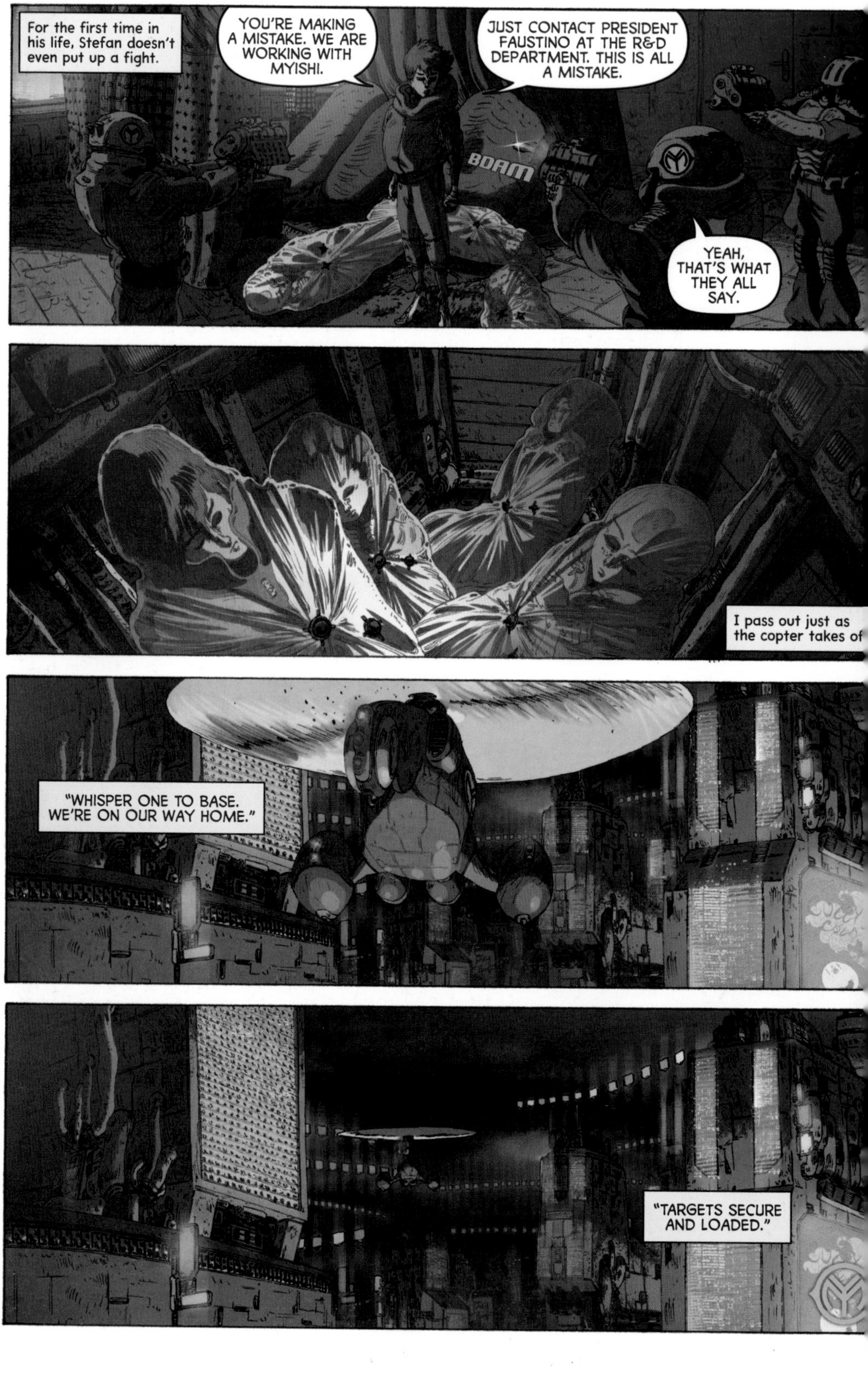
For the first time in his life, Stefan doesn't even put up a fight.
YOU'RE MAKING A MISTAKE. WE ARE WORKING WITH MYISHI.
JUST CONTACT PRESIDENT FAUSTINO AT THE R&D DEPARTMENT. THIS IS ALL A MISTAKE.
BDAM
YEAH, THAT'S WHAT THEY ALL SAY.
I pass out just as the copter takes of
"WHISPER ONE TO BASE. WE'RE ON OUR WAY HOME."
"TARGETS SECURE AND LOADED."

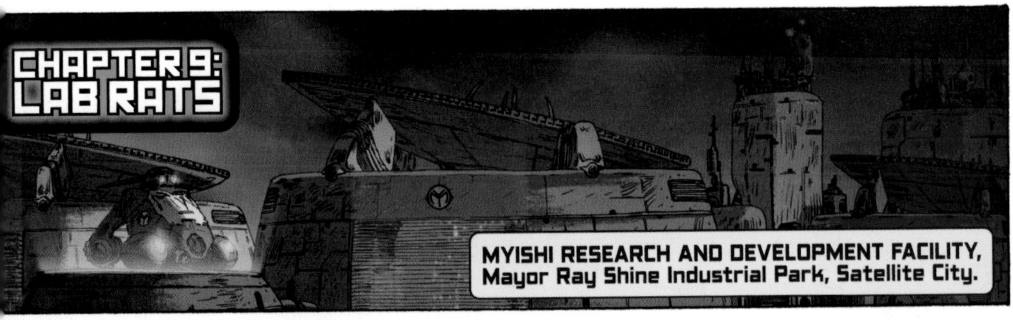
CHAPTER 9:
LAB RATS
MYISHI RESEARCH AND DEVELOPMENT FACILITY,
Mayor Ray Shine Industrial Park, Satellite City.

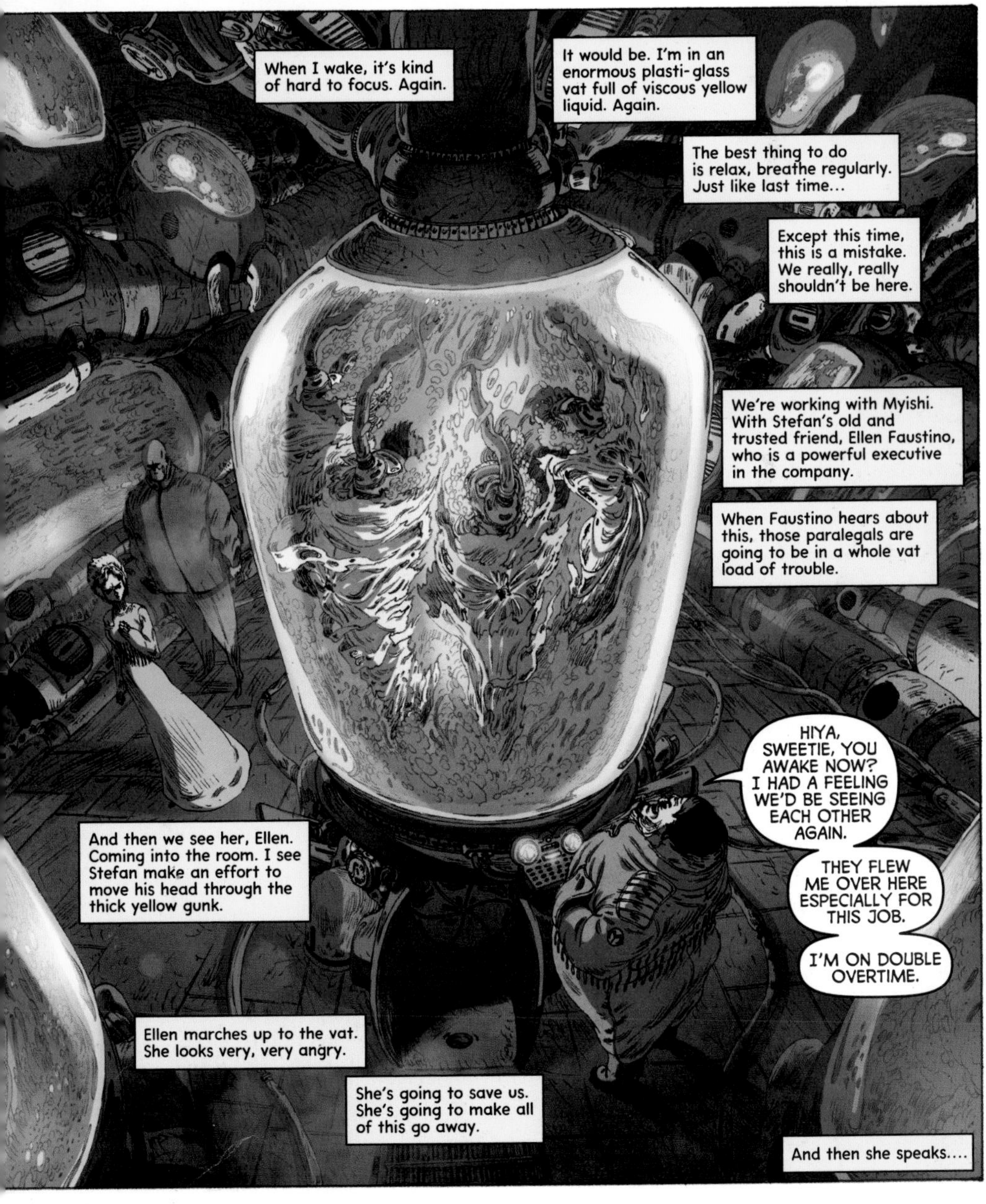
When I wake, it's kind of hard to focus. Again.
It would be. I'm in an enormous plasti-glass vat full of viscous yellow liquid. Again.
The best thing to do is relax, breathe regularly. Just like last time...
Except this time, this is a mistake. We really, really shouldn't be here.
We're working with Myishi. With Stefan's old and trusted friend, Ellen Faustino, who is a powerful executive in the company.
When Faustino hears about this, those paralegals are going to be in a whole vat load of trouble.
HIYA, SWEETIE, YOU AWAKE NOW? I HAD A FEELING WE'D BE SEEING EACH OTHER AGAIN.
THEY FLEW ME OVER HERE ESPECIALLY FOR THIS JOB.
I'M ON DOUBLE OVERTIME.
And then we see her, Ellen. Coming into the room. I see Stefan make an effort to move his head through the thick yellow gunk.
Ellen marches up to the vat. She looks very, very angry.
She's going to save us. She's going to make all of this go away.
And then she speaks....

WHAT DO YOU THINK YOU'RE DOING? THESE PEOPLE ARE NOT SUPPOSED TO BE IN HERE.

She's going to set us free.

THESE FOUR ARE SUPPOSED TO BE *DEAD*. ALL I WANTED TO SEE WAS FOUR LIFELESS BODIES SO I COULD BE SURE.

SADLY, THESE ARE CLEARLY VERY MUCH ALIVE.

What?

Inside the vat I see Faustino's words cut through Stefan's daze.

This must be a mistake.

Stefan tries to speak, but his breath barely ripples his cellophane wrap.

"SO YOU'RE AWAKE, STEFAN. DO YOU UNDERSTAND WHAT'S HAPPENING HERE?"

"THESE LAST WEEKS, YOU'VE BEEN WORKING FOR ME, DOIN[G] THINGS THAT MYISHI WOUL[D] NEVER ALLOW ME TO TRY."

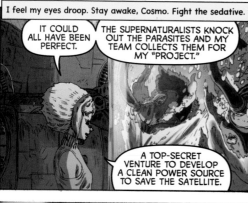

I feel my eyes droop. Stay awake, Cosmo. Fight the sedative.

IT COULD ALL HAVE BEEN PERFECT.

THE SUPERNATURALISTS KNOCK OUT THE PARASITES AND MY TEAM COLLECTS THEM FOR MY "PROJECT."

A TOP-SECRET VENTURE TO DEVELOP A CLEAN POWER SOURCE TO SAVE THE SATELLITE.

BUT SUDDENLY, AFTER ALL THESE YEARS, THE OBSESSED STEFAN BASHKIR CHANGES HIS MIND AND DOESN'T WANT TO FIGHT PARASITES ANY MORE.

NOW THE SUPERNATURALISTS ARE NO LONGER ASSETS. THEY ARE LOOSE ENDS.

AND WE KNOW WHA[T] HAPPENS TO LOOSE ENDS...THE[Y] GET CUT.

STRUGGLE ALL YOU LIKE; IN A FEW HOURS' TIME THERE WILL BE NO TRACE OF YOU OR YOUR GROUP LEFT.

THERE ARE TWO MORE THINGS I WANT YOU TO KNOW, JUST TO PUNISH YOU FOR INTERFERING WITH MY PLAN.

"FIRST, YOUR LITTLE COLLEAGUE, DITTO, IS ABSOLUTELY RIGHT. UN-SPEC 4 ARE NOT PARASITES THAT SUCK LIFE FORCE.

"WE RAN LAB TESTS YEARS AG[O] ON...AH... VOLUNTEERS, A[ND] FOUND THAT THEY DO TAKE AWAY PAIN FRO[M] PEOPLE WHO ARE SUFFERING[.]

AND YOU'RE REALLY GOING TO LOVE MY SECOND PIECE OF NEWS.

"IF YOU EVER BOTHERED TO CHECK, STEFAN, YOU MIGHT HAVE NOTICED THAT AROUND THE TIME OF YOUR ACCIDENT, SEVERAL OTHER CADETS FROM OUR STATION ALSO SUFFERED NEAR-DEATH EXPERIENCES."

"WELL DONE, THE PENNY DROPS..."

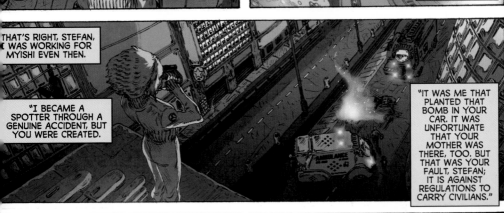

THAT'S RIGHT, STEFAN, I WAS WORKING FOR MYISHI EVEN THEN.

"I BECAME A SPOTTER THROUGH A GENUINE ACCIDENT, BUT YOU WERE CREATED.

"IT WAS ME THAT PLANTED THAT BOMB IN YOUR CAR. IT WAS UNFORTUNATE THAT YOUR MOTHER WAS THERE, TOO. BUT THAT WAS YOUR FAULT, STEFAN; IT IS AGAINST REGULATIONS TO CARRY CIVILIANS."

YOU LOOK CRUSHED.

WHAT A SHAME.

KEEP THEM IN THERE UNTIL THERE'S NOT SO MUCH AS A TOOTH LEFT.

DISSOLVE EVERYTHING.

YES, MA'AM. ALWAYS A PLEASURE.

llen Faustino walks way, leaving us all o dissolve in acid.

AND EXPECT A LITTLE BONUS IN YOUR PAY PACKET.

We are completely and utterly dead.

Of course, dissolving is really the least of our problems.

We'll all suffocate long before the acid gets us.

The others are all unconscious. I've been wrapped three times now, and I guess I'm building a resistance to the sedative in the cellophane.

"MY NAME'S MONA, BY THE WAY. NICE TO MEET YOU. WELL, WHAT'S LEFT OF YOU.

"WE PATCHED YOUR FRACTURED SKULL WITH A COUPLE OF ROBOTIX PLATES. THAT'S THE MATERIAL THEY MAKE ASSAULT TANKS FROM. DITTO SAYS YOU'LL BE ABLE HEAD-BUTT YOUR WAY THROUGH A BRICK WALL."

HEY, SWEETIE. ARE YOU TRYING TO ESCAPE? I'M AFRAID SKIN AND BONE ARE NOT GOING TO DO IT.

NOTHING SHORT OF A TANK IS GOING TO GET THROUGH THAT PLASTI-GLASS.

WHACCCKKKKKK!

"HEY YOU, STOP THAT!"

I'm the last Supernaturalist standing.

Think, Cosmo, think.

Use your head and come up with an—

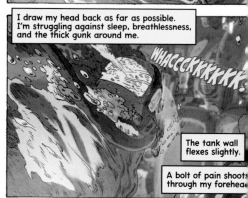

I draw my head back as far as possible. I'm struggling against sleep, breathlessness, and the thick gunk around me.

WHACCCKKKKKK

The tank wall flexes slightly.

A bolt of pain shoots through my forehea

We both see it at the same moment.

A crack.

A tiny crack.

One more. I have enoug breath for one more try

CRACKKKKK!

The crack races across the glass spreading like a silver web.

There's just enough time for the Vat Man's jaw to drop open in disbelief.

Then the tank blows...

...several thousand gallons of thick yellow acid explodes outward...

HOW DID YOU...

WHOOA HLOOP HALLOMPHHH

...and smashes into the Vat Man as hard as a truck at full speed.

We're dashed onto the tiles like unwanted fish from a catch.

My eyes finally close.

I may as well go to sleep now. Everybody else has.

DRIPP!

DRIPP!

DRIPP!

AUSTINO...

WHAT DID I TELL YOU? WHO'S THE TRAITOR NOW, EH? HER, NOT ME.

UGH! HOW DID WE GET OUT OF THE VAT ANYWAY?

I THINK THE ROOKIE SAVED US AGAIN. HE USED HIS HEAD.

WE NEED TO FIND OUT WHY ELLEN FAUSTINO IS COLLECTING PARASITES.

THAT MAY HAVE TO WAIT A MINUTE. I THINK I'M GOING TO BE SICK.

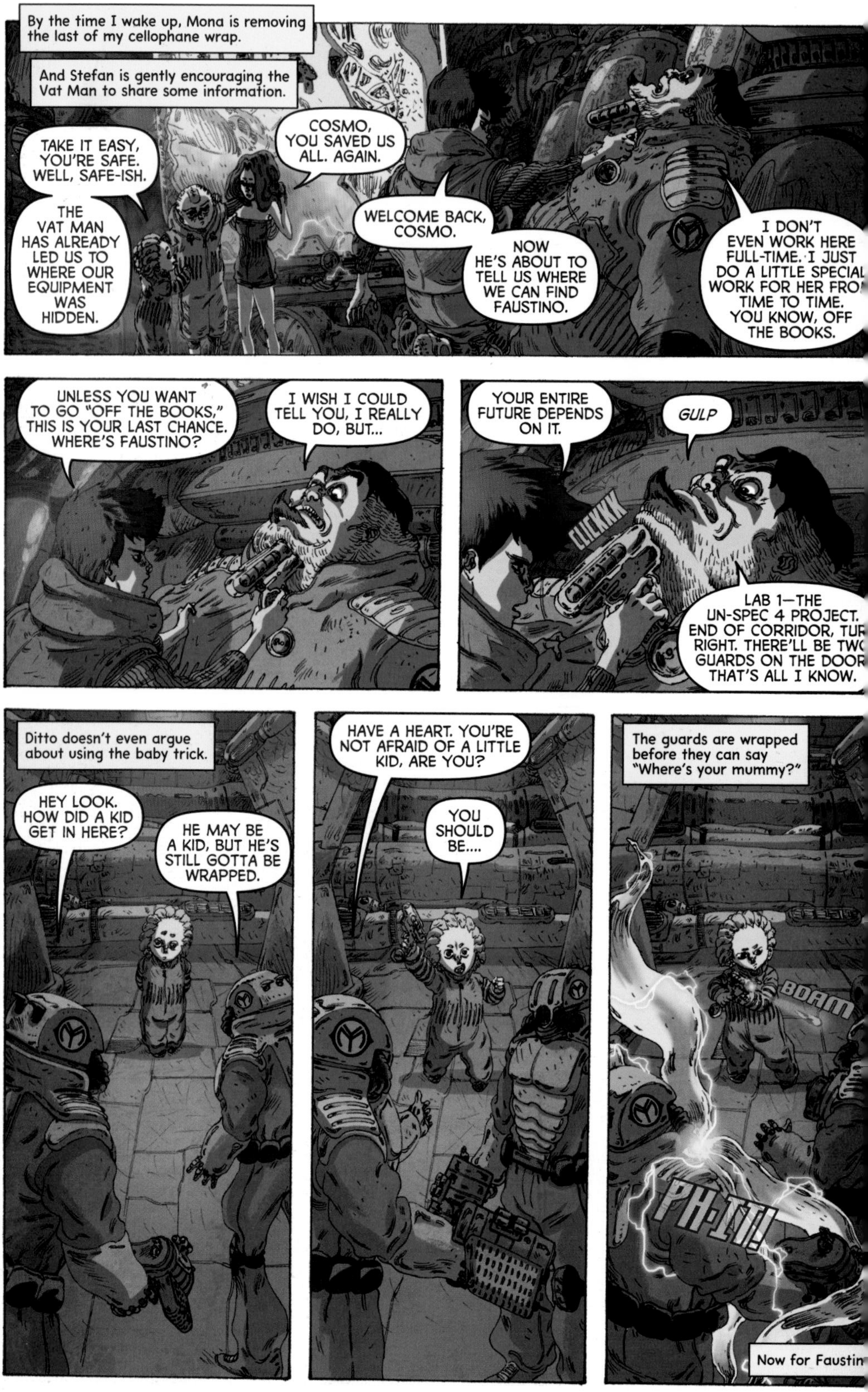
By the time I wake up, Mona is removing the last of my cellophane wrap.
And Stefan is gently encouraging the Vat Man to share some information.
TAKE IT EASY, YOU'RE SAFE. WELL, SAFE-ISH.
THE VAT MAN HAS ALREADY LED US TO WHERE OUR EQUIPMENT WAS HIDDEN.
COSMO, YOU SAVED US ALL. AGAIN.
WELCOME BACK, COSMO.
NOW HE'S ABOUT TO TELL US WHERE WE CAN FIND FAUSTINO.
I DON'T EVEN WORK HERE FULL-TIME. I JUST DO A LITTLE SPECIAL WORK FOR HER FRO TIME TO TIME. YOU KNOW, OFF THE BOOKS.
UNLESS YOU WANT TO GO "OFF THE BOOKS," THIS IS YOUR LAST CHANCE. WHERE'S FAUSTINO?
I WISH I COULD TELL YOU, I REALLY DO, BUT...
YOUR ENTIRE FUTURE DEPENDS ON IT.
GULP
CLICKKK
LAB 1—THE UN-SPEC 4 PROJECT. END OF CORRIDOR, TUR RIGHT. THERE'LL BE TWO GUARDS ON THE DOOR THAT'S ALL I KNOW.
Ditto doesn't even argue about using the baby trick.
HEY LOOK. HOW DID A KID GET IN HERE?
HE MAY BE A KID, BUT HE'S STILL GOTTA BE WRAPPED.
HAVE A HEART. YOU'RE NOT AFRAID OF A LITTLE KID, ARE YOU?
YOU SHOULD BE....
The guards are wrapped before they can say "Where's your mummy?"
BDAM
PH-IT!
Now for Faustin

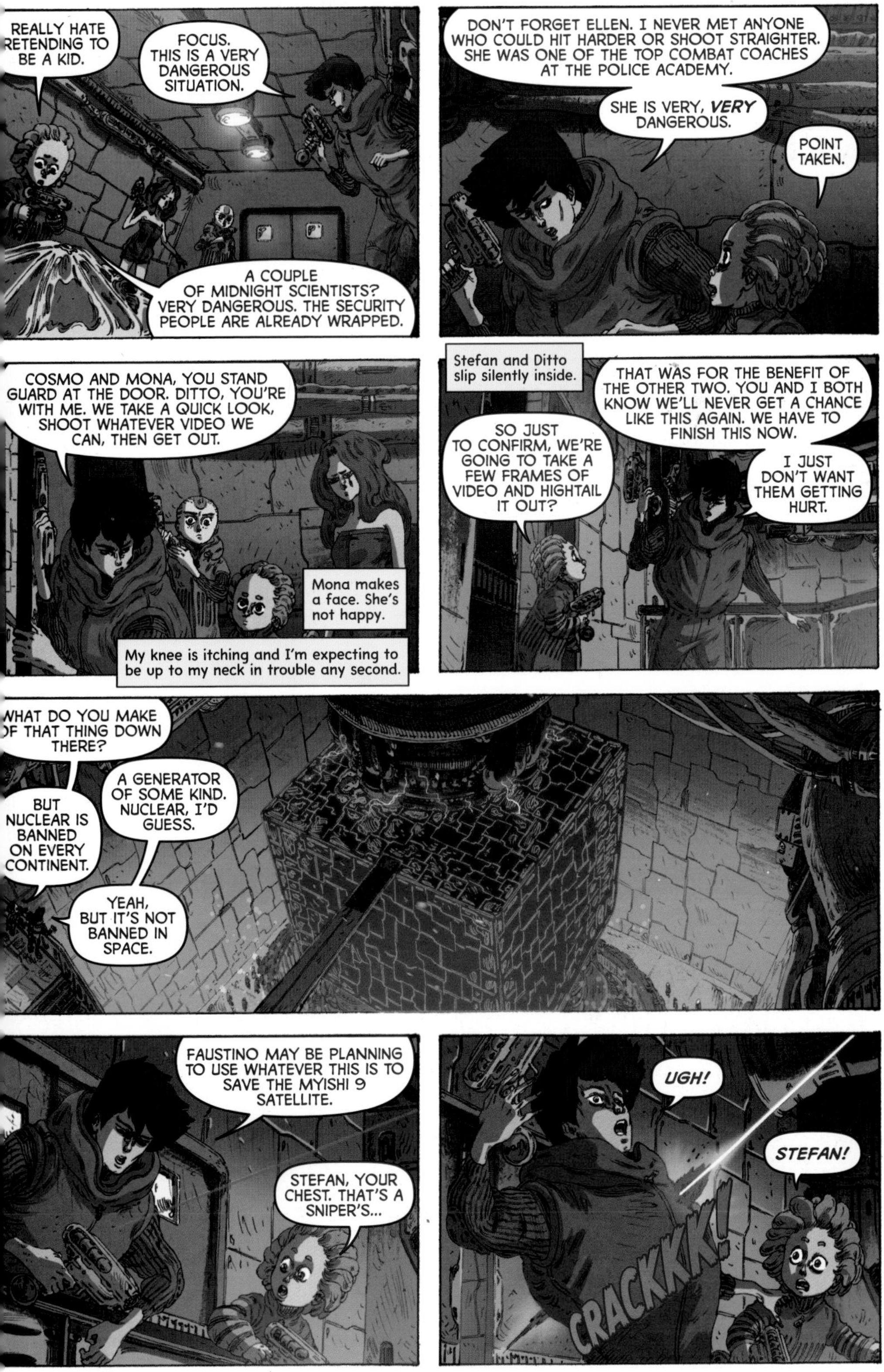
REALLY HATE RETENDING TO BE A KID.
FOCUS. THIS IS A VERY DANGEROUS SITUATION.
A COUPLE OF MIDNIGHT SCIENTISTS? VERY DANGEROUS. THE SECURITY PEOPLE ARE ALREADY WRAPPED.
DON'T FORGET ELLEN. I NEVER MET ANYONE WHO COULD HIT HARDER OR SHOOT STRAIGHTER. SHE WAS ONE OF THE TOP COMBAT COACHES AT THE POLICE ACADEMY.
SHE IS VERY, *VERY* DANGEROUS.
POINT TAKEN.
COSMO AND MONA, YOU STAND GUARD AT THE DOOR. DITTO, YOU'RE WITH ME. WE TAKE A QUICK LOOK, SHOOT WHATEVER VIDEO WE CAN, THEN GET OUT.
Mona makes a face. She's not happy.
My knee is itching and I'm expecting to be up to my neck in trouble any second.
Stefan and Ditto slip silently inside.
SO JUST TO CONFIRM, WE'RE GOING TO TAKE A FEW FRAMES OF VIDEO AND HIGHTAIL IT OUT?
THAT WAS FOR THE BENEFIT OF THE OTHER TWO. YOU AND I BOTH KNOW WE'LL NEVER GET A CHANCE LIKE THIS AGAIN. WE HAVE TO FINISH THIS NOW.
I JUST DON'T WANT THEM GETTING HURT.
WHAT DO YOU MAKE OF THAT THING DOWN THERE?
A GENERATOR OF SOME KIND. NUCLEAR, I'D GUESS.
BUT NUCLEAR IS BANNED ON EVERY CONTINENT.
YEAH, BUT IT'S NOT BANNED IN SPACE.
FAUSTINO MAY BE PLANNING TO USE WHATEVER THIS IS TO SAVE THE MYISHI 9 SATELLITE.
STEFAN, YOUR CHEST. THAT'S A SNIPER'S...
UGH!
STEFAN!
CRACKKK!

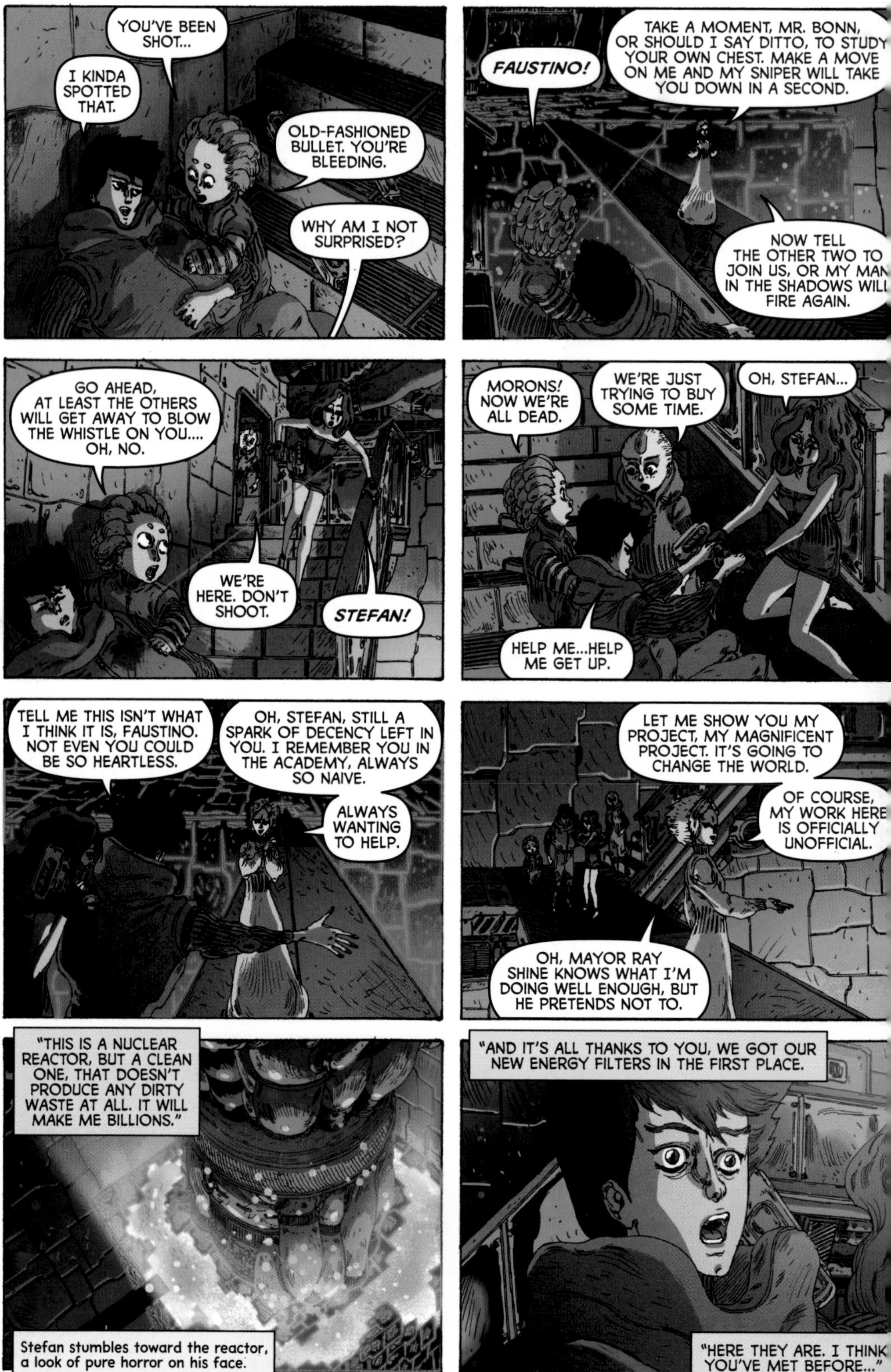
YOU'VE BEEN SHOT...
I KINDA SPOTTED THAT.
OLD-FASHIONED BULLET. YOU'RE BLEEDING.
WHY AM I NOT SURPRISED?
FAUSTINO!
TAKE A MOMENT, MR. BONN, OR SHOULD I SAY DITTO, TO STUDY YOUR OWN CHEST. MAKE A MOVE ON ME AND MY SNIPER WILL TAKE YOU DOWN IN A SECOND.
NOW TELL THE OTHER TWO TO JOIN US, OR MY MAN IN THE SHADOWS WILL FIRE AGAIN.
GO AHEAD, AT LEAST THE OTHERS WILL GET AWAY TO BLOW THE WHISTLE ON YOU.... OH, NO.
WE'RE HERE. DON'T SHOOT.
STEFAN!
MORONS! NOW WE'RE ALL DEAD.
WE'RE JUST TRYING TO BUY SOME TIME.
OH, STEFAN...
HELP ME...HELP ME GET UP.
TELL ME THIS ISN'T WHAT I THINK IT IS, FAUSTINO. NOT EVEN YOU COULD BE SO HEARTLESS.
OH, STEFAN, STILL A SPARK OF DECENCY LEFT IN YOU. I REMEMBER YOU IN THE ACADEMY, ALWAYS SO NAIVE.
ALWAYS WANTING TO HELP.
LET ME SHOW YOU MY PROJECT, MY MAGNIFICENT PROJECT. IT'S GOING TO CHANGE THE WORLD.
OF COURSE, MY WORK HERE IS OFFICIALLY UNOFFICIAL.
OH, MAYOR RAY SHINE KNOWS WHAT I'M DOING WELL ENOUGH, BUT HE PRETENDS NOT TO.
"THIS IS A NUCLEAR REACTOR, BUT A CLEAN ONE, THAT DOESN'T PRODUCE ANY DIRTY WASTE AT ALL. IT WILL MAKE ME BILLIONS."
Stefan stumbles toward the reactor, a look of pure horror on his face.
"AND IT'S ALL THANKS TO YOU, WE GOT OUR NEW ENERGY FILTERS IN THE FIRST PLACE.
"HERE THEY ARE. I THINK YOU'VE MET BEFORE..."

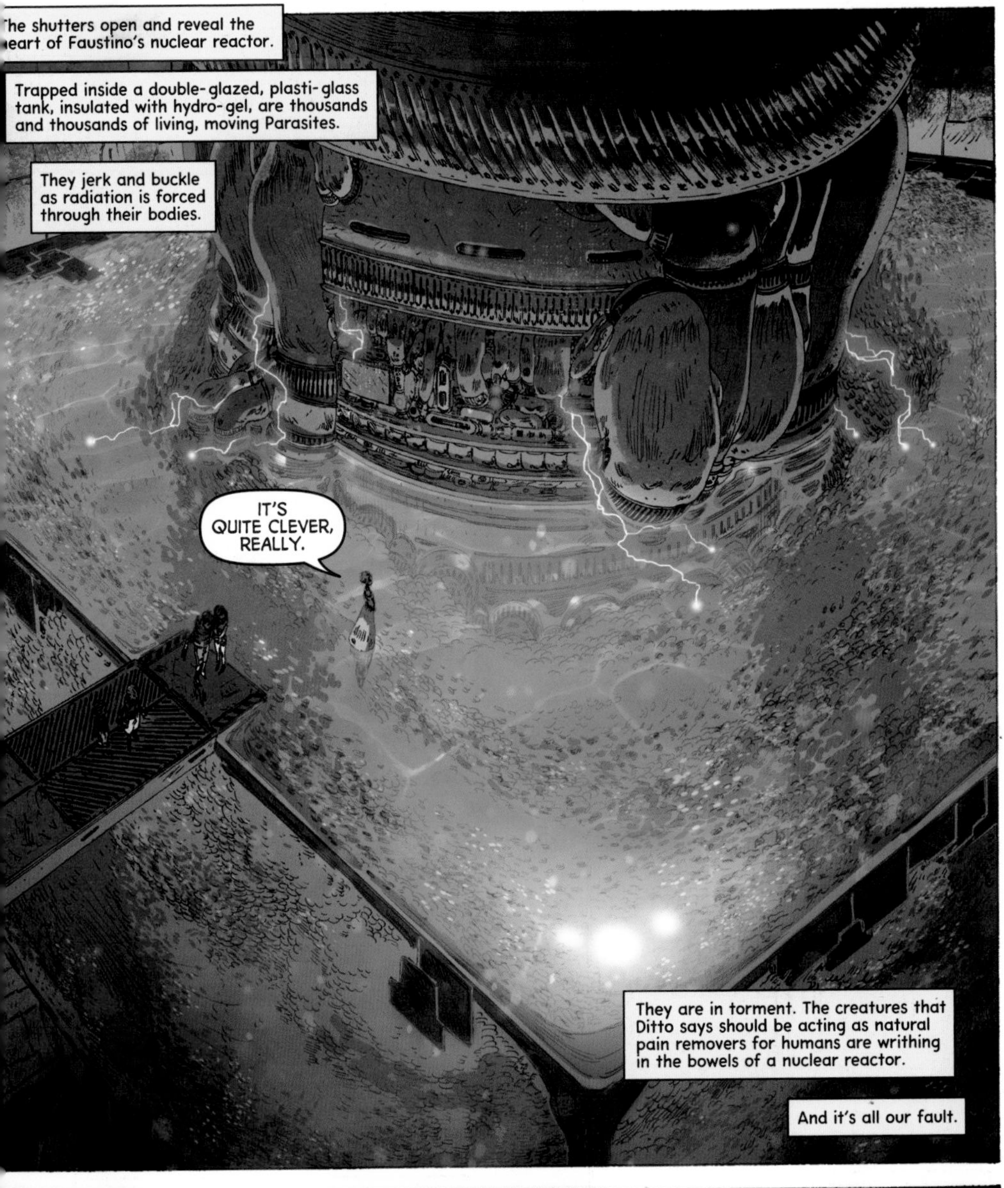
The shutters open and reveal the heart of Faustino's nuclear reactor.
Trapped inside a double-glazed, plasti-glass tank, insulated with hydro-gel, are thousands and thousands of living, moving Parasites.
They jerk and buckle as radiation is forced through their bodies.
IT'S QUITE CLEVER, REALLY.
They are in torment. The creatures that Ditto says should be acting as natural pain removers for humans are writhing in the bowels of a nuclear reactor.
And it's all our fault.

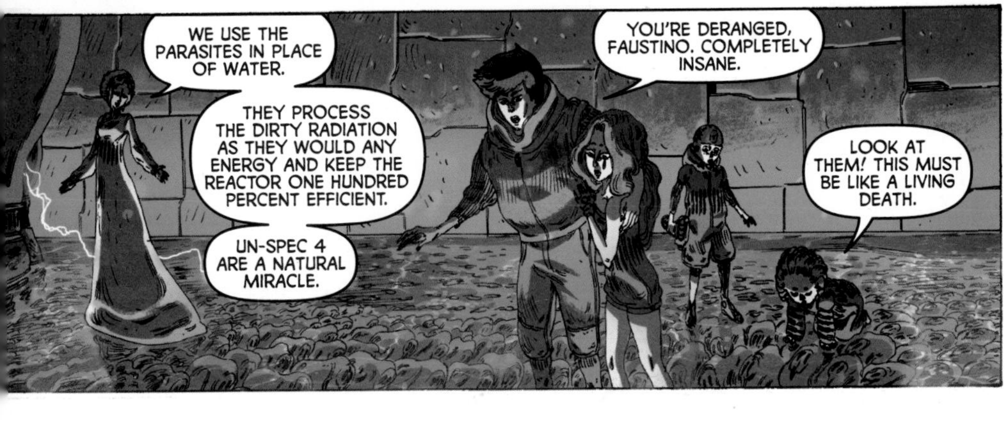
WE USE THE PARASITES IN PLACE OF WATER.
THEY PROCESS THE DIRTY RADIATION AS THEY WOULD ANY ENERGY AND KEEP THE REACTOR ONE HUNDRED PERCENT EFFICIENT.
UN-SPEC 4 ARE A NATURAL MIRACLE.
YOU'RE DERANGED, FAUSTINO. COMPLETELY INSANE.
LOOK AT THEM! THIS MUST BE LIKE A LIVING DEATH.

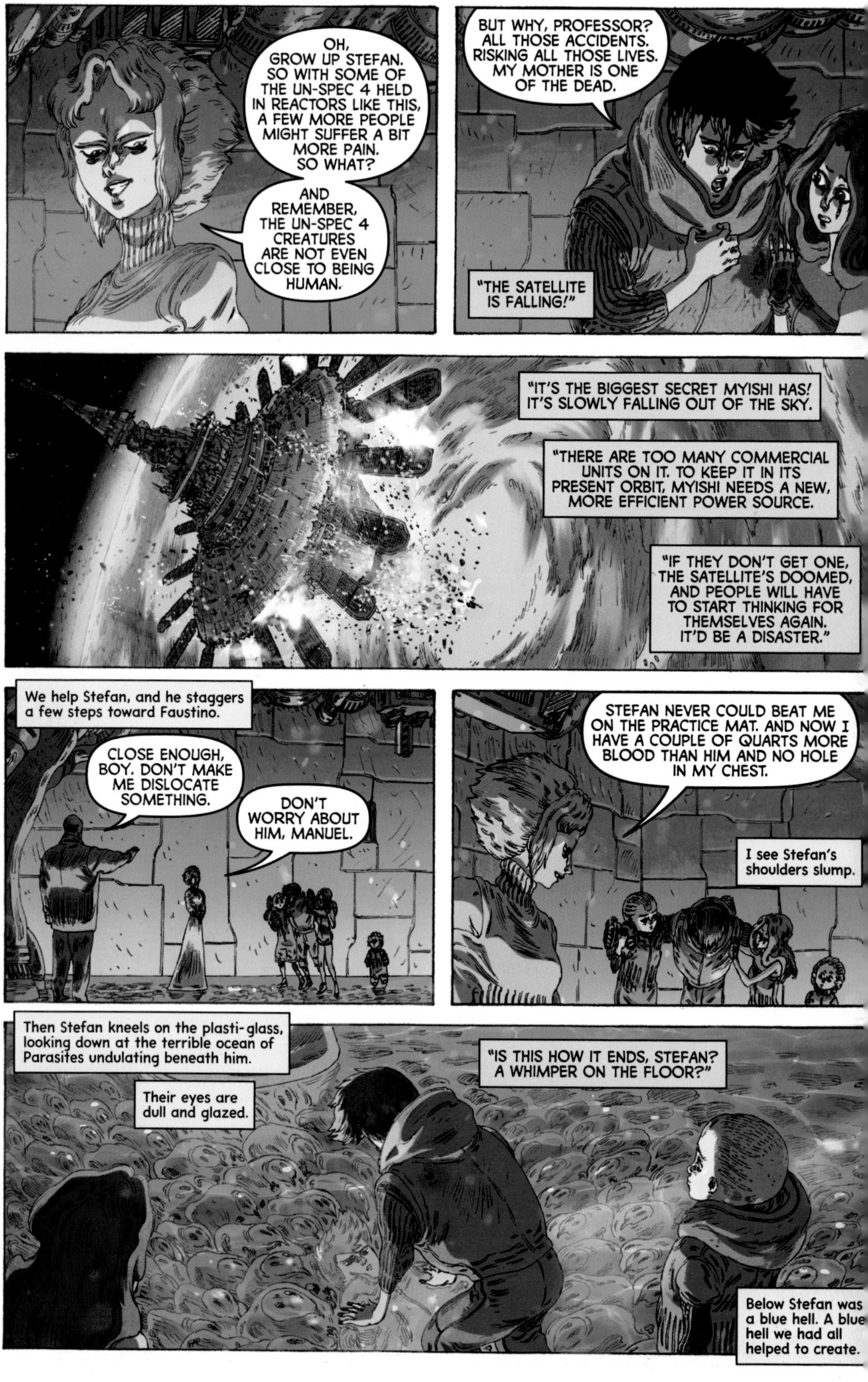
OH, GROW UP STEFAN. SO WITH SOME OF THE UN-SPEC 4 HELD IN REACTORS LIKE THIS, A FEW MORE PEOPLE MIGHT SUFFER A BIT MORE PAIN. SO WHAT?
AND REMEMBER, THE UN-SPEC 4 CREATURES ARE NOT EVEN CLOSE TO BEING HUMAN.
BUT WHY, PROFESSOR? ALL THOSE ACCIDENTS. RISKING ALL THOSE LIVES. MY MOTHER IS ONE OF THE DEAD.
"THE SATELLITE IS FALLING!"
"IT'S THE BIGGEST SECRET MYISHI HAS! IT'S SLOWLY FALLING OUT OF THE SKY.
"THERE ARE TOO MANY COMMERCIAL UNITS ON IT. TO KEEP IT IN ITS PRESENT ORBIT, MYISHI NEEDS A NEW, MORE EFFICIENT POWER SOURCE.
"IF THEY DON'T GET ONE, THE SATELLITE'S DOOMED, AND PEOPLE WILL HAVE TO START THINKING FOR THEMSELVES AGAIN. IT'D BE A DISASTER."
We help Stefan, and he staggers a few steps toward Faustino.
CLOSE ENOUGH, BOY. DON'T MAKE ME DISLOCATE SOMETHING.
DON'T WORRY ABOUT HIM, MANUEL.
STEFAN NEVER COULD BEAT ME ON THE PRACTICE MAT. AND NOW I HAVE A COUPLE OF QUARTS MORE BLOOD THAN HIM AND NO HOLE IN MY CHEST.
I see Stefan's shoulders slump.
Then Stefan kneels on the plasti-glass, looking down at the terrible ocean of Parasites undulating beneath him.
"IS THIS HOW IT ENDS, STEFAN? A WHIMPER ON THE FLOOR?"
Their eyes are dull and glazed.
Below Stefan was a blue hell. A blue hell we had all helped to create.

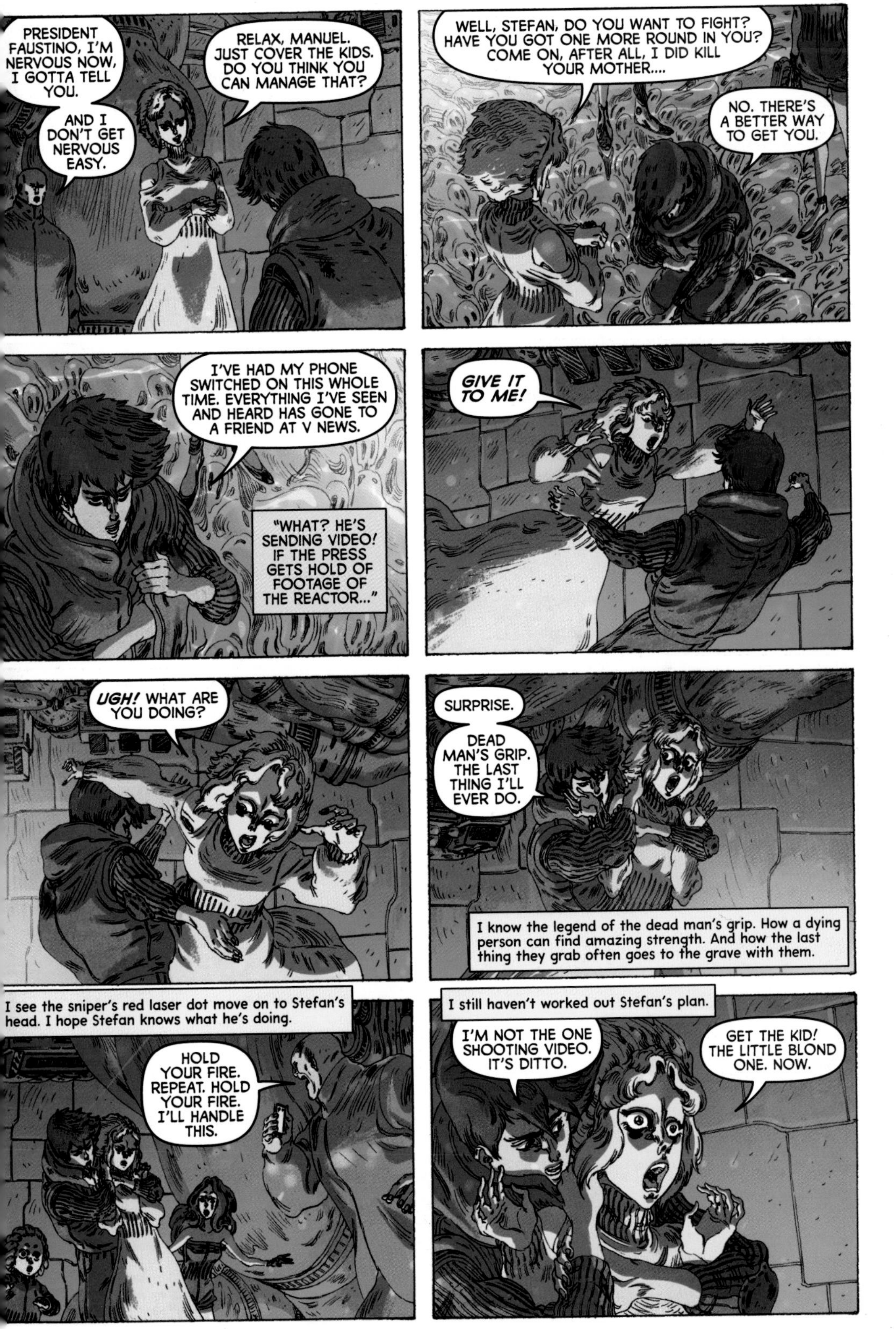
PRESIDENT FAUSTINO, I'M NERVOUS NOW, I GOTTA TELL YOU.
AND I DON'T GET NERVOUS EASY.
RELAX, MANUEL. JUST COVER THE KIDS. DO YOU THINK YOU CAN MANAGE THAT?
WELL, STEFAN, DO YOU WANT TO FIGHT? HAVE YOU GOT ONE MORE ROUND IN YOU? COME ON, AFTER ALL, I DID KILL YOUR MOTHER....
NO. THERE'S A BETTER WAY TO GET YOU.
I'VE HAD MY PHONE SWITCHED ON THIS WHOLE TIME. EVERYTHING I'VE SEEN AND HEARD HAS GONE TO A FRIEND AT V NEWS.
"WHAT? HE'S SENDING VIDEO! IF THE PRESS GETS HOLD OF FOOTAGE OF THE REACTOR..."
GIVE IT TO ME!
UGH! WHAT ARE YOU DOING?
SURPRISE.
DEAD MAN'S GRIP. THE LAST THING I'LL EVER DO.
I know the legend of the dead man's grip. How a dying person can find amazing strength. And how the last thing they grab often goes to the grave with them.
I see the sniper's red laser dot move on to Stefan's head. I hope Stefan knows what he's doing.
HOLD YOUR FIRE. REPEAT. HOLD YOUR FIRE. I'LL HANDLE THIS.
I still haven't worked out Stefan's plan.
I'M NOT THE ONE SHOOTING VIDEO. IT'S DITTO.
GET THE KID! THE LITTLE BLOND ONE. NOW.

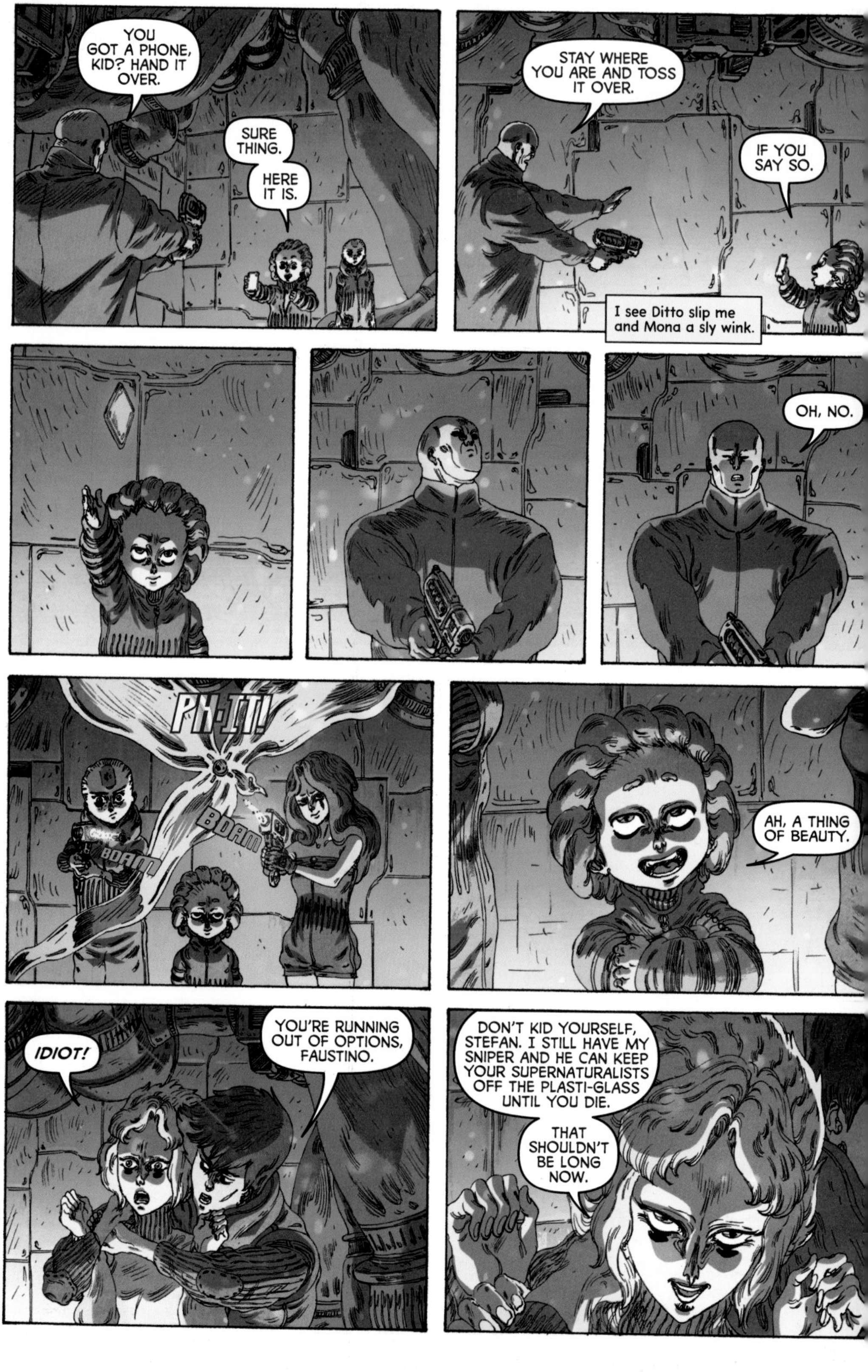
YOU GOT A PHONE, KID? HAND IT OVER.
SURE THING.
HERE IT IS.
STAY WHERE YOU ARE AND TOSS IT OVER.
IF YOU SAY SO.
I see Ditto slip me and Mona a sly wink.
OH, NO.
PH-IT!
BDAM
BDAM
AH, A THING OF BEAUTY.
IDIOT!
YOU'RE RUNNING OUT OF OPTIONS, FAUSTINO.
DON'T KID YOURSELF, STEFAN. I STILL HAVE MY SNIPER AND HE CAN KEEP YOUR SUPERNATURALISTS OFF THE PLASTI-GLASS UNTIL YOU DIE.
THAT SHOULDN'T BE LONG NOW.

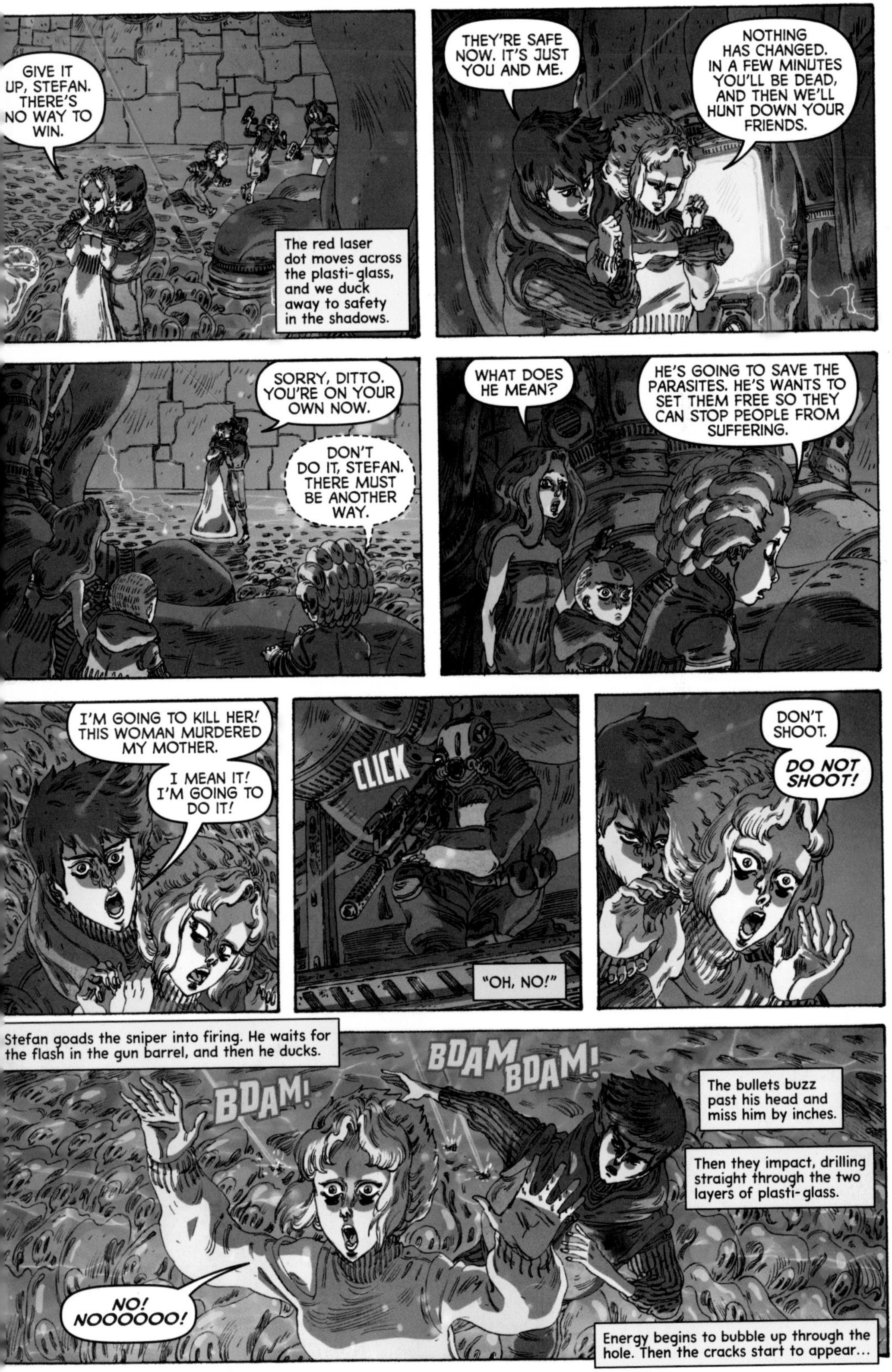
GIVE IT UP, STEFAN. THERE'S NO WAY TO WIN.
The red laser dot moves across the plasti-glass, and we duck away to safety in the shadows.
THEY'RE SAFE NOW. IT'S JUST YOU AND ME.
NOTHING HAS CHANGED. IN A FEW MINUTES YOU'LL BE DEAD, AND THEN WE'LL HUNT DOWN YOUR FRIENDS.
SORRY, DITTO. YOU'RE ON YOUR OWN NOW.
DON'T DO IT, STEFAN. THERE MUST BE ANOTHER WAY.
WHAT DOES HE MEAN?
HE'S GOING TO SAVE THE PARASITES. HE'S WANTS TO SET THEM FREE SO THEY CAN STOP PEOPLE FROM SUFFERING.
I'M GOING TO KILL HER! THIS WOMAN MURDERED MY MOTHER.
I MEAN IT! I'M GOING TO DO IT!
CLICK
"OH, NO!"
DON'T SHOOT.
DO NOT SHOOT!
Stefan goads the sniper into firing. He waits for the flash in the gun barrel, and then he ducks.
BDAM BDAM!
BDAM!
The bullets buzz past his head and miss him by inches.
Then they impact, drilling straight through the two layers of plasti-glass.
NO! NOOOOOO!
Energy begins to bubble up through the hole. Then the cracks start to appear...

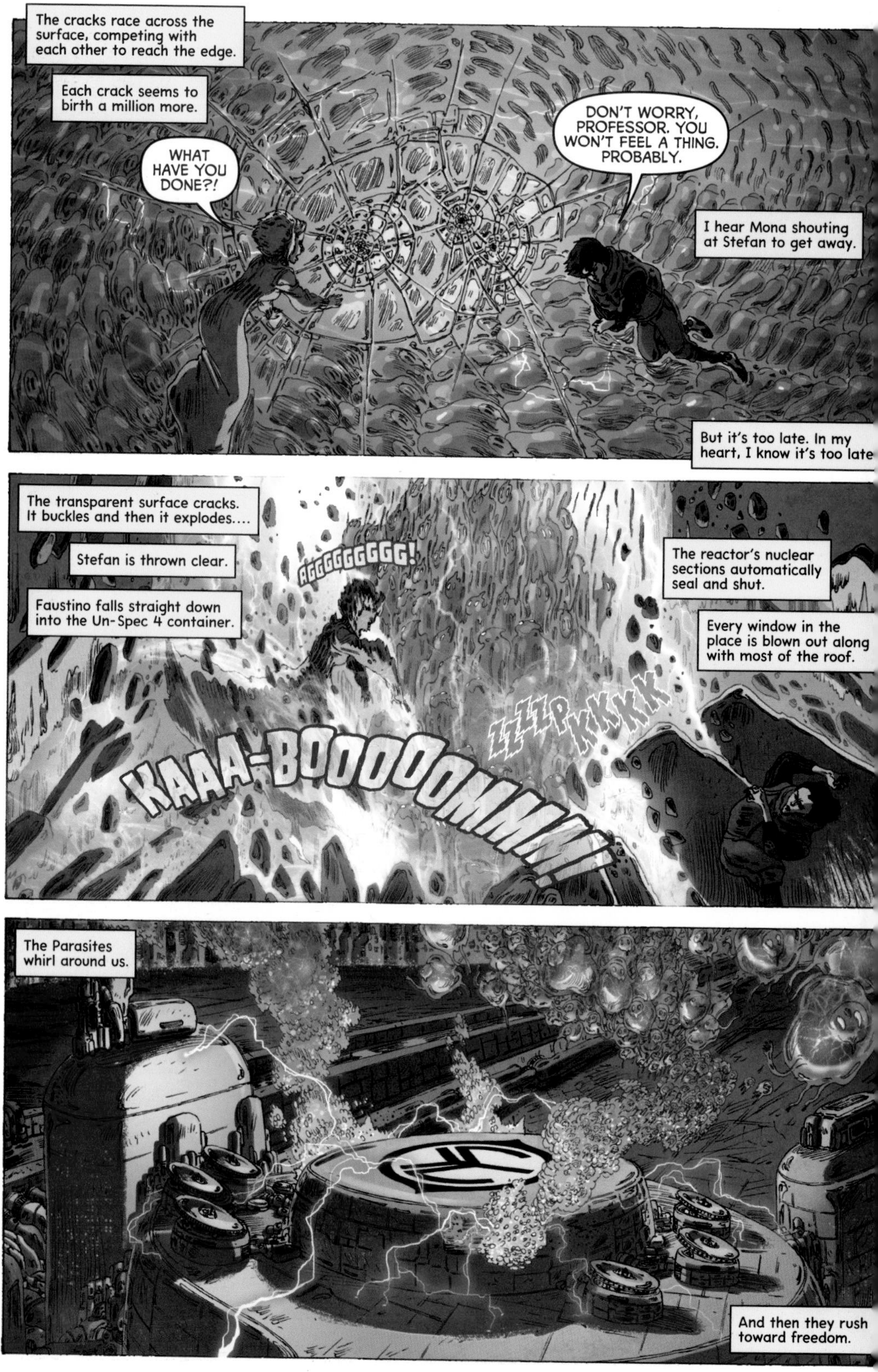
The cracks race across the surface, competing with each other to reach the edge.
Each crack seems to birth a million more.
WHAT HAVE YOU DONE?!
DON'T WORRY, PROFESSOR. YOU WON'T FEEL A THING. PROBABLY.
I hear Mona shouting at Stefan to get away.
But it's too late. In my heart, I know it's too late
The transparent surface cracks. It buckles and then it explodes....
Stefan is thrown clear.
Faustino falls straight down into the Un-Spec 4 container.
AGGGGGGGGG!
The reactor's nuclear sections automatically seal and shut.
Every window in the place is blown out along with most of the roof.
ZZZZP KKKKK
KAAA-BOOOOOOMMMM!!
The Parasites whirl around us.
And then they rush toward freedom.

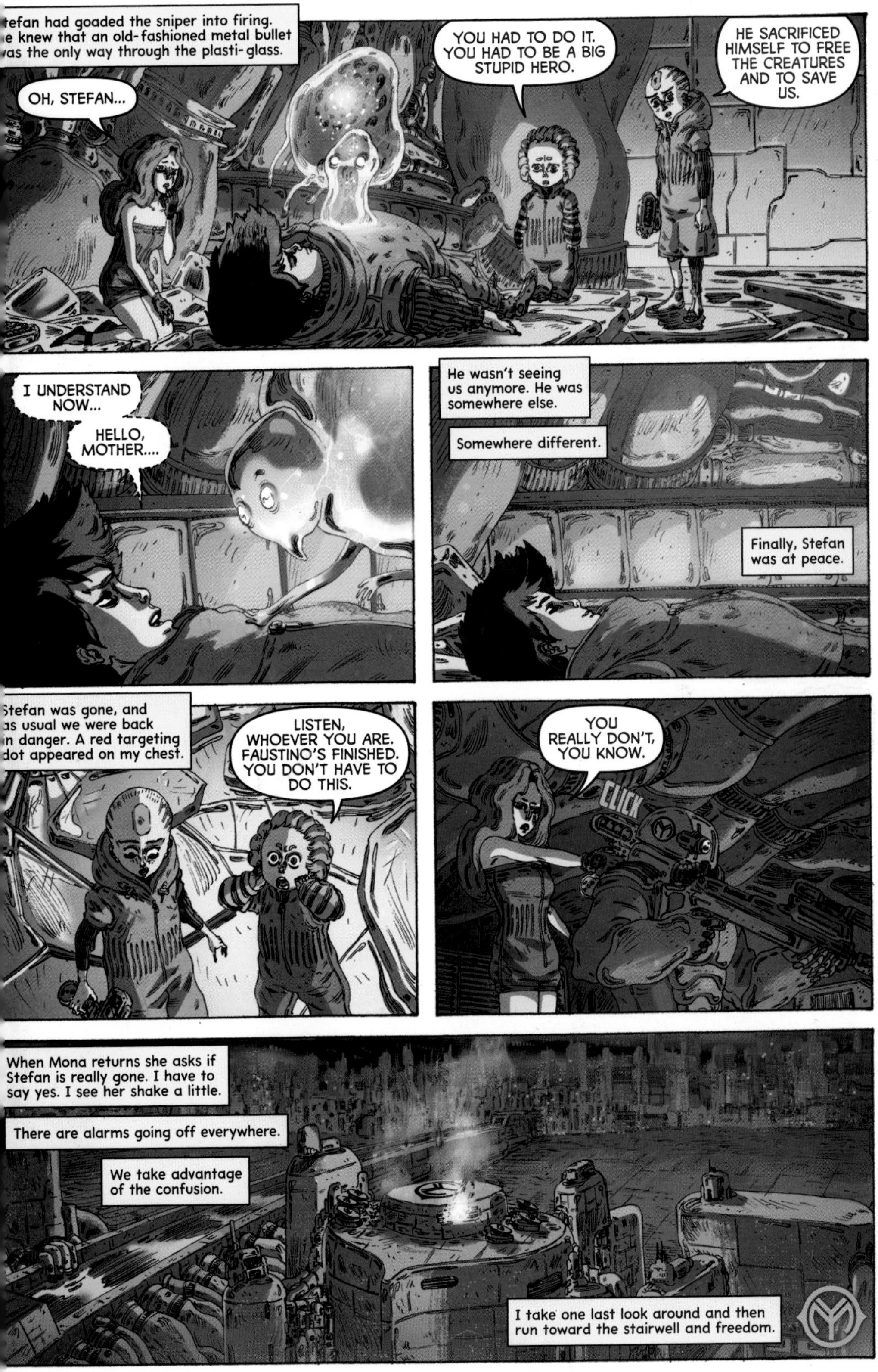
tefan had goaded the sniper into firing.
e knew that an old-fashioned metal bullet
as the only way through the plasti-glass.
OH, STEFAN...
YOU HAD TO DO IT. YOU HAD TO BE A BIG STUPID HERO.
HE SACRIFICED HIMSELF TO FREE THE CREATURES AND TO SAVE US.
I UNDERSTAND NOW...
HELLO, MOTHER....
He wasn't seeing us anymore. He was somewhere else.
Somewhere different.
Finally, Stefan was at peace.
tefan was gone, and
as usual we were back
n danger. A red targeting
dot appeared on my chest.
LISTEN, WHOEVER YOU ARE. FAUSTINO'S FINISHED. YOU DON'T HAVE TO DO THIS.
YOU REALLY DON'T, YOU KNOW.
CLICK
When Mona returns she asks if Stefan is really gone. I have to say yes. I see her shake a little.
There are alarms going off everywhere.
We take advantage of the confusion.
I take one last look around and then run toward the stairwell and freedom.

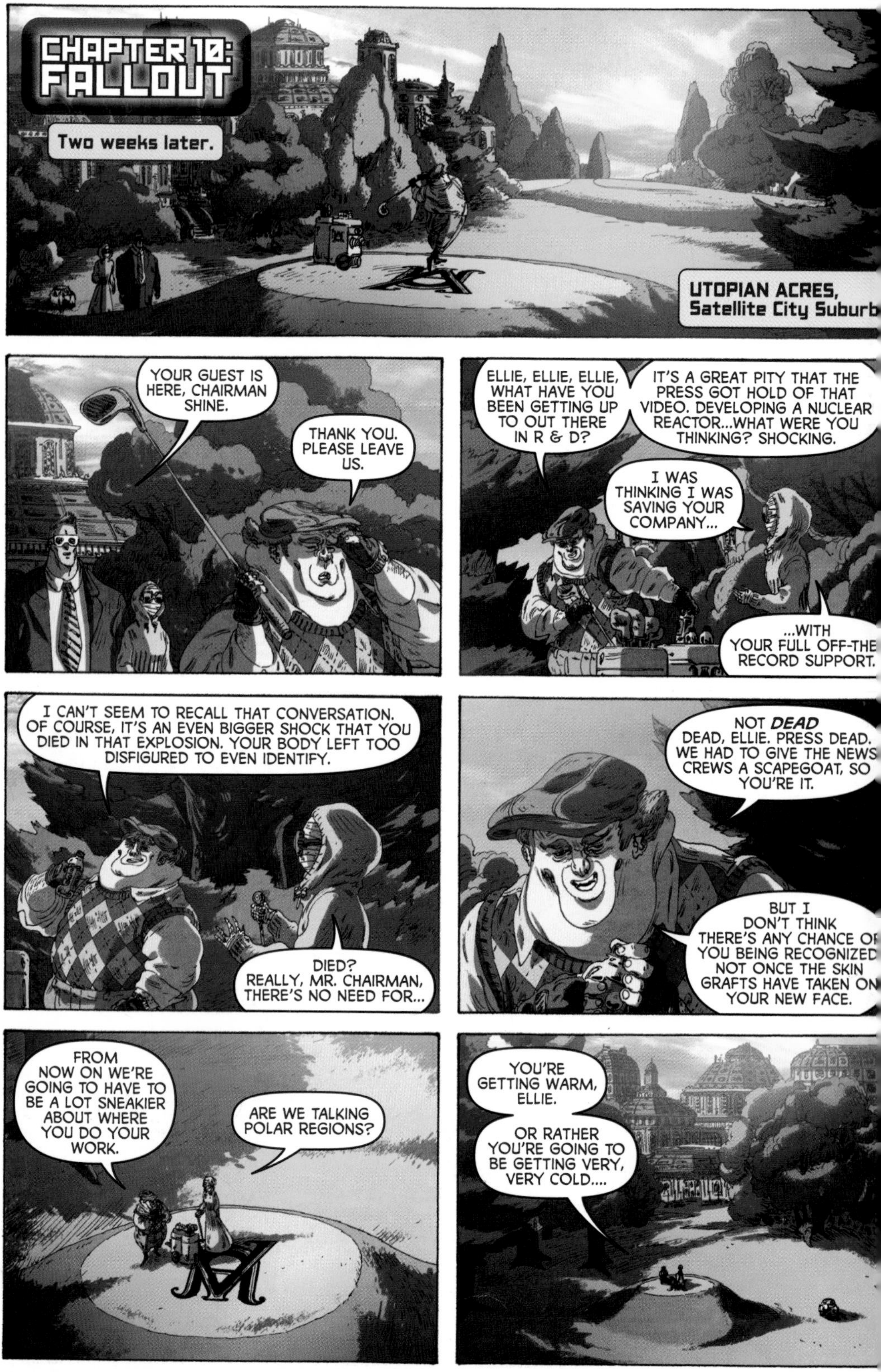
CHAPTER 10: FALLOUT
Two weeks later.
UTOPIAN ACRES, Satellite City Suburb
YOUR GUEST IS HERE, CHAIRMAN SHINE.
THANK YOU. PLEASE LEAVE US.
ELLIE, ELLIE, ELLIE, WHAT HAVE YOU BEEN GETTING UP TO OUT THERE IN R & D?
IT'S A GREAT PITY THAT THE PRESS GOT HOLD OF THAT VIDEO. DEVELOPING A NUCLEAR REACTOR...WHAT WERE YOU THINKING? SHOCKING.
I WAS THINKING I WAS SAVING YOUR COMPANY...
...WITH YOUR FULL OFF-THE RECORD SUPPORT.
I CAN'T SEEM TO RECALL THAT CONVERSATION. OF COURSE, IT'S AN EVEN BIGGER SHOCK THAT YOU DIED IN THAT EXPLOSION. YOUR BODY LEFT TOO DISFIGURED TO EVEN IDENTIFY.
DIED? REALLY, MR. CHAIRMAN, THERE'S NO NEED FOR...
NOT *DEAD* DEAD, ELLIE. PRESS DEAD. WE HAD TO GIVE THE NEWS CREWS A SCAPEGOAT, SO YOU'RE IT.
BUT I DON'T THINK THERE'S ANY CHANCE OF YOU BEING RECOGNIZED NOT ONCE THE SKIN GRAFTS HAVE TAKEN ON YOUR NEW FACE.
FROM NOW ON WE'RE GOING TO HAVE TO BE A LOT SNEAKIER ABOUT WHERE YOU DO YOUR WORK.
ARE WE TALKING POLAR REGIONS?
YOU'RE GETTING WARM, ELLIE.
OR RATHER YOU'RE GOING TO BE GETTING VERY, VERY COLD....

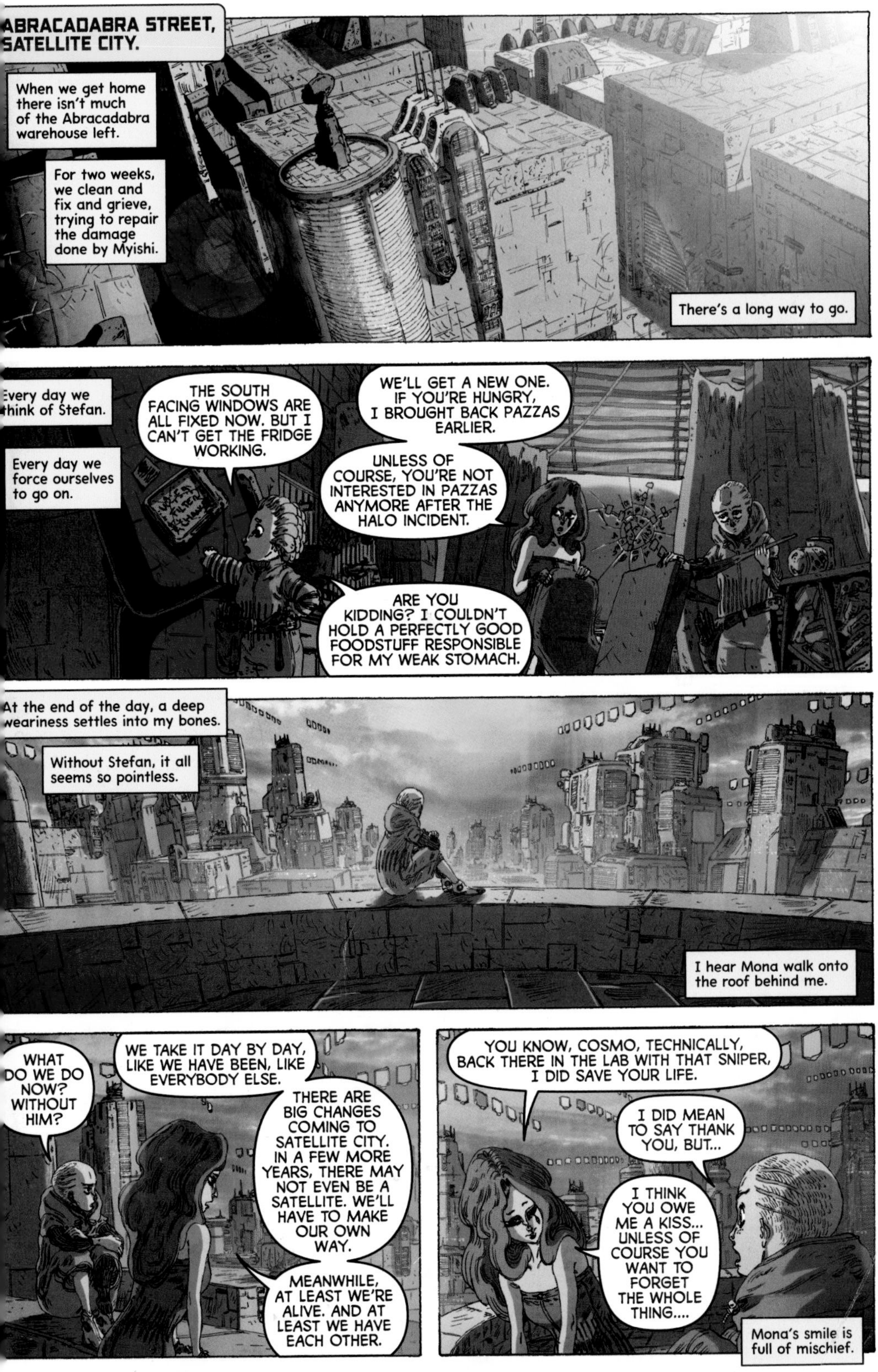

ABRACADABRA STREET, SATELLITE CITY.
When we get home there isn't much of the Abracadabra warehouse left.
For two weeks, we clean and fix and grieve, trying to repair the damage done by Myishi.
There's a long way to go.
Every day we think of Stefan.
Every day we force ourselves to go on.
THE SOUTH FACING WINDOWS ARE ALL FIXED NOW. BUT I CAN'T GET THE FRIDGE WORKING.
WE'LL GET A NEW ONE. IF YOU'RE HUNGRY, I BROUGHT BACK PAZZAS EARLIER.
UNLESS OF COURSE, YOU'RE NOT INTERESTED IN PAZZAS ANYMORE AFTER THE HALO INCIDENT.
ARE YOU KIDDING? I COULDN'T HOLD A PERFECTLY GOOD FOODSTUFF RESPONSIBLE FOR MY WEAK STOMACH.
At the end of the day, a deep weariness settles into my bones.
Without Stefan, it all seems so pointless.
I hear Mona walk onto the roof behind me.
WHAT DO WE DO NOW? WITHOUT HIM?
WE TAKE IT DAY BY DAY, LIKE WE HAVE BEEN, LIKE EVERYBODY ELSE.
THERE ARE BIG CHANGES COMING TO SATELLITE CITY. IN A FEW MORE YEARS, THERE MAY NOT EVEN BE A SATELLITE. WE'LL HAVE TO MAKE OUR OWN WAY.
MEANWHILE, AT LEAST WE'RE ALIVE. AND AT LEAST WE HAVE EACH OTHER.
YOU KNOW, COSMO, TECHNICALLY, BACK THERE IN THE LAB WITH THAT SNIPER, I DID SAVE YOUR LIFE.
I DID MEAN TO SAY THANK YOU, BUT...
I THINK YOU OWE ME A KISS... UNLESS OF COURSE YOU WANT TO FORGET THE WHOLE THING....
Mona's smile is full of mischief.

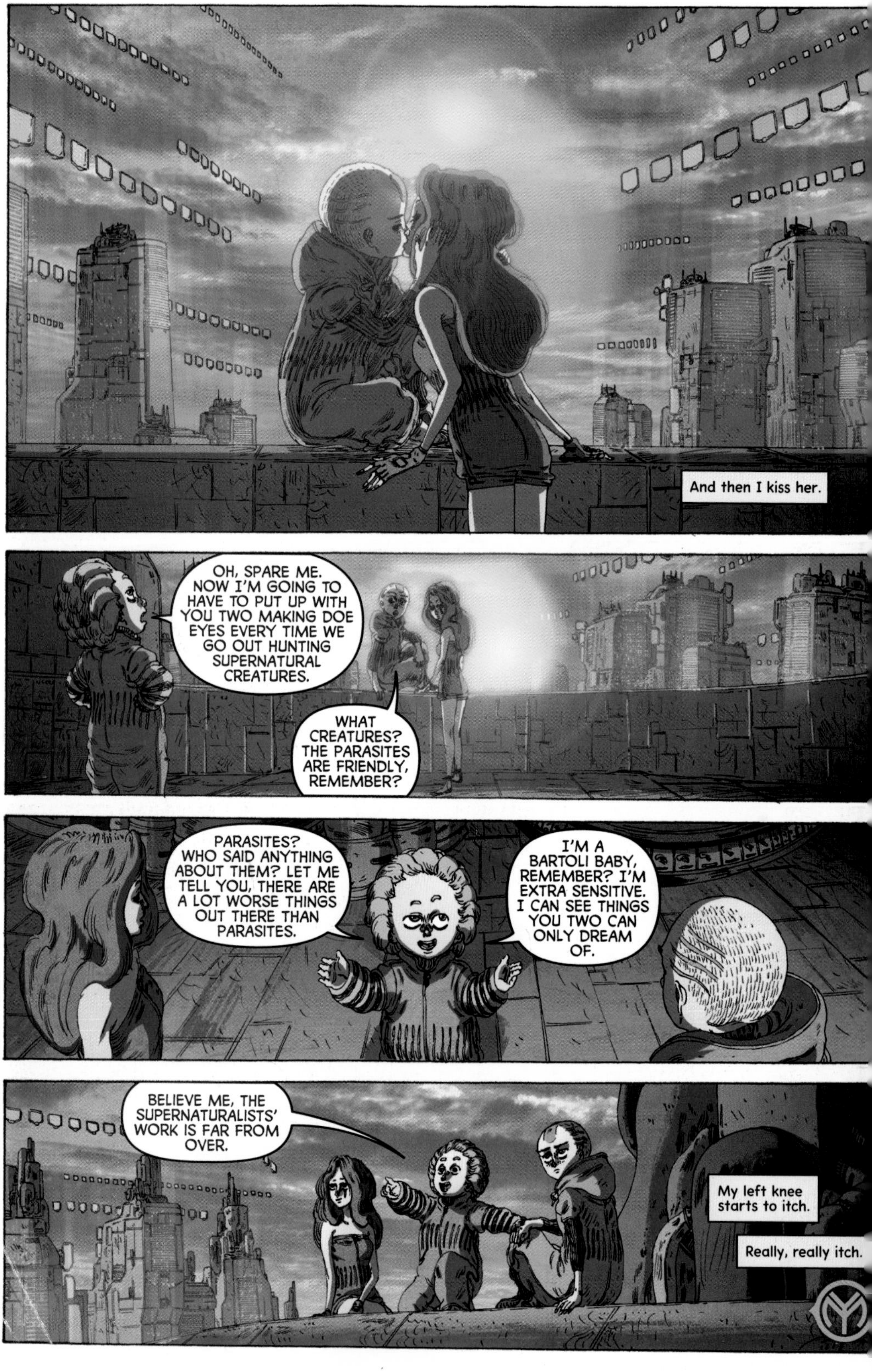
And then I kiss her.
OH, SPARE ME. NOW I'M GOING TO HAVE TO PUT UP WITH YOU TWO MAKING DOE EYES EVERY TIME WE GO OUT HUNTING SUPERNATURAL CREATURES.
WHAT CREATURES? THE PARASITES ARE FRIENDLY, REMEMBER?
PARASITES? WHO SAID ANYTHING ABOUT THEM? LET ME TELL YOU, THERE ARE A LOT WORSE THINGS OUT THERE THAN PARASITES.
I'M A BARTOLI BABY, REMEMBER? I'M EXTRA SENSITIVE. I CAN SEE THINGS YOU TWO CAN ONLY DREAM OF.
BELIEVE ME, THE SUPERNATURALISTS' WORK IS FAR FROM OVER.
My left knee starts to itch.
Really, really itch.

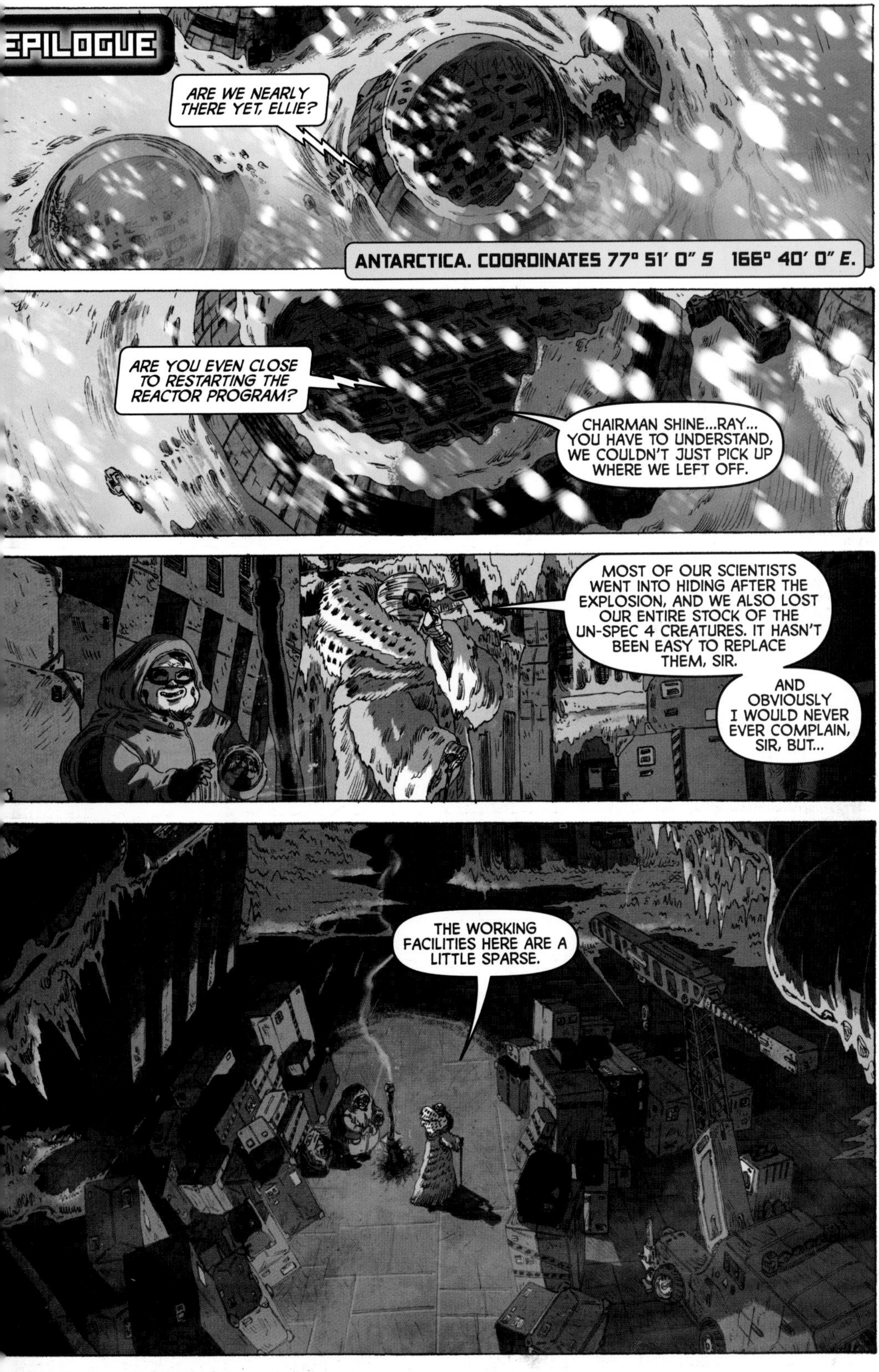
EPILOGUE
ARE WE NEARLY THERE YET, ELLIE?
ANTARCTICA. COORDINATES 77° 51' 0" S 166° 40' 0" E.
ARE YOU EVEN CLOSE TO RESTARTING THE REACTOR PROGRAM?
CHAIRMAN SHINE...RAY... YOU HAVE TO UNDERSTAND, WE COULDN'T JUST PICK UP WHERE WE LEFT OFF.
MOST OF OUR SCIENTISTS WENT INTO HIDING AFTER THE EXPLOSION, AND WE ALSO LOST OUR ENTIRE STOCK OF THE UN-SPEC 4 CREATURES. IT HASN'T BEEN EASY TO REPLACE THEM, SIR.
AND OBVIOUSLY I WOULD NEVER EVER COMPLAIN, SIR, BUT...
THE WORKING FACILITIES HERE ARE A LITTLE SPARSE.

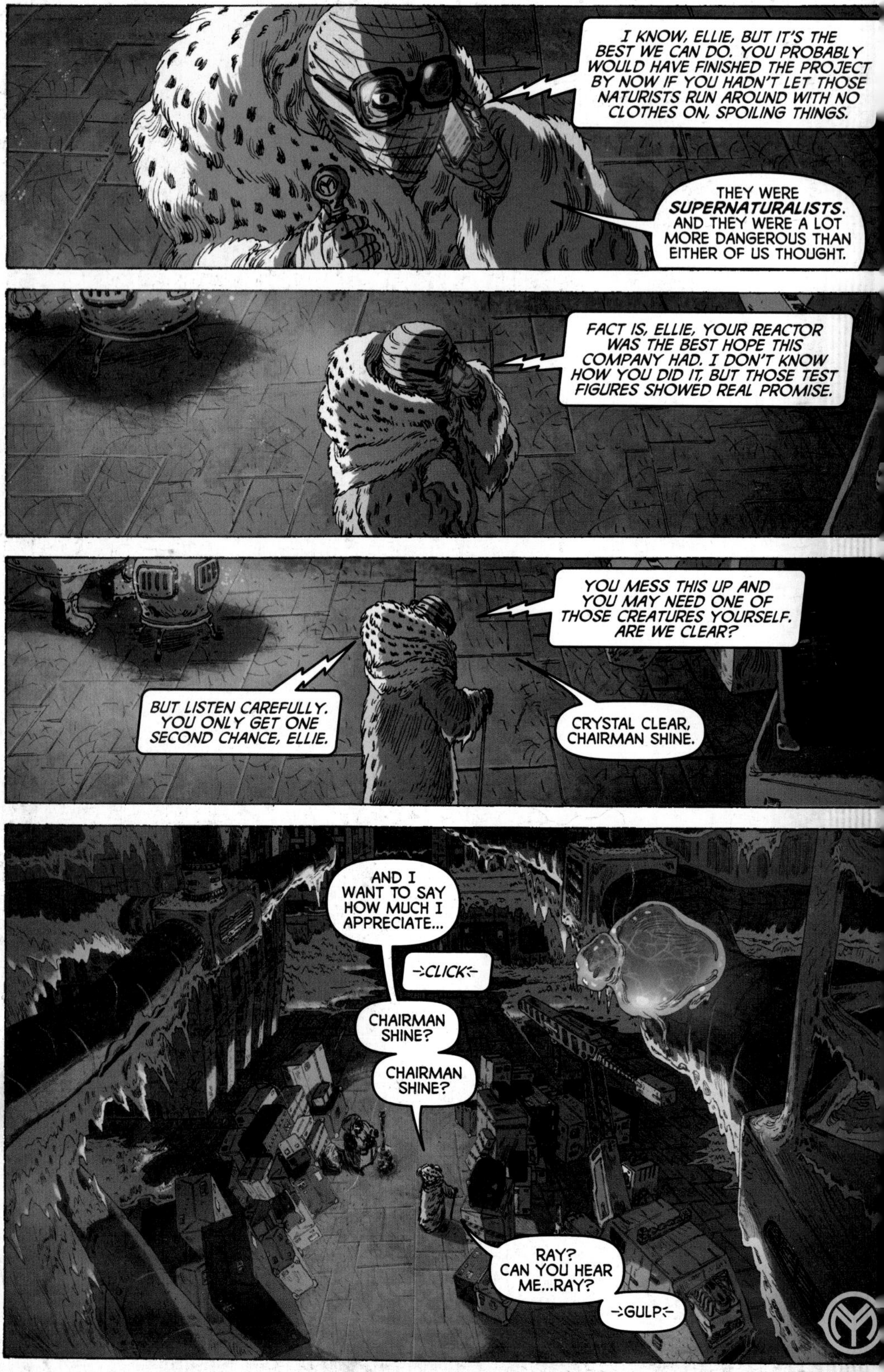
I KNOW, ELLIE, BUT IT'S THE BEST WE CAN DO. YOU PROBABLY WOULD HAVE FINISHED THE PROJECT BY NOW IF YOU HADN'T LET THOSE NATURISTS RUN AROUND WITH NO CLOTHES ON, SPOILING THINGS.
THEY WERE **SUPERNATURALISTS**. AND THEY WERE A LOT MORE DANGEROUS THAN EITHER OF US THOUGHT.
FACT IS, ELLIE, YOUR REACTOR WAS THE BEST HOPE THIS COMPANY HAD. I DON'T KNOW HOW YOU DID IT, BUT THOSE TEST FIGURES SHOWED REAL PROMISE.
BUT LISTEN CAREFULLY. YOU ONLY GET ONE SECOND CHANCE, ELLIE.
YOU MESS THIS UP AND YOU MAY NEED ONE OF THOSE CREATURES YOURSELF. ARE WE CLEAR?
CRYSTAL CLEAR, CHAIRMAN SHINE.
AND I WANT TO SAY HOW MUCH I APPRECIATE...
-CLICK-
CHAIRMAN SHINE?
CHAIRMAN SHINE?
RAY? CAN YOU HEAR ME...RAY?
-GULP-

For information address Disney • Hyperion Books, 114 Fifth Avenue,
New York, New York 10011-5690.

First Edition
Printed in the United States of America
10 9 8 7 6 5 4 3 2 1

Library of Congress Cataloging-in-Publication Data

Colfer, Eoin.
The Supernaturalist: the graphic novel / adapted by Eoin Colfer & Andrew Donkin; illustrations by Giovanni Rigano; [color by Paolo Lamanna; lettering by Chris Dickey].—1st ed.
p. cm.
Summary: In futuristic Satellite City, fourteen-year-old Cosmo Hill escapes from his abusive orphanage and teams up with three other people who share his unusual ability to see supernatural creatures, and together they determine the nature and purpose of the swarming blue Parasites that are invisible to most humans.
ISBN 978-0-7868-4879-9 (hardback)—ISBN 978-0-7868-4880-5 (paperback)
1. Graphic novels. [1. Graphic novels. 2. Orphans—Fiction. 3. Friendship—Fiction. 4. Science fiction.] I. Donkin, Andrew. II. Rigano, Giovanni, ill. III. Title.
PZ7.7.C645Sup 2012
741.5'9415—dc23 2012003835

Visit www.disneyhyperionbooks.com

SUSTAINABLE FORESTRY INITIATIVE
Certified Chain of Custody
At Least 20% Certified Forest Content
www.sfiprogram.org
SFI-00993